PRAISE FOR *BENEATH THE RISING*

"*A* wonderful genre-defying adventure, rife with strange heart and weird horror. But most notable is its particular, careful attention to its characters. Premee Mohamed is a bold new voice."

Chuck Wendig

"A perfect balance of thriller, horror and humour; reminded me of *The Gone-Away World*."

Adrian Tchaikovsky

"A galloping global adventure where privilege and the lies we tell others are as great a villainous force as the budding cthulonic forces the heroes must rush to stop."

Brooke Bolander

"One of the most exciting new voices in speculative fiction."

Silvia Moreno-Garcia

"Premee Mohamed writes with a joyous velocity that careens through genre-lines, whipping the reader helplessly after her. One of the most exciting voices I've heard in a long time."

John Hornor Jacobs

ONE OF *THE WASHIN*
BEST SCI-FI AND
BOOKS OF THE

T0002120

"One of those wonderful books that keeps peeling back layers, not of some cosmic mystery, but of its two main characters. Nicky and Johnny end up being much more complex and ambiguous than they appear at the start of this book, and every reveal is gasp-out-loud astonishing."

Charlie Jane Anders

"Gripping from the first, arresting sentence to the last, this is unsettling, mind-devouring cosmic horror at its best, wrapped around one of those captivating *noooo-this-is-a-terrible-idea-but-why-what-noooo* relationships."

Jeannette Ng

"I wish I could provide a short and pithy blurb for this novel, but I can't. It's too involving a book, too *good* a book for that. It quietly drills holes in your expectations, sliding demolitions charges into them, running the wires back to a detonator, and then—when you reach the climax—it quietly says 'You can't say you weren't warned' (and you were), before quietly leaning on the plunger, at which point, things stop being quiet at all."

Jonathan L. Howard

"This book is the offspring of *A Wrinkle in Time* and the Cthulhu mythos, raised on epic poetry, the love songs and rock ballads of the 00s, and the inescapable rhythm of *Gitanjali* if it were a gory tentacle-sprouting punk anthem."

Likhain

First published 2021 by Solaris
an imprint of Rebellion Publishing Ltd,
Riverside House, Osney Mead,
Oxford, OX2 0ES, UK

www.solarisbooks.com

ISBN: 978 1 78108 875 3

Copyright © Premee Mohamed 2021

A CIP catalogue record for this book is available
from the British Library.

Designed & typeset by Rebellion Publishing

Printed in Denmark

A BROKEN DARKNESS

Premee Mohamed

SOLARIS

For the friends who left
And returned as strangers

CHAPTER ONE

I SPOKE THE words of power, and brought into being a perfect void.

The small impossibility hovered weightless and self-sufficient, fueled by strange particles, carrying impossible light, bound by rules not of our world but of worlds alongside ours, unseen and untouchable, worlds of endless abyss.

It was also about the size of a grape. Was it *supposed* to be that small?

I flipped through the deck of index cards containing my scribbled notes, but it was too dark inside the closet to read them. The only light—strange, headachy, and faint—came from the void. It was practically at my eye level, and I didn't like the look it was giving me.

Don't look, I knew that much. Don't make eye contact: it didn't like to be stared at. And don't breathe on it. Human breath worried it.

"So it's like a tarantula?"

"That is quite enough back-talk from you, Nicholas."

I kept my eyes meekly down while I set the cards aside. It was dangerous in the first phase of creation, and vulnerable (maybe even *nervous*: who knew) while it grew its coating of reality, the hardened skin of molecules and time on this side of the boundary. Unstable, basically, in every sense of the word. Easily offended, capable of great harm.

But when it was all done, toughened up, wised up, it would be the first watcher I'd been allowed to create. An incredible honour (as my instructors kept telling me) for someone in such a junior position. Maybe even a first. *Don't let it go to your head*, they said.

Not yet, I thought. Not while it was still raw and angry. Maybe I'd let it go to my head after, when the watcher was working, part of the global monitoring network, a blob with a job, like me, floating invisibly around and speaking in its inaudible and incomprehensible way to the other watchers. When it was more than just a gyrating grape shedding flecks of weird spectra. Lopsided, too. If it were a real thing, it would have been making a little *woob-woob-woob* sound as it lost its spin.

My back teeth hurt. Well, I'd been warned about that: you pay the price for the spell, as it took whatever it needed from you as well as whatever nearby magic was around. First thing the training had covered.

"And you'll teach me to do… magic?"

"That will be the first part of the training. Not everyone has the capability, you know. And of those, the few that can be trusted to use it properly…"

Don't think about it, don't think about it. I rubbed my jaw and watched the void rotate faster, squeeze into a proper sphere, sprout tiny crackling spires of glassy, bluish light, the first stages of its armour. The spikes flickered, steadied, and sharpened themselves against one another just at the edge of hearing, the sound not like music but the massed voices of a choir heard from far away, sweet and high.

I didn't know what would happen to me if I failed this spell. If the watcher didn't work or, God forbid, decided to leave, or got itself caught somehow. The Society wasn't real big on telling you about consequences in any kind of detail. Only that they existed: only that to violate the Oath would not result in anything so mild as being written up or demoted or disciplined in the way I understood from ordinary jobs. Because the Oath was "To protect the sources of magic and of magical knowledge; to acquire and guard whatsoever artifacts and devices which comprise the same; to uphold the system of watching and knowing which preserves the security of mortal life on Earth." And at the end of the ten- or fifteen-minute recital, you had to say: *With my entire being.*

With my entire being.

My new employers were powerful. Always had been, to a greater or lesser extent, and in inverse proportion to their visibility. And now that I worked (I refused to say *lived*) in the bright upper-atmospheric cloud of that power, looking at the world I thought I knew from fifty thousand feet, I no longer felt awed by it.

Awe had lasted about a week. Now it was fear, pure and simple. Fear of the true and unfathomable strength of their grip, held in check till the Oath was recited and signed, and only then revealed: a hold that would not break even if you fought it with all your strength, or all your wiles, or all your money, or all your allies. Not even (someone had hinted) death could release those coils. And what the hell did *that* mean?

Still. To be so high up. To be raised so high, in such secrecy, lifted alone into this bright place, to look down on where I had been before they had arrived, even for the terrible reasons they had asked, the worse reasons I had accepted….

The void swayed and sang, sang and swayed. I monitored it out of the corner of my eye, seeing only glimpses of a thing like a solar eclipse: a feathery ring of light surrounding a perfect orb of darkness. It's fine, it'll be fine. Trained for weeks. Wrote the sigil a thousand times on the whiteboard.

And after this, who knows? Sky's the limit, baby.

My heart pounded as the watcher rose slowly over my head, and settled into a kind of questing, steady flight, no longer rotating, the spikes quiet. I exhaled slowly, and reached for the whiteboard again. The second part of the spell would b—

"Nick? Can you come up? The boys won't let me record my show!"

The watcher flinched in midair, jerked towards the door. Towards the voice of my sister.

Before I could think anything more coherent than *Get the fuck away from her!* my hand snapped forward and closed around it.

Roar of pain. Invisible explosion, trapped and rebounding from unbreakable walls, darkness whirling, a *crack* as something broke.

Under the surging noise I barely heard Carla's socked feet pattering down the steps, and I wrenched my fingers open, shaking my hand. But it was too late. This was no crushed bee, dead after its single-use weapon. The watcher had... popped, or something, and an agonizing wave of cold crawled up my arm, burning and freezing and breaking and pulsing like lightning.

No time to suffer, only enough to conceal. My legs weren't working; I staggered up from the floor, crashing first into the door then through, shoving it shut just as Carla entered my bedroom.

Her nervous, angular little face seemed startled in the reflected light of the stairway. "What were you doing?"

"Work."

"With all the lights off?"

"What were you saying about the PVR?" I shepherded her back to the stairs and we climbed to the living room, following the familiar sound of the boys shouting.

"I wasn't going to bother you," she mumbled. "It's just, I wanted to set it up to get the new *Futurama*, and their turn is *over*, and the rules say—"

"Okay, okay. TV cop."

"...I'm sorry."

"It's okay."

"Were you super busy? I shouldn't have said anything."

"No, it's okay." I sat on the couch, poking one of the boys—I couldn't tell who—with my toe. They both remained glued to the rug, staring up at the TV. "Hey, you butts. Why're you being butts this time? Why're you doin' buttly things to your saintly sister?"

"*Thank* you."

"It'll only take a second!"

"We just wanted you to see one thing! We found it on the news!"

"And Cookie is a *tattle*."

"You're supposed to say *nark*."

"*You* don't even know what that means."

"*Neither* of you knows what it means!"

Chris turned, agitated; their usual bickering seemed strangely on-edge too. And what the hell could a couple of ten-year-olds worry about, I thought with a sudden flare of irritation? What was so important in their goddamn lives? It wasn't like they'd just fucked up the most major task they'd ever been trusted with, it wasn't them who'd have to explain... my God, and the phone was already beginning to buzz in my pocket, and I didn't even dare take it out to look at the number. I knew who it would be, and the questions he would ask, and how weak my answers would sound.

How could you be so careless (the kids were busy and Mom was asleep, I thought I had time to), why were you doing it inside the house (I didn't want to die of hypothermia), what other places would have been dark enough to perceive the necessary spectra (none, I checked, honestly I did), did you even bother to erase the sigil (no, whoops). Jesus Christ.

My brain felt like it was in two places at once, and I only half-heard Brent saying, "Hang on, I gotta fast-forward through the boring stuff."

"Yeah, yeah," I said. My boss had recruited me, trusted me, placed me carefully into the global network of knowledge and safety, found me a spot in the system. And I'd just squished part of that system.

It wouldn't matter to him that I was paying a price of my own; the Society would need to extract their own later. How long would I have? My phone fell silent at last, and through tears of pain I tried to focus on the TV, which both twins were pointing and yelling at in unison. Carla turned on the closed-captioning, which simply said *[AUDIENCE APPLAUSE]*.

The cold, mercury-heavy weight in my arm faded; my fear receded; my ears rang. In a cartoon, I thought deliriously, in a comic, there would be golden stars and chirping birds and little pink hearts (no, not hearts, goddammit) orbiting my head like planets.

Because there, on the TV she had bought us (using the electricity she paid for every month, in the living room of the house she had given us) was Johnny Chambers, former child genius, prolific inventor, world-class researcher, scientific celebrity, noted asshole, and once the kids' favourite aunty and my best and only friend in the world. No longer. And never again.

It wasn't that I had been avoiding her for the past year and a half, only that I had, as much as possible, gone out of my way to not talk to her or think about her. Or see pictures of her. Or video. Or respond to her phonecalls or ICQ messages. Not *avoiding*.

And anyway, even if I had, what else did she deserve after what she had done to me? To us? To the *world*?

All the same, I couldn't blink, couldn't even look away from the small familiar face, coin-sized on the huge screen. My heart was still beating somehow, but my blood had turned to ice. I imagined it as the river glimpsed from a passing train: sludgy with cold, thick and still. That was how you knew it wasn't love. It was its opposite, as far as you could get.

"What's she doing?" said Carla.

Chris said, "You'll see in a *second!*" at the same time Brent said, "It's a *secret!*"

I rubbed my temples. All right. Stay: because they want you to, and because they're excited, and enough feelings have been hurt and trust has been lost; let them have this. It's a shitty gift, but you still have to show appreciation for its giving.

Push the memory down. That's over, it's all over. That was another world, and she was another person, and so were you. And if you had a moment, a split second, when the spell was cast and her job was done and you could have let her die, and maybe you should have, not for revenge—no, of course fucking not, *no*, not that—but for justice, to pay the price for what she had caused... Stop it, push it down.

Don't let the kids see. Look past the TV, don't look at it. Yeah. That should work.

The camera pulled back, clearly trying to impress us with the size of the crowd: people in black coats with black umbrellas packed onto a flat concrete platform, so that against the indistinguishable silvery mass of sea and sky it seemed like footage from an old movie. The girl, too, in black at the podium, the big man in black beside her, and above them a hundred wheeling gulls whiter than chalk. Was it raining? She stood unprotected in it, face shiny and hair dull.

"...*gratitude to the government of Scotland for their dedication and hard work,*" Johnny said, half drowned-out by the waves. It was easier to read than to listen, but that meant losing sight of her face. The face I had loved, the face we had all loved, beautiful, serious, sensitive, interested, intent on her speech. The face of a traitor and a monster. When was the last time I had seen it even on a screen? Months, I thought. Longer. Maybe a year.

Thanks droned on. The high-precision laser-level startup. Tolerances to within a thousandth of a— Construction process of the—Trust the science to— Permitting process of—Public consultation extremely gratifying and—The reaction of Edinburgh in general to the—A tribute to the many—A fitting—

"*I'd also like to thank everyone who came today, what with the rain,*" Johnny said, to a faint squelchy chuckle from the crowd. "*You're part of history now, you're part of science—you're part of a better future. Part of*

*the world getting back on its feet. And that makes you
no different from me. Thank you."*

Oh you fucking little liar. Nice words. But you don't
really think *anyone* is like you.

She jumped down from the podium and ducked under
her assistant's umbrella; a tall, broad-shouldered woman
sporting a crystal brooch the size of a tennis ball stepped
up and began her own speech. The mayor, I gathered.
Or another politician. Good voice, nicely enunciated.

I glared at Johnny, huddled in her sodden coat. Innocent,
and confident in her innocence. God, you could see it in
the way she was standing, without a word being said.
As if she herself had not been made by the monstrosities
she called the Ancient Ones, as if her experimental clean-
energy reactor had not first attracted Their attention,
then handed Them the keys to enter our world.

What she had caused—what was eventually dubbed the
Dimensional Anomaly—had, in less than two minutes,
killed hundreds of millions of people; and aside from the
deaths, the aftereffects still poisoned the planet like deep
peat burning far below the charred trees of a forest fire,
the very land itself smouldering out of sight, ignored by
those who saw only a landscape that seemed safe from
further flames. *Nothing* had been unaffected, and the
rebuilding, in dozens of countries, still went on. Wearily,
painfully, the long drudgery made bearable only by her
handouts and her tech. She had been hailed as a savior,
and accepted the invisible crown of everyone's gratitude,
and said sweet modest things. If only they knew.

She had nearly ended the world. And half against

my will, I had worked with her to save it—at the last minute, by the skin of our teeth. But nothing else had been saved. My job, my family's safety and privacy, their trust in me, my only friendship, sleep, sanity, everything we thought we knew about each other, ourselves, the universe in general.

For months after our return, all I could think was: No one else knows what I know. No one was there to see. No one knows. No one will ever know. A monotone filling every waking hour, drumming out thought. As if I'd visited some planet that scientists denied even existed, and I had brought no evidence back, nothing but stories.

We never made a pact, not like when we were little kids playing blood brothers with the knife and the signed papers; nothing had even been spoken aloud. In our heads we simply said: Don't tell. Don't tell anyone.

We couldn't talk about what had happened.

We couldn't talk about what it had cost.

And for all the time we *could* have said something— alone, unwitnessed, recuperating in the warm dimly-lit hospital in Baghdad—we still had not. All burnt and blasted and busted up inside from the kickback of the spell, with my chipped and fractured bones (ribs, pelvis, left arm) reassembling themselves, waking in the dark to realize she was still sleeping in the chair in the corner of my room.

When we were both awake, bandaged and shiny as robots with silver burn ointment, we spoke little, and watched old movies on the TV bolted to the ceiling. Ignored the hum (whose exact frequency and pitch I knew I would never forget) of the bone machine, sitting closer to me than her, and even more her than she was, somehow, a white box with the bright C and L intertwined on the side, Chambers Labs. Stitching my bones back together with nanoceramic, stronger than the shielding on a space shuttle.

Any time I could have woken her up, whispered to her in the dark. But I was rattled by drugs and pain and shock and fear of the future, and I did not yet know that it was hate I felt. Nor that I had sworn off the old love forever. Both seemed too impossible.

For months I woke screaming with nightmares, staying up as long as I could to avoid a moment's sleep. Even Mom, of the school of 'Try thinking positive thoughts' and 'Maybe you just need a vacation' had suggested therapy or drugs.

I insisted on moving to a new house. Johnny's people arranged it in days, as part of her reparations (I refused to believe she felt guilt about what she'd done to us, but she felt *something*, and she paid up). A fresh start: but it hadn't helped. With the hate, or with the noise in my head.

Then last year, just as I had begun to think frankly alarming thoughts like *What would fix this? What would be a way to solve this problem for good?* the Ssarati Society came to me with their job offer.

Times are tough, they'd said, not with condescension; just a straight-up statement of fact. *Times are tough. How are you making ends meet? You leave the house, you drive around for hours, you tell your mother and your sister and your brothers that you got another job. You don't tell them about the money that appears in your account every month, do you? Wouldn't you rather earn your own, doing honest work again?*

What honest work?

Let's say… information management.

Low rank, but a rank nonetheless, without which you could not operate in the strict hierarchy of the Society at all; and a title, a paycheque, a cover story. What had I known about them till that moment? Nothing except what Johnny had told me (a vague story of their mission to preserve and study knowledge); and what I had seen for myself the moment they had refused to help us on our frantic, half-deranged sprint to assemble the weapon we needed to save the world. Hell, if anything, they had tried to stop us, under the guise of 'protecting' us, and who knew how that might have gone if we hadn't squirmed free?

But the most important thing I knew about them was the one thing they did not say in that long conversation: that they did not like Johnny, and they did not trust her. And that was enough for me, without hearing anything else at all.

Give me that. I'll sign it. Snatched the heavy beautiful fountain pen I did not know how to use, and scrawled my name in blood-thick ink. As if they might snatch away the offer, whip the paper out from under my hand. Spat out the Oath, not listening.

And the drumbeat in my head stopped dead, instantly, and I could sleep again.

On the screen, Johnny raked her hands through her wet hair and returned to the podium, digging in her coat pocket. Out of old habit, not expecting it any more, I glanced at her left hand: but there it was anyway. Our secret sign, unhurried, and making sure (how did she always know?) that the camera caught it—the signal she had been giving me since kindergarden to tell me she knew I was watching.

My eyes filled with furious tears, and I turned reflexively, as if avoiding a kick. The death of love felt an awful lot like a cracked rib.

But if I lived to be a thousand I would never love her again. Never trust her again. Still and always wish her revealed, humiliated, imprisoned, even dea—

"Nick! It's happening!"

"Are you watching?"

"You gotta watch! This is the best part!"

The device in Johnny's pocket had been a remote; as the noise from the crowd mounted into a steady roar, she raised it into the air, paused theatrically (of course), and pressed the button.

Far out to sea, something leapt silently into life; for a second I thought lightning had struck, but it was something else, a made thing, a lit skyscraper surging up through the waves like a breaching whale. It had been there all along, of course. Switched off and so giving the illusion of invisibility. Now it was a tidy array of golden lights, blurred by the rising storm, arranged inside a square gray building perched on a square gray island.

"See how cool?" Brent whispered. "They said it was a power plant. How's it work?"

"Why's it on an island?"

"Yeah, that's weird. Where do the wires go?"

"I dunno. They put her wind turbines out in the middle of the ocean, too," I said.

The camera panned over her shoulder, closed in on the sparkling building, then whirled back out and swivelled nauseatingly over the city skyline, all soaked buildings drooling soot and smoke, everyone still clapping, waving, tilting back their umbrellas... and then a smaller shock, *another* face I knew in the crowd.

Was it? No. Couldn't be her.

Someone who looked like her, that's all. You goof! Paranoid much? The rest of the world getting to you?

The girl in the crowd yanked her scarf over her face, even raised an arm, as if the camera's gaze were not only perceptible but the disagreeable breath of a comic-book heat ray. In moments she had shoved through the mass of people and vanished off-screen, leaving her dropped umbrella, still open, spinning forlornly on the cobblestones.

And then it was all over, a quick shot of Johnny climbing down from the podium again, the politician and her bodyguards trailing them, everybody piling into gunmetal gray government cars, a sudden gust of rain. The entire segment: speech, ceremony, light-up, crowd shot—had barely been as long as a commercial break.

The last shot was of security drones, deceptively

dainty-looking with nothing around them for scale but probably eight or ten feet across, blinking red as they flew tight laps around the lit-up building, and the two long-range observation towers, instantly familiar—the same everywhere you went. Looking for enemies that they would never, *could* never detect.

I took the remote from Carla and rewound it, ignoring the whining about her show, to pause on the face in the crowd.

No, it *was* her.

Huh.

"My turn!" Carla grabbed the remote back, and the *DELETE THIS SEGMENT?* menu popped up. A second later it was gone, and the *Planet Express* zoomed confidently across the screen. "Are you okay?"

"All good."

Jesus. If I'm right. If. What does it mean? The pain in my hand, the mistake still burning there, as if it were eating away the bones. The boys so excited to see Aunty Johnny again, never knowing that two people who should have been a world apart were in the same place at the same time. Not a coincidence. Nothing was a coincidence any more. Think, focus. The phone buzzing again in my pocket, like a hornet.

Don't say anything. Got enough problems. But if I—

No. The coward's way out. Trying to distract my boss with this? Like waving a laser pointer in front of a cat? He's not a cat, they're not cats; they know there's nothing there to catch, that it's an illusion. They'll know what you're doing and it's utterly transparent, it's so transparent it's actually fucking pathetic, like the old days, bringing Johnny home with you when you know you're in trouble, knowing Dad won't yell at you if there's a guest… is that what you want them to see? You being like this? Trying to weasel out of what you did?

No! No.

Her fault anyway. Her fucking fault all this happened. Some genius.

I realized I was panting; the kids were staring at me. What would happen to *them* if something happened to me? No, don't say anything. Keep your head down.

Outside our cosy box of blankets and light lay the solid wall of night that had settled in hours ago, streetlights gleaming on fresh snow, my car huddled in the driveway with the black umbilicus of its extension cord snaking back to the house, bright and ordinary stars gleaming through the trees in the yard. Everything back to normal. The scattered black plastic bits of the boys' new Xbox, not cleaned up from Christmas; Carla's books neatly stacked in the corner; Mom's shoes gleaming and new on the shoe rack by the door. We'd never had so many shoes that we had needed a rack before. We'd never even had a Gameboy.

"Are you gonna get that?" Carla said tentatively.

I touched my phone, a bolt of pain shooting up my arm. A new normal. The world a little rattled, sure. First contact bound to be a shock. No business of mine. And now we were closed up, everything shut, locked, bricked over. A clean start, free of the enemy.

Yet a world in which the Ancient Ones posed no threat

was still a world in which plain old humans could get up to all sorts of evil.

Okay, but. Listen. But that's been the case since forever. Since we crawled out of the oceans and began to lose track of one another's business.

This is nothing, this doesn't mean anything. Not seeing her there and not seeing *her* there either. Can't you just hate without doing anything about it? Look at this, at all you've been given. The house and the job, the trips, everything the kids want, everything Mom's always coveted to be like her friends, the shoes and DVDs and makeup and perfume, the safety, the quiet. Given to you. And all you have to do is keep up your cover and do your job. Your little, insignificant job. That they only gave to you because you knew her. That you should not, *cannot*, risk for her.

Cannot.

And yet.

Nothing is a coincidence. Not any more. Not even if you hate someone does it make anything they do a coincidence. If I… you would not have to stick out your neck *very* far. Because you're far from the only person who hates her.

"Nick?"

Three faces turned to me, lit in the flickering blue of the screen. "Good for her," I said, slowly rubbing my aching hand. Something cold and hungry still writhed in it, not stopping. The proof of my mistake. Maybe the last mistake I'd ever make.

They were still staring. I said, "Come on, guys. Clean

electricity. Super good for the planet. Thanks for letting me see that, seriously."

Don't say anything. Don't say anything.

Twelve hours later, I was on a plane over the exact centre of the Atlantic Ocean.

CHAPTER TWO

IF ANYONE KNEW what I knew, they'd say, and rightly so, *You knew everything. She told you everything, at the last. And you took this knowledge purchased literally with your life and you did nothing. It's not too late though. Call the cops. Call the FBI. Call a priest. Arrest her! Do something!* But you didn't talk. *And she didn't talk.*

We didn't talk. But we'd have to talk tonight, for as I laboured up the slope towards the entrance of the castle, everything made certain to remind me, in case I managed to forget for one second, that this was her party, it belonged to her, she'd paid for it, was the guest of honour, the hero of the hour, and the world's first official Chambers Reactor powered the lights and music.

A lightshow rotated on the damp stone of the castle walls: flags of Scotland and the European Union and the City of Edinburgh, and a tangle of crests, tartans, logos, brands, mascots. Spinning unicorns corkscrewed into a half-dozen Chambers Industries graphics: Chambers Labs. Chambers Energy. Chambers Biomedical. I imagined a half-dozen interns jealously duelling it out at the projector deck like rival DJs fighting at a rave, elbowing each other aside to get their particular division on the program.

Which was hilarious, because tonight I was pretending to be an intern too: for BGI, the big tech conglomerate. I'd been assigned the internship as a cover (as well as a branded t-shirt, mug, baseball cap, cell phone, and five hundred business cards that I never handed out). Only Society members were supposed to know if you were in the Society or not.

BGI was a good choice. Their employee base worldwide numbered in the faceless and anonymous thousands, and they were recognizable enough to be 'prestigious' to Mom and, grudgingly, in our infrequent phone calls, Dad too. They had a vague idea what my job description meant ("Quality assurance and quality control") and were merely proud that I had gotten such a well-paying job in the gap between high school and, they assumed, university.

I hoped I could lie fluently about being in Edinburgh on a work conference, sent as a last-minute replacement for my boss (which was more or less true). Meanwhile, I'd told Mom and the kids I was in Orlando for a different conference (user interface design? something like that). The Society had even figured out how to get my name on the web page; I knew Carla would peek right away. She tried to resist, I knew, but was always cross-checking my movements to see if I was lying to them again. I felt terrible about her compulsion, but I could never tell her the truth; who knew *what* they'd do if I did.

Really though, in my (rented) tux, I was pretending to be James Bond. Like Jude Law in *The World is Not Enough* or *Die Another Day,* sleek and arrogant and able to brazen his way through anything. Hadn't mentioned that on the phone to my boss, of course. There hadn't even been a space to apologize for what I'd done to the watcher, nowhere to fit words in through the Niagara-like, billion-ton waterfall of his anger. Only when he had paused to catch his breath did I mention that his daughter, whom I'd thought was studying in Spain, was now in... Edinburgh? Coincidentally, at the Chambers Reactor ribbon-cutting ceremony, to which tickets had been assigned months in advance? What a lucky young lady she was...

Lucky, Louis had said, drawing the word out, and hung up on me.

As I had stood in the kitchen, staring blankly at my phone and trying to think of how to communicate my last wishes to my sleeping family without actually telling them why I might be doing such a thing, he had called back.

Louis's assistant had been quietly calling around; both Sofia's residence manager and her dorm-mate said she had dropped out. Sofia hadn't been seen in weeks, despite the fact that at every call with her father, she had chatted chirpily about her classes and exams.

And one thing had led to another, and here I was, the instigator of this tangle of boss, daughter, nemesis and myself, struggling in the middle of their web like a very confused, though dapper, fly.

From Louis, I had understood, clearly and a little insultingly, that my commitment to the Society was not *distrusted* exactly, but (and I would admit this) undeniably strained: both from the conditions of their discovering me in the first place, and the incident with the watcher. *Do you know what used to happen to people who did what you did? In the old days? Mm?*

Fuck you, I should have said. You're not paying me enough to threaten me.

But I hadn't, and had sat there instead, frightened and fuming, absorbing the familiar refrain: Just pay your dues. Serve your time. I could be so much more than a mere Monitor. I could rise in the ranks. Other people had. I could be prestigious, respected, like the others.

Remembering the kids beaming through their envy, demanding souvenirs from the Kennedy Space Center and Disneyworld. Mom ruffling my hair, running her thumb over my ear. *I'm so proud of you, baby. That's a good sign, when they start giving you more responsibilities.*

Liar, liar, liar, liar. And I'd come back without a tan, too. Just tell them you were listening to talks the whole time, Louis' assistant had said. A strong implication of: Do I have to think of everything? Can you not lie on your own? A Chambers Labs subsidiary was presenting at the conference in Orlando, I had noticed: Lazuli Software Solutions.

Johnny was everywhere, she was like mold spores in the air, nowhere was free of her. You couldn't take one breath without drawing her in, having her grow inside you. Making you sick.

A nasty realization had built while I writhed unsleeping on the plane, and it worsened now, as I joined the line of people waiting to get in, shivering in the cool fog. If it really had been Sofia, her dodging the camera suggested she didn't want to be spotted there. Yet she must have known the ceremony would be filmed—not only that, but broadcast worldwide. Millions, even billions of people must have seen that footage. And she knew that, she would have known that. So why had she gone? What was she up to? And why hadn't she told her dad?

I hadn't seen her in person for months, not since my last training trip to Chicago; she'd been distant, even cool, yet somehow had contrived to run into me, with or without her dad, about a dozen times a day. Afterwards, she kept messaging me on ICQ, a half-hour of cautious small talk each time. We were, I thought, in that uneasy space between strangers and friends, but since I'd never really had friends except Johnny (ow—that stab of hate again), I couldn't tell.

The beams of the lightshow stabbed up through the fog like knives, a guard of honour as I approached the front of the line. Like photos of royal weddings, walking under the bridge of blades. Good thing Louis's assistant had called to get me a tux: under laughably heavy coats, many trimmed with fur or velvet, most people were in tuxedoes too, or else floor-length dresses in a dark rainbow of hues. I hoped no one would look at my boots.

The lady taking names with her laptop stared up at me far too long. I met her eye, daring her to say something, tell me I didn't belong there. Go on. You'll see. The Society is full of these little tricks.

"Nicholas Prasad," I repeated, leaning down. After she looked at my driver's license, she gave me a paper wristband and waved me through. I swiped my sleeve over my face, barely dislodging the clammy mix of perspiration and precipitation.

God, why had I agreed to this bullshit? Some vague impulse fueled by who-knew-what, something I hadn't been able to resist, giving the impression that it was not large but fast-moving, too quick to dodge, about how a man's got to do what a man's got to do, but was this, in fact, *it*?

If it was, I decided, what a man had to do was *incredibly* bad planning.

All the same, what was the worst that could happen? Two girls might be mad at me, and I could call Louis back and confirm that his darling only child was fine. And then home on Monday, with Society-provided memorabilia, mouse ears and rocketships and little bits of gator-shaped tat and glitz. Job safe. Everything fine, and the boat that I had set rocking with my mistake (not to mention ratting out Sofia) would be settled again, safe again.

I walked under a stone arch into a cross-road, thick uneven walls against a clouded sky, feather-soft and without a single star. People milled, murmured, smoked, laughed. There was a strong smell of money; you got it at Johnny's place sometimes, and always at her mother's house. Cigars, cryo-treatments, Botox, lip fillers, hair transplants, expensive perfumes and colognes, aromatherapy orthotics, drycleaning chemicals, real leather, jewels kept in storage. I didn't have that. Would they sniff me out, turn on me? Rented tux, hotel soap. Smell of jetlag. My watch still on Edmonton time.

Metal signposts pointed to *PRISONS OF WAR* and *WAY OUT*, mostly obscured now by large laminated sheets that said *CHAMBERS REACTOR GALA FEBRUARY 6 2004* with a big reflective arrow.

I liked the tall blocky towers, their windows crisscrossed with lead. The stones were all different colours, like camo-print. It wouldn't help if you were being invaded, I thought, but maybe the visual effect would screw up the aim of folks with projectile weapons. How old was this place, anyway? Its age pressed down like the weight of a thunderstorm. *I have everything you don't*, it seemed to say: *mass, history, dignity, culture*. And by 'you' I thought it meant both me and where I was from. No castles back home. Rightly so, I wanted to explain: the land was swindled or taken at gunpoint from people who neither built nor needed them.

Need has nothing to do with it, I pictured the castle replying, *and I will be here for thousands of years more, needed or no*.

Conversely, I didn't like the arches, which seemed too heavy to stay up, itching to fall on some tourist. Indoors was a relief despite the monumental slap of heat. Unofficially, I knew, the party filled the entire grounds, and I had seen a few forlorn-looking string quartets and appetizer stations outside in the fog, but in practice, it was cold and grim enough that everyone had crowded into the Great Hall.

The room was half-painted in deep red, half panelled with wood; the stained-glass windows had been strung with small white party lights, bringing their colours to life. Polished armour and dozens of weapons hung on the walls, baroque blades and spikes arranged like fireworks. That was good, actually, very handy. When either Sofia or Johnny started asking the hard questions, I could just run myself through. Die of blood loss before dying of embarrassment. True, the Society would lose its deposit on the tux, but...

Before I really realized what I was looking at, my body jolted minutely, like the electrical shock of a dry winter day. The hall was lined with nooks like restaurant booths, which I figured were off-limits during tourist hours but were now open; and one of these was occupied by Johnny, lit all gold and dark like an old painting under several skinny standing lights. She was being simultaneously photographed and filmed by two people, and interviewed by three others, pivoting back and forth at their conflicting cues and the demands of the lenses.

I parked myself behind a big guy in a white jacket who was offering trays of what Johnny called 'tiny bits of junk on sticks' (her nemesis; she always ate before parties). The crowd eddied like one of those fancy aquariums in the mall, deep water of tuxedoes, bright coral of gowns, jewelry like darting fish. Hm. Save up, get a suit like that back home: silky blue or green or violet under the lights, black in the shadows. Couple of iridescent ties. Start going to clubs.

Some people stared despite my tux, but after I snagged a glass of champagne, I abruptly achieved invisibility; their gazes hit and slid off. I held my nose over the cold skinny glass, enjoying the tickle of the popping bubbles.

The lighting left the musicians (six of them—what was that? a hexet? a sextet?) and the high ceiling in darkness. In the center of the room, someone had poised a spotlight on something I couldn't see through the crowd, glassy-looking, maybe an ice sculpture. Like that one Nobel-watching party we'd gone to at the university, where we had gotten kicked out after she—

That sting again. Stop it, stop remembering her as human. It was all lies, goddammit. You know that. Stick to your job.

I scanned the room for Sofia and gingerly let my champagne soak into the apparently parched scrubland of my tongue; it had no taste at all, only texture, as if I had drunk a mouthful of tacks. Two mouthfuls later I was thirstier than before. I glared at it.

"Want some smoked salmon?"

The fourth sip exited my mouth in a fine mist; Johnny evaded it absentmindedly, and held up her plate.

"Come off it," she said. "Like it's so shocking to see *me* here, with my name all over the signs. What are *you* doing here? How did you get in? I didn't put your name on the list."

"Don't just sneak up on people like that!"

"Uh huh. Should I call security or what?"

I glanced around in automatic alarm. The security I had expected, her assistant Rutger, who first of all didn't like me, and secondly was about twice as big as me on every axis, was nowhere to be seen. The two dark-suited people behind her were unfamiliar—stiffly alert, watching me with Rutger-caliber disdain.

She followed my gaze. "He's back at the hotel. Wanted to review some data. You know Elizabeth and Wayne."

I nodded as if I did. While I waited to see which of my various sphincters had either fused shut from shock or were on the verge of letting go, she complacently made a tiny burrito out of a pancake, some smoked salmon, a scoop of caviar, and pickled onion. "Here. Eat this."

"Where did you get this?"

"Buffet at the back," she said, expertly wrapping up another one. "Asked the caterers for it. Can't stand that little-shit-on-sticks situation."

I glared downwards. Her boyish, Gap-commercial haircut had been recently touched up; the ends seemed fresher, brassier, like fine wire. If she'd done her own makeup, she'd done a piss-poor job of it; the gold glitter on her eyes had escaped into her eyebrows and even her nose and chin. Under a weirdly short but long-sleeved sweater, her knee-length black dress was belted with a chain of Oreo-sized golden discs. It made me think of ancient Greece: a famous vase, maybe, or a picture in one of the kids' books.

Her eyes, steadily meeting mine, were the same as ever: that sinister green, the green of a Disney villain's eyes, if anything more yellow than I remembered. Sickly, even inhuman. Like an animal. I reached inside myself, felt for the old love, the new hate, and felt only revulsion, the instinctive recoiling from a monstrous stranger who had stolen a beloved face, a familiar voice, and now wore them proudly, showing them off to the horrified survivors.

"Okay, listen," I said.

"Listening." She took my champagne glass and drained it, then handed it to a passing server without looking.

Something warm slid through my arm and grasped my wrist, and this time I yelped out loud and jerked backwards into the wood panelling. The thing clung like a tentacle, but in the split second before I drew my fist back (good God: to do *what*, exactly?) I realized what was happening and tried to recover, picturing how it must have looked—the squawk, the sluggish flinch and twitch, the noise (had I imagined it?) as my head hit the wood. I hoped no one had been filming us.

Face hot, double-0 status revoked, I crooked my elbow where Sofia had taken it, and managed something that I hoped looked like a smile. She was a shimmering presence at my side, like a mirror, or those polished refractor things the ancient Greeks or whoever aimed at ships during wars to burn them up; I couldn't look directly at her.

"Sofia!" Johnny said. "What a nice surprise! And holy shit, your earrings. And your *dress!*"

"Thank you! I just bought it this afternoon, especially for tonight!"

"Glgk," I said.

Sofia went on, smoothly, "And thank you for being flexible about the guest list! Security is so important these days."

"Yeah, can't be too careful. Any sort of riff-raff might just wander in."

To her credit, Sofia didn't even glance at me. "I agree, you do not want questionable people at something like this."

As they chatted, I slowly put it together: two Society members were supposed to have been here tonight, but couldn't make it (I wondered if Sofia had pushed them into the ocean). Sofia had been sent unexpectedly at the last moment instead, but Louis had been unable to make it.

"Everyone was very insistent that the Society be represented tonight. It's an historic event! And you were kind enough to ensure we got in. And of course," she added, squeezing my arm, "I hope you do not mind that I used the other ticket for my love here, even though he is not with us! I was hoping we could get some photos while we are all dressed up."

"Of course I don't mind. Two surprises for the price of one. Oh, you should go pose with the armour!" Johnny pointed back at the alcove she'd been in. "The light is still set up, the photographers are paid all night, and you get the painting too. You'll just have to wait for... who is that, is that the Princess of Monaco?"

"No, that's her sister."

"Doesn't that make her a princess too?"

"Not after what happened last week."

I wondered if this was death, if my soul was even now leaving my body, floating up into the ceiling, passing through it sadly into the sky (or, let's be realistic, down into the Earth's core to be incinerated). How was I supposed to figure out what Sofia was doing now? Louis wouldn't care that I'd been set up somehow, or by who. He'd just kill me. If you could kill someone who was already dead, which...

Sofia surreptitiously pinched my wrist, producing a bolt of pain from my fingertips to my ear. "Sounds good," I croaked.

"Well, you both look like a million bucks," Johnny said, reaching out surreptitiously to tug up one side of my cummerbund. "You should *totally* get some nice pictures. Especially you, Nick; you're always on the wrong side of the camera, you got all those photos of the kids and none of you. Your mom deserves at least one nice shot up there somewhere. Like, *one*."

"Mmpt."

"And maybe Sofia has a comb you can use?"

"Eckff."

"I'll see what can be done," Sofia chuckled.

Belatedly—possibly because, as far as I could tell, I was dead—Sofia's absolute conniving cleverness dawned on me. How else would you explain me being there?

Her, you could explain. She wasn't a Society member, but she was a representative all the same; in fact, Louis had always tried to keep her as far from their business as possible. She was just the eternal and permissible coworker's kid, allowed at their events and parties since she had been little, the way the dealers and bartenders had fondly looked away when Mom used to bring me to her shifts at the casino.

I realized that I had been expecting, for at least a couple of minutes, to see something resembling irritation or jealousy on Johnny's face, and then was annoyed at myself, and then was annoyed that I was annoyed. I tried to freeze my face into an expression of pleasant unsurprise.

Sofia announced, "Let's go see if the photographer is free!"

But a moment after we wandered away, the smile dropped off her face with an audible thud. "What are you doing here, Nicholas?"

"Uh, having a panic attack."

"Oh, God," she groaned. "You can always trust boys to have the stupidest answer out of a choice of millions... I recommend you *try again*. And *fast*."

"Are you about done? Jesus. Your dad sent me. Obviously."

"What? Why?"

I blinked. Had I not said *obviously?* I was sure I had. "Because he was worried about you. Because he called campus, and they said you dropped out. Why do you *think?*"

"I assumed you were here for *her*. Why wouldn't you be?"

"Lots of reasons," I said.

"My father has no need to send... nannies after me. I'm not a child."

"Nobody said you were! Calm down. He's worried, he says you were lying to him. About being in school. They said you dropped out. He was going to come find you himself, but he couldn't make it. What are you trying to pull, anyway? They're not gonna do anything to you, but who even *knows* what they'll do to me?"

She blinked, having clearly stopped listening to me halfway through my rant. The anger drained away from her face, leaving a terrible uncertainty and betrayal, the expression of a kid promised something only to have it suddenly yanked away. A moment later it was gone, and she was all business again.

Somehow, even in formalwear, she looked businessy too: the long, silvery-blue dress was cut like a suit at the top, and she was wearing heels so high we were eye to eye. Makeup too, dark lipstick and eyeshadow, metallic on her deep brown skin. Her long hair was tied back, the curls in front ferociously bobbypinned; the crisscrossed metal resembled a secret language. A cuneiform curse, no doubt.

But her face. Don't lose track of that. Saying into the silence: *He sent you? After all I did to rig it so that he would be here tonight?*

I said, "He said he was going to send his new... what do you call it. Secretary?"

"*Ass*istant."

"Yeah, Sherwood or whoever. Is that his first name or his last name? Anyway, Louis thinks he's too new. So he sent me. So it would be less weird."

It's still weird, her sneer said. "Let's look over here instead!" she announced, pulling me further towards the perimeter of the room, then hissed, "I'm on spring break. I'm allowed to go on holiday, you know!"

I shook my arm free. "Look, are you going to tell me what you're doing or not?"

"Nothing! This is unbelievable. He sent you all this way, and you—you said yes, you agreed to come all this way! To what, spy on me? It's *nothing*, I got a cheap flight, and I had plans with friends, they did not work out this week, then I decided I would still come by myself."

"Okay," I said. "You know. For the weather. Which is so nice. In Scotland. In February."

"People don't travel for the *weather*, Nicholas."

Johnny was wandering back towards us, the blonde head bumping through the crowd. Like the shark from *Jaws,* but little. I held down a laugh that I knew would come out in a donkey screech.

"Now knock it off or I'll tell her everything," Sofia whispered, and smiled again, brilliantly, as she took my hand.

"Me? You're the one who—"

"Yeah, and on *top* of the bull," Johnny was saying even before she reached us, "we're actually being audited by the IARE too. It started off as just a health

44

and safety thing, but they've got the entire ethics department involved now. They think multiple facilities are falsifying and publishing data. Can you believe it?"

"Incredible!" Sofia shook her head.

I pursed my lips. Johnny had been audited before, though mostly for safety stuff; it was both horrifying and unsurprising how many accidents she'd had, apparently thinking that safety standards were something for other people. They hadn't found anything at her facilities as a result, but at a *minimum* I knew she'd been burned by acid, had a few solvent inhalation incidents, got blasted with one of her early particle accelerators (luckily at low power), been on the sharp end of ten or twelve explosions—I'd lost count—poisoned herself, fallen off ladders, cabling, catwalks, rigging, and bookshelves in her ridiculous house-slash-laboratory, been electrocuted about six times, and Chem-Bot had accidentally sampled part of her arm once. And that entirely left out the dozens of incidents where genetically-screwed-up insects and plants had escaped 'containment'—usually a carelessly-lidded plastic tub, as I'd discovered more than once while scavenging for a snack.

She ran her empire in roughly the same fashion as ancient kings insisting on going to war personally rather than staying in the castle and moving pieces on the map with a wooden stick. But that was something. The audit... why would the Society be here for that?

"There's a completely private one for my personal guests," Johnny was saying when I tuned back in. My watcher-wounded hand had started to hurt for some reason, quietly building, as if ice were forming from some tiny core within it. "Down that hallway, and you'll see a guy in a dark green suit? Tell him I sent you, and say 'Independent review.'"

"What?"

"You'll see," she laughed.

Sofia disentangled herself, gave me a peck, and slipped through the crowd, her dress a trickle of mercury through all the dark fabrics. Where her lips had touched my cheek felt like a cigarette burn.

"Let's go get some more food." Johnny wriggled out of her sweater and handed it to Wayne, who folded it neatly to the size of a paperback book and placed it inside his own jacket pocket.

The crowd parted almost frantically around us. Her touch phobia, which to this day I wasn't sure was real or staged, was well-known, in fact had literally been the subject of a documentary once, and although many palms hovered in congratulations over her bared shoulders, people probably knew they would have set off, at best, a crying jag and a swift retreat, or, at worst (and it had so often been worst) a couple of swift blows ending in broken collarbones, fingers, or jaws. Even a dislocated shoulder once, I remembered. An older man had touched her from behind and… bad angle. Bad land. She struck out like a wasp, not strategizing, just looking to jam in her sting and flee. The phobia had disappeared after the Anomaly, or her stubborn maintenance of the act had slackened off, but no one else here could know that.

Near the fireplace, the room was stifling; sweat gathered in my hairline and crawled down my face. I heaped up plates of random food in the low scarlet light, handed one to Johnny, and, although I was beginning to suspect she was already a little drunk, let her get two more glasses of champagne. Or no, what was the word…?

"Flutes, Nicky," she said airily, as if I had projected it from my head like the lightshow outside. "Chug, chug. It won't go flat right away but it's kinda gross when it gets warm."

Her tone was affectionate, familiar. If I hadn't spent so long remembering and recreating everything she had done to me, it would have been so easy to just… tell her everything. Fall back into the deep permanent me-shaped rut that she *wanted* me to see was still there, and still perfectly intact, even though we were both so different now. *Look*, she was saying. *I won't treat you any differently. Everything you miss is waiting for you. Everything you've been missing during this long cold self-enforced solitary sentence. See, I don't even mind your girlfriend, or you not telling me. Because we're best friends. Blood brothers. Aren't we?*

I took the glass and we wandered away from the fire into relatively cooler air. I'd play along, no more. Couldn't she see, she who had known me all my life, that I wasn't hers any more? That she had thrown me away by telling me the truth? At the very least, could she not fucking tell that I had a higher mission now than being her *pet*?

Anyway, I'd put something on her plate that I hadn't put on mine, and I wanted it. "What's that?"

"Stuffed mushroom, I think."

"Stuffed with what?"

"Haggis."

I frowned, and stabbed it with my tiny fork. "I thought a haggis was a whole... thing. Like I'm picturing an animal the size of a volleyball."

"I think that's a weirdly common misconception."

I drained my flute, the bubbles crackling between my teeth. The second glass of champagne, I decided, was better than the first. More like fine-grit than coarse-grit sandpaper. But it still left me desperately thirsty. "What's *in* this stuff?"

"I know, it does the same thing to me. I think it's a rich people conspiracy to sell more champagne."

"You're a rich people."

"No, I just have money. *They're* rich." Her apparently casual gesture at the crowd somehow managed to hand off her empty glass and swap it with a full one; she gave it to me. I wiped my face with my sleeve again. My left hand hurt so badly it was taking an increasing amount of concentration not to clench it into a fist, and break the delicate glass.

"So," she said. "You and Sofia."

"Uh."

"Is that what you were going to tell me earlier?"

"No."

She smiled, a careful selection from her arsenal, one I knew well: sly, self-satisfied, slow, only wavering for a second when it seemed I wouldn't react to it.

"I thought it was so *romantic*," she breathed, "the way she came in half an hour before you did."

"What? No she didn't."

From her belt she unclipped a phone case I hadn't noticed, black leather with a glittery unicorn sticker on it. "So, the station up front where you got your wristband? That laptop is synced up with my records. Neat, huh? And so nice to see that you... managed to reunite after meeting once? It's like something from a movie. Like *Cinderella*. You Prince Charming you."

You know what? You're one to fucking talk. You were sneaking around behind the scenes for my entire life, making sure anyone who might have loved me or even liked me suddenly had to move away or switch schools, got fired from their jobs or transferred to another country. You think I've forgotten? Or you're forgiven? Looking up at me like that, so innocent?

But we couldn't talk about it. Still. Never.

The room swam with heat and pain as I tried to focus on a real response. Of course Johnny thought we'd only met once. In Fes, when Sofia had appeared out of nowhere, saving both our asses. What was the obvious...? "Okay, not that it's any of your business, but yeah, she did find me afterwards. It wasn't like you made me hard to find. We talk a lot on ICQ and stuff, this is the first time we've seen each other in... listen, the main thing is, we have to keep it on the down-low from her dad. He doesn't want her to date while she's in school. He'd be pissed. *Pissed*, she says."

"Totally hear you," Johnny said. "He used to say it all the time. Even when she was little. You know. *No boys. Keep your eyes on your books. Boys are evil. Only after one thing.*"

"Yeah, you get it."

"Mm. So that must be why she took you to this party," she went on, jerking her chin at the room. "A big, public event, with scientists and celebrities and politicians and royalty. Where you'd be filmed together. And photographed together. And that the Society's had two tickets to since last September. Makes perfect sense."

"None of my business," I said again. "I got nothing to do with those weirdos. I'm here for the free food. And what's that over there?" I gestured at the pedestal in the middle of the room.

"Nice subject change. Come look at my pride and joy," she said. "You may as well, since you came all this way just for... the party. I'll show Sofia when she comes back from the bathroom, too. Not everybody is getting the personal tour, you know."

"Poor them."

It wasn't an ice sculpture as I had thought, but a glass dome over a tiny model of a building, perched atop an island the size of a paperback book. It might have been made out of paper-thin folded metal. "What is this, a reactor for ants?" I said.

"I know, right? The thing is, the working part of the real reactor is about the size of a hockey puck, but you can't just put something that small out there. It needs to look legit. People get nervous if it doesn't."

She tapped the dome with her glass, making everyone around us cringe at the noise. "*This* is my favourite thing. We're not doing a lot of transparent nanoceramic because of the interactive bond-degradation problem, but I begged them to make enough for the model. It took months. I utterly degraded myself. *We're not worthy, we're not worthy!*"

"Yeah. I bet."

"And then I came over and me and Wing ran it over with one of the lab trucks to see if it would break. It was awesome."

"...Ran *this* over?"

"We buffed out the tiremarks afterwards. You could blast this with a railgun and it probably wouldn't break." She paused, thinking, and sipped her champagne. "It might chip. Anyway, generation is fully automated, but there's remote control just in case. See, there's the signal array. We used the experimental molpoxy on it, the entire roof will rip off before that dish does. On the building, I mean, not here. *This* is all held together with superglue. The torus and shielding goes there, under the red X. Except I forgot to put one on the mockup so I had to borrow some nail polish from one of tonight's makeup guys."

"A professional did your makeup? I hope you didn't pay them."

"Shut up. I kept touching my face during the photoshoot. Anyway, I made sure the reactor is about the size of a golf cart, and the rest of the building is mostly safety stuff in case of storms or seismicity, and smart grid control systems to regulate the undersea cable distribution load and deal with surges. And make sure that it's tuned to... to avoid... the problem we had when it was initially developed."

"The," I said slowly, "problem."

She tilted her chin defiantly, as if one of us had said, *Are you referring to the 'problem' that accidentally but very nearly ended the world?* "I've had trial versions running with no issues, no harmonics. Oh, and down there, that's the pod system for personnel in case the drones can't reach the island."

"And what's that?"

"What's what?"

"That," I said, touching the top of the dome, where a half-dozen small, shiny orbs had been meticulously painted on the underside. "Is it for measurements or whatever? Wind? Waves? Are those weather balloons?"

She blinked. "Those are a reflection."

As one, our chins dragged themselves to the vertical, pinning our horrified stares on the high, crossed beams of the ceiling where the light refused to go.

"Remember that one time we rode our bikes north of town," she whispered, "and—"

"—went to that old grain elevator because—"

"—I wanted to test my cyclonic densities detector, and it was full of..." She carefully put her glass on the pedestal, without looking down.

"Oh man," I said, still staring. "It would be *awesome* if those things were bats."

And, as if it had only been waiting for us to meet its gaze, darkness descended.

* * *

THE THINGS BILLOWED down in silence, formless and lazy as parachutes, so that for the first moments people smiled up at them, maybe thinking it was some kind of art installation. But Johnny dove to the ground, rolling away from the roped pedestal, and I did too, just as the screaming began: one high, terrified note, quickly joined by dozens of others.

"Everybody outside!" someone cried, but it trailed off into an awful, wet gurgle. Ballgowns and shining shoes flowed past us like water, confused with other bright things: eyes that were not eyes, just membranous lights; hair that wasn't hair but strings of slime; feathers as far from feathers as anything you'd see in a nightmare; and worst of all, recognizably human, or imitating a human: familiar skulls, femurs, eyes mindless with pain. Feet hammered against my shoulders as I rolled into a ball, watching for Johnny, the bright winks of her metal belt.

Many of the creatures were pulsating far outside the normal spectrum, hues you'd only see in sigils. The palms of their hands stuttered and flashed like strobe lights, sending people unseeing into the walls, to be quickly picked up by scavenging beasts while they lay stunned. Others extruded what I took to be streams of bubbling liquid but quickly proved to be tentacles, stabbing through clothing and into spines, wearing people like dangle-legged puppets high in the air, screaming and scrabbling for their pierced backs.

People fell, were swarmed at once, flung into the air,

released to fall howling into thrashing nests of teeth and limbs, splattered ichor, humans and human-monsters trading identical blows. The hall echoed with voices, the clang of dislodged weapons, crash of broken wood and bone. Someone pulled the fire alarm and that did it: time slowed to a crawl, and everything glanced off the surface of my eyes instead of sinking in.

Up, one hand crunching over broken crystal: the bloodied rainbows of a highball glass etched with thistles. Where had Johnny gone? Her security people surely—no. Smothered in flapping wings and claws, two gunshots virtually unheard over the noise of the alarm, three shots, four, a spray of them, why would you *stop* shooting once you'd started, why did they have *guns?* Something whined past my nose: not a bullet but a human head, bodiless, mouth filled with tentacles, the tiny wings behind either ear pitted and oozing.

A semaphore of flashing discs: there. Johnny hadn't gone far, only crouched behind the pedestal with a silver hors-d'oeuvre tray. Good idea actually. I picked one up myself and ducked instinctively as something swooped over my head, catching in my hair for a moment with a skittering *skritch* that told me it had hit scalp. I flailed at it, snarling, but it was long gone, lost in the commotion.

What spells did I know to fuck something up in here? I couldn't remember. Maybe they hadn't taught me any. Probably for the best. My brain was flying in a million directions, couldn't even focus to see properly, my vision seemed washed out with fireworks of panic. At least the room was still emptying, the walking-wounded dragging the just-plain-wounded, occasionally picking up a monster that seemed more human than the others, releasing them with a cry of disgust. The escape was jittery, stop-and-start, chaos as people stopped to fight the creatures at the doors, creating bottlenecks. The human puppets swooped down, away, back, mobbing, screaming, scrabbling at people's faces and tossing them aside.

Johnny squealed as someone descended on her, clawing at her bare shoulders. As she kicked it away, I walloped it with the tray, casting around for a weapon—the *walls*, for Chrissake!

I made it about two steps before she grabbed my wrist, and I turned in surprise only to realize that it actually *was* a tentacle this time. Hitting it did nothing; I turned my head away, shouting helplessly as the mass of purplish bulges and glittering teeth began to drag me away from the sword-covered walls. Its face was half-familiar, bearded, all too human except where the eyes had been replaced with something else.

Flailing at the thing with my free arm, I unexpectedly fell on my face as it crashed into something and lost its grip, leaving my wrist with a burnt-looking ring and a dozen spots of bloodied flesh. Broken? Hope not. I spun again while it was distracted and wrenched a sword loose from its display—massive, ancient, blunt, with a chipped metal handle that stuck at once to the oozing cuts on my palm.

Then it came into crystal focus, like a lens had swung down; Johnny met my eye and I heard her think it too, clear as words. Oh shit. Oh Christ. It can't be.

The monsters weren't trying to kill her.

They were trying to *capture* her.

(And maybe me, judging from that last grab.)

And if we didn't escape them we'd better figure out a more drastic solution, because any reason they wanted her *alive* meant death was the *better* option.

Things flew, banked, crashed to the floor in cocoons of slime—half-here, half-somewhere else, unreal, flickering in sync with their battle cries. Wide slicks of food, liquor, blood, other things (don't think about it don't look don't touch it) impeded the last few people racing through the doors, hampered in dress hems and coattails, dropped jackets. The cold, rotten reek of magic mixed with the smell of whiskey, and some small, still functioning part of me thought: *Well, that's that; I'll never have a sip of the stuff in my life.*

"Go!" Johnny gasped, pointing at the door. "Quick!"

"You go first!"

"I'm right behind y—"

She cried out as something huge and scaly dropped, really fell this time, as if it could not fly at all, clumsily flattening both her and the pedestal; the domed model rocked, wobbled, recovered, and then, impaled abruptly by the thing's claw, exploded into a billion glittering shards as if it had only been waiting to be relieved of some impossible level of internal stress.

The creature towered over us both, studded everywhere with the starry bits of broken dome, a collection of human faces stretched over its wings—or not wings, but flat membranes extending from its back. Its dozen thick limbs were all occupied in pulling the struggling Johnny from the floor. And failing: horrifyingly, there was so much blood on her bare skin that it couldn't get a grip.

My vision narrowed to a pinprick. I ran roaring at the thing, swinging the sword, feeling my thumb wrench back with a pop as blade met scale.

Something dug into my throat, something else seized my jacket; something that felt horribly like a *beak* crunched into my ear. They all felt very far away. All that mattered was the noises Johnny was making, noises that even I, who had heard her scream at least once a week for most of my life, could not tolerate with any degree of rationality.

I was being dragged backwards, but my sword was stuck in the monster, a real hit, and greenish liquid was pouring onto the floor, and Johnny was alive, rising, running. Towards me, and then past, grabbing my sleeve. I twisted free from the things behind me, shuddering at their highpitched wail that was so nearly human speech, and then we too were through the doors and outside, plunging through the icy fog at a dead run.

"Keep moving!" Johnny panted, glancing back as we threw ourselves down the hill towards the main road, sliding on the wet stone. "Can't let any escape. Move outta range!"

"Out of range of *what?*" I shouted, but she was sprinting back towards the Great Hall, unhooking her belt.

I swore, a nonsensical string of syllables, and began to run after her. Later on I would remember how slow it felt—lumbering and clumsy, like a plane taking off next to a songbird. Five steps, six. Seven. A blossom of lightning-hot darkness.

Familiar. Where had I. Oh yes. The couch. The—

The explosion knocked me off my feet, allowing a surprisingly long time, as I flew, to imagine how expensive these special effects would be in a movie, unless you used computers, I supposed, and moreover that the *Mythbusters* had proven that in such close proximity to an explosion you would just turn to jelly, not become airborne and weightless, but my boots left the ground and the cool wind of my flight cradled me and all around me in a dense cloud like guardian angels flew chips of stone and glass and wood and metal and, I supposed, transparent nanoceramic, and monsters made to look like us.

That wasn't out of range, was it, I tried to say, but I was too sleepy and the words wouldn't come.

CHAPTER THREE

I WOKE, OR came to, what seemed like a few minutes later. The blackout had possessed a strangely infinite quality, as if it had been not months or years but an immeasurable amount of time, too long to capture in numbers, compressed into a period of perfect darkness unrelieved by a single mote of light. I felt like I had been running for the entire time, ruining my feet, wrecking my back. Thought about school, phys-ed class the last year of high school, when they couldn't really think of what to do with us, grown men, and just made us run.

No more school. Real world. Sun doesn't revolve around the earth, earth doesn't revolve around you. Get up. *Up*.

Everything hurt. I lay on the cobbles, my field of vision filled with the strangely broken sky. Something wrong with it. Hard to see with eyes. What other senses to use? Like pigeons maybe: magnetic fields, the pull of something other than light. Blurry stone walls crowded me on three sides, like worried bystanders.

Standing took a while and there was plenty to look at while I clawed my way up the wall. The Great Hall, for example: the glowing heap of wreckage, still encircled by a few stubborn stones, was sort of on fire—greenish, fading as I watched to gray, and then nothing, only a curious shimmer above it, like heat haze. The stench of something not quite magic, but not quite not, hung in the still air.

That strange flame. Was something still burning under there, something that would burn without light or heat? Those monsters, pretending to be people. Or people made into monsters. Or... whatever they had been. The fear shuddering inside me felt oddly familiar, and I thought if I had been a peasant in, say, fifteenth-century Europe, born after the big outbreaks and only knowing horror stories of the plague, I might feel something similar if someone had staggered out of the woods in front of me covered in black buboes and dropped dead. Something known and unknown; something that should not have happened, something I had been told *could* not happen.

Yeah. Told by who?

Maybe some of that flame had been Johnny, trapped and burning under the wreckage. Or what was left of her. And if she was dead, how would I... how would the *world*...?

I stood there unable to move for so long that eventually the paramedics found me themselves and walked me gently down the hill, their voices audible, even recognizable as English, but incomprehensible through the roar in my head.

The white pop-up party tents that had held DJs and speakers and appetizers and ice buckets brimming with beer bottles had all been commandeered, converted to impromptu medical stations crammed with medics and stretchers. Down the road, sirens sang through the fog, sending up fans of blue and red light.

No, I'd know if she were dead. I'd know. Don't think about it. Think about what to do next.

What the hell did she *do?*

Don't think about it.

As I walked, each step sent electricity through my body, hairfine crackling pain ricocheting from heels to forehead and earthing in the bloodless wound in my left hand. Serves me right. My fault. Tried to fix that mistake by cringing like a kicked dog, and going here where I was sent. And see how that turned out. I didn't even know where Sofia was. Louis was going to kill me. If he hadn't been ready to kill me before (himself, or in some worse, official fashion, involving the entire Society), he'd definitely do it now. I'd just be *disappeared.*

Calm down. Don't say anything. Something can be salvaged, something can always be salvaged. There's no one to yell at but yourself now.

Okay. Okay.

Inside the tent I sat as directed on a shaky pair of stacked coolers. Five other people lay around me on stretchers shoved between small folding tables still laden with cold food. It smelled powerfully like bacon, and under that a thin sickly current of blood, rubbing alcohol, vomit. The champagne in my stomach gurgled loudly, which I ignored.

"Deep breath, little pinch."

I breathed, and held very still, and accepted the murmured praise. Someone stuck a small round patch on the back of my hand, and warmth crept up my arm, settled into my chest.

"Give me that hand, love."

Glass removed. Expensive crystal shards. Nanoceramic too, probably. That un-shatterable dome.

"Now the other one."

A gravel pit's worth of tiny rocks had to be painstakingly mined out and scraped free, pattering stickily to the ground from the tweezer's tips. How had it gotten so deep?

"Eyes closed."

Cuts glued shut, strange smell of mint. Why not make a medicinal glue smell less medicinal? Not herb or solvent, something else, something nice—think of it later. Hum of a device along my face: I opened my eyes despite my instructions, saw the Chambers Medical logo, black ink on gray plastic, drive past my face. Instant, disconcerting tightness of the skin knitting itself shut, embracing, hands across America. Sky-blue tape around my wrist and thumb. A different device, white. Cloth on my face.

You think you can get away from her, but you can't. But what does it *mean* if we all get away from her?

Look at this fucking thing on my face. Look at it simply and seamlessly sticking me back together. Like special effects. Did we get away from her? Is that what we did? What happens now?

"Can you press on that? Press on that, my love, for a minute."

She wasn't dead because I'd know if she was dead. That was all. That was the entirety of it. She was not. And anyway, even if she was. The Society would... they'd fix this. Whatever *this* was. Power in numbers.

"Press hard! That's right. Keep the pressure on."

She was not dead because *something would have told me* if she were dead and I didn't care what that was. Along all the ways that we were (not *used to be*) connected I felt that none were severed. In my head I walked along them, plucking them like a spider testing the strands of its web for soundness.

Not by the bonds of our covenant, nor by the bonds of trauma, by proximity; not by time, love, hate, or blood were we apart. We were *not*.

And anyway, some fucking genius, setting off something she couldn't escape. Her ego wouldn't let her even consider dying like that. Would it. Not for someone who kept saying she wanted to *save the world*.

I talked to myself in silence, moving my lips without breath, holding the cloth to my nose as the medic did something cold and painful to my left ear. They let me go half an hour later, after an unbelievable amount of paperwork, and I staggered outside and instinctively looked up: framed by stone arches, a hole had been punched in the clouds, edges razor-sharp, containing within it like the deep still water of a well a smattering of stars... and an enormous violet-blue aurora crossing the darkness like a malediction, a no-smoking sign. Banned, barred. *You cannot come here. You shall not pass.*

The castle grounds were busy, orderly, the earlier chaos giving way to shellshocked obedience. Police filed up and down the slopes holding clipboards like leafcutter ants. The hot white reflections of their safety gear kept reminding me of the explosion: like a nuke, an anti-nuke, releasing darkness rather than light, hurtful to the eyes. Everything wrong about it. What *had* Johnny done? I hoped no one would arrest me and ask the same question. Witness to the crime. Present at ground zero. Accomplice, possibly. Maybe it would be *better* if she had taken her secrets to the grave.

No such luck. She was outside a tent, gadgets dangling from fingers and chest, getting nebulized and crying a little bit, tears cutting through the dust and blood on one side of her face and bumping over dozens of tiny cuts on the other.

I stood well back between two canvas walls, watching her while she couldn't watch me, trying to get my brain around the edges of what I was feeling. Whatever it was, it was sharp enough to cut, it hurt me in places where I thought the nerves had died, it clenched my just-repaired hands into fists that broke the cuts back open.

I thought about her destroyed model, stainless steel and superglue and nail polish under its supposedly indestructible dome. Years ago, in her passion for what she called the 'iterative economy,' she had cooked up a thousand low-carbon and biodegradable substitutes for plastic and styrofoam, but had never managed to duplicate glass, only things that looked like it.

"It's too weird," she had told me once. Sitting on her balcony in the middle of the night, cherry Slurpees, grass stains on our knees, mosquitoes around us disoriented and colliding in the field of her repeller. "I mean weird in the physics sense. *Wyrd*, maybe. It's a matrix, it's a slow liquid, it's a glacier moving at its glacial pace and scale; but it's also a crystal, it's also a galaxy. Basically it's a jerk. I can't engineer the same chaos. It does it by itself."

Yes. I am the only thing you ever made that turned out the way you thought it would. And now I too am unmaking myself. And one day everyone will know you are a monster, not just me.

When they took her mask off, I took a deep breath, smoothed the anger from my face, and headed towards the tent. She met my eyes just as a tall thin policeman stepped in front of me, holding a clipboard as big as the serving tray I'd lost in the Great Hall.

"Sir? Like to come with me for a minute?"

"I have to check on my friend," I said. "She shouldn't be alone." *It's dangerous for people*, I almost added.

"Wasn't really a request," he said, then glanced over his shoulder. Johnny gave a minute head-shake, almost too small to see, not even dislodging the pendant of bloodied tears hanging from her chin. But the officer saw it, and wandered off. Not far, I noticed: maybe not close enough to eavesdrop over the noise of sirens and engines, but close enough to watch us.

"You okay?" Johnny said hoarsely.

"Better than you."

She wiped her face on the blanket, leaving a smear of slightly less muddy skin; her eyes glittered like broken glass. "Really? You look like hell. Where's Sofia?"

"She texted me. She's okay. Went back to the hotel."

"Is she."

"Sure is."

The paramedic still taping up her arm made an extremely good show of not paying attention.

"Nick," she said quietly. "What are you *really* doing here? And if you say that you wanted a Scottish holiday in February with your secret girlfriend who's in the middle of exams, I will literally stick a scalpel in you."

"Can't have one," the paramedic said.

"I wasn't asking."

Wisely, he turned her loose. We retreated towards the castle, away from the flashing lights and headlights and flashlights and the new onslaught of photographers and reporters and cameramen. Drones were approaching from the city, still dots for now, their rotors sending ahead of them a kind of jaw-numbing hum of compressed air. "Up," she said. "It might be safer."

"Good, 'cause I got some things to say to you," I said.

"Totally, but keep your voice down."

Crunching over the broken glass, we ended up next to the cannons, looking down at the dog cemetery, a semicircular patch of turf edged with flowers. Miniature tombstones ringed the wall, epitaphs illegible in the shadow of the wall.

War dogs. There was really nothing people wouldn't do if they wanted to kill someone, was there? There really was *nothing*. They'd even throw *dogs* at them. Dogs, the purest, kindest things humanity had ever managed to produce. Throw *dogs* into battle, and then bury them under small versions of human monuments as if that made up for it. They'd never know. Only that they had done what their people asked. Out of love, out of hunger to please, out of something else they did not even know they suffered from, the desperate fear of being turfed from the pack.

Before she could open her mouth again, I said, "What the *hell* just happened, and don't you think that's more important to answer than what I'm doing here?"

"Of course it's important!"

"*More* important, I said. Look, I know you're probably jealous or whatever—"

"Of what?"

I paused, and recalibrated. One thing I had learned, or that we had been forced to learn, two years ago, was how little actual adrenaline people usually operated with; and how badly your brain worked when your body was flooded with the stuff. "Look," I said. "What happened? What the *fuck* did we just see? I thought you said nothing could ever come back here!"

"I did say that!"

"So you were lying? Like you lie about everything?"

"No!

Jesus Christ. I waited out a hideous wave of vertigo, clinging to the stone wall till something new broke open on my palm. "Just tell me."

"I don't know what happened. I really don't. That's the truth."

"Uh huh. So those things just randomly showed up right where you were. Right after you activated the reactor you said you fixed. And not anywhere else. In the whole world. And you don't know what happened—you, who knows more about anything, and definitely more about Them, than anybody else in the world. Absolutely. Makes perfect sense to me."

"Listen. There haven't been any reported sightings," she said. "Okay? *That's* true. They clearly came in from somewhere. But it doesn't matter where They started off, because all the options are impossible. The spell I cast locked all the gates. Broke the keys off in the locks. Made them unusable."

A house with all the doors shut, the bolts shot home, I thought. But you never knew who had owned your house before, did you? For billions or trillions of years, or more, maybe before time began, the Ancient Ones had existed; and even if They had slept or fought or dreamed for most of that time, who knew what They did when They weren't sleeping? Our little blue marble hanging in space, its water, its life, everything being watched from somewhere both very far and very near... if you were one of those things, and you lived next to something teeming with life, how tempted would you be to break in if you couldn't get in any other way? "Is there a way to get to Earth without a gate?"

"I don't think so. I've never read about one."

"Well, people don't put everything in *books!*" I took a deep breath and tried to lower my voice. "We both saw what we saw! Everybody saw! Hell, it's probably being broa—" I stopped, horrified. *Broadcast all over the world.* What if Mom had seen that, the kids had seen that? There had been cameras in the room, I had seen them, a half-dozen, easily. If they knew I was here, instead of where I said I was, my cover would be blown, I would…

Johnny, apparently not noticing my internal screaming, said, "The thing is, Their matter doesn't really work like ours, I don't think. A lot of the writing, the thinking about it, has been lost. When They show up in dreams, are They real? Is anything in a dream real? Or in a coma, or delirium, or when you're high. There have been sightings of all of those. But where are They, when you see Them in a dream?"

"Oh my fucking God."

She shook her head, the side of her bloodied lip twitching, revealing a flash of incisor. I glanced down at her torn dress, billowing in the cold breeze; her arms were covered with goosebumps. And what was that on the back of one arm? It couldn't be… no. Darkness playing tricks on me. Reluctantly, I gave her my jacket, ignoring her nose-wrinkle as she put it on. The damp air soaked instantly into my sweat-sodden shirt and I began to shiver. "So you're just going to stand there and tell me to believe you," I said, "about the reactor."

"Yes."

I looked out at the city for a minute, dazed. Warm, lit windows; cars moving slowly down the roads; cranes near-invisible further out, just their lights gleaming far above all the rooftops like fallen stars. A lit and pillared building like Greek ruins. A clock in a domed tower, telling the wrong time. Or had my watch stopped? It was a nice view, if you didn't look straight up. I couldn't help but feel that it was listening to us, that rip in the clouds. As if it were anything more than water vapour arranged in the most menacing possible configuration. "You knew this was going to happen."

"What?"

"You blew up a castle! You didn't even have to go back to the car or anything! You were already carrying a... what was that, anyway?"

She patted her belt, which had four neat parallel scratches down one of the discs, just visible in the dim, lilac light. The disc next to it was missing, revealing a short length of chain and two small strips of dangling duct tape. "Built a one-shot plasma fusion field generator into the back of that one."

"...The issue here being that you *had it on you.*"

"Yeah. Just in case."

"In case of what."

"Just in case."

"There's no reason you'd need a, a, a weapon of mass destruction on you unless you thought something like this was going to happen, Johnny."

"I know what it looks like. But it's not for... *Them.* It's for anything."

"You could have killed people. A lot of people. Why the hell would you carry something that could do that if that wasn't what you were going to do?"

"Well I just *proved* what I'd use it for, didn't I?"

Her phone buzzed; belatedly, I realized it had been buzzing the entire time we'd been speaking. Not ringing, at least; I was pretty sure if we got caught, we'd be escorted back down, none too gently, for being smack in the middle of a crime scene. "Are you gonna get that?"

"No point. They've shut down the reactor. Taken it completely off the grid. Everywhere else is starting to shut down construction on theirs. Singapore, Sydney, Berlin. They're invoking the Act of God clauses in their project insurance. They're saying it's because..." She forced out a laugh, somewhere between a cough and a sob. "Because they think the reactors are causing interference with the long-range detection systems. That they're a security risk."

"Wow. They could not possibly be further from the truth if they *tried*." I rubbed my temples, still shivering; the rain was getting heavier and colder, turning from a mist into fat sparse drops. And what the hell was I going to do now? What was *she* going to do? Were the two even related? I just... had to find a quiet spot, call Louis. Or his assistant. No. Wait. Couldn't do that until I knew where Sofia was, what had happened to her. Otherwise just wasting everybody's time. Christ, why had I agreed to this, why was I so far from home, why... "Get back here. You'll ruin my jacket."

"It's already ruined. You're not getting your deposit

back." She climbed onto a heap of wreckage, dug from it a dramatically bent sword, looked at it, put it back down. "This is impossible."

"You don't care if you ruin other people's stuff, that's your problem. Plus, that word has kind of stopped having any meaning for me?"

"No, I mean *literally* impossible. We are no longer living in a universe that *can* have this happen. And the other thing I don't understand is—*ulp!*"

We both jerked backwards reflexively as the stones began to shift a dozen paces away, clattering and clinking like bells, a bluish, abyssal glow oozing across the cobbles towards us. Johnny toppled backwards from her perch, and I grabbed her reflexively, hanging onto the loose fabric of the tuxedo jacket as we froze, half on and half off the heap.

For several seconds, nothing moved: not us, not the rubble. And then it began again, a stealthy sound, the leathery noise of something soft scraping against stone. Unsteadily, swaying, someone rose from the wreckage. I opened my mouth to call out to him, a short man in a tuxedo, almost invisible in the dim light except for the white of his shirtfront, but Johnny, rigid against me, inhaled sharply: not to silence me, a different warning. *Stay still. Don't let him see us.*

No sound but the faint squeal of her breath, something she couldn't control, coming from her chest. From the city, a hum of approaching drones, still distant. The man dusted down his sleeves, patted his face—and flopped backwards with a guttural grunt, his body limned with blue light. Don't look, I thought urgently, though at whom I wasn't sure: Johnny, me, the world. Don't look, don't look, don't look.

He twisted, writhed; a rising scream was cut off abruptly by something wet and toothed jutting suddenly from his mouth, a sinister plant that flowered into a dozen slender tentacles. Bones cracked and broke as he tried to stand again, his hands flailing in the darkness, as if reaching for help. Wings sprouted from his back, pointlessly small, barely bigger than his hands.

The rain divided around him, became mist again, small vortices of it gleaming in a halo around what remained of his head. And then he turned, as I had known he would somehow. Towards us: not eyes seeing us but something else, that too like a deep-sea fish, no need for sight when you had other senses, when you would snatch and eat anything close enough, if there was something there, don't let him realize something is there, the something is us—

His legs weren't working properly. He managed one step, another. I inhaled deeply, tightened my grip on the jacket, prepared to run. Like in the movie: you were safe if you stayed still only for so long. And definitely not if the T-rex was moving towards you. Our smell, our heartbeats, neon signs showing him the way.

"*Attention! Please exit the area. This area is not safe. Attention!*"

This time we both screamed, and I overbalanced and fell onto the cobbles, Johnny just staying upright, losing one of her shoes. The monster started, flung itself into the darkness, gone in seconds. Above us, the hubcap-sized drone dropped nearly to head-level, its tiny light erasing our night vision, multiplying our shadows into strange curls on the stone. Then it drifted slowly off, as if to remind us that it had a camera, we were being watched.

Johnny snarled under her breath, picked up her shoe, and followed me back down the hill, sliding on the damp stones.

"It sort of looked like a—" she whispered, but was cut off by another bleated "*Attention!*" this time close enough to blow back our hair with the drone's rotors. We let it escort us all the way to the medical tents again before it soared off with the others. The policeman I had spoken to earlier frowned, but did not approach us again.

We stood for a moment under the awning of one of the tents, on the far side of all the drone lights and headlights of the police cars and ambulances that kept pulling up, our shadows from the legs down long and crisp on the wall next to us.

"It looks like a…?" I said under my breath.

She clung to the wall and put her shoe back on, then glanced warily up at me. Her face had nearly been washed clean in the rain, leaving only a few streaks of dried blood and the blue adhesive on her cuts. Under her lank bangs her eyes appeared bright yellow, holding light from somewhere else, not this enclosed place. "Look," she said. "Whatever this is. Whatever's happening. I've got this, okay?"

"You *what?*"

She gestured vaguely at the still-smouldering heap of wreckage up the hill, pluming a thick transparent of smoke into the dark sky. "I don't want you to get involved. Last time, I... we..."

My stomach revolted. We don't talk about it. We never talk about it. We never said we wouldn't talk about it. We... Stop it, focus.

"The least I can do," she said, "is try to minimize collateral damage. I'm going to get to the bottom of this, yeah. If there are any answers to be found, I'll find them. But you, you stay out of this... be safe, go home. Be with your people."

I stared at her, at a genuine loss for words. A couple of years ago, if you had told me that she and I would ever have a single awkward silence, I would have laughed at you. That there would ever be a moment that we could be together and not be joyfully babbling over each other's words, not finishing each other's sentences so much as never letting each other start them...

For just a second I fought down a powerful urge to just tell her everything, start to finish, everything I hadn't been telling her while I'd been trying to pretend she didn't exist. It shouldn't be me, I never should have come. They could have taken you and flown you back to wherever the fuck They came from. That place in the dark where a circle's worth of angles doesn't add up to a real number. Where you came from, in a sense. Where you really belong. Your homeland. "I think I saved your life a little while ago. Again."

"Yeah. Thanks. Again."

And you don't get to tell me what I should and shouldn't do. Not anymore. Not now that I know what you are. But I didn't know *what* to do next, and realized that part of me had been waiting for her to tell me. Which she had, and the anger beginning to smoulder under my ribcage told me that all the other parts of me had wanted a different answer. It wasn't her I was mad at, not really. It was still and always me.

She glanced over my shoulder. "There's my ride," she said tonelessly. "I'm at the Sheraton. Are you close? Do you want a lift back?"

"I'll walk," I said, even though I was thinking again of the man in the tuxedo cracking and twisting, transforming in front of us, before thinking that could be me, on the walk back, ambushed and wrenched apart into a shambling monstrosity, how many people had that happened to already before the ambush tonight, how many had it *failed* for, how many *pieces* of people might be in the city, rotting under bushes, washing into the gutter... "You said They couldn't come back. Not wouldn't. Couldn't."

"I know what I said."

"But what are you going to *do?*" I waved a hand, feeling again that brief cold stab of pain where I'd seized the watcher. Do about the police, I meant to say; and the reporters, the photographers, the drones, the ambulances, the still-smoking rubble, the fact that she had blown up part of a castle, the fact that she was alone, that we didn't know that all the monsters were destroyed or gone, everything.

"Do you know what plausible deniability is?"

"Sort of."

She took off my jacket and handed it back to me, ten times heavier than when I'd put it on, soaked through. "Then let's just say it's my consolation gift. For tonight. Because you didn't get to enjoy the party. And just... stay away from me. I mean *keep* staying away from me. You were getting really good at it."

What would James Bond have said? Something snappy. *My pleasure, madame.* Something like that. *We'll just see if you can stay away from me, ha ha, check and mate.*

Instead I shrugged, and walked back down to where the road was level, slipping easily behind the frazzled-looking line of police and medics trying to keep reporters and photographers from getting in. The rain eased off, and I resisted the urge to look up, see if that rip in the clouds was still there.

Back at my hotel, the temptation to sniff the jacket in case it smelled like her was so strong, and so infuriating, and so fucking pathetic, that I forced myself to throw it into the shower and crank the spray to full blast. Specks of broken glass jumped up like crickets as the water struck, and the sodden fabric spun in a reddish vortex. I dumped one of the tiny shampoo bottles onto it for good measure.

There. Fixed.

CHAPTER FOUR

NEITHER MY BODY nor my brain knew what day it was or what time it was supposed to be, but I dozed restlessly for a couple of hours and woke before dawn, disoriented and cold. The paramedics had given me a pocketful of extra patches to help get me to sleep, help with the pain of the healing bruises and scrapes, but they hadn't put me far enough under, and I remembered too much when I woke.

Bad dreams, like the old days. Messages encoded in buildings and landscapes, instructions I was supposed to infer from the placement of certain stones on a beach whose sand was the crumbled bones of sea serpents. I blamed the light: while I had been on the phone with Mom, then Louis, I had turned on all the lights in the room, even the extra ones in the bathroom that lit up the counter and the interior of the shower; I had not wanted any dark angles, no places I couldn't see into, quantify, name.

Because something was moving. Something was moving that I couldn't see and Louis couldn't either, that neither of us could even sense. Something like bees nesting in the wall of a house, but silent, not even dripping honey, not buzzing. Just clinging there together, in unnatural order, disobeying their instincts to dance and fly and feed.

Do as you wish, he'd said. *I am not authorizing anything you wish to do. But if you are suspected, and you say anything...*

He hadn't needed to finish the sentence. And that was how you knew it was a real good threat. At least in *Mission: Impossible* they told you you'd be disavowed.

Why were two Society members supposed to be at that party?

If you were allowed to know that, you would know.

No pause, nothing. Shame darkening my cheeks. Know your place, his tone had said.

The Society was, they'd said, a microcosm of the world. Hierarchies, ranks, layers. But nothing so opaque or difficult to understand: no, they wanted everything to be clear and easy, so that there wouldn't be misunderstandings. At the very bottom, me and my fellow Monitors. Then the Mentors, Instructors, Investigators, Counselors, and Archivists. Above them, the Governors, like Louis, each with one Advisor. And at the very top, the Director. Know your place: one brick at the base of the pyramid, one book on a bookshelf, like that. Holding up the rest of the structure. But you'd know exactly what was in your book and nothing else, as best they could manage it.

Idly, I wondered if Johnny would tell me. *If,* I told myself sternly. But she's not gonna, because I'm not gonna ask. There's other ways to find things out. And maybe one day, not a Monitor but an Investigator, and... well, let's not get ahead of ourselves here. Don't hope too much. Never pays off. Better to want something else, something reasonable.

Everything still hurt, but I had to admit that at least it was all different things now. Nice to get some variety. I got up creakily, glancing back at the spots of blood and dried glue left on the white sheets, and unplugged my phone from its charger, thumbing it open. One incoherent text message from Carla—something about some limited edition 'sapphire blue' mouse ears—and one from Sofia simply stating 'I am fine,' and no missed calls.

I didn't think Louis' assistant would be able to dig up the ears. I'd just have to tell Carla I hadn't had time to find them. A little disappointment, soon forgiven. Not like Louis's, not like the Society's. At what I had done to the watcher. At what I had failed to do here, my chance to redeem myself.

But if I could give him something only I could give. If I could convince him of that. And that I was not doing this out of revenge, or because he had slighted me... Some people, I had learned very young, were *allowed* to be angry; and some would be slapped if they showed it, or beaten down. And some would be laughed at. I had never been allowed to be angry in all my life. So I had pushed it down, and pushed it down, and pushed it down, and it had no use, could never serve as fuel. I couldn't let it now. If anyone brought her down, it would be the Society.

Witness meant two things, her face had said last night, in the flickering light of the ruined castle. A verb: to witness. But it was also a noun. Both of us watching and watchers so that now, in the aftermath, *only* we knew what she had done; and *only* we knew how I had factored into that, voluntarily or not. I could say nothing without jeopardizing myself, and vice versa. No one else. No one in the world. We had both armed and arranged nukes pointing directly at one another's faces: friendship as mutually-assured destruction.

It has to be us, I could say, and she'd believe it; out of shame, and out of necessity, and out of the thing she couldn't resist: the unknown. But I'd be damned if I begged her to tag along. Such a thing as dignity. No.

I drummed my fingers on the windowsill, seeing and not seeing the first hints of dawn, not real light yet, just a pale silvery glow illuminating the black branches that pressed against the window. Who knew how monsters worked, how these monsters specifically worked... like cockroaches, maybe? The saying about how if you saw one, there were a hundred more hidden somewhere? In what world would you be able to see one cockroach and think, There he goes, the brave explorer, all by himself, the only one in my house? Surely those creatures that had ambushed us in the Great Hall weren't alone either.

If you were allowed to know that, you would know.

If you were allowed to know *anything*. Why were only some people allowed to know? I stared at my face in the brightly-lit window, refocusing past the darkness outside. Dozens of tiny cuts, mouth drawn down at either corner, dark hair floppy and dull. The same look of exhausted paranoia I saw whenever I bothered to check, which wasn't often. I was tired of my entire face and just as tired of trying to change it.

I tried, anyway, though I couldn't shave with all the little wounds and didn't bother trying. Wetted and combed my hair, creakily put on clean clothes from my suitcase, breathing the smell of home: the new-drywall odour of my closet, bright chemicals of detergent. What was it, Mountain Spring or Mountain Breeze...? No matter where we went, how many times we moved, Mom insisted on buying the same scent and the same brand. Even during our two brief stints in shelters she had lugged a bottle of it back and forth in a plastic bag.

One more look in the mirror before I left: better-framed—a big gilt thing artfully speckled with age—than the window, but the reflection itself not any better. Do I dare?

Do I not?

Downstairs, I leaned over the cold marble counter of the concierge desk, and cleared my throat to wake him up. "Hey. Yeah. Sorry. Where's the Sheraton?"

* * *

OUTSIDE, THE COLD air made my watcher-wounded hand feel better, and dulled the faint but persistent pain. To soothe it I walked with one hand in my pocket and one out, trailing through the low thin fog.

Practically the first thing I saw after I left the lobby was the castle, perched defiantly on its hill and swagged with high-viz crime scene tape. The wreckage still emitted a stream of dark smoke, a straight undisturbed pencil-mark in the pale sky. Drones orbited it, occasionally harassed by crows, and the metal and glass of monitoring devices winked down like secret code. Other flickers of light might have been police or investigators with cameras, clipboards, other gadgetry. They'd be looking into it for months. I wondered what the 'official' investigation would find—about the monsters, probably nothing; but the explosion was a different matter.

On the other hand, it wouldn't be like Johnny to design something that might incriminate her. Too preoccupied with her image for that, and justifiably so; to keep up her hero costume, she had been working at a breakneck pace on electric cars, electric planes, and bio-plastics. Phasing out fossil fuels to burn meant phasing them out of the manufacturing cycle too, so she had devised ways to recycle all the existing plastic by breaking it down to its molecules, what she called molcon. Made for a booming economy in a lot of places now. Anyone could do it, mine out the landfills, collect scrap, divert stuff from the back-end of factories, beachcomb for it. The tide was rising, she said; and unlimited cheap electricity would bring everybody up together.

The city was somber under a misty, bright sky; after last night's rain, it felt fresher, clearer. Big electronic billboards proclaimed *PHASE 1 ALERT IS IN EFFECT*. Something strange about the letters, maybe a projection lens slipped out of true. Below in a smaller font, virtually unreadable, scrolled the same information as the card the concierge had given me as I'd left: no large gatherings; some bus routes cancelled; entertainment, fitness, and recreational facilities closed; no boating; ferry service and airport still operational; some roads closed. Tour groups permitted for fewer than 15 people. Curfew not to be instituted till Phase 2. Refresh the supplies in your go-bag in case there's a power cut.

Some city planner somewhere, I thought, was scared out of his wits but secretly grateful that there had actually been a use for all the new protocols and systems that most countries had scrambled to develop after the Dimensional Anomaly. Most had created them with phases (back home, it was colour-coded for some reason, rather than numbered), after the initial panic and draconian captivity of the post-DA hours.

It wasn't that keeping people in their houses would prevent attacks, since the appearance of creatures had been fairly limited, and only in certain areas (yes, I would have pointed out: precisely along the route of travel that Johnny and I had taken). But it might be better, everyone reasoned, if this were going to happen again, to keep the population dispersed instead of frenziedly clogging the roads, or caught by surprise in arenas or movie theaters. Same principle as blackouts during the Blitz, people said. Don't clump, don't concentrate. Stay apart, get your go-bag, be ready to move, but don't interfere with defense operations, and stay out of the line of fire. It kept cities from tying up soldiers or public servants trying to manage the movement of entire populations. Hence: shelter instead of evacuation. And it was easier to practice in drills, too.

There weren't many people out, not much traffic either. People looked harried, rattled. I knew the look. Panic curdled quickly, as if the body were trying to hold up too heavy a weight, and became this expression: grim annoyance. One guy on the corner, shivering in a t-shirt and zebra-print parachute pants, was screaming about the reactor and the end of the world. Around him, pedestrians passed without even glancing up. Flyers stuck hastily onto the walls said much the same thing: *END TIMES!* and *THEY ARE LYING TO US ALL!* and *WORLDWIDE COVER-UP OF ALIEN FIRST CONTACT!* I wondered if the screamer had put them up.

Two days till my flight home, playing spy in a strange city, killing time till I thought Johnny might emerge from her hotel. I felt ridiculous, still wished I had brought Carla's little digital camera; my phone took lousy photos. Old stone churches and squat towers, sculptures everywhere, the trees all slick and dark against the pale sky, a few looking ready to bud, grass and weeds already going green. Some places had set up sawn-in-half wooden barrels by their doors as planters, many with strappy leaves that I thought might be tulips later. Funny, back home we were still snowed in; you wouldn't see a flower till May.

Gates, I kept thinking. Gates, doors, locks, keys.

Maybe we were looking at the wrong thing. Maybe we always had been.

Keys. Locks.

A corner store had shingled its windows with today's papers, clipped to thin chains: last night's torn sky, that terrible streak of light, the purple and green even more lurid in print. The headline took up more than half the page and read simply: *IT'S BACK*. Unable to resist, I went in and got a chocolate bar and a copy of the paper, folding it into the inside pocket of my coat.

The city had a hell of a lot of stairs and slopes, I realized as I ate my candy and wheezed up flight after flight, sometimes stopping in stores just to catch my breath. "When did ye arrive in the city?" a girl asked me behind the counter at a scarf place, and I managed, "Look, I used to have a lot more active job, okay?"

Many of the stairs were barely wide enough to admit my shoulders, leading into strange little courtyards, the backs of buildings, some with fountains or gardens, more just a meeting place of stairs that went other places. The problem with North America, really, was that you didn't have enough old buildings to look at...

I thought about the castle, built so you'd have to run uphill to reach it in the first place. Then the thick walls, the arrow-slits barely wide enough to fit a hand, the cannon protruding from the stone. Spikes on the gates and no clear lines of sight, a hundred places to split up your foe, pen them in, slaughter them. *You'll never get in here, we are ready for you.* Watchtowers, cameras. How had last night happened, *how?* Hundreds of people going over the place with a fine-toothed comb to make sure it would be safe for the party. We should have taken a cannonball in with us, I decided.

Eventually a group of tourists in bright windbreakers pushed past me, their leader announcing something garbled about a war museum, and I followed them for something to do, ending up not quite back at the castle, under some huge pointy stone thing, smeared pitch black all over as if it had been burnt. Conical speakers had been wired to the top of it, labelled with the city crest, like the ones they'd put up in Edmonton on various buildings and trees. We'd taken down the tornado sirens years ago, Dad had said, because they'd use radio, TV, the internet, or your cell phone to let you know there was a warning; now, new ones were going back up. But no one was worried about tornadoes any more. Bigger concerns these days. With tentacles.

Johnny's hotel reminded me of her house: broad, heavily decorated with stonework like a frosted cake. I moved carefully behind the illuminated concrete sign near the lobby doors, my jeans immediately soaked by the dripping hedge next to it. Right; I had killed enough time, I thought, for someone who habitually slept in (and who had stayed up late, I knew with rock-hard certainty) to wake up and leave the hotel. And why did we say 'killing time' anyway? Godawful saying.

At any rate: maybe she would spend all day indoors on her laptop, and in that case I imagined that when she did eventually leave I'd have died of a heart attack from sheer frustration. But I didn't think she'd find the answers she needed that way, and I wanted to be ready when she did. I had two plans, basically.

If she walked, I would tail her to see where she was going. If she drove, which she couldn't do, she'd have to wait in the lobby while a valet or somebody brought the car around (rented, oddly Popemobile-like—giving every impression it was coated in a thick layer of bulletproof glass; I'd seen it last night). That would give me time to sneak out and leap into one of the cabs waiting at the hotel's cab stand. It was perfect.

Follow that car, I'd say. Growl, like a private detective in an old movie. And hope they took credit card, because not only did I not have cash in whatever currency they used in Scotland, I didn't even know what it might be. I hadn't looked it up before I flew out.

The cold crept up through the soles of my boots, the thin fabric of my jacket. Back home, it wouldn't even have felt that cold. Not a dry cold but damp, clinging. Only a few people walked in and out of the glass doors of the lobby, not glancing at me where I stooped behind the slightly-too-short sign. Because there had been no further attacks, as far as I'd heard from eavesdropping on people on the walk back, the city planned to stay in Phase 1, without too many restrictions on movement and businesses. But people clearly didn't want to leave anyway. Maybe she'd…

Nope. Ha. Even before I saw the face, something about the hair, posture, coat, size—everything fractured behind the decorative patterns on the glass—told me it was her. She stepped outside for a moment, trailing Rutger, then nodded to him and went back in, broken into shards again by the designs.

Okay. So they were driving, were they? Well, there were two cabs at the stand, both empty. All I needed was for…

"All right, let's keep moving."

I jumped, and spun nearly into the chest of a black-uniformed security guard, built not quite to Rutger-scale but tall enough to loom into the fog so that I could barely see his face. His hands were clasped politely behind his back.

"Oh, uh," I began, backing away, trying to stay between him and the lobby doors so Johnny couldn't see. "Sorry, I uh, I dropped my phone and I was looking for it."

"The phone you're holding?"

"Uh." Christ! Come on, come on, thirty seconds and she'd leave. Then I could make some excuse and get away from him, into a cab. "Yeah, funny isn't it, when you travel, the jetlag, hard to think."

"Pack it up. Go on, gerroff." His voice was pleasant and level, but his mouth had drawn into a tight bloodless line in his ruddy face, fog swirling around the top of his head so that I couldn't see his eyes.

"Okay, okay." I held up my hands in a gesture of surrender, and made the mistake of looking over at the lobby doors.

"Is… is that what it is, then? Eh? Violatin' the privacy of our guests? One of them creepers, come here to spy on that little girl? What, to get pictures? *Eh?*" He snapped out a hand to grab my phone, and when I yanked it out of the way, seized my wrist instead, painfully tight.

As I tried reflexively to twist it out of his grip, someone else took my other one, and for a second I had a sense of *déjà vu* that froze me to the spot just long enough to realize that he had let go.

"Morning, Miss Chambers," he said. "Just gettin' rid of a pervert here."

"Thanks, Jim," she said. "I'll handle this."

"You'll… er, I mean…" He gave up and headed back inside, making a little futile gesture at the valet who pulled up with their car, Rutger sitting shotgun.

I pulled my sleeve out of Johnny's hand. "Th—"

"What do you *want?* And what part of *stay away from me* didn't you understand?"

"It's a free country! I can walk where I want!"

"Not only was that not an answer, but it didn't even make sense!" She took a deep breath and, with a visible effort, lowered her voice. "What, I'm supposed to believe you just went for a walk and got… caught by a security guard outside my hotel, by coincidence?"

"My hotel is like two fucking blocks away, thank you."

"*Your* hotel? You can't afford to stay within two blocks of this place."

"How do you know what I can afford or not? Oh, let me guess. You invented some great new machine that lets you look into people's wallets and check their account balance, that's gotta be it. Not just *assuming*—"

Somebody—I hoped the valet—honked the horn.

Without looking back at them, Johnny flipped them the bird, then returned her hands to her pockets and glared up at me. Her face was a patchwork of cuts and bruises, including a real whopper across the bridge of her nose that had blacked both eyes as well. She looked like she was wearing ski goggles. Inside the sepia cups, her irises glittered like broken glass.

"I'm too busy to have you tagging along with me anyway," she said. "Go back to your hotel."

"*Tagging along* with you. Is that what you think I want. Is it?" I felt woozy, dizzy; I felt the sudden weight of *we don't talk about it, we agreed never to talk about it.* Fuck it. "You, who fucking *made me* tag along with you for your whole entire life, who picked me out like a designer puppy from a store, who spent more than a decade breaking and disappearing everybody else I could have made friends with, took away everything else that might have competed for *one second* for my attention, because you wanted it all, all of it, *you, you* of all fucking people, think I want to *tag along* with whatever you're doing? Is that it?"

She flinched, nodded, looked down at the ground. Anger still seethed in me like lava, or like vomit; I wanted to keep going, let it all out. Her head snapped up as I was fighting it back down, and she said, "Okay, well give me a better reason then. You don't have one. I saw you hiding behind the sign. You were waiting for me to come out. I saw you. You were trying to spy on me, weren't you? And doing the worst fucking job of it I've ever seen in my life. Even Boris and Natasha would have been less half-assed at it. What were you thinking?"

"Maybe I was worried about you!"

"Oh my *God*, that's such bullshit. Even if you were, there's nothing you can do about any of this."

"How do you know I can't?"

"There isn't! Okay? Christ! My businesses are falling apart, I have to talk to lawyers every five minutes, which by the way, you're making me *late* for, the fucking *Vatican* is mad at me, the Ancient Ones might have figured out a way back here, or They might not have, who even knows, and every arrow is pointing at me, and why can't you just let them? Why do you want *any* of them to point at *you*?"

"You know why!"

The one thing we weren't supposed to say. The thing we thought and never said. For a second I clearly pictured us both with our hands hovering over the red buttons marked *FIRE*. Mutually assured destruction. Those last hours in Nineveh. That if I had come back sooner, or if I hadn't left at all, the Anomaly might not have happened. That there had been time before the alignment to fuel the spell. But I hadn't. Not till after the last minute. Not till it had been too late, and all those millions and millions of people had died. Her fault as much as mine. Mine as much as hers. And we both knew it.

Her face said, *If this is blackmail, I have no idea what you think you're going to get out of it*. Her mouth said, "Let's just go get some breakfast."

"Don't you have a meeting with lawyers?"

"I hate lawyers. I like breakfast."

* * *

"STOP SCRATCHING."

"Up yours. You don't know about stubble. It's *itchy*."

"Just grow a beard then."

"Beards are for old dudes." I squinted at the menu, a sticky laminated sheet. Our breakfast venue was a typical Johnny place: pitch-dark, near-literal hole in the wall. Outside, it gave no indication of existing. Just a door whitewashed to match the wall, set beneath a wooden sign the size of a playing card; then up two flights barely wide enough to walk facing forward. It stank of beer and cigarette smoke and bacon grease.

Rutger in theory liked places like this, because weirdos and paparazzi had trouble finding them; but in reality he hated them, because if you did get caught, you'd be cornered. He sat across from Johnny and me, back to the wall, his broad bronze face composed and watchful. Despite the pleasant neutrality of his expression, everything about his posture suggested he'd rather be fed into a woodchipper than be here right now. I knew the feeling.

True, there was something to be said for familiarity: for Johnny frowning over the menu, for something in this strange city that was if not comforting at least known, quantified. The physical bounds and limits of her the same as always, the mental ones even more delineated now. And the familiarity of the hatred too, of someone who had never stopped hurting me, the damage and the pain and the insult of it still inside me like shrapnel, no different from the thing in my left hand, quiet now. Would it ever heal? Would any of it?

Mom would have said: Not if you don't quit picking at it.

Johnny would have said: I'm working on a device for that.

"Wayne is not yet discharged from hospital." Rutger frowned at his beeping Blackberry. "Elizabeth says she is ready to return to duty."

"Tell her not to," Johnny said. "Back to the hotel. That's an order."

Rutger grunted, a noise of frustration rather than assent, but slid out the keyboard. Typing was a laborious and delicate effort under his huge thumbs. What did he know, I wondered? About last night, about the DA, about her. What had she told him? Everything?

I didn't think so. Whatever else she felt about the truth, there was so much shame attached to it, so much guilt, that she'd spent her entire life hiding it. All her life had been devoted to controlling it. Wanting it buried with her, like an Egyptian pharaoh: hide it from the sight of others and the flow of time, and she would reckon up on the other side where no one could see. The more people knew the truth, the more she feared its consequences.

And she was right to do so, I had realized. If people knew what she was, what she had caused, yes, absolutely, they would take the truth, melt it down, forge it into a guillotine blade to end her. If people knew what she had done.

She pointed at the menu. "Let's just get two of these."

"What? You can't eat all that."

"No, it's fine. I've been here for five weeks. Optimizing the process. What you do is, right, you eat the full Scottish, with a ton of coffee, and then you don't need to eat again till the next day. Saves all the time you'd waste with restaurants and stuff. Good for hangovers, too."

"You should've figured this out by now," I said patiently. "Wasn't your first hangover when you were like eleven?"

"Twelve. Yeah, but I never did Robbie Burns night here," she said, pronouncing it *Rabby*. "Nights, actually, plural. I accepted about ten invitations over the course of the week. Overdid it a little bit."

"Little bit."

She blinked innocently at me, all sweetness and light. The Anomaly, I thought. You. Yours. The Anomaly, the Event, the Intrusion, the Invasion.

Merely in the hours afterwards, they figured about three hundred million people had died: most bewilderingly without cause, simply dropping dead from a sickness that took over their entire bodies. The rest by suicide. In the weeks after, while Johnny and I had been in hospital, about two hundred million more. Impossible numbers. From plagues that had no name, racing through countries like wildfire; from accidents, panic, tramplings, botched evacuations, fires; from other disasters terrible to imagine. Crops rotting in seconds like timelapse footage, livestock galloping in terror from invisible predators. Their corrupt bodies, once captured and slaughtered, revealed to be inedible, hoofed poison.

Even friendly fire, the worst and stupidest oxymoron, had taken uncounted lives: people shooting guns into the sky for those two minutes, at things they did not realize were not happening directly overhead them but surrounding the globe. Worst of all, a couple of countries had even managed to crack open their nuclear briefcases and special phones of various colours, sending up nukes that rebounded off nothingness and toppled onto neighbouring lands.

All the deaths would not be correctly counted for years. Entire governments had fallen, borders had been redrawn. And people were still dying.

The world had looked up and howled at what it had seen; and even if you had not looked, you still suffered. Worse for those who had already been suffering and lacked the infrastructure to take the hit and roll. They had struck at terminal velocity, and the survivors were still climbing out of the pit of madness and despair. Not quite two minutes. A hundred and eleven seconds. Her fault. Her doing.

And that *I* knew what she had done, and what she was—that she had been forced to reveal it—was the greatest shame of her life. The thing she hated the most.

And that I had been involved was the thing *I* hated the most.

Johnny sipped her coffee and said, perhaps misjudging the expression on my face, "Anyway, this morning I asked Sofia if she would help me investigate—"

We waited till I was finished coughing; Rutger, mildly appalled, refilled my cup.

"Come on," she said. "I knew *you* wouldn't ask her."

"Why *would* I? Why would *you?*"

She counted off, her fingers crisscrossed with blue medical glue like she'd been scribbling on them with a ballpoint pen. "First off, no matter what she says, her dad educated her better than most. She can do *really* heavy spells if there's enough magic around; we saw her do it in Fes. Front-row seats. Secondly, she's in town already. Third, she saw everything happen; she knows exactly what we're dealing with. It would help if I knew what she knows. Fourth, she clearly doesn't give a shit about missing school; she's here because her Dad asked her to spy on me and the reactor, or she isn't, and I don't care which, and she knows I know."

"...She... She came for the party, though. That's why we're here."

"Is that what she told you? Yikes. Come on, Nick. Don't let's have another fight about how stupid either of us thinks the other person is." She gulped the last of her coffee, and waved the heavy white mug hopefully in the air, although as far as I could tell there was only one waitress, and she wasn't around. Fair enough, for just three customers. "No, here's what I figured happened. Two *other* Society members were supposed to be there last night, to talk to Cardinal Geary, right? *Not* as part of the formal negotiations, just... you know. Being social. A pre-meeting. Sofia figured that out, or was told by Louis, and got to them somehow, convinced them not to go. Then she came instead, using their tickets."

"Louis didn't tell her to go," I began, then clamped

my mouth shut before I could say, *That's why he sent me.* Okay, don't talk. Don't say anything. Just nod.

She stared at me for a second, asking the obvious question. When I didn't answer, she went on, "Anyway, her spying got interrupted last night. Interesting that she was in the bathroom when everything happened, wasn't it? And then this morning, she's not feeling well, she says. And there's you, outside my hotel, like an idiot."

"...You think she put me up to spying on you?"

"Well, *you* haven't come up with a good reason to explain why you were out there."

I sipped my coffee and tried to think. When you laid it out like that, something I had been avoiding, it felt a bit like that *Star Trek* episode where Scotty had been found with a bloodied knife in his hand and a woman dead of stab wounds in his arms. You could plead innocence, sure. You could plead coincidence. But it *looked* pretty damning.

"We're all Scotty," I said, ignoring her confused blink. "Anyway, she didn't. She's not a member. And I'm staying *way* away from all that cult crap."

"So you abandoned your girlfriend to come spy on me of your own free will?"

"That is *not* what I was doing."

"What were you doing then?"

I opened my mouth and closed it again. A path was becoming evident, a very distant light a million miles away, which was probably an oncoming train. All I could see of it were tangles of lies, which she would see through (I had always been terrible at lying, particularly to her), and acting, which I was also bad at. But if she had created me, I thought with a brief surge of anger, if she had *designed* me, then she had made this path, too. I said, staring down at the table, feeling her eyes on my face, "You're not gonna like it."

"You wrote a whole speech about it, didn't you."

"Yeah."

We fell silent as our food arrived. The answer to 'How can you eat at a time like this?' turned out to be 'Ravenously.' Rutger scrolled on his Blackberry between bites of pancake; Johnny and I ate in jaw-snapping, cheek-bulging silence, budgeting our last bites of scone and bread to mop up the egg yolk, bean syrup, and tomato juice that had escaped absorption by other items. She pushed aside her three little black pucks, which I had discovered I liked even though I had no idea what they were, and I forked them into my own plate to finish them off. Waste not, want not.

"Look," I said, when we were starting to wind down. "Can we talk in private?"

"No," said Rutger, not looking up.

Johnny gave us both a pained look. "Just summarize it," she said.

I took a deep breath. Do your damn job. Had I not done it already? Simply by seeing Sofia? No, goddammit. Be a fucking grownup. Had enough of being a child and a coward both. They're watching you; they want to see what you'll do. Protect humanity. They can't do that without information, can they? And Johnny does everything alone. Wants to do everything alone, always has: except for me. The real right-hand man.

The entire history of human evolution. You don't do things alone. Strength in the group, power in numbers, even when the number is *two*. Don't go hunting mammoths alone. Bring someone with you when you pick berries, in case they're poison. And later, sick of the sticky tumbled bodies in the cave, sneaking out to watch the stars: and secretly pleased when Og or Yug came out to sit next to you.

Scary things. The breath in the night only bearable if you weren't alone. Who would she want with her now but the person who'd been with her for other scary things? The first thing people do as soon as there's a disaster is reach out for a hand to hold. Regroup, rebuild, clump together after being spread apart, share stories and art, know that you could survive if you made some numbers. Made a community.

She hated community. But she *had*, all the same, asked for a pet. Long ago. And knowing that I was all she had was that light in the distance.

I said, "Okay. Short version. I missed you, I worried about you doing this on your own. Whatever this is."

Her pupils dilated with visible speed, like a drop of ink had been placed in each. Shakily, she put down her cup. Oh God, it was working. You monster. No, keep going. That's what you do with monsters. That's what monsters are for: to expose, and then to destroy.

"You're never going to find answers on your own," I said. "Are you? Maybe you are. But what if you need a backup? You already thought of that, right? Why you asked Sofia. But she won't."

She nodded slowly, still staring at me through the mask of bruises.

"I'm here. Sure, I'm not as good as her. I can't do magic. I don't know what she knows. But I know what *we* know, I know what... what we'd never tell anybody else. And that means I can get answers too. You told me to stay out of this: fine. But I'm already in it. I got skin in the game. Those things were trying to get *both* of us. Weren't they."

"Maybe," she finally said. "I think so. I need more co—"

"Do *not* drink any more coffee."

The waitress came by anyway, and refilled both our cups. I pushed mine carefully away.

"But you're on holiday," Johnny finally said.

"I can change my flight."

She curled her hands around her cup. For a moment I could hear nothing except my heart beating—not her, not the traffic outside, not the sound from the kitchen. "Well," she began.

"There is not time for this," Rutger said, replacing the phone in its case at his hip. "There has been another ethics complaint. Substantial inconsistencies are being reported at Segobriga, Fortier, and Wulworth Keep. Not in the calculations. In the raw data. In the seeing."

"Is the degree of observed inconsistency internally consistent between the three?" Johnny said, instantly switching attention.

Rutger stared at her, then exasperatedly got the Blackberry back out. "It is more important to fulfil the requirements of the audit than to... obsess over the incident last night. We have a great deal of work to do before we can issue even the preliminary audit report for the Astrophysics and High-Energy divisions. And those only encompass eight components. And no supplemental information requests."

"You don't think a potential repeat of the Dimensional Anomaly also needs a great deal of work?"

"No further events have occurred," Rutger said. "It's likely that it was... an aftershock. An isolated incident. Underberg hasn't alerted me to anything. No diseases or deaths have been reported. The local police are looking into it, and the UN Department for Dimensional Research is sending a team of twelve subject matter experts."

"*I'm* a subject matter expert. Look, it could be an aftershock. Isn't that a cool word? Wouldn't that be great? Or it could be a *pre*-shock. I won't know unless I dig into it."

"It is not your responsibility to dig into it. Your responsibility is to this audit and the subsequent continued operation of your research facilities. Enough has been impacted already. Contingency plans were not in place for such a sudden shutdown; it's meant to take between ninety to a hundred and twenty hours of operational preparation and emergency response planning. And, as I have said, there have been no further events. Anywhere."

His voice was perfectly level, neutral, as always; you would not have realized how upset he was unless you knew him well. Johnny had hired him when she had been very little—six or seven, I thought. Found him as a grad student in a physics lab, then whisked him away, paid for his PhD, handed over the reins of a thousand things: hiring, negotiation, scheduling, acquiring. He ran a number of individual divisions just on his own, I knew, overseeing and vetting their research personally. Material physics and high-energy physics and astrophysics and something else; and he had singlehandedly coordinated most of their emergency response to the Anomaly while Johnny and I had been in that hospital in Baghdad.

How possessive would you get of those, I wondered, if you had been doing it long enough? How much would you believe yourself (rightly) to be the hero of the hour when your employer had disappeared, and you had watched her go at the airport? When you had *let* her go, and blamed yourself for not stopping her?

Her empire was not crumbling, but it was under close watch, being picked apart by outsiders, and I was sure he felt that he was a part of this, had a *right* to be a part of it; but none of this showed on his face. He was absolutely immobile in the gloom, a handsome and symmetrical mountain, the face and hair nearly the same golden-brown so that he resembled a statue or monument plucked from a city square. Bodyguard, negotiator, research assistant, guardian. Secretary. *Secret*ary: keeper of secrets. I wondered if he hated her too.

Johnny paid for breakfast, but followed that up with an incredibly awkward, half-whispered fight with Rutger in the doorway as we left, which trapped me on the stairs just high enough to not be able to hear what they were saying except in fits and starts, too embarrassed to either push past them or retreat back up.

Rutger didn't want her out of his sight, and wanted to assign another employee to guard her; Johnny didn't want anyone near her; yes, but you've got *him* near you and *look what happened last time*; well that's *not going to happen this time* and go *back to the hotel and I'll see you tonight*. How can I *do my job* when you act like this. *Your job is to do what I tell you to do that's your whole entire job*. Well what you tell me to do and what's *best for you* are two different things. Well what's best for *you* is to *stop telling me you know what's best for me*. Well—

Well, you can't pay people to think what you want, I thought, and stuffed my hands into my pockets and waited for them to finish. When they eventually stopped talking, I wasn't sure the fight was over. I felt heavy, sleepy. Maybe Johnny had been right about the coffee. The sun was fully up, bright through the thin clouds; the sky was a hard, chalky blue. Around us, the fog-soaked buildings and their stone and moss and ivy seemed delineated in ink, painted with dark tones against the pale sky. No one was around, every window unlit except for a convenience store far down the block sending a little stream of pink neon onto the gray sidewalk.

Something crackled against my ribs as I shifted. When Johnny returned, having sent Rutger on his way with the car, I dug in my jacket and took out the folded newspaper. "You're on the front page again. You want it for your scrapbook?"

"Nah," she said gloomily. "It probably says I'm the Antichrist."

"Well, maybe you are the Antichrist."

"I am not!"

"No wonder the Vatican put a hit out on you," I said, tossing the paper into a recycle bin chained to a stone post on the corner. "The Pope's probably gonna come for you himself."

"*Nic*holas."

"Tase you and throw you into a van. Yep." I hesitated. "We didn't cover Catholic bounty hunting in school, I admit, but…"

She laughed, then winced and touched her cheek. For too long we stared at each other: reluctantly, like reading something against our will, a technical manual or a description of something painful. Her bruising was nearly the same colour as her navy coat, there was dirt on her ears, and her hair looked dull and greasy. The only shine in it came from bits of broken glass. Had she even showered last night?

It struck me with an abrupt wave of nausea that this was why my face had seemed strange last night in the mirror, this morning when I tried and failed to shave, why I thought something had happened to it: because all my life, I had been looking at *her* face, not mine. Some fucked-up little part of my brain, responsible for telling me who I was and what I needed to do next, had just rotted away. Decided she would take that spot instead of me, identified her as me, and simply atrophied and died. All those years making sure she was next to me, watching out for her but most importantly, *watching* her.

After a moment, I said, "Have you… gotten shorter?"

Patiently, she said, "I think it's *slightly* more likely that you grew since the last time we saw each other."

"That doesn't sound very scientific."

She smiled, and gave the sudden head-toss that indicated that she'd arrived at a decision that was going to get us at best grounded and at worst killed. "Come on."

"…What?"

"Come *on*. We're going back to the Castle. I'm Sherlock Holmes, and you're John Watson."

"*You're* John Watson."

CHAPTER FIVE

IT WAS A long walk, but Johnny said she knew the way; she'd been in the city, as she explained, for more than a month, and had made a half-dozen other trips during the construction of the reactor. We moved through empty streets, waited obediently at car-less crosswalks with the other tourists while the locals walked across, heads down, hurrying to get inside. I jumped every time the sidewalk vibrated lightly under my feet, indicating that the light had changed. Drones hummed overhead, ranging from the size of a dinner plate to as big as a pool table. Johnny glared up at them occasionally.

"Paranoia," she said. "Unscientific. They're looking down, they're looking up, they can't see or hear or sense in any way what caused the Anomaly."

"Yeah, but nobody knows that except us. And we're not telling."

"What's the point? The gates are shut. It can't happen again."

"So again I gotta ask: then what happened last night?"

She growled with frustration, her face reddening. For a moment I was reminded of an incident five or six years ago, when she had somehow caused two supercolliders to literally collide *with one another*—her own facility in Boston and another lab's facility in Lisbon or something had tunneled straight towards each other and crashed something like three kilometers below the Earth's crust, not to mention several kilometers of ocean. It had taken more than a year for salvage teams to travel along both tunnels and try to recover some of the more valuable components. Physicists were still arguing about how it had happened, apparently, but the main image I always had was her in a sunny courtroom somewhere in Europe, face beet-red, fuming and squirming at the far end of a black-and-white marble floor like the world's smallest, maddest chess piece.

"Okay, so," she said, "last year I walled off the whole Creek, put up surveillance, electric fencing—well actually to keep out bears and cougars and stuff too, you know how they get. And built a new facility in the East Field, where the old CN turnaround used to be. Not even Rutger knows about it. Do you know how hard it is to hide spending from him? I wanted a dedicated space to come up with a... a magicometer, I guess."

"What?"

"Like a... a magnetometer. Or a Geiger counter, let's say. What do you do when there's something around you that you can't see, but you need to know if it's there or not, and once you know if it is, you want to measure it? Gravity's one thing, magnetism's one thing. Radiation: tricky. You can't sense it, you can't prove it exists with a simple demonstration like iron filings or something." Her phone rang. "Gawd! Hang on. Hello?... No, I'm sorry, don't laugh at me, okay? I'm *super* busy. Yes, I'm okay. *Yes*, we can work on it, absolutely."

She snapped the phone shut and ran both hands through her hair. "Sorry. David Bowie. Anyway, the point is—"

"*What?*"

"The *point* is," she said, "we, and by we I mean humanity in general, have never had a way of telling whether the amount of magic was increasing, decreasing, or staying the same. Did you know that the Ssarati have supposedly amassed something like eight thousand known spells, and *none* of them can quantify magic? We don't know anything about it, not really. Not where it comes from, what happens when it's used, how to regenerate it, how to control where it goes. We just know it's real, and it moves. Now how the hell's that gonna help anybody in the world except make them freak out about it? Everybody's paranoid enough already. Look at these stupid things."

I squinted up at the hubcap-sized drone that had just hummed past us, shaking glassy droplets of rain loose from the bare trees. "That's got a Chambers Aerodynamics logo on it."

"Not the point. The point is, no, everybody doesn't

get to know everything, and everybody doesn't get a vote on everything. What kind of world is that? Every single Canadian doesn't get to cram into Parliament to make the laws. Every single... every single person in a restaurant doesn't get to go into the kitchen to decide the menus. Some people have to do the knowing and the choosing, and some people have to stay out of it. Especially with magic. I don't trust the Society farther than I can throw them, but they've got the right idea."

"So you're just gonna profit off it in the meantime."

"Yep. Money buys science, science answers questions."

I rolled my eyes, but she wasn't looking. We rounded a corner that looked slightly familiar, and I glanced up instinctively past the sharp peaks of the roofs around us to see the castle high on its hill, still rippling with the reflective tape and orbited by drones and crows.

"When you said go back to the castle, how exactly did you think we were going to get in?"

"Well, it's not exactly..."

"Oh, for God's sake. You have no idea."

"I *do* have an idea! Why would you think I wouldn't? I mean, maybe *you* didn't have an idea. But it's not—"

"You're about to say *legal*," I said. "Or, um. Nonlethal? Both maybe?"

"Maybe both." She got her buzzing phone out, and turned it off with an impatient flick.

"This is great," I said, looking up at the castle again. "You know, *The X-Files* taught me that criminals often return to the scene of the crime."

"They better just try it," she said darkly.

"I was referring to you."

We had huddled out of the wind behind a high stone wall, the main street ahead of us and a shorter, ivy-covered alleyway at our backs. A black cab slowly ticked past; a little group of tourists trailed after a tour guide with a small microphone clipped to her scarf.

"You have to ask yourself," Johnny said, and hesitated.

"Why here," I said. "Why now. If They've developed the ability to go anywhere."

"Yes." She swung her bag around to her back, the same shapeless waxed-canvas sack she'd been carrying for years. It looked like a dirty ottoman. "Feels a little personal. And no other incidents, *really?* None? So last night was, what, a hit-job? They could have killed us. But They didn't. They tried to kidnap us. Incompetently. What does it mean?"

"Dunno."

"Rhetorical question. But there might be clues at the castle, they might have left something behind, we just need to…"

I turned when she did at the scrape of shoes on the cobblestones behind us, but it was only a couple of middle-aged women, tourists I thought, with practical runners in bright shades of neon, each with a large backpack. One had a paper map folded tightly to the size of a paperback. "Excuse me," she said in a broad American accent, I couldn't tell from where. "Do you mind? We're a li'l bit turned around."

"Don't look at me," I said. "I don't even know what time zone I'm in."

"Where are you trying to get to?" Johnny reached for the map, and froze, her hand out.

Both women began to tremble, then shimmer, as if viewed through flowing water. The woman holding the map collapsed dramatically, her legs giving way, and hit the cobblestones face-first with a sickening crack that I quickly realized was the least of her problems, as dozens of amber-coloured, spiked legs began to tear through her skin, spraying blood and other fluids into the air.

I didn't wait around to see what the other one was turning into, but grabbed Johnny by her sleeve and ran the other way. Dead-end, of course, and I cursed myself: I'd seen that when we came in. Back, towards the main street—

Johnny twisted free and pointed back at the entrance, where more things were gathering, some still recognizable as people, others less so. They moved towards us in lurches and skips or slithering on the cobbles and walls; some had managed wings that kept them a few inches off the ground. Worst of all, they were entirely silent except for the sound of their scales or claws on the stone.

Could we climb the walls? I might, I thought, but I didn't think Johnny could. Nothing to do but follow her at a dead run down the alleyway, longer than it looked, towards the darkness at the end: the opening of a round tunnel or storm drain, half-covered with dangling ivy but fully covered, I realized, with a thick iron grate. "What the fuck? Did you know this was here?"

"Of course I did, but I thought we'd have more time to—"

I nudged her aside and put my shoulder to the spot she was futilely shoving, near the ancient but sturdy-looking hinges, not hoping for much. They bowed at once under my weight, though, revealing that under the hefty metal they had been attached to the stone with much more recent, and thoroughly rusted, thin iron nails. We swung the grating open just wide enough to get through, grunting with the effort, and shoved it back into place, bracing it at an angle on the wet stone on our side. It would fall at once if pushed, but it might buy us a minute or two. But to do what, exactly?

We splashed quickly through the trickle of water running down the center of the tunnel, the already-dim daylight disappearing much more quickly than my night vision could compensate. In moments all I could see was the gleam of a buckle on Johnny's bag. She darted suddenly to the left, down another tunnel, and I followed, cursing and tripping on the broken stone.

"You didn't say we were getting in through the sewers!"

"This isn't a sewer pipe!"

"Smells like one," I said, but actually the odour of urine at the entrance had faded; people must have been pissing against the grate.

"They call these the South Bridge Vaults. People used to live here, I mean, initially they used to like work here and stuff. Shops. But after the plague started coming, it was mostly people who didn't have anywhere else to live. The main thing about them is that there's a lot of them, and only part of it is open to tourists these days, and we're not in that part."

"I *thought* we were pretty far from the actual castle. Huh. Also, by *people* do you mean, like, millions of plague ghosts?"

"Well there's *probably* a few ghosts, I'm not saying there's not. You know Burke and Hare?"

"No. Should I look them up if we live?"

"Extremely no." She got out her phone and turned it back on, illuminating low arches, crumbling stone, indecipherable graffiti cut into the rocks themselves, and some soft-looking wooden supports. The stink of piss had been replaced with the mouldy funk of stagnant water.

"And these lead back under the castle?"

"Pretty close, yeah." She took a deep breath and immediately coughed. The weak square of light bobbed in front of us, glinting off the water at our feet. "Can you hear those things? I can't hear anything. Which is, like, the worst."

"Yeah. That's, like, right before a jump scare."

"No, the first jump scare is the cat."

"More like a rat, down here." I took out my phone too, and turned to cautiously check behind us, shading it with my fingers. No monsters, no people, no ripples in the small slow stream. My heart was still pounding. "What the fuck *was* that, anyway? Can They turn people into monsters now?"

"Maybe. Looked like it. That's the lowest-energy option, I think. Alternatively, somewhere They're making monsters that look and sound like people, and sent them here when they were done." She paused to run her fingers carefully across a carved wooden beam, half-familiar letters—English or Latin—barely legible. "I nearly peed myself."

"Surprised you didn't, with the amount of coffee in you."

"This way."

"Are you sure?"

"Why wouldn't I be sure?"

Don't strangle her, don't strangle her, don't strangle her... serenity now! Serenity now! I stifled a small, horrified laugh, and kept trudging after her, turning continuously to check the way we had come.

"Do you have any, you know, secret weapons in case those things follow us?"

"They're not exactly the easiest things to make, you know."

"I thought you were some kind of genius."

"Not the weapons kind."

"Have you ever considered," I said, "that about two years ago was a *great* time to start becoming the weapons kind?"

"The gates. Are. Shut."

"You keep saying that like it changes what's happening." Why us, I kept thinking as we twisted and turned in the stone tunnels, climbing up sudden shin-tearing steps, sliding unexpectedly down crumbled slopes of stone. Why us, why here, why now? Why not everywhere?

Don't think about it. The kids, Mom. The house. Don't think, Why not there. Call down trouble, as all my aunties would say.

Why us. Why us *again*. Why... where *was* Sofia, anyway?

And why had I just thought that?

"That magic detector of yours," I whispered.

"I never got it to work. Never."

I blinked at the venom in her voice, and enjoyed the small, mean pang of satisfaction. "Okay, okay. So you ran into a problem you can't solve and your feelings are hurt. What were you expecting? It's *magic*, not science. How did you think you were going to study it in a lab? It's... what do you call it. Apples and oranges."

"It's not about my *feelings*. And they're *not* different. I know they're not. And there's a difference between a problem that can be solved with enough money and time and eight hundred thousand kilos of thrust, and a problem that can't be solved," she snapped.

"Well, maybe you should pick a different problem."

"No. I have to solve this one. *Humanity* needs a solution." She stopped and turned her phone so she could see me; startled, I did the same. Her burglar-masked face was jittery, flushed. "What do you think will happen to us if we can't understand magic? If we don't know how it gets in, how it's used, wasted, controlled, generated, broken, accumulated, channelled?"

"How did we survive it before?" I retorted. "Isn't that Their whole thing? They've been here before. They've been kicked out before. We've always survived. *Humanity*. Listen to you. Like you're the only person who's ever existed in the history of the world."

"We had outside help," she said. "And millions of

people, maybe billions, *stopped* surviving. What's wrong with your hand?"

"Uh." I glanced down at the back of my left hand, where the silver tray from last night had gone awry somehow and left a triangular black bruise surrounded by swirls of ornamentation. But I had been rubbing it against my leg without realizing it, because my palm bore a perfectly round bluish bruise of its own where the watcher had gone in. And it had begun to hurt again, like putting too much weight on a hairline fracture. They hadn't taught us what happened if you touched a watcher. Maybe everybody else had died. "Nothing. Bruise. Look." I showed her the top of my hand.

She lost interest at once. "Anyway, the way you figure out how much magic in the world is by doing a small spell, then a larger one, then a larger one, you know? But that process uses up magic. And you can't calibrate what's left until you try a spell that doesn't work. It's like driving in a car with no fuel gauge. Trial and error? We can't live like that. We especially cannot live like that now, after the... after last time. Because this is something They understand and use intuitively, and that intuition isn't something we can develop. It might not even be something humans are physically *capable* of. It's like They can sense things with their skin, like sharks, that we can't."

"Ampullae of Lorenzo."

"Lorenzini. Yeah." She stopped again, and looked up at the ceiling above us, shining her phone on it. Something small wriggled there, eye-level with me, perhaps a foot above her: a small, startlingly magenta worm that must have burrowed through the wood above us. It flinched from the light, opening a line of jewel-green eyes with tiny, sticky pops, one by one. "Ew. What kind of weird-ass bug—"

I poked her in the back with my elbow, hurrying her along. "That was a *tentacle*, genius. Are we close?"

"What in the hell is happening," she muttered. "What is happening. What could They possibly... *How*..."

The next whiff of breeze brought a thread of different stench our way: the rotten, sour, and above all unmistakeable smell of magic. We both caught it at the same time; Johnny stiffened, sniffed, held her breath. And behind us, something plopped into the water.

"Quick!" she whispered. "We'll lose them in the castle."

"That could have just been a rat!"

"How is that better?!"

We sped up, stumbling and even tripping now, cursing softly as we took the hits on our cut palms and sore wrists, trying to spare our phones, the only source of light. All around us the carven stone, the crumbled doorways and columns, the fallen beams, choked off the path through which we ran. More of the waving things—limbs, eyes, teeth, claws—stirred minutely as we passed.

"I've seen this movie," I panted. "The whole hallway comes alive."

"Don't think about it," she gasped, rounding one last corner and skidding to a halt at the edge of a deep, still pool. The ceiling had opened out into thick grayish curves of stone, humped in the middle, like ribs. All around us hung rags of moss and other... things, some craning to watch us, our two little lights in the cavernous space.

"Are these clues? Do these count as clues?"

"Yes, they're still clues if they're staring at you."

There was a strange smell now, or not strange at all really—only strange in the sense that it seemed out of place, as we had once, a long time ago, been alerted that someone was creeping up behind us by the cigarette smoke on his clothes. Here, it smelled of the sea, the unmistakeable sharpness I remembered from my very few encounters with one. Beached seaweed, the stinging odour of the water itself, things disintegrating to bones and ammonia on wet sand.

"Is... this place built over a—" I began, and Johnny whispered, "There's the door!"

I liked doors; you could shut a door. We edged quickly around the pool, heading for the oddly comforting outline in the distance, labelled *ELECTRICAL B3-2*. An ordinary thing, recognizable, reassuring.

Behind us, splashing footsteps, the clatter of broken stone. Murmurs, all too human. What were they saying? Something or someone laughed, a hysterical cackle that echoed around the space like the cry of a hyena. We were cornered.

"We're *not*," Johnny whispered, as if I had spoken. "Keep going."

The door swung open silently, giving way into a smaller darkness inside it, something strange about it, thick, moving. We stopped, pressed our backs to the wall. Our pursuers fell silent too, and for a moment I heard nothing but Johnny's fast breath.

And then a faint, distant rushing. The iodine smell struck us in a cold wave, and pressure came with it, like the heavy minutes before a storm.

I didn't panic until I turned and saw that the way we had entered had vanished, replaced by a thick mass of trees, birches, their pale trunks gleaming in the jittery light of Johnny's phone. They grew straight through the muddied flagstones of the floor, tilting them up and splitting their mortared joints.

And still the dark crawled on, the dark and the smell, till we cowered in its shadow, a tsunami bigger than the stone roof, bigger than the castle, than the hill, the clouds somewhere outside, Johnny still holding her phone up, shining it straight into the darkness, the light disappearing into it and showing nothing.

Just before it reached us, she closed her eyes. I did too.

Don't look away, you need to see it come at you, need to see what's hitting you, was this a trap? Do you know what traps look like now?

Did she—

THE DARKNESS HIT like a true splash of water, cold, humid, not like the still stuffy air of the vaults, shocking my eyes open.

Light returned slowly, sallow and dim, like the green-tinted minutes before a tornado. Ahead stretched a long uneven slope of charcoal-coloured sand, packed hard near the water, a horizon-spanning expanse of oily-looking waves of a chemical or even electric green. Where the beach became impressionable dozens of huge footprints marked it, all different sizes and shapes. In lines, or ranks, so many in the same place they had rutted the ground like tiretracks.

Instinctively, like a blink, I looked down and to my left for Johnny: gone. But the motion had revealed something else, or maybe it hadn't, maybe I was just losing my mind rather than whatever the alternative was. That the painfully-green sea wasn't a sea at all, but the foot-deep pool of water in the center of the room that Johnny and I had entered; that the sand wasn't sand, but the crumbled and weathering remains of the floor and walls that had connected the vaults to the sub-level of the castle.

I moved my head again, cautiously, then shut my eyes. The sound of the waves. Hissing across the hard, rutted sand. And that sea smell, not like the fetid, decades-old water infiltrating soil and stone.

But. But. When I opened my eyes again there was a flash, like before, of the uneven walls, the toppled furniture, the arched ribs of the roof above. Even the E and the L of the word *ELECTRICAL* on the door.

I turned to see that the way we had come in was gone (of course), replaced with a thick birch wood, the canopy interlaced overhead and shading the undergrowth into a hazy mass, the thick pale leaves steadily waving. Worryingly, because everything was worrying, there was a path, bare of the usual forest debris, leading into it. And did the curve of the branches look like the curve of a roof, carved and assembled by human hands? Did the dirt trail look like a corridor leading into some other place?

From certain angles both these things were true, as if all around me were mirrors—not real ones, more like the hypothetical ones Johnny talked about for some of her labs: her wish to have a mirror that wasn't a real, solid thing with thickness and weight, but just a reflective pane, perfectly reflective. But here it would be six or ten or a hundred of them, placed at angles to one another that created a whole new image somehow, and behind them, or even behind *me*, what was real.

Worse yet, somehow, was the crawling realization that though there was no wind here, the leaves of the canopy thrashed in an irregular, but clearly perceptible rhythm. Not a single hair moved across my forehead in the cool, still air. I stared up suspiciously into the greenery. Giant spiders, right? Like from the movie. Up there chittering in their own language, waiting for fresh prey. And every time I moved my head a certain way I caught that glimpse, just fast enough to process, that the silvery-white trunks were carved stone marked with lichen, that the leaves were hanging moss, the branches the remnants of doorways and tables, chairs and beds, the items abandoned when the place I had been a minute ago (and still was, maybe?) was abandoned.

You didn't move an inch.

You moved into another dimension.

Better dry land, at least. It was warmer in the woods, and the packed dirt of the path, interrupted only by occasional roots, continued on its way so smooth it looked swept clean. And it was something to do, aside from panicking; you may as well panic while you walk. I debated calling for Johnny, but had a flash, maybe from a movie, of birds rocketing from the trees, and somewhere, an eye opening up, swiveling, focusing, the pupil slitting... where had I gotten that idea from? Anyway, the silence was too thick and unbroken to interrupt. Nothing but the soft constant sound of leaves brushing against one another. (Or it might have been legs. Hairy legs. *Lots* of them.)

On either side, the uneven masses of trunks receded into the distance, thick and close, showing no other paths. Herded, I thought uneasily. No two ways about it. They know you won't walk into the water. Maybe They don't know much about us, but They count on that, they count on Their dim memories of human limitations.

And then this. Human preferences. The warm damp air, the smell of sap, the safe, flat pathway. How easy to steer people around when you only give them one way to go.

My left hand began to throb, a slow metronome of cold and pain, faint and irritating at first, rising in a steady wave till I could no longer ignore it. I stopped to examine it: nothing. Bruise on one side, bruise on the other. But it had started to do that back in the tunnels, hadn't it? Then stopped, for no reason I could determine.

The watcher doing something, maybe just squirming, angry at being trapped, or maybe just its ghost, if I had killed it; or an early warning system, responding to something nearby.

Or *calling* to it.

Panic rumbled low in my gut, as if held in the cup of my broken, knitted pelvis, and as I began to walk again I cursed myself softly under my breath, all the words I could remember, all the ones I'd picked up from Johnny's multilingual swearfests over the years, everything I'd heard on TV. Why had I grabbed the stupid thing? Maybe it wouldn't have done anything, maybe it would have just burst into fragments as soon as it got too far from the sigil I had drawn to summon it, first stage of the spell, right, it's fragile, they said so, they taught me...

Something in the undergrowth gleamed like bone: a long fallen branch, sheared away on one edge to a razor point. Damp and fresh (don't think about what that might mean) but sharp enough to do some damage. I tugged it free, snapping it loose from the last shreds of bark. It was unpleasantly warm to the touch, warmer than my hand, and I immediately wanted to put it back, but if I *was* being herded, I planned to gore something at the end of the chute.

No birdcalls, no bugbuzz. My boots were silent on the soil. How long had I been going? I couldn't hear the sea any more over the hissing leaves, only the noise of my heart, the scrape of my wooden spear on the path.

Fucking Johnny. Led us under here, straight into this.

Had she known it was here, and lied to me? Had she known last night was going to happen? That weapon on her belt, that... whatever the hell she had called it. That sci-fi bunker-buster not even in her purse but inches from her hand, all night. She knew, she must have known. Lied to me like she always lied to me, for years and years and years, since day one. Maybe everything part of a trap. The party itself. The fight at breakfast, staged.

But she would slip up at some point, and now I was employed by the people who could actually *do* something about it, not just a bewildered loner out there in the salt and the sand... She'd slip up, and the world would know what she had done. And I would get credit for it, and my job would be safe, family taken care of, whatever godawful punishments the Society had planned would evaporate.

This too was a story I needed to tell myself as I walked and muttered, and it was a story with a bad ending, an old-styley Brothers Grimm ending, like the book I used to read to the twins. Her downfall wouldn't make up for everything that had happened to us, let alone the world. But it would feel like justice. It would feel more like justice than this. This, whatever this was, letting her, and Them, jerk me around like a horse on a lead.

Her *and* Them.

The party, the dome. Earlier. The reactor. That They wanted, that she denied Them. What did it...

Around me the leaves fell still, all at once, a silence like the obediently bated breath of a concert crowd when the lead singer raised a finger to the lips. I stopped, startled. Somewhere to my right a small noise began, a howl not quite human, more like an animal or bird imitating one, rising in moments too high for me to hear, followed by others, a half-dozen keening harmonies. And then, much closer and even more surprising, very clearly, the slamming of a door, cutting off a ringing cell phone.

My *phone*. Ignoring the noises for a moment, I hauled it from my pocket, juggling it in my eagerness. Why hadn't I just—no, it refused to power on, and the screen was filled with something that looked like mercury, a heavy silver oblong moving reluctantly from corner to corner when I tilted it. I snapped it shut, debated putting it back in my jeans pocket again (too close to my junk? better not risk it) and slid it into an inner pocket in my jacket instead.

The cry began again, behind me, and without meaning to I sped up a little, trying not to make noise, trying not to look up at the stilled, watching trees, trying not to think about what had happened to my phone, it's just magic, just *magic*, something I was supposed to be friends with now, something that's supposed to be *mine*...

Remember. Don't forget. Sometimes They want you to move forward, sometimes They want you to turn back. Always They steered you with the simplest physiological alchemy: fear here. No fear here. And you would go where They wanted you to go.

If you let Them.

A trap, of course it was a trap.

My left hand thudded angrily with every step, that

small furious star of pain in my palm threatening to go supernova. Low down, something darted away from the path, rabbit-sized, a spangle of surfaces mostly reflecting the white bark, the green leaves.

And something else.

Don't turn and look. Run.

But I turned and looked anyway.

Behind me, absolutely silent and nearly close enough to touch, something watched and smouldered—a writhing, near-invisible mass of darkness crowned with a thousand horns, dripping blood and fire from one set of eyes into the set beneath them, so that the featureless face filled in turn and spilled over. Its feet, undefined columns of darkness, like the birch twigs in which it stood, were on fire, burning with a sickly, reddish flame. I froze.

She brought me here she brought me here and she knew she must have

I brought the wooden spear up straight ahead of me, the old signal or the old threat, the same length and weight as my old stick playing street ball in the old neighbourhood: *This hockey stick is between you and me. Not one more step.*

It shuffled forward one step, another. Heat wormed from it, sticky and rank, like breath rather than flame. Just before the branch would have reached its chest, I stopped moving too, and we stared at one another, my back-brain screaming *Don't look! Don't stare! What are you doing? Don't you know that's how all those people died?*

The eyes of fire, weeping down its face and into its

throat, like the spill of lava down a volcano at night, and the furious darkness of it unlit by the flames, and the horns each as sharp as a knife, so that they sliced even the air above it. Slowly, I held up my left hand, and it did as well, and then it sketched something in the air that vanished in a second: a burning rune, a vertical streak of fire with a couple of branches. As I stared at the empty air, it stepped off the path and melted into the woods.

For a minute I stood there, staked in place with disbelief, my heart hammering so hard it seemed to echo through my whole skull. Why had I done that? Why had *it* done that?

Find Johnny. Get out of here. Find her and get out. Get back. Reckon up on the other side.

I cupped my hands around my mouth and called, listening for what seemed like forever between each shout. Jesus Christ, other rich people had those trackers implanted in their bones, the ones she'd developed for Chrissake, so you didn't lose them for one second, and Rutger begged her, nagged her, yelled at her, but she never *wanted* one, she was *special*, she was—

There: a break in the trees, not quite noticeable unless you had been walking for long enough seeing nothing but the near-identical trunks, till the eye had got used to it. Johnny wouldn't have gone that way, would she? But the leaves were indeed stamped down, branches freshly dangling, even sending a faint fragrance of sap and— unless I was imagining it—her acidic, chrysanthemum-smelling sweat. She had been running.

Don't leave the path. Don't leave the path.

They did this to herd you: split you up. They knew you would try to protect her because that is what she trained you to do. Don't fall for it.

I plunged into the shrubbery, forearm over my face to protect it from the branches. Not a path but a trail, narrow as a rabbit run, almost invisible in the thick gloom.

My boots slid under me; I grabbed a branch, which snapped under my hand, and rose, gasping for air. The ground below my feet was no longer slick with fallen leaves but was damp turf, turning into mud and large stones—the built-up bank of a small stream. A real stream, a real place? Or some kind of set-dressing, the way I had thought the sea was the pool... there was no way to tell. The stream looked real. Slow, clear as glass, trickling past in sedate silence.

A moment later, Johnny crashed out of the bushes and skidded to a halt in the mud just as I had, pinwheeling her arms to stay out of the stony fringe of the little stream. "Jesus *Christ*, what the *absolute fuck*."

"Are you okay, are you hurt? Where were you?"

"There was a thing," she panted, putting her hands on her knees, the asthma wheeze just at the edge of her words. "A thing with a... face like a... I don't know. About the size of a shih tzu, to be honest, but you know the rule."

I did know; it was a very good one, known between us and the kids as the Joanna M. Chambers Unbreakable Law of Proportional Body Size and Personal Danger, and it went, *If it's bigger than you, it's stronger than you; and if it's smaller than you, it bites.*

"And it was on the path right in front of me, till suddenly it wasn't, and I just ran off the path and into the trees. Not thinking, I guess. On the other hand, I haven't seen any giant spiders. Yet. I'm still gonna say 'yet.'"

I nodded as she spoke, and stooped to pick up a rock at my feet, gently wriggling it loose from the mud like a tooth from a socket, feeling to make sure it had at least one sharp facet, running my thumb along it, and when she paused for breath, I did too.

Then I slammed the rock into the side of her head.

CHAPTER SIX

BLOOD SPRAYED IN a fine mist, coating my face and hair; I coughed, spat, frantically scrubbed it off with my sleeve.

The thing slumped in the reeds, its front half bobbing in the stream. Blood jetted into the still water, a disc of red glass rotating lazily in the dappled sun.

Holy shit. Jesus Christ. I was wrong. I was so wrong. I thought—

Stars flashed in front of my eyes, a warning clear as a billboard that I was going to pass out. My entire arm hurt with the force of the swing, the sensation of something *giving* under the stone. My vision began to dim.

Oh God what am I going to do what have I oh God I was wrong I was wrong I

What am I going to do when I leave this place they'll arrest me and I'll try to tell them that I was wrong but monster they'll say monster you killed her you cannot explain yourself the Society won't help me my family won't help me they'll what am I going to do I'll have to disappear run away but I can't I can't leave them I'm all they have I have to go back to them they're my responsibility I—

Across the stream, the woods flickered—a thousand faint eyes glowing two by two in blue and green, red and white. A blink, or a wink. Then they were gone.

Something flitted past my eye, and I jerked my head back reflexively. A wasp? A leaf? No, something else. A chip of something the size of a penny, tearing itself out of the woods and stopping, not hovering but apparently stuck, adhering to something I couldn't see.

And then another, and another. Beelining past me, whispering like paper as they cut the air. I turned to see where they were coming from, but couldn't tell other than, impossibly (*but nothing's impossible now, is it? nothing is, not now that the line has been crossed, the line of murder, death the one thing even she cannot cure*), the woods themselves, the lush green-and-silver wall.

A portrait. Chaos to order. The black fork between two branches became a pupil, the underside of a leaf an iris; colour flew from dried grass and broken branch to form blonde and brown hair, shadows to rebuild a navy coat, the green stripes in a scarf.

Finally remade, rebuilt on thin air, thrown together from the darkness of the woods, she turned to me, dazed. "Nic—"

And she keeled over backwards, so that I had to dive to reach her before she hit her head on the stones.

IN A MOVIE, I'd have splashed her with the stream water (full of blood: no) or slapped her (asking for a punch in the face: no) to bring her around; I settled for pulling her into a sitting position and jiggling her shoulder. I would never speak of those moments of doubt. Couldn't. Or what I had felt when I realized that I had been right, not wrong.

Her eyes, once open, took forever to focus on my face; her pupils were the same size, but as big as dimes. "What...?"

I pointed at the stream. The thing had unprettily and completely disintegrated, leaving only long sticky runnels of white and crimson that eddied around the rushes like yarn. "I hit it in the head." I thought for a moment, then added proudly, "With a rock."

"Killed it?"

"Well, I assume..." I trailed off uneasily. But there *had* been a couple of minutes, when my brain had shut down from panic and my vision had been darkness and sparkles, like someone had set off a flare in my face, and I hadn't been able to see. Of course, there was no good way to say that.

"If you smacked it hard enough, it probably did die," Johnny said. "Inasmuch as a czeroth *can* die, in the human sense. That is, I suspect what makes it 'alive' isn't much different from what makes us alive, if you want to talk about the very basics of differential electrical or magical potential across membranes. Anyway, it's dead, or it managed to get back to the place we came through..."

"Or it stayed here, circled back, and is waiting to hit *us* with a rock."

"Maybe," she said. "As you know, most people who have met us want to hit us with a rock."

"Check."

"Check."

I helped her up, and she wobbled away from the gory stream, bracing herself on a tree. "How did you know it wasn't me?"

"What?"

"...You don't know what those are. Right." She inhaled shakily. "Come here. Get your back to something. I didn't see who cast the spell. Or what. Listen, they're an exact copy in a way that even twins aren't exact, in the way even a clone wouldn't be exact. It's a physical snapshot down to the subcellular level. No one can tell one from what it copied."

"What are you *talking* about?" I leaned on the tree next to her, the bark so warm that it paradoxically made me start to shiver. "Of course it wasn't you."

"I don't... understand," she said, after a pause long enough that I almost started talking again. I'd never seen the look she was giving me, her face rippling like the uneven sunlight, anxious, unbruised places marble-pale, a small localized conflict. I wondered what the two sides were. "No one can tell. That's not how the creature works. There isn't even a spell to tell it apart from the copy; you just have to wait for it to fall apart. And *definitely* nobody could tell by looking. It's not possible."

"I don't know. It just wasn't you."

"Even *I* thought it was me."

"*I* didn't think it was you. It wasn't you."

Yeah. Let's just keep saying that. And let's never talk about those moments of doubt afterwards. Not before: there was none. And not because I changed my mind at the last second, but because the stone in my hand was moving too fast. Struck without thinking, the way you might slap an insect on your arm before seeing if it would bite or sting if you touched it. Let's not talk about those seconds when I decided I was a murderer, the blunt blade of some monstrous assassin that knew everything would happen just as it foretold, and swapped you and the double maybe at the exact instant the rock hit...

No. I had known. If she had been swathed in burlap from head to toe, and silent, and a hundred miles away, I would have known it was her.

But how?

My mind flip-flopped between certainty and doubt like a metronome: Was it *magic*? Had I been able to tell because of my training, because of my ability to do magic, the thing she believed only she could do? Or was it the watcher—that venomous void leaving a signature, or a mark, or an (oh God) *egg* in my hand?

Or was it absolutely secular, if you could call it that, was it simply that she had been my only friend for my entire life, and that alone gave me secret knowledge? Would she have been able to, if it had been me?

Stop it. Remember what you're doing. She's still the enemy: this doesn't change it. Or at least, doesn't change it for the better.

"Are you okay?" I finally said, unable to stand the look she was giving me. "What was it like? Are... Does it hurt when it does it? When it copies you?"

"I'm all right. I blacked out after a couple of seconds." She stared up at the leaves. "This... isn't where I came in."

"Where *are* we? I kept thinking..." I trailed off. *That it was a trap, that you did this. But looking at your face, the face of a liar...* "That we never left. That we're still under the castle, somehow."

"Me too. You know what it was? It was when the..." She waved her hands vaguely. "The dark came at us. For a second I thought *it* wasn't moving, I thought *we* were moving, being moved into it. I put my hand on the wall to see if we were moving or still, and right under my fingers, I swear to God, I felt the wall change. From stone to metal, small cold metallic shingles, smooth as a fish, but dry. I looked down but the dark caught up and I couldn't see anything. When the light came back, I was in a..."

She pointed back at the birch wood I had stumbled through. "A room, a big one. But not like the rooms we were going through. It was metal, a plain metal box shingled with a bunch of little hexagonal pieces, with four doors leading outside. I walked around and looked through them, and it was the same on every side, flat fields, this kind of purplish grass. And the grass kept moving, swaying, but there wasn't any wind."

"I saw the same thing, going through the woods. The leaves were moving on their own."

"Yeah. Creepy as hell. I kept thinking there was something in the grass, something coming at me... I called for you, but that was actually *more* creepy, it was so quiet. But I didn't want to stay in the room, either. I felt trapped. Started walking, and spotted the woods in the distance, maybe these ones, I guess. I saw a thing like a..." She laughed uncertainly. "Okay, so maybe we're somewhere else? Maybe we're here? What tipped me off was I saw a thing like a rabbit, all broken glass, kind of, both clear and reflective, and lots of teeth, but as I turned to get away from it, it looked like a rat. I mean, an ordinary rat. A regular rat."

"From a certain angle."

"Yeah. But then I couldn't get the angle back. And I was running anyway. Like a girl in a cartoon," she added, disapprovingly. "A housewife standing on a table with a broom... and it's not like I haven't worked with rats."

"Lab rats aren't regular rats," I said.

"Anyway. It was sort of two things at once, I mean, whatever it was. And I heard other things for a second—a car horn, people talking. Just ordinary people. In English." She chewed gingerly on her lip. "Like in *The Matrix*, you know? Two places at once. You're in the 'real' world and you're in the Matrix too. You can be in one without being in the other just one way: being in the real, not being in the Matrix. But you can't be in the Matrix without being in the real."

I stared dully at her. In the stream, the last of the blood and remains finally unhooked themselves from the rocks and the reeds and floated away. The rock I had used (both a perfectly ordinary stream rock, and a cut rectangular cobblestone), still stained with blood, gleamed in the grass. "*If* we're in the Matrix, how do we get back to the real?"

"I don't know that there's a way to get back if we haven't left."

"What?"

She closed her eyes, leaned her head on the tree. Her eyelids, streaked and speckled with broken blood vessels, trembled like the leaves above us. I waited out a wave of sudden nausea, as I thought she might also be doing. Wait it out, let it break over you.

If we had crossed dimensions, I thought, there were ways to tear open a path to get back to our own; not a gate, more like kicking a hole in the drywall—she had told me that once, I had heard it too in my training. And within a dimension, you could move around if you had to, though that too was energetically and magically costly, not necessarily a spell a single person could do, and certainly not with so little magic in the world now. But this, unsure of where we were, of whether we had even moved or not? I had never read about it. And, with a sinking feeling, I thought Johnny hadn't either.

She opened her eyes after a few minutes. "Maybe we should keep moving."

"Yeah. We walked in here, right? Maybe we'll just walk back out."

WE STUCK TO the banks of the stream for a while, following it downstream, till it turned back nearly on itself and the ground got too wet. After shoving our way through the brush for a while we squeezed through two closely-twined trunks towards a patch of brighter light, finding an empty, thickly-grassed clearing, humming with fat bumblebees and carpeted with multicoloured blossom. There was something calculated about the sunlight through the leaves, something Disney-ish. Planned to put us at ease. As if, I thought, anyone who watched as many animated movies as we did wouldn't notice. Tiny birds undulated overhead, chirping and flirting their tails.

"*Wow*," I said, at the same time that Johnny snorted, "*Nice* try."

We looked at each other. "Nope."

"Absolutely not."

It was harder to walk, sticking to the edges of the trees, but there was no way we were walking into that inviting meadow. Gotta remember who sent the invitation. "So you never saw who did that spell," I said. "To make the... the thing. The double."

She shook her head, pushed down a branch, waited till I took it so it wouldn't snap back into my face. "It's a *hell* of a lot of magic, though. Nothing a human could do. Maybe eight or ten people, working together, siphoning magic and life from one another... or maybe not a human."

I took a deep breath, and told her about the burning thing I'd seen: Ghost Rider, I said, trying to laugh, but like a deer. But not like a deer *really*, not with horns. They were made of wood. I left out the way it had raised its hand to me, mirroring mine.

"The Burning King," she said, glancing up at the trees as if he might drop out of them. "Around 800, they say, near Lindisfarne, the monks reported 'fiery serpents' flying above the abbey. Disaster, fires, the well ran dry. And then a Viking raid, on top of everything."

"Are we sure they were Vikings?"

"You get it. Anyway, the serpents were supposedly led by a man 'with the head of a stag,' with his eyes and his feet on fire... The records are so muddled. They called him the Burning King, and people were claiming they still saw him after the serpents had left. In the woods, chasing people down and eating them. Even if they were on horseback. But he'd usually let the horse go."

"Very considerate of him," I said. "Could *he* have done that? Made the double?"

"Maybe."

But I knew what she was thinking, as we walked in silence, crunching through the twigs, dodging the huge suspicious fungus. That the spell, costly or not, had not been cast for nothing. That someone, or several someones, had intended for the double to deceive me, and for Johnny and I to be split up here, wherever here was. And that raised the question of why. And neither of us wanted to ask that, in case we found out the answer.

Quietly she said, "They're so disorganized, They're so chaotic. They don't follow rules, only laws, and we don't know those. It's hard for some of Them to even *think*. I keep remembering the history books, the ones saying when They've come, it's just been random, angry, like..."

"Raccoons getting into the kitchen."

"What? Yes, okay. Because They're not really intelligent, most of Them. They *react*, it's all based on emotions, insults, impulse. But if They had a plan... if they were being directed, somehow. If they had... organized..."

Yes, I thought. But if that. If you were bees, bees in the wall. Bees waiting silently in the walls, moving. The soft sound of feet only other bees could hear.

There was a small path at the end of the clearing, branching into three parts; Johnny stepped gratefully into the cross-roads, dusting her clothes free of leaves. "If They—"

"Wait," I said. "Don't move."

She froze obediently, eyes wide. There had been something at the head of one path, the rightmost one: slight, delicate. But not just that. It had also carried the Burning King's sign: the vertical line, the others sprouting off it, glimpsed for just a second as I had looked up. For both of us to find, I thought, but for only one of us to be caught by it, because the other had been warned. I gestured for Johnny to stay put, and edged towards where I thought I had seen it.

A second later I crashed into something so hard that I found myself facedown in the undergrowth, arms still moving as if they could break my fall. "Motherfuckingsonofafuckingbitch!"

I rolled over, rubbing my shins through my muddy jeans, gritting my teeth; it felt like I had walked into the razor-sharp edge of a coffee table. New scars right over the ones she'd paid to have laser-erased from our last gong show. But there was nothing there.

"The *fuck*. Did I just trip over a *dimension?* Because I swear to God, if They're setting up *math* traps now, I quit. I'm going home. Fuckers."

"Oh my God, dimensions aren't *math*. Don't get up." Johnny edged cautiously out from the crossroads, craning her neck; after five minutes of heron-like posturing, bobbing, weaving, and covering one or both eyes, she said, "Okay, come here. But carefully. And go like this."

Her instructions made no sense, and it took several minutes, but once it happened, it was as if a filter had slotted down over my eyes and I could see it—albeit blurrily—without having to stand in precisely the right pose and place.

I had pursued, and tripped over, the outcrop of an invisible stone... or not invisible, exactly. It was both clearly exactly where I had fallen over it, with a little shred of bloodied cotton on one bastard-sharp edge, and clearly *not*. Like her long-wished-for nonexistent mirror, reflecting only the stone, had been planted in the ground, and so it had no more depth than a reflection, possessing only height and width.

Somehow, and without contradicting itself at all, it also looked intimidatingly solid and real. Shaped like the jagged tooth of a tiger shark (edge within edge within edge), the bulk of it reared high above us, mottled bluish-white and spotted with silvery lichen and fresh smears of something dark and iridescent, like engine oil. The rune on it was carved so deeply I could have put my whole hand into the chiseled stone.

But something else about the stone bothered me, not merely its invisibility, or half-visibility; not merely its vaguely menacing shape. More that it seemed strangely familiar, and I had never seen it before.

No.

I had. Not in a dream but a vision, given to me by Their minions or messengers, when I had been asleep, or entranced, or perhaps They had just taken my consciousness and pressed it through something—who knew how They worked, even They did not, I thought— and I had flown, and in a terrible field of barren ground I had seen stones like this, sharp as knives, white-blue, arranged in repeating semicircles and aligned and staggered like teeth seen from above, the unbreakable teeth of some buried behemoth not as dead as the legends believed it to be...

"I think it's an altar," Johnny said, looking around us, and thankfully not up at me: I had no idea what my face was showing. "It's always said They insisted on... payment. Protection money. A life was best: then you could get both the sacrifice's time and their... whatever. Vital energy. And willingly given. They loved volunteers.

Supposedly. A lost life gave immense power."

I stared at the stone, waves of hot and cold washing over me, crackling into the fresh cuts on my shins, dribbling into my socks. "Hey, uh," I said. "What the *fuck* does that mean?"

"Ss... several things, I think." She glanced around us, as if an entire battalion would come crashing through the trees, from the warm blue sky, straight out of the stone. "Um, but if it means that this is a gathering source of magic, then... maybe there's enough to... get us out of here."

"Oh hey, there's an idea."

She got her laptop out of her bag, but before I could say something unhelpful she had wrestled the heavy oblong onto its side and ejected the CD drive, which contained not a disc but a flat plastic envelope.

Opened, its contents turned out to be a handful of laminated square cards bearing hand-drawn sigils: magic circles, the channels that would funnel magic into shapes that could do work, needing only the correct words to activate each. I didn't recognize any of them. Of course, I only knew a few by memory, but these were far more complex than any I'd seen while training.

She caught my eye. "Just in case."

"I saw you draw magic circles while we were in... while we were... doing stuff last time," I said slowly. "Why are you carrying them with you?"

"I just told you."

"You told me They'd never come back. What would you need these for?"

"Can you *quit* asking that? You never know when you'll need an emergency spell. Like now."

Next to the altar-stone, she outlined a circle in the soil with her shoe. I stepped into it, taking the far side of the card she was holding. My heart was pounding; whatever fear I'd felt at the dark coming at us, my quasi-murder, the dead king, sank under a leaden wave of fresh terror. Johnny was shaking; I felt it through the card.

But that was what They liked to do too, the fuckers. Like life. Give you a choice that wasn't really a choice. Force you down the path you never wanted to take. The last time she had done this, we had ended up under a sky that was eyeballs all the way to the horizon.

And it was then that she knew what They had done to me. What the mere fact of Their approach and request had done to me: how it had burned into and corrupted me, tainted me. She felt her wards trying to throw me away from her. And she said we would talk about it later. And we never did. And we never will.

She didn't see the Burning King spare me.

"Wait," I said. "Maybe this is... maybe this is what They want us to do. I mean, if They trapped us here, maybe getting out is a trap too."

"Oh, okay. I guess we'll just live here forever then. Hope you like eating leaves."

"I'm not saying I have any better ideas," I said, annoyed. "Just, are you sure this is our only option? You're the genius. Supposedly."

"It'll be okay," she said. "I mean, if all of our particles make it."

"Yeah. I mean, what do people need, y'know. *Particles* for, anyway."

"Particles are bullshit too." She laughed weakly, and added, "By the way, none of the spells on these cards have been tested. Just modelled. They're actually not pre-existing spells, I wrote a program to—"

"Johnny."

"Oughta work. In theory. Don't let go of that card."

"I won't let go."

She whispered the words, soft and fluid, the spell coalescing around us cold, burning, heavy as lead, clear as glass; I opened my eyes, saw the staring mass of darkness across the clearing, shimmering through the burgeoning power, the face aflame, the feet aflame, watching us, but it was too late to say anything. Every direction yanked on us at once, and I instinctively held my breath.

WHICH TURNED OUT to be the best thing I could have done, as the air pressure vanished, returned, snapped back into place and threw us both upwards and sideways, somehow, into the utter shock of clouded, icy water. Small objects swirled glassily around my face, and I flailed for the surface of what fortunately turned out to be just a few feet of water: a fountain, finished with small blue hexagonal tiles. The things I had seen were coins, stirred up when we hit.

Spitting and coughing, I climbed out and tried to snort water out of my burning sinuses. Johnny swore as she shook water from her bag; the waxed canvas was water-resistant, I thought, not water-proof, and her laptop must have been soaked.

The fountain marked ground zero of a large courtyard, enclosed by tall, intricate stone buildings and floored with concave cobblestones. Each held a round puddle in its center that reflected the crimson glow of either a sunset or sunrise. I looked around to get my bearings, see which way the shadows were going: not a cloud in the dim, coral sky.

A burst of lightning flooded the square, so bright and close that it seemed for a split second we'd been submerged in white-hot liquid. Thunder hit hard enough that I felt my internal organs jiggle, and right on its heels, three more pillars of lightning, splitting the sky into segments. One must have earthed close by; behind the walls, I heard a clatter like roof tiles hitting stone.

"Bad sign," Johnny said, when the noise seemed to be over; we had unaccountably found ourselves sheltering under a stone archway across the square, for what little protection it would give.

"Yeah?"

"Listen, there's a... you know, the reason we're alive, basically, when you get right down to it, is that our bodies, and Earth, have approximately equal amounts of positive and negative charge on most of our particles, and the attractive and repulsive forces are close to canceling each other out, right?"

"...Sure?"

"Even a small imbalance can lead to... well, local

effects. Trying to balance out. Lightning is one you can see: it gets unbalanced in the upper atmosphere, then it restores itself."

"Oh, okay," I said, uncertainly. "So this is natural, then?"

"It might be, it might not be. Maybe there's an imbalance building up somewhere else. Or in some other place that's... that's affecting us." She took off her scarf, folding it and wringing out the last drops of water. "I'll see if I can figure out where we are. Earth, I hope."

"...What."

"Can you get me some coins from the fountain?"

"Can you go back to what you said a second ago?" But she was already fiddling with her laptop, not listening. I walked back to the fountain and scooped up a handful of change.

She pored over them, frowning, then held them out on her palm for me to look at: blank discs of metal, though with edges clipped or serrated as if they were real coins. *You fucked up*, I almost said, then bit my tongue. Stick with the mission, can't get information if you lose your temper at her. "Let's go see if we can find some street signs or something," I said.

"No, hang on," she said slowly. "I asked the spell to take us back to the... to the last place that *that* place had led to. Which I assumed would be where we came in."

I looked around, cautiously, in case the sky wanted to fry my eyeballs again. It looked like the little of Edinburgh I'd seen so far, I had to admit. The shape and size of the buildings, their architecture, the cobbled ground, even the fountain. The only weird thing about it was the apparent lack of a way in or out, though perhaps that was common for courtyards, maybe you just used the doors. You wouldn't have built anything wide enough for a car if you were just going in and out of the buildings on foot...

"Maybe we're back," she said, "but not *exactly* where we came in. Maybe while we were walking, we came out somewhere... from the vaults, I mean. Not under the Castle any more. But..."

She fell silent too, thinking. I hoped we weren't thinking the same thing, though without much hope. The sea, the pool of water, the trees, the roof. That last glimpse of the sign on the door. Not *The Matrix*, but the Matrix.

I said, "I don't think They did get back. I think They figured something else out. How to... *turn* things. Into Themselves. They started with... well, who knows, probably too gross to think about. I don't know. But at some point They tried it with people. Those things at the party, those tourists we saw. And it's... not just people. I think it's things, too. Turning our stuff into their stuff. Turning Earth into..."

And then I really did have to stop, because I had no idea. There was nothing like this in the books or the stories, or nothing I'd seen anyway, from the histories of Their repeated invasions and attempts; which made sense, I guessed. No time for small-talk while you're getting killed and eaten. "Over there," I said, when Johnny still did not reply. "Their dimension. Their place."

She nodded, still playing absently with the handful of blank coin-things. "Theory five," she said at last.

"What?"

"That spell felt practically effortless," she said. "It shouldn't have. There was a lot of magic, free magic, right where we were. And with the gates shut, there should be virtually none on Earth. So did we leave our dimension and go somewhere else, or did a lot of magic flood into ours somehow? I'm thinking the second. So, theories. But let's look for a way out while we theorize."

"We?"

"I was being generous. Theory one: those things were hiding here, left over from the Anomaly. Except the spell I used at the alignment in 2002, the Heracleion Chant, that's designed to tag and eject Them to the far side of the gates before shutting. And the gates did shut, so the spell must have succeeded."

"Okay. What's theory two?" The air was damp, heavily charged; it was hard to breathe, and crackled in our lungs like it was forty below. We moved methodically around the cobbled square, checking for a way out. The things that looked like doorways were actually just arches filled with stone, corner-to-corner, like the plaster decorations placed as faux-fancy architecture in chain restaurants. One of the walls was crosshatched with chisel marks if you were being generous, claw marks if you weren't.

We gave that one a good long look. Eventually she said, "Theory two is that some of Them were in some kind of... suspended animation, or a juvenile form, or a spore. We don't know much about Their biology, because They're not really biological creatures as we understand them, Their physics don't work like ours, how They experience time, gravity, electricity, light, magic. But supposing They were in a form insensible to the spell, or had been shielded somehow, perhaps in an artifact, a hoar-stone or a statue or a geological formation, supposing They weren't *alive* enough for the spell to work on them."

"I don't like that theory much."

"Me too. Or three or four, either. Theory three, something like accidental transport. But I've only ever read that it's extremely difficult. You can only get through a gate under the correct conditions, and if you know the spells to make it open. And even then, crossing it is dangerous and exhausting, apparently. Like squeezing yourself through a revolving door that's moving too fast, They get battered, beaten up, drained of magic and life force, or whatever They call it. Four, deliberate transport, but outside of a gate. A dimensional tear, perhaps. Like walking through the drywall instead of using the door. But They've always used gates because gates, frankly, work. Did They find out, figure out, something else that did? Maybe. But if so, why not launch a full-scale assault? Why this... this piecemeal, half-assed, picking on *us*?"

We were back at the fountain. I sat on the edge and looked around again, trying to surreptitiously relax my painfully-clenched jaw. Why us. Why us in this perfect square, something off-putting about the way we had been placed in it, had walked its perimeter and crossed it. I thought of the summer Johnny had taught Carla how to play chess; Carla had immediately turned around and tried to teach it to me and the twins, but only Chris had figured it out.

I don't get it, Carla had said, baffled, a kid of nine or ten gesturing past her long tangled curls at the orderly squares. *They can only move one way.*

I know, I'd said; I know, I still don't get it. I couldn't understand why Chris got it, either. Carla was the only one Johnny liked to play. I knew that the pieces only moved a certain way; I just couldn't figure out how to make them move in a way that was useful for what I thought I wanted to accomplish. The pieces didn't know what they were doing either, and couldn't stop someone if they were breaking the rules.

Who was moving us now, I wondered? *Someone* was. Pawn, knight, bishop, queen, king. We were only moving in the ways we were allowed to move. I was sure of it. Or if they were not yet, if they had just begun to watch us with a kind of horrified amazement, accidentally going places that we were not supposed to be, then the game would start very soon. Now that we had been spotted on the board...

"Theory five," I said. "They couldn't get here from there, so They just started turning here *into* there."

"Yes. Is that the winning theory? I don't know. I need more information. And we need to get the hell out of here. How'm I supposed to do anything stuck in a courtyard? This is worse than the woods."

"Yeah, we can't even eat leaves here."

"I could eat you."

"I'd eat you first." We began another circuit. "If we'd ended up in a city that looked like Edinburgh," I said, "maybe exactly like it, but it *wasn't,* would we know?"

"Maybe."

"Maybe?"

She shrugged, and knocked on the stone inside an arch with her knuckle. "If we were in an Edinburgh in a dimension a lot like ours, but not exactly."

"*Are* there dimensions like that?"

"Probably."

"A long time ago, you told me..." I paused at the next arch, which was particularly deep, and pushed experimentally against it, to no effect. "That the universe was a certain shape because it wouldn't work otherwise. But you also said every universe in which a spell is cast is... is a completely different one from the universe that existed before it."

"Yeah. And we should both probably stop saying 'the' universe. You mean *ours.*"

"So... what happens to all those old universes? Do they disappear?"

She blinked. "I don't know. I don't think so."

We walked for a few minutes, as she grew increasingly agitated, till I could nearly hear the gears in her head moving. "I don't know. Like, there's only so much energy and mass, so you'd think... but that's not true either, when you think about it. That's never been true. There's both energy and mass coming in from somewhere else. Somewhere outside."

"Outside where?"

"Outside everywhere. Where They come from. And a lot of other things. Things we don't know about. Things They fear, because They can't control them."

I didn't ask where she had learned that, but filed it away to panic about later. "If those universes still exist, and you can travel to them, we could have ended up in one of them. Right? Is that what you're saying?"

"Well, I don't think we did, actually."

"But are they all *exactly* the same except for the spell? Or are they different in other ways? Are there ones where... I don't know. That guy didn't get shot and World War One didn't happen? Or like... U2 stayed together? Maybe one where the terrorists *did* fly the planes into those buildings in New York?"

"I suppose anything's possible. You can't account for knock-on effects after a single change; sometimes there probably aren't any. Maybe there are billions or trillions just like ours, maybe there are an infinite number that only differ in a single point in history that affected everything after it. Or all those might be unstable and gone."

I thought about that for a minute. "Do you think there's one where you're not a huge asshole?"

"Maybe. Infinite, remember?" She paused under the stone arch we'd hidden under originally, staring up at it, flexing her fingers.

"No," I said, patiently.

"Hold my bag for a second."

"We are *not* climbing out of here."

"That's the thing," she said, sliding the bag off her shoulders and putting it on the ground. "I don't think we can. I think we're in a kind of... pocket. It's not an entire universe, but it's a *piece* of one that fulfils all the requirements except coordinates. It's a place but it's not *in* a place, if you know what I mean."

"I do not."

"And in theory, if it's the specific pocket I'm thinking of, what we just did was impossible, because no one gets in or out. It's not a place *between* places. It's its own place. So if we got in, what does that mean? Boost me up."

"What part of 'no' did you not understand? And also, pockets *have* an opening."

"Well do *you* have any other—eep!"

I caught her as she tripped backwards over her bag, resulting in a brief but paralyzing moment of terror as I felt her full weight descend on my forearm. The plain stone had begun to... sprout, there was really no other word for it. *Grow*, twig by twig, rapidly and sinuously, from the cobblestones up to just over her head. The twining wood extended tiny sprigs that met, clasped, rustled into place, till finally it was a bristling but solid oblong in the shape of a door.

I knew better than to reach for it, and waited patiently next to Johnny until it opened from the inside, golden light flooding out onto the gray stones. It was strange, I reflected as we waited to be invited inside, how quickly you recalibrated your entire existence. Before the Anomaly, I'd have thought I was losing my mind. But now, like the rest of the world that had survived, I knew better. Nothing could be disbelieved and nothing could be dismissed. Everything had to be investigated. You couldn't walk away from anything any more; you had to walk towards it, so that it couldn't sneak up on you.

A querulous voice said, "Did you know that the original meaning of *prodigy* was 'an unsolicited message from the gods'?"

"We can just talk here," Johnny said.

"...In."

The door nearly shut on my face; I had to shove my foot into the opening, breaking a handful of the twigs. The woman inside stared up at me as I apologized, then let me in.

"Of course," I said into the silence.

CHAPTER SEVEN

THREE SPIRALING STAIRCASES of brass and wood rose into the impossibly high ceiling, connecting dozens of catwalks, ladders, and cables between hundreds, maybe thousands, of bookshelves. Bats formed small joyful tornadoes in the highest part of the ceiling, where a dozen ornate chandeliers, chains glittering between them like spiderwebs, supplied most of the light.

The woman who had let us in was short and elderly, with a ragged halo of silvery hair, clearly in a pair of green-and-white striped pajamas under a thick scarlet robe. She was also, forgivably, holding a cricket bat. "How the *hell* did you get in here?" she said to Johnny, her accent not, I thought, Scottish, nor English, but some muddle between the two. "You working for them shifty buggers now? Eh? Is that it?"

"We didn't come on purpose," Johnny protested. "It was an accident."

"Was it now."

"Nick, this is Dr. Huxley," Johnny said unhelpfully, gesturing between us. "Dr. Hu—"

"I know who he is. Take your shoes off, you're tracking in half the outdoors."

Still carrying the cricket bat, she led us under the stairs and down a hallway also lined with bookshelves, past rooms filled with heaps of scrolls and huge tomes, crumbling zig-zag creations stitched and stapled together like Frankenstein monsters, tiny books stacked like bricks and making little houses on their shelves, books on chains, books under glass domes, books clearly designed to look like other things: a small chest-of-drawers, a safe, a gargoyle. I wasn't sure how you would read that one, but it clearly had pages, old and yellowed, and a cracked, gold-stamped binding. I wondered what the walls looked like, behind all the knowledge.

Eventually, we reached a relatively book-free room (only six shelves), a small kitchen with a low wooden ceiling and plaster walls. Somehow this was more disorienting than the sudden transition from tunnel to forest, or forest to fountain; I leaned heavily on the doorway and rubbed my temples.

Huxley lugged a large plastic kettle to the sink, filled it, and turned it on, muttering to herself as she got out three mugs. Even though we were out of sight, I felt oddly watched by all the books, as if they weren't just inert paper waiting to be bought, nor yet (as I often felt) sleeping until they were selected and read, but as if they were *listening*. There was a weight to them that felt like the weight of a crowd, sweaty and alive and attentive. I thought of the worms I had seen as we had walked through the vaults: watching, turning to watch.

"You don't get here by accident," Huxley said, not turning. "As you bloody well know, because I happen to be the one charged with keeping out the rabble. Which is you. What were you really doing?"

"We got stuck somewhere else. Like this."

"And you got out how, precisely?"

Johnny stared intently at the floor. "Um, the Distortion of Adar."

"*Bloody* hell. And they let you go around calling yourself a genius. Christ! Drink this." She slammed a thick white mug of Ovaltine onto the table; I sat and helped myself as Johnny continued to stand awkwardly in the middle of the room.

"Uh," I said, when no more information seemed to be forthcoming. "Ma'am, where are we, exactly?"

"Disneyland. Behave yourselves and later on you'll get an ice lolly and a photo with Bugs Bunny." She put another mug down, this one prominently emblazoned with the Olympics logo and a little *MOSCOW 1980* plaque. "You're in a place that doesn't exist. Where d'you *think*?"

Johnny swayed a little, and managed to sit in one of the stiff-backed wooden chairs, curling her hands around the mug. I looked out the lace-curtained window over Huxley's shoulder, not very surprised to see more books.

"I never thought I'd see this place in person. I wasn't even sure we were here," Johnny said.

"Damn right you thought. 'S why they put it in a bloody remnant, isn't it? Formerly the Rodhalazz Repository, now known officially as the Huxley Archives, lucky me, ho ho, ha ha. That's sarcasm, by the way, go on and laugh. Books here from places you'll never go, places that don't exist yet, and places that quit existing on a timescale we can't even know. You know what it cost them to keep this running? No? Me neither. You know what they'll do to you for this? Eh? They don't tell you, y'know. And why all the lightning?"

"Dr. Huxley, I'm *not* working for the Society! I'm not here for them!" Johnny said.

Huxley snorted, and leaned against the counter with her own mug. Her eyes were nearly the same colour as her skin and hair: a reflective, pearly white. "Mm. Very convincing. If you're not on the job, then just what the hell *are* you up to, gallivanting around in remnants? Tell me that."

Johnny opened her mouth, but Huxley cut her off before she could speak. "No, you'll just spew bullshit all over my nice clean kitchen, and I don't want to have to clean the Equalizer again," she said, apparently referring to the cricket bat. "You," she said to me, "*you* tell me."

I cleared my throat and straightened up. Johnny, meanwhile, adopted a posture so exaggeratedly casual and relaxed that I half-expected her to slip off the chair. "Ma'am, if you don't mind, who *are* you?"

"Don't answer a question with a question, Nicholas."

She snapped her fingers at me. "Now."

I gave up. "We were at this party... well, the one at Edinburgh Castle. Which you maybe heard about already on the news? Don't know if you get the news here, wherever this is? Anyway, in the Great Hall, we were looking at..."

"I changed my mind," Huxley said, and turned back to Johnny. "Well?"

Johnny gave me a helpless look, and then recounted a reasonably accurate story, I thought, though with several major lies of omission (a concept I had to re-teach the twins about once a month or so), beginning with the attack at the party.

Huxley listened without interrupting, somewhat to my surprise. When she was done, the shocked silence stretched out for what felt like forever, but I was getting used to those now.

"You hit the *czeroth* with a *rock?*"

"Yes'm." I lowered my face into my cup; all the same, I felt two alarmingly hot spots on my forehead where her eyes were drilling into me. She glanced between us, clearly aware we were lying, unsure about what, and unsure what to do about it. I knew that feeling. Curiosity, out of everything you ever felt, was the hardest to push down, file away. It was the one thing that had gotten not just us but the entire human race, I was pretty sure, in more trouble than any other trait, and there was nothing we could do about it. Finally, she sighed, ending in a growl that sounded like resignation as well as anger.

"...You've lost a day. It's Sunday evening. The eighth. Come with me."

Johnny took her mug; I left mine on the table, not wanting to drop it on the obviously old, grubby, but intricately mosaic'd floors. We trailed Huxley down a short hallway, turning into a small bedroom, all dark wood panels and tumbled piles of clothes; it smelled powerfully of Vicks VapoRub and stale cigarette smoke. A small, ancient TV perched on the dresser opposite the bed; flipped on, the sound took several seconds to arrive, as if traveling at the real speed of sound rather than the airwaves or cables. "It's late, but there should be something still. There's nothing else on the news, that's all they're showing. You, go on."

Half-hypnotized, Johnny pressing so close that her malted-milk breath fell on my wrist, I turned the dial, heavy clonks that reminded me of the TV in my uncle's house in Toronto, so old it had been in a wood frame too heavy to move.

Every channel was the same. A monster movie: a Godzilla production. Skies not dark but brilliantly lit, like the terror of radiation, unseen poison, brighter than a thousand suns. With each clonk of the dial, the pale image rippled before settling, and in some cases did not stop, because it was the world that was out of focus.

Tattered skylines like burning lace, wings and claws battening leechlike on them; cargo ships toppling with startling speed for their bulk, crushed by the embrace of translucent tentacles, full shipping containers flying like spilled rice; some city unfurling a huge white flag in a field, rippling like silk, as if They would know (or care) what it meant.

Americans in Confederate t-shirts firing variously at the oncoming creatures and into the sky, spurts of slime jetting up before they fell, trigger-fingers twitching, transforming. The chaos of crowds, a mass of people plunging into the sea from a collapsing island, many swimming to the surface as something else. The air full of burning oil or broken gas lines, lakes and rivers burning under a thin slick of hydrocarbons. Oil tankers going up in darkness, streaming liquid fire. A beach somewhere in grainy grayscale security footage, palm trees twisting like snakes, opening mouths, pulling themselves from the white sand. A thousand people, perhaps half looking not quite right, still clawing and trampling each other to get away from something that didn't show up on the camera.

Wobbly aerial footage of empty streets—locked down, or everyone dead or gone?—shivering, changing, things bursting from roofs and driveways like fungus. A contagion, ripping through the world like the plague that had come after the Anomaly. Or perhaps it hadn't ended, perhaps this was its resurgence, a tumour lying in wait for some signal or chemical or moment of radiation...

"Jesus fucking Christ," I heard myself say, though my lips were numb and I thought I hadn't spoken. "In one day? All this..."

"They can be killed," Huxley said, and dialed down the volume. "Supposedly. Except it seems when you kill 'em, you catch it."

"It?"

She shrugged.

Johnny whispered, "Chevauchée."

"What?"

"Old idea. I mean, old word. You... you're attacking a fortified place. Maybe a castle. The gates are locked, you can't get in. So you make your army back off, then you go raid the countryside around the castle, kill villagers, loot and plunder and torch the fields. So then your adversary is forced to leave their fortifications and come out to defend their people." She sounded as if she were reading off a page, her voice high and steady. "Old idea. Still clever. Still works. And this, see." She tapped the glass. "Like... panicking a herd of something so it stampedes off a cliff. If you know it'll stampede, and not just turn and attack you. If you know the gates will never, ever, ever be unlocked. You lure the other side outside."

Huxley said, "You think that's what They're doin', eh? Because They tried to invade a couple years ago, and got Their wrists slapped? And now They're trying *tactics*? Bullshit, Chambers. They're not that bright. Never have been, or They'd have succeeded by now."

Right, I thought. That was true; we'd already said it. So what had changed? What?

I barely heard them arguing about tactics; I was still staring at the text crawler at the bottom of the news channel, moving so fast I couldn't read it. Nothing about Canada, about St. Albert, but no news didn't mean nothing was happening. Mom. The kids. The house.

As I fumbled for my cell phone, Huxley grabbed my wrist; mud flaked onto the floor.

"You'll never get a mobile call out from here. This ain't a place, understand."

"You still haven't said where we actually *are!* And—"

"Oh boy." Johnny turned up the volume, a little too late; I looked up just in time to see a moment's footage of the big familiar man, dark coat flapping gracefully behind him, lit by lightning or flashbulbs. Rutger: walking into a prominently signposted police station. Had he been handcuffed? I couldn't tell. I looked down at Johnny, her face calculating, not yet panicking. The face of one of the twins, trying to get away with something.

"If They can't get in, how are They doing this?" I turned the dial one last time, landing on another bit of footage, wobbly and high up, slimy sheets racing over a high stony slope and flowing down the far side, crashing like an avalanche into a village, as people flooded out the other end. It all looked strangely fluid, boneless. A mountain become flesh.

The question landed with a thud. They exchanged glances that to me seemed out of all proportion to what I had said: Johnny looked cagy, Huxley irritated. We trooped back to the kitchen, leaving the TV on. By way of explanation, Huxley said over her shoulder, "I ain't supposed to, and I'm not gonna. I'm throwing you out of here as soon as I figure out how. End of story."

"Which is absolutely fair, and I get that," Johnny said sweetly, "but can we talk to the books first?"

"Nope."

"Why not?"

Huxley laughed, and turned to look at us; I piled into both of them in the hallway, Johnny juggling her cup to keep it from spilling. "You've got some nerve, Chambers," she said, sounding honestly delighted. "After all those years of *volunteering* for them out of the *goodness* of your golden little heart, you're going to look me in the eye and say you're not with them at last? You? Look at you, got a face like a weasel. A nice weasel," she conceded, seeing Johnny's affronted pout, "one of them pet-store, maybe purebred weasels; but up to no good. You think, *Oh, she can't keep me out'n the archives just for my face, can she*, but you bet I can.

"Nobody's saying anything, but everybody's talking. And you know that, bein' what you are. Some coincidence, it goes—that an outsider, a non-member, starts callin' around saying the world's gonna end, and while everybody's trying to figure out what's happening and how you'd know, you run off with a boy, simply vanish into thin air, get a *reward* put on your head, and a couple of days later, what do we get? Eh? The Event, the Invasion."

Huxley looked up sharply at me, and I braced myself for a similar tirade, but she was just reading my face, I thought—like a book left on a desk, opened to an incriminating page.

"Collusion," Johnny said. "Is that what they're accusing me of?"

"Nobody's saying anything," Huxley repeated. "Drink

your drink. I have to look up how to get you two out of here."

WHILE HUXLEY ROAMED the stacks, we were allowed to wait near the front door, which had vanished back into a smooth wall of gray stone. Johnny and I sat on the bottom steps of the middle of the three staircases, covered in threadbare red carpeting tacked down with small brass nails. The nailheads clinked against the rivets of my jeans as I shifted.

"You mean *read* the books," I said. "Not talk to them."

Johnny rocked her hand in the air: *sorta*. "They say the books here do talk. Some of them. And more than that, they can talk to books that aren't here—not just in other libraries, I mean, but other dimensions. I don't know if that's true, but if it's not true, there's about five thousand years of stories about it. People asking the books what other books know. Getting answers they couldn't possibly get."

"She's looking after this place for the Society. Right? Like, that's her job."

Johnny nodded. All around us the books fluttered, riffled, which at least this time you could explain with the thin steady breeze that swirled around us, probably to keep the dust off them. It sounded like the whispers of a crowd in a theatre before the movie started.

"So many books have been destroyed over the years," Johnny said, looking up at them. "Books specifically about magic, about Them, what happened when They came. Religions and governments of all kinds said: no magic, divination, sorcery, prognostication, witchcraft, necromancy, idolatry. Nothing like that. The Society has always protected what it could, but sometimes there was no way to save things without outing themselves and being killed or exiled. Books, temples, records, tablets, even tombs, art. Statues. Tapestries. Wherever they could hide knowledge, encrypt or encode it, it would be found and destroyed. Finally, they just started trying to put things... entirely out of reach."

"Here. In a different dimension."

"Pocket universe. Yeah. Now they're safe."

"But no one can read them."

"There's some kind of lending scheme," Johnny said. "The Society allows limited access. Just to the books, not to the entire place."

"She really hates the Society, doesn't she?" I said quietly, just in case Huxley came unexpectedly around the corner or down the stairs. "But she's protecting their books, working for them."

"People work for people they hate all the time," Johnny said. "You always do."

I got my phone out, unfolded it again, out of habit: the screen was dead, but an ordinary kind of dead, not the way it had looked in the birch wood. I put it away. Somewhere outside of this place was a huge fancy hotel, my room, my little rolling suitcase, my phone charger, my rented tux... my brothers, my sister, my mom, my dad. Waiting for me to fly back tomorrow with stories and souvenirs. And Louis, waiting for me to report back with what I had learned about Johnny's scheme, if she had one (and, just as Huxley had instantly realized, I knew she did). What was it?

People work for people they hate all the time. Yes, they do. And in a sense, she had been working not quite for Them, but on Their behalf, the entire time, hadn't she? Not quite a monkey chained to a typewriter in a closed room, with scientists watching on cameras to rush in and snatch away the sheet of paper on which it had typed some piece of brilliance, but... not *very* different, I thought. They had made her, and then They had watched her. Knowing something would come out of it that They could steal, twist, corrupt.

The breeze inside began to pick up, stirring our hair, raising the noise of the fluttering pages into a roar. We looked around, confused. Johnny stood up, clinging to the bannister, then ducked as a book flew off a shelf and nearly hit her.

I stood too, trying to look into the upper darkness where the chandeliers' light couldn't quite reach. The books were trembling, jiggling, more and more leaving their shelves, flapping heavily in agitated circles. A scroll unwrapped itself as it flew, undulating through the air like a kite. In the empty spaces above the remaining books, bats huddled in terror, their tiny eyes winking back at us as if asking for help.

"Um, Dr. Huxley?" Johnny called, cupping her hands around her mouth.

Huxley emerged a few minutes later through the storm

of books, furiously waving an arm above her head. "What the hell did you do?"

"We didn't do anything!" I said. "What's happening?"

"Never seen 'em like this. Don't like it." She too ducked as a large, heavy book skimmed over the top of her head and crashed into the floor, flopping open with a *crack* as the spine separated from the pages. This seemed to be a signal, or just too much for the other books to take; the wind died down, and several dozen more books fell to the floor. In the sudden silence, a small, piping voice came from somewhere, in a language I didn't know; but Johnny and Huxley looked up alertly, staring around the shelves. The room filled with the mouldy smell of magic, making me cough.

"Okay, fine," I said. "Don't tell me what's going on then."

"They want to talk to *you*," Huxley said tartly. "God only knows why."

"Can... you ask them?"

"They already said they wouldn't tell us," Johnny said. Her face had crumpled with jealousy, and I felt a mean thrill to see it. You spend your whole life being the special one, the famous one, the cameras always pointed at you, the face on the newspaper... and suddenly you're not, and all the lenses are pointed at your shadow instead. There, I thought. Serves you right. Something finally going through the impenetrable layer of ego you wear like a bulletproof vest.

"They want to tell me something?" I said.

"Sounds like it," Huxley said. "You'd better not,

though. It's not good for regular people to try it. You have to be trained, experienced. *And* you have to be able to use magic. Not everybody can, you know. You could end up with your brains all over the floor. Or worse yet, flattened into a book."

"See if you can convince them to let *me* talk to them," Johnny said, bouncing on her toes. "It'll be safer."

I glanced at Huxley. "No. I'll do it."

She sucked her teeth, then gestured me deeper into the books after her, leaving Johnny silhouetted by the staircases, clinging to the bannister with both hands.

"Quit looking back at her. Get out of this if you can," Huxley said quietly as the light faded, blocked by the shelves. "As soon as you get back to the world, wherever you are. Leave her, my lad. Leave."

"I can't."

"You can't? You better. They're watching her, they're watching the both of you, I don't know what she's got you around for—muscle or whatever, a lookout—it's clear you're torturing yourself to be here. Look at your face! You don't even know what it looks like, do you? Why, I wish you could've seen yourself back there in the kitchen. How you must *hate* her."

I stared down at her, into the colourless eyes no longer concealing their urgency and terror in the dim golden light. She grasped my wrist, her fingers cold and far stronger than I had guessed. "Why do you keep her secrets for her? She knows how you feel. Can you live like that? With someone who looks past your hate and doesn't care?"

You don't know us, I wanted to say, and then, You don't know me. I don't trust you. But it was so hard to live like this, keeping not just her secrets, but everyone's, mine, the world's. I couldn't tell her the truth. "The world's ending. She says she can stop it. What the hell kind of friend would I be if I didn't at least try to help? What kind of *person*?"

"The world did end. We're living in a new one. She thinks she can... what, turn back what's happening? If she just asks the right questions? Use your damn head."

"You think she can't?"

"Of course she can't. And she won't. You'll see how it works out, in the end."

"Won't? What do you... why would you say that?"

"I'm not helping you," she said, and gave me a push in the small of the back, towards a little hexagonal-shaped alcove lined with the usual bookshelves. Another chandelier, small and hung with crystals, threw off a low, rainbow-spangled glow. I could barely see my hand in front of my face. "I'm not *allowed* to help you. All right? She knows that, she clearly didn't tell you. All I'm saying is, you can't live in the hope that you'll be able to force her to do the right thing. Go, before she ruins your life."

"She already did. How did you get out of the Society, Dr. Huxley?"

"None of your business. But they've been as good as their word. As good as gold. Get in there, close your eyes. The light's bad for you."

Before I could speak again, she had swiveled out of the

alcove and shut a hidden door behind me, also books, completing the hexagon. I waited in the dark, hands in my pockets so that I wouldn't clench my fists. Brains all over the floor, she had s—

We knew you would come here
We knew you had changed
Let us introduce ourselves

IT WAS TRUE, the light burned and stung, I had no eyes to close and the pain built as the brightness built till I could not see with whatever I was using to see, I flew bodiless over the streets of a city made of shadows, and I was hunted by things I could not see, that could not see me, and I hunted things myself, and the books ran with me, not shaped like books, not shaped like anything, only bright points of urgent light. I screamed to let out the pain and they screamed back and it was a song, and they demanded I remember it when I was released, *This is what we must give you*, they said as we rushed above the patterns of the streets, *and we are very sorry, but we knew you would come*

Why not her? I howled. *She is here too!*

No

No

No

No

No, *not her*, no

And I knew that my hatred was right, and my hunger

for revenge was right, it was better than any other hunger I might ever have in my life (for money, for women, for knowledge, but also for those things it would be noble to starve for, like honour, like duty), if the whole world hated her, if this unseen universe of knowledge had been whispering to itself that if it got the chance to speak to someone, it would *not be her*—

Sing back to us

So we know you remember

Then we will tell the others that you know what is needed to be known

I sang it back into the thousand towers curved at their tops into craters of light, and it bounced back, rebounding, the soundwaves precise, visible, all in formation, and the reflection hit me, knocked me out of the air, towards the brightest light of all, parting, opening, to reveal a safe warm darkness, silence, relief, the end of pain.

WHEN I WOKE up, I was stretched out in the bedroom with the tiny TV, on but muted. Someone had put a mildewy-smelling wet rag on my forehead. I pushed it off, followed voices back to the kitchen. My legs felt shaky, tense; I had carpet-burn on both palms, and my left wrist ached. Must've fainted onto the floor. Lucky to not land on my face.

Huxley and Johnny were eating toast and oranges at the table, not looking at each other. Between them, separating the butter dish, jam jars, and three more mugs of Ovaltine, lay a thick open book, but a strange one—printed like normal, but scribbled over, vandalized really, in blue ballpoint. There were two sigils on the page, complicated and badly smudged.

"Okay," I said, sitting down. "Somebody talk."

It was a long time before Huxley sighed, and tapped the book. "You said your piece."

"I what?" I stared at the blue writing. It wasn't in English. "I wrote that?"

Johnny nodded. "We opened the door up when the lights stopped, and you came out babbling for something to write on. So I gave you a pen, and you grabbed a book off the shelf."

"...Did I write anything useful?"

They both nodded.

"And is someone going to fucking tell me what that *was*, because I could have died in there, and you said so yourselves. I risked my ass for this!"

"We have to get out of here," Johnny said, "is the short answer. I can tell you the rest on the way."

"The way to where?"

"Prague."

"...What?"

BACK AT THE entryway, we put our coats and boots on again, and Johnny tied on her green-and-red scarf. There was a strange new nastiness between her and Huxley, very different from the generic, former-coworker hostility they'd had when we had arrived. What had they talked about while I had been away, I wondered? She would never have told Huxley the truth about the Anomaly, but the old woman must have guessed it anyway, perhaps thrown it into Johnny's face. What good would denial do at that point?

"Prague is dangerous," Huxley said, getting a piece of chalk from the desk. "Low spot. One of the lowest spots now, built over one of them—what do you call it. Not a gate, but one of them big tangles that sops it up. Collected all sorts of things over the years."

"A nexus," Johnny said. "You've never gone?"

"Never needed to. I got everything I need here." She laughed, an oddly bitter sound, and chalked a circle on the stone wall. "And safe as houses. The wards they put on this place..."

We all paused at the same moment, sniffing the air. Wet, mouldy smell of magic. But something else. Ozone, a thick reek of musk, like the enclosed smell of a zoo.

And smoke.

Johnny froze, mouth open. Behind Huxley, in the darkness of the shelves, light flared—white, as hot and fierce as lightning, fading to scarlet—and we all began to cough. The shelves trembled, swayed, and began to fall away from the walls, rocking around us, raining books and scrolls onto our heads; I covered my head with my arms, and we ran to get our backs to the stone wall, the only place in the room bare of shelves.

As I turned, a tremendous head burst through the darkness above us, tangling on the chandeliers till they tore loose from their wires, plunging us into darkness except for the shivering glow of the approaching flames. Black-glass teeth snapping and champing, iridescent scales, the scrabble of huge claws ripping up the tiny tiles on the floor, spraying them up like raindrops.

A *dragon*, impossibly wedged in the tiny place, shouldering aside shelves, walls, warping the bright brass of the railings, books dropping onto it and bouncing off. And kneeling on its head, clinging with an arm like black smoke to one of its horns, was the one Johnny had called the Burning King.

"You *dare!*" Huxley screamed, then doubled over coughing; the heat was growing so intense that I half-instinctively shoved her and Johnny behind me, closer to the wall, as if it would help.

The dragon squeezed through the railings, snapping and biting at the brass; the tip of a tooth broke off and whirled over my head like a bullet, audible even over the crackling roar of the burning books. One enormous limb worked free, scrabbled for a second on the tiles, and stretched towards us, flexing and clenching. Cornering us: no way out, burning the only escape into the maze of books. The Burning King had no face with which to smirk, but seemed to be anyway: gloating already, his prize nearly in reach, feet from the snapping teeth of his mount.

Someone screamed behind me, the voice already too broken by smoke to figure out who, and a blast of green light enveloped the dragon, its rider, the books, the flames, everything, in a wash of brightness that turned the entire place inside-out and blew it to pieces.

CHAPTER EIGHT

Wherever we had ended up, a streetlight still glowed, though it was tilted at a hilarious angle—nearly parallel to the road. Enough light remained for us to creep back towards what was left of Huxley's pocket dimension: a pyramid of rubble and ash, disintegrated bricks, pages smouldering as they blew lightly across the street, a few twisted pieces of brass that must have been from the chandeliers, the small faun statue that had crowned the fountain. Mosaic stones littered the ground like busted windshield bits after a car accident. I stooped, unable to stop myself, and picked up a few, their edges softened by heat.

Johnny was still coughing, bent over; I moved her arm, unzipped the front pocket of her bag, and handed her the sticker-encrusted inhaler.

Huxley was incandescent with rage, the anger visible

even as she slowly, even menacingly, picked up a fragment of binding with a few pages attached, still on fire. Somewhere sirens began, spiraling towards us, still distant. It was night, deep and clear, a sky glittering with stars. I wished I could identify any of the constellations. Wished I had anything telling me where and when I was.

"Dr. Huxley," Johnny croaked, "*I* could have got us out."

"Not in a thousand years," Huxley snapped, dropping the burning book. "I *told* you, the wards on that place was cooked up for it special. Prodigy? Genius? You're a scientist, not a sorcerer. All you'd have done was dithered around and we'd ha' got roasted alive."

That probably wasn't true, I thought, after everything Johnny had seen and memorized; but there was no point in arguing it. Johnny flopped onto the edge of what remained of a low brick wall, and took another hit from her inhaler, the little electronic voice counting down its numbers primly between the approaching noise of the sirens.

"It followed you here." Huxley glared at me, sparing Johnny temporarily while she was dealing with her inhaler. "*You*. There's no other way it could've found this place. Damn near ten years this place's been running. Not a rumble, not a whisper. Not even during the Incursion. You fucking *bastards*."

Johnny said, "I can..."

"You can *what?* No amount of *money* will replace those books."

I stared at her, numb; it was all very familiar. Maybe

everyone Johnny knew would have to say that to her at some point. And what could I say to the accusation? Of course it had come for us. Huxley had only managed to save us, as far as I could tell, by destroying the entire dimension, courtyard and all.

Where were we? I had no idea. Big, old stone buildings around us, three or four storeys. A steeple nearby, neatly blocking out a narrow triangle of stars. It wasn't all that cold, but I began to shiver, and sat down heavily next to Johnny, making the little pile of bricks wobble alarmingly.

"You know what really pisses me off?" I said to the street at large. "This isn't even like... the *fifth* worst day of my life."

"Not by a *mile*," Johnny said, through chattering teeth.

"Fix your scarf. What are we going to do now?" I added, as Huxley returned to the heap of rubble and began methodically pawing through it, kicking aside flaming piles with her slippered foot.

"We? Fuck you, sonny. I'm going to get as far and fast away from the two of you as possible. After beating you to death with the Equalizer, if I can find it."

That sounded pretty reasonable to me, and when Huxley eventually unearthed the ashy but intact cricket bat and approached us, all I could manage was, "Her first."

"Rude."

Huxley stopped, sagging, then began to sway as if drunk, and I got up so she could sit down in my spot.

She covered her face, leaning one arm heavily on the handle of the bat. "*Christ.*"

I closed my eyes. The sirens were getting closer. Let them arrest us. Arson, or whatever. Let someone else do this. Take over. Let the grownups handle it. I just saw what we already knew: the satellites never saw anything, the proximity alarms were never tripped, because the creatures weren't coming from space. Of course they fucking weren't. Everything pointed straight up: but that's not where They come from. They come from over *there*. Under *here*. Just *there*. Watching us so closely we probably leaned on Their eyeballs at one point, separated by a membrane so thin our molecules touched. Seeing nothing.

I thought: Something's coming? Wrong. Something came. And They're moving in, because soon our world will be just like Theirs. Redecorated to Their exact taste. Just like that. And They will get rid of the pests living in it, if They don't turn us into things that are not pests...

Waves of red and blue light appeared down the hill, inching their way towards us. This address, I thought, probably hadn't existed a minute ago; neighbours would be calling it in using their own. Shouts, car horns in the roads around us. Lights in the windows, curtains being pushed back.

The first fire engine rounded the corner a moment later, a storm of noise and light so that for a moment I couldn't see or hear. Two police cars, bright blue and yellow, pulled up next to it, adding to the light. Doors slammed, feet scuffed on the asphalt. "Don't move!"

I put my hands up, not looking to see what the other two were doing. Whatever (let's face it) pleasure I had felt at the thought of forcing Johnny to slip up, bring herself down, at impressing the Society, whatever it was I thought I had been doing, felt very far away. Rutger was somewhere spilling his guts, why wouldn't he? I'd just do the same. Tell them everything, and deal with the consequences. Maybe they'd think I was nuts and lock me up. That would be fine. The kids could come visit on weekends.

The cops ringed us, surprising me a little with their getup: radios, no guns. Two of them pointed Tasers at us though, and someone shouted "Don't move!" again, despite the fact that I hadn't. I resisted a powerful urge to look behind me and see if Huxley or Johnny were moving. What would I need to be arrested properly? To go limp, first of all. They would help me out with the Taser if I wasn't submissive enough on my own. And to not speak when they started to fuck me up, if they did (and these cops not having guns was no guarantee of anything, I knew). And my wallet, probably, to show them my ID… still safe in my back pocket? Yes, it felt like it. What else? I supposed they could look at my dead phone, if they wanted to.

"Hands in front," one of the cops said, and approached me with the cuffs out. People had started to open their windows, interestedly, watching the show. I supposed they thought a bomber or something had been caught, given the explosion. A trio of bombers.

"Am I being arrested?" I said.

"Shut up. Hands front."

I held them out at my waist, and looked closely at him. He was about my colour, about my height, a bit bulkier; his high-vis jacket was unzipped over a thin bulletproof vest marked *CHAMBERS ENGINEERING*. Of course.

Without meaning to, I jerked my hands back when he touched them. "*All* right," he began menacingly, but I didn't even hear what he said next, and began to backpedal, back towards Huxley and Johnny, who had realized the same thing I had: some of the cops weren't human. The firefighters, who knew, too far to see, doing stuff with hoses and axes so that the smouldering remains of Huxley's archive wouldn't catch anything nearby, but the cops, no, the one who had almost cuffed me had not been holding the cuffs in hands but something else, something with claws, and a few of the others had thin silvery tentacles snaking from their backs, eyes in their cheeks, glistening in the headlights.

"Get back here!"

I ignored him, kept backing, heart hammering. Great, extremely great. The dragon didn't catch us, but *these* guys—yes, excellent, perfect way to end the night. They hadn't surrounded us, only partly flanked us, there was room to run, the empty street behind us leading back into the maze of houses, but Johnny surely couldn't escape, and what about Huxley? I couldn't leave her.

"Halt! Or we will activate non-lethal weapons!"

"What?" said Huxley.

"Well, they don't have guns," I said. A moment later, she pushed something into my hand, something heavy:

the cricket bat. *We're not fighting our way out of this,* I almost said, and then without looking brought it up, slapping the prongs of the Taser high into the night sky, entirely reflex, not even hearing the bang as it went off. Someone else fired another one, which spiralled randomly somewhere to our left, and then they were closing on us, cautiously, as I swung the bat around my head. Not quite enough of a threat: one man darted at me, trying to go low. I brought the bat down across his shoulders, hard enough to make him grunt, not hard enough to stop him, and squirmed out of his grip.

Johnny's breath wheezed rapidly, cleared, wheezed again. There was a small, out-of-place noise: a zipper. And a second later, two gouts of blue fire whooshed past my shoulders, flattening the cops and making the cars rock so violently that their tires cracked and deflated. I blinked away afterimages, shouldered the Equalizer, and turned. "Run!"

HALF AN HOUR later, we fetched up in a lightless little park under a couple of dead, intricately-rusted streetlamps, at the top of a steep hill that gave us a view of an unrecognizable city, mostly low buildings, no skyscrapers, golden-lit windows smeared by fog. Johnny's breath sounded a bit better; Huxley had not spoken.

I turned to Johnny, a dark lump in the starlight. "Do you mind my asking..."

"What?" She tensed up, shivering.

"How come you cured practically everything except fucking *asthma?*"

"…Oh that. Well, the organoids I came up with, they're great for organ-focused diseases like Alzheimer's or diabetes. 'Oh, but asthma is just lungs': no it isn't. Turns out it's a full-body autoimmune response dysfunction. Organoids don't have a fully-functioning immune system, so it's tricky to research autoimmune disease. The system is hard to turn it on, even harder to turn it off, and both of those could kill somebody while you're still frantically trying to flip the switch."

"You could just test stuff on monkeys or humans or whatever. Like normal labs."

"I don't like the wait times for approval."

I nodded, and listlessly spun the handle of the cricket bat between my palms. My skin still seemed lightly slimy or sticky where the monstrous cop had touched me. That's how it is, I thought. They figured out how to *infect* us with Themselves. If it's a war, that's how it'll be won: annexation, assimilation. Just like in school. I wondered if I too would turn, then decided that if it was going to happen, it would have happened after the attack at the party.

Still no idea where we were. The cops' accents had sounded a bit like Huxley's: not English, not Irish. Funny of the Society to put a pocket dimension exactly where her original house had been. Must be why she got cable, but you couldn't get a cell phone call out.

"If we—" Johnny began, then looked down blearily; the bench she was sitting on had grown a couple of small, luminescent tentacles, waving near her shoulders and piping a faint unpleasant song. She got up and moved to my bench. "If we live through this, I'm never leaving the house ever again. I swear to God."

"You won't have a house," I said. "It'll be a monster. It'll be turned into a monster. It'll just be a... a house, shaped like a monster."

"Like in that movie."

"Yeah. But fancy."

"Wards are being removed," Johnny said, closing her eyes. "The books said. I mean, you said the books said. Worldwide. Dug up, chiseled out, burnt down, picked apart."

Huxley nodded. "Someone's not doin' their job."

"Mm. Could be. And that volcano," Johnny said. "In America. No seismic indicators at all. And there's six new hurricanes forecasted. February isn't hurricane season... and there have been earthquakes, tsunamis. Those aren't necessarily... signs of something happening, like the way people used to take the appearance of a comet as a harbinger of plague. Sometimes they're a result of... of dimensional shifts. In unmonitored places. Like deep in the ocean, or below the crust or the mantle. Knock-on effects. But crucially: unseen. Unseen, always. Things aren't responding to the changes in the world, they're responding to something else that's responded to them. But what?"

"What kind of weirdo uses the word 'harbinger' when they're just talking to ordinary people?" I said.

No one laughed.

"If I were going to start a war," Johnny said slowly, "I'd want to win it right away. In fact, if I could fight a war without fighting at all, I'd do that. Then I'd get the win, and all the things that go with the win, without having to lift a finger."

"Okay," I said. "You could get your enemy to join you. And then you'd win."

"Then I'd win."

Huxley's head swung back and forth between us, her face inscrutable in the faint light. "It's not a war," she said. "It's done. You talk about it like it's still going."

Johnny said, "No. It's not done." She closed her eyes and slumped back on the bench.

Mom, the kids. The kids, Mom, the house. Our little neighbourhood, safe and quiet under the protecting trees. Rutger back in Edinburgh, spelling everything out in his precise, methodical way, probably drawing diagrams. The encircling rings of FBI, UN, CIA, whoever, God only knew, closing in on us, us specifically, no one but us. The Society doing the same. Flanking us, looping tight, pulling till we had no air. Putting two and two together and coming up with four: the Dimensional Anomaly, and now this, days after flipping the switch on the reactor. The dragon and the king that rode it, the humans around us not even human, stone no longer stone, metal no longer metal. Monsters coming for the only people I loved. The only people who would notice if I died in this war.

The only thing we could do was to keep moving so that we could fight.

I rubbed my eyes, itchy and red from the smoke. "How are we going to get to Prague?"

"None of my business," said Huxley.

"Come with us," I said. "What've you got here? With everything burned, everything gone. You could go somewhere else, start over. Wait for the problem to solve itself. Or you can help us find some answers. And get Johnny out of here."

Huxley glared at me, her crimson eyes streaming with tears. "Jesus *bloody drooling fuck*. There are *thousands* of people whose sole reason for existing is to fight this fight. And they certainly do not need a couple of bloody children running about the place, crying for their mamas and getting underfoot. What do they need *her* for?"

"They don't. We do. Why? For whatever reason the Ancient Ones are trying to take her," I said, dragging up each word from the pit of my frozen stomach. "For *whatever reason* They want her alive. *That's* why. We can't let Them have her. And we can't let the Society have her either." And the Society *can* kill her, I almost added. The Ancient Ones can't. Not part of the deal.

Huxley watched me, breathing hard. With a barely-audible *pop*, the concrete garbage can next to her changed to something dark-red and polygonal, like the shell of some huge insect. Legs began to grow from its circumference, rustling quietly. She glanced at it, back at me.

I said, "For what it's worth, and I know it's a bullshit thing to say, I'm sorry. This is absolutely our fault. And we'll never be able to make it up to you. What was in there… I know it can't be replaced, not ever, no matter what happens in this fight. I know this is a disaster on a million levels. And it was your home."

"It wasn't my home," she said. "It was just a place where I lived."

"You have to at least *pretend* you heard the rest of that."

"*She's* not apologizing," Huxley said stubbornly. "Notice that?"

"I can probably make her," I said, "if that's what it takes to get you to come with us."

"I'm not dead, you know," Johnny said, without opening her eyes.

"Yeah, and you're not sorry, either," Huxley said. "Do you know the difference between guilt and shame? Hmm? Jesus. This is why I never had kids. Up. Get up. If we're going, we're going now, and we're going my way."

We got up, avoiding the trashcan creature, which had started to shuffle clumsily along the path, and stood facing one another. "The Adversaries," Huxley said, her voice oddly cadenced, as if she were reciting something or teaching something, "obey inhuman laws. By inhuman, I mean not laws as we understand them: ours are formalized, created, and disseminated for broader obedience. Their laws are limited and proscribed by magic, and so they can be broken or bent in many ways. Perhaps it's better if you think of them as scientific laws, like gravity or thermodynamics. The only catch is that to break one of their laws, you must discover *how*. It cannot happen by accident."

"That doesn't make sense," Johnny said. "A broken scientific law happens by accident all the time. It just means we didn't understand it well enough to know where the failure was in the theory. You make it sound like magic has to give consent for the law to be broken."

"That's a good way to think about it," Huxley agreed. "But as it happens, that's the only law They cannot break."

"...Are we about to break one now?" I said.

"Ah, paranoia," Huxley said approvingly. "Very good."

"It's not paranoia if someone's actually out to get you."

"Also true. Anyway, yes, in some respects. We're going to do something that only They can do. Or let's say, that They have been known to do, in the past. Ride the leys."

This meant nothing to me, although the word 'leys' sounded vaguely familiar... not from my training, but from something else. And not in the context of 'riding.' Johnny, though, visibly started.

"But people can't... oh."

"There, that's genius for you," Huxley said. "Come on. You got some paper, a pen? You're the one who memorized it, you said, so I hope your memory's as good as you say it is."

I opened my mouth and closed it again as Johnny got a notepad and pen out of her bag: a blue ballpoint. "The books told me how to do it and I wrote it down, didn't I?" I said.

"Yep," Huxley said, watching Johnny meticulously draw out a small but wildly complicated sigil, so dense that as she worked, it looked as if she were colouring in a circle. "One good thing about the leys, they're like rivers. Magic's often like that: flows downhill, to the lowest point. Prague is real low. So in theory we wouldn't be travelin' against the current."

"You said only They could use this?"

"Mm. Historically."

"Anyone who's tried it has died," Johnny said, still drawing. "Sometimes bits of them wash up in the low spots after a couple of weeks."

"Uh," I said.

"But this is a new sigil. I've never seen this before, these components. I suppose the books put it together from one another. This could work."

"Could."

"Won't know till we try," she said. "The ol' spirit of scientific investigation. Here. I hope you copied it down right and I hope I remembered right *and* I hope I copied it down right too. On the other hand, my will and business plans are all drawn up in case I die unexpectedly, so there's that."

"I don't have a will," I said, gripping the notebook when she held it out.

"Well, you don't have any stuff, either," she said. "I'll do the spell, Dr. Huxley."

"I wasn't gonna volunteer."

THIS TIME THE motion was less wrenching, and much slower than I thought it would be. I unclenched everything and cautiously cracked my eyes to see lights flickering on all sides, curiously familiar from a hundred sci-fi movies, reassuring even though I knew we were traveling by magic and would probably fly apart at some point, if it had really killed everybody else who had tried.

The light was cool, streaky white, with glimpses of colour behind it. I wondered what they were. Something real, or something from space? Warp drive, FTL engines, dilithium crystals. Punch it, Chewie! "My God," I said. "It's full of stars."

"Why *does* she keep you around?" Huxley said crossly, then reached out to get an arm around Johnny, who had begun to sag. "Oh no you don't, Chambers. We're nowhere near yet."

I got a good handful of coat, keeping her upright. Huxley let go and glanced around interestedly; for the first time I noticed that her white, dandelion-like hair was spotted with ashes, and burned away in several spots to reveal pink scalp. "Bloody hell, there *is* a lot of magic about."

"Where does it... come from?"

"Magic? Who knows. Folks've been trying to figure that out for a while now." She raised her voice over a low, deep hum that had begun under our feet, as if we were standing on train tracks. "Some folks thought it was generated by the turning of the Earth, or maybe the orbit; but it waxes and wanes, and nobody's ever been able to reck the pattern of it. It's always been pretty minimal, except when the Adversaries are about, wrecking the place. It's like we're... walled off from it. And only a little ever seeps through."

I looked down at Johnny, and flinched: her eyes were shut, mouth open, a thick dark liquid that shimmered like mercury draining from both, and her nose, and her ears, soaking into her scarf and running over my hand where it was locked onto her coat. I pulled her to full vertical, a flood of the stuff darkening her chin like ink and running over my wrist. "Um, Dr. Huxley..."

"It's fine. It'll empty out."

"What is it?"

"Dunno. You're the one who wrote down this would happen."

"The books... oh, forget it." It was terrible to watch, but I didn't think I could stop watching either, just in case her thick, bubbling breath suddenly stopped. Like sitting with the twins when they were babies, if one of them caught something the other inevitably did too, and they would lie there, feverish, staring at each other in the crib, so that you felt like you couldn't leave the room, leave them there with nothing but each other.

"Ignorant folks destroyed records about Them for years," Huxley said quietly. "Said they were evil merely to keep around, and would spread evil by existing. Even the Society, sometimes, took things to ashes... believin' that just having the words writ down would attract Them back. Even if no one spoke them out loud. Even if no one drew the circles. Even if there was no magic around, just the little bit of background magic. They were wrong, they were fools. I don't mind sayin' it. We needed all that knowledge, all of it, and the reason we needed it is 'cause we didn't *know* when we would need it again. And it's gone forever."

I nodded. *Just in case*, Johnny kept saying. *Because you never know*. What she'd meant to say, and couldn't, in her arrogance, was *Even I don't know, and that's why*. I had suspected her of... what? Having predicted that it would happen? But maybe she really didn't know.

THE LIGHT FADED to reveal that we were in an alleyway; it was night, or still night, clear white streetlights shining in the distance. And it was snowing, very lightly, slow fat flakes the size of golfballs. Keeping one hand on Johnny, I let go of the notebook with the other and held my sleeve out, seeing if it would accumulate. If we weren't on Earth, I thought, at least we were somewhere Earth-ish enough to snow.

"Can't believe she managed it," Huxley said around her chattering teeth, looking around. "Honestly, thought we were being had. Hey. Hey, Chambers. Snap out of it! No, she's blacked out. Jesus. Lightweight."

I sighed. "I can probably carry her. Do you want my coat?"

"Don't patronize me. This way."

"I'm *not!* It's cold, and you're in pajamas... Man, girls always think you're talking down to them," I muttered.

"Watch it," Huxley said. "Girls are one thing. But you're not gonna live long enough to see one naked unless you realize that old women know things no one else can know. And most of us have killed a man."

"...What makes you think I've never seen a naked girl?"

"I can tell."

I awkwardly got Johnny over my shoulder, liquid splattering to the cobbles behind me, and followed Huxley. Outside the alley were more streetlights—dozens maybe, small and very bright on decorative black-painted posts, like stars. A huge church, illuminated with deep amber spotlights, loomed across a bridge from us, spiked and toothy against the low skyline.

We were alone. I looked up leerily at the sky, half-expecting to see that oval tear again, like an eye watching us. Just a thin layer of cloud, faintly orange from the streetlights bouncing back up. Perfectly normal, but silent, still.

"Are we in the right place? Is it under alert, do you think?"

"I'd expect so," Huxley said. "And they'll have a curfew. And that means fines, and we don't have any money. Not that I'd pay. Come on."

"How do you know where we're going if you've never been to Prague?"

"I read."

I couldn't really argue with that, and we crossed the empty square, then a bridge, lined with big statues that looked down at us interestedly the entire way. I thought again of the lightshow at the castle, the beams visible in the fog. Honor guard. Meant to say: *I protect and condone this endeavour. Whatever it is.* Royal wedding. Ribbon-cutting. End of the world.

On the far side we walked for another half-hour, no sound but our breath, far-distant traffic, the hum of drones. The snow was too light to accumulate, and blew around us like poplar fluff. We moved from cement sidewalk to cobblestones, asphalt, cobbles again. I felt slightly unreal from disorientation, or whatever it was inside my barely-evolved lizard body that knew it wasn't ideal to fall asleep on a log or something and wake up five thousand miles across the ocean on a whole new beach. My cells, maybe my genes, cried out against it, and wanted to know when we would all go home again. Knock it off, I told them. I don't care if you used to be a lizard, we're on a *mission*.

"How do you know Johnny?" I whispered as we walked. "Or how does she know you? Is it just, what do you call it. Her usual thing?"

Huxley chuckled, surprising me. "You mean by reputation? No, we've met. Maybe... a half-dozen times. She'd remember the exact number, no doubt. What, she didn't tell you? Thought you were s'posed to tell your boyfriend everything."

"We're not dating."

"That's the only good news I've heard all day."

She went on, keeping her voice so low I could barely hear. The first time, in Lagos, Huxley had been introduced to an improbable new member of her project team: a blonde child who had apparently memorized every scrap of parchment, every clay tablet, every lead sheet, in fact every codex, scroll, book, half-glimpsed business card, and conversation she'd been allowed to encounter. Though skeptical, the doctor had heard stories of this particular below-the-table assistance—of the prodigy scientist who, strictly owing to an eagerness to help and a belief in the shared goal, had initially done translations for the Society, and begun to help them acquire rare manuscripts and artifacts, track down experts, and, unbelievably, and rapidly, and apparently effortlessly, connect all the dots between primary sources hundreds or even thousands of years apart. Dazzling new constellations of research opened up to the Society, doors opened that had been shut for thousands of years, scholars from every country and every era beating their heads uselessly against it until she had opened it for them.

I nodded listlessly as Huxley described the impossibilities she'd seen Johnny perform, like the miracles leading to the declaration of a saint. A fragment of brick from a long-buried temple, a single torn page of a codex from an Italian monastery, a Roman curse written on a sheet of lead and buried under a tree in Egypt, a painting in a mausoleum in Singapore, sixteen pictograms tattooed onto the wing of a mummified bat in Uruguay: from these, no more than a handful of legible words on each, had been assembled the only extant copy, now locked in the Society's vaults, of the most powerful known spell for resurrecting the dead.

"She's good at that," I said dully. "Like assembling a puzzle."

Huxley shrugged. Her own research, she went on, was

primarily lithothaumatological—magical stones, both naturally occurring and manufactured artifacts. And in this respect Johnny had proven to be literally invaluable: the Society's resources were shadowy but vast, but even they could not, without revealing themselves, acquire the physical material and access to dig sites, quarries, and mines that Huxley needed to buy or steal the stones for the Society's archives.

At this she paused again, and looked at me. "You don't seem shocked."

"She told me stories. And anyway that's what she said the mandate of the Society is."

"Mandate. Mm. I like that. We never used that term. Go on: what did she say?"

"Well, basically the... the safeguarding of knowledge. Right? So the collection and, um, centralization of... of everything that's historically been known about Them. Keeping it all together with the people who... who know. So they can keep up the wards and stuff."

"And you never asked yourself: why the secrecy? Why not let it out into the open?"

"None of my business. I'm not involved with them."

She sighed. "When the Incursion happened... I thought of her at once. That little girl. And I couldn't imagine why. I hadn't seen her, heard much about her, for three or four years. It wasn't till later that I saw that she had gone missing just then. 'Ditched her minder and run off with a boy.' All right, a tad scandalous, but nothing worse than the heiresses and nouveaux-riche do all the time; little brats scampering about on Greek islands and their silly parents, the baronets and minor dukes, pretending to be appalled, announcing they'll write them out of the wills for the tabloids... kind of impressed, really. You know, except for all those accidents, she'd always seemed to keep her nose clean.

"Nothing, you understand, would have linked the two events in my mind except that they happened at the same time. But afterwards, it seemed like everyone in the Society had thought the same thing I had, and come to a lot of different conclusions. Everyone who knew anything about the history of the Ancient Ones. Everyone who knew anything about the Society; and everyone who knew anything about her."

"Mm."

"So. When that happened. What *were* the two of you doing? Sitting at the beach, no doubt, drinking a beer? Getting a suntan?"

I inhaled, exhaled. Johnny was unconscious: was she unconscious *enough*? Was Huxley *really* not with the Society any more? She still seemed to be connected with them, at least with the whisper network, the unofficial gossip body. It would be like them, I thought bitterly, to ask someone to fake it to get information... look at how easily they had gone along with what I had thought was my brilliant, original idea to spy on Johnny. They'd probably been waiting for me to suggest it, as a step (not an early one, either) in some much longer checklist. Chessboards, pieces.

But you had to trust *somebody;* and the fewer lies I had to keep straight the better. "Saving the world."

"*You* two? Nope. Shutting *all* the gates? There's only one spell can do that. The Heracleion Chant takes between twelve and twenty trained adepts," she said dismissively. "Most of whom would be expected to sacrifice themselves to finish it. And anyway, it's not complete. Everybody knows that. Not even she could get around that. Only the Society could muster up enough brute manpower to do what was done there, and that assumes they had the missing parts t' begin with."

"No, we found the... Look, Johnny said she modified it. Not just to like... brick up the gates. But take away their ability to be opened. Even if all their conditions were met, everything. As if they were gone."

"Which I don't believe for a second; and even if I did, it doesn't explain how the *two* of you managed. And lived."

"I don't think she knows either." I hesitated, and said slowly, "She blames herself for it happening in the first place."

"Nonsense," Huxley snapped. "Typical ego. *One* person is never responsible for a disaster. You know that. There's always dozens, hundreds of people behind everything, and you often don't have to trace it back that far." She paused, curiosity overtaking her face. "And why would she say that in the first place, hmm?"

"Oh, uh. You know. Because we... because she didn't do the spell in time. Because the Anomaly happened. And everything that happened afterwards..."

"Mm."

Two minutes. Not quite. A hundred and eleven

seconds. We had saved the world, we said; but we had only saved some of it. It had still ended. No part of me, not even the part that hated her for what she'd done to me specifically, could even acknowledge that she had accidentally had caused that many deaths. Or that the deaths were beginning again. Or that perhaps they had never ended.

"Here," said Huxley. "Hope he left the lights on."

'Here' was an ordinary wooden door, set into the stone wall of a windowless one-storey cinderblock building. Ordinary in every respect, that was, except for not having a handle. She didn't even bother pushing it, but knocked lightly in a strange rhythm till it swung open, outwards. Inside, small lights began to glow, incandescent bulbs in wire cages strung on a thick black cable along one side of a concrete staircase. Dust lay heavy on the steps, a thick silky layer, undisturbed. On the other side of the stairs was darkness: a sheer drop.

"You have got to be kidding me," I said.

"Down you go."

I still hesitated. "How do I know we can trust you?"

"Well, you don't. And I happen to not trust you, either," she added severely. "Why d'you think I'm still carrying the Equalizer? You two, and your dragon problem, have a lot of explaining to do. Get in there."

"If you don't trust us, why are you helping us?"

"Pretty personal question to ask a stranger, don't you think? Now move."

We had to stop several times to cough, and after perhaps half an hour, with my thighs and knees screaming, I swung Johnny down and leaned her on the wall. At last she turned her head, drew a long rattling breath, and spat into the thick dust, the dark liquid refusing to disperse, sitting there obstinate and mounded as mud.

"What the *fuck*."

"I don't know," I said. "Dr. Huxley said it was normal."

"I didn't say it was normal," Huxley corrected me. "I said it was fine. By which I meant, survivable. Come on."

"She can barely walk!"

"Barely is still walking."

"I can't see either."

"It's just stairs. We're not warded till we get into the bunker and shut the door behind us, you know."

Carefully, as if protecting the easier targets of my fingers from a dog I knew would bite, I put my forearm under Johnny's chin and tilted her head up so I could see her face. Her eyes were cluttered with the stuff, drifting across the white in symmetrical strings, but where I could see her irises and pupils they looked about the same size, and sort of lucid, inasmuch as she ever did. Her teeth were the colour of charcoal, apparently still coated with the liquid. If she did bite me, I didn't want to think about what would happen.

"Can you manage stairs?" I said, as she irritably shook me off, sending the blobs darting across her eyes like the gloop in a lava lamp. "Hang onto my coat."

"Where are we?"

"Prague," I said. "If Dr. Huxley isn't bullshitting us."

"Headed down into Sparrow's place," Huxley tossed over her shoulder. "If he's still alive. He might be a mummy down there."

"Ew. What's that noise?"

"My knees," I said.

"I'll buy you new knees."

The stairs went on and on, one bulb about every twenty steps. How deep were we going? I was so hungry and tired I felt a little caved-in, twisted even; my ears were ringing. I imagined fainting, rolling down the endless steps, which couldn't be endless really, of course, but if everyone agreed that the laws of physics had been broken during the Anomaly, then maybe some of them were still broken and no one had noticed, maybe the steps knew that, and would just go on and on forever...

Bunkers had become a big thing after the Anomaly, but this didn't seem to be one of those. And I understood the impulse, I understood everybody's impulses afterwards, I even understood the period where people just went absolutely numb for a couple of months and would do virtually anything they were told without resistance; I had felt it too. People had begun to hoard things, including guns and weapons, on a personal or household basis, as well as on a national basis: stocking their bunkers even if they didn't have one. Mutual-aid and mutual-death societies sprang up everywhere. Everyone assembled a go-bag and a shelter-in-place bag, and rushed out to get first-aid training. Millions of people tried to get permanently sterilized, or did it themselves (gruesomely, in many cases), arguing that they did not want to bring children into this terrible new world in which we had discovered the worst thing about the universe.

And cults, and miracle protection devices against the effects of witnessing future Anomalies like special sunglasses or contact lenses, personal orgone generators, the sightings of long-lost local saints, it all made sense to me. But *especially* bunkers. Because it had happened so fast that even the ultra-rich did not have time to get into theirs. So there was equality, finally, or maybe for the first time in human history: all you had had to do was look up at the wrong moment, no matter where you were or what you were.

After about an hour, we reached a square landing a few yards across, and a door, also concrete. Johnny touched it tentatively, her hand small and pale on the dark, sooty surface, which was burned in a great curling leafy flare as if there had been a small explosion on the floor. I turned and looked up at the stairs rising into darkness behind us, a thin waterfall of fine dust falling from one to the next to the next as I watched. No way out.

Well, one way out.

The door was half-open, showing itself to be a couple of feet thick, and reinforced with rebar that gleamed through the dull gray like bone. "In we go," said Huxley, brandishing the cricket bat. "You want answers? You go to the guy who's watching all the questions."

"*I* don't want answers any more," I pointed out. "I want to go home."

"Must be nice to have one that wasn't blown up."

"All right, all right."

Inside was concrete too, a short hallway leading to a large, low-ceilinged room full of plastic tables and chairs, lit with dull fluorescents. At the end, something like a large parking kiosk covered in faceted panels had been installed. Windows halfway up the concrete base framed a chair upholstered in orange vinyl or leather, and several consoles that looked interestingly like the ones in photos I'd seen of nuclear control rooms. Or no: more like the bridge of the starship *Enterprise*—the old version, not the newer ones. I desperately wanted to go in and flick all the switches.

A man, tall and gangling, dressed in a thick white sweater and puffy blue vest, waved at us from the back of the kiosk. One of the panels swung open and he emerged.

"Sparrow," said Huxley.

"Ah, Dr. Huxley! What a pleasant surprise, seeing you on the stair camera. It has been a long time since our last visit. Boston, was it not? The conference?"

"Could be."

"So, you are reinstated with...?"

"That'll be the day," she said pleasantly. "That'll be the bright new dawn. We won't be long. A few questions, that's all, about what you've been seeing."

"Let me get you supper, at least. I am about to sit down myself." He beamed at us, and held out a long, cold hand. "I do apologize, I am not permitted a human name any more; 'Sparrow' has so far not raised any objections."

We introduced ourselves, Johnny's hand hesitating in the air for a moment a before he realized what was happening, captured and shook it. He was far blonder than her, his hair nearly white; he might have been in his mid-thirties. I couldn't place his accent. "Come eat, please. And if there is any way I can help with what you are doing here, you must tell me."

"We will," Johnny said, "but I gotta warn you, every time somebody says that, it ends super badly."

"It also ends badly if you don't," Huxley said. "Ask me how I know."

"...Come eat."

The bunker was in surprisingly good shape; I supposed it had never been used for what it was meant for, which I vaguely imagined as weeks of increasingly worried, smelly, and strung-out government officials packed in close quarters after a nuclear war. It showed tasteful traces of Sparrow's habitation—neatly-framed posters and paintings; a full laundry hamper; a turquoise-framed mountain bike mounted on wall hooks, five helmets hanging next to it.

After we washed our hands and tried to scrub some of the stains off Johnny's face, he served us tea, then ham and pickle sandwiches on buns and thick potato soup reheated in a gigantic industrial microwave.

"It's too bad," he said, sitting back down and pushing a huge blue-and-silver tin across the table. "Have a biscuit... It's too bad, I mean, that you are here in my beautiful city, during mask season too, and we are all told to stay in our homes..."

"Have there been attacks here?" Huxley dug into the tin, and put three cookies on Johnny's plate.

"Yes. So they say; I have not been above for weeks. Yesterday, we were in Phase Amber. Now, we are in Red. The appearance of creatures, and other..." He waved his hands. "I don't know. Eccentricities."

"We've seen 'em," Huxley said grimly.

"I am very interested in your being here," he said after a moment. "I watch the news, I watch the internet, even the radio. I make calls. No one is allowed in or out. They have put guards on the roads. When those are eaten, fresh guards. The airport is closed. Everywhere, street fighting against things of all sizes. If you go to Old Town, you will probably have a grenade in your face. And yet..."

"I've got a lot of resources," Johnny said chirpily.

"And an official bull was issued," he added, almost apologetically, dipping his head at Johnny. "It says..."

"I know what it says," Johnny said, picking up a cookie with reasonable accuracy and blinking furiously at it for a moment. "They let me read the draft wording."

"Just a damn minute," I said. "You know, I never did find out why."

"I'll tell you later."

"Well, you made a good choice, coming here. We're very safe," Sparrow said. "Much safer than above. There's been a volcanic eruption, you know, in America. And hurricanes, tornadoes. Landslides. Lots of things. They are saying the UN is working with Chambers Labs to rescue, they are using dogs, robots, helicopters..."

"Yeah, we have a dedicated emergency response division," Johnny said. "For natural disasters and stuff.

They're kept in reserve, but they can deploy quite a few units when they're called up. Stabilization, then extraction, rescue, medical assistance, evacuations, shelters, and then food security, potable water, hygiene and waste management."

"Faster than local government, of course."

"Anything's faster than government."

"And all for free."

"Crassus has never really been a role model of mine."

"Stay here until we are back in Phase Green," Sparrow urged, leaning over the table. His eyes were very dark under the blond brows and lashes, earnest and fretful. "All the people out there, it's hard to get them to comply with the rules! The older people remember life under... various regimes, and they become angry when it seems this new freedom will be taken, they want to go out and shop. The younger people think it's a joke, because anything the elders fear is automatically funny... we've had drills, like everybody else. Nobody paid the penalties from being out during the drills, even though we were told to act as if they were real. The bureaucracy ate the fines. Offices eat things. That's what happens if you don't watch. So no one paid anything, and everyone laughed at them."

"It's hard to convince people to take things seriously," Johnny agreed, placidly buttering another roll. "The roof nearly needs to fall in on them."

"Around the world, too, there are things like... Crusades. They wander around, like the Middle Ages, like the engravings you see, in the last few days. Where do they all come from? They say they will worship the... invaders, they will... well, they don't know the history, of course," he added, hastily, as Huxley began to speak. "Anyway. Neither they, nor the invaders, can bother us here."

Something about his voice was setting me on edge, even though it was so pleasant, eager to help. I thought about the endless staircase, the faint but necessary glow of the lightbulbs. Going dark with a single flip of a switch in his control room. Imagined him keeping us, imagined dying down here, in the cool, constantly-moving, filtered air. Would you rot or mummify? Huxley seemed confident about the latter. The twins had just done a unit on it in social studies class: the conditions under which you would mummify, fossilize, decay. How you could rig it so you'd be more likely to last.

"You wished to ask me...?" Sparrow said, delicately.

Huxley gave him a look. "Look, I'm English," she said. "I like the social niceties even more than you do. But I'm just gonna say: why the hell do you *think* we're here? It ain't for the soup."

"The soup was very good, though," Johnny said.

Sparrow stared between them with his round, dark eyes. Birdlike, I thought, and maybe that was how he had given himself the name. And had he said he wasn't *allowed* a human name any more? That wasn't something you could and couldn't give permission to have. Was it?

(Yeah? Who do we know that tries to dictate things like that?)

(Shut up.)

(It's in the oath. It says your blood, your life, your whatever, anything, *anything* they want of yours, they can take it away to save the world.)

(Shut up, I said.)

And for a moment I almost felt sorry for Sparrow, an uncomfortable kinship manifesting itself in a pang of real pity as well as pain, somewhere under my ribs. Clearly he had been with the Society once, I thought, just like Huxley. Maybe they had even worked together. But unlike Huxley, who had escaped via some kind of formal arrangement—her archive guardianship less a reassignment than a prison sentence, I suspected now—he had been disgraced, ejected, had his name taken from him, was probably being monitored, like her, to stay within certain bounds, some kind of... of severance contract. But he still had value to them somehow, at least a little, and he wanted to use this scrap maybe not to get back in, but at least buy his way back into their good graces. And there was only one way to do that with the Society. With knowledge. No different from me. Not really. Not in any way it mattered.

Huxley must have known all this, I thought, glancing at her stony, scorched face. Did Johnny? She clearly knew *of* Sparrow, but that didn't mean much. As a contractor, she would have met or heard of a lot of Society members over the years. It didn't mean she trusted him. But Huxley, I thought, whether she trusted him or not, would not have dragged us down here if it wasn't useful, and if the books hadn't suggested it to me, through me, for reasons that I hoped we could trust.

Sparrow said, "I thought perhaps you wished to stay here for a little time. Because it is safe. And outside is not safe. No one knows what is happening or when it will stop."

"No one's ever known that," Huxley said, exasperated. "Stop dancin' around it. We need to use the Seeing."

"Oh," he said. "You mean, I am sure, the external monitoring system, the…"

"No. The Seeing." Huxley jerked a thumb at Johnny. "And right quick, too." Johnny nodded; another droplet of dark liquid oozed out of her ear and soaked into her shirt. Sparrow stared at it in poorly-concealed horror.

I got the feeling that while this was the question he had been afraid he'd be asked, he also knew there was really no other reason for Huxley, or indeed anyone, to show up on his doorstep. I watched his face writhe for a moment while he debated denying that whatever she was talking about even existed.

"I'm afraid I cannot let anyone else use it," he said. "Really, to be honest with you, it would be dangerous for them, it would be dangerous for the system… It is calibrated and tuned very carefully, and particularly at this… time, I think it's important that its operation not be jeopardized. However, if you gave me a general idea of what it is you are looking for, I could retrieve…"

"I don't work in general ideas," Johnny said. "Sparrow, listen, please. We were told to come here, and to use the Seeing to help us figure out what's going on up there. I won't take long. I promise. And I won't change any of the settings. Your setup really will make a difference in what happens next for everybody, for the whole world."

"I truly cannot," he said regretfully. "I hear what you are saying. And I appreciate you asking so nicely," he added, raising his voice a little on the last word, as if Huxley would care. "But, as I said, if you tell me what you would like to use it for, I can do so on your behalf, and bring back the results. And then we will both be happy. No?"

Johnny shook her head. That, I thought, wasn't part of what the books had told her. She just didn't want Sparrow watching her while she used whatever it was they were talking about. For good reason: what else would he do with it but turn around and run to the Society? Just like I was going to do when I had access to a phone again? Whatever she was doing, she wanted to do it outside of their purview.

She said, "You know, if it's compensation that's the issue, I'm happy to help out with that."

He smiled. "What use do I have for money? I have everything I need here."

"Then what do you want?"

He spread his hands, still smiling. "I want only to help you, believe me. But you must understand, the machinery is such that we must do it under my terms, or not at all."

"Neither of those is an option," Johnny said patiently.

"I am very sorry about that." He sighed, and helped himself to a biscuit from the tin, dropping big granules of sugar on the table that landed with audible *ping!* noises. He frowned, swept them into his palm, and went to empty it in the sink. "Ants," he said, when he returned. "Nothing gets in here. No outside air, no water, no radiation, no signals, no bacteria, no anything. But ants? How do they get in?"

Johnny and Huxley watched him without expression. He glanced at me as if I could help, then went on, brightly, as if he had just thought of it, "There are, I think, many... extremely qualified persons in the city, who might be able to help you in other ways. In fact, I think they have been... called into service finding solutions to the problem. They would be grateful, I am sure, for any assistance you can provide."

"Uh huh." Johnny dabbed at her ear with a paper napkin. I thought about something Huxley had said about the Society while we were in the ley: *Oh, they'll have their field staff everywhere, they'll empty out every one of their bloody offices, down to the last ninety-year-old who once went on a trip in the 'sixties to check out a runestone dug up in a churchyard five miles away.*

"Perhaps I could put you in touch with them," he said. "No sense running over the same ground, of course. A waste, duplication of effort."

"No thank you," Johnny said. "We're making our own inquiries."

"Well. Perhaps I will contact them anyway," he said. "And let them know that you are doing so. In case they have information that could be... useful. To you."

Johnny, who did not seem to have blinked in a solid minute, narrowed her eyes so minutely that for a moment I thought I hadn't seen it. "It would be better if you didn't. Don't you think?"

Was that a threat? It certainly sounded like one; and like one of her usual ones, too, which left the actual consequences unsaid. I glanced between their faces, unmoving now, unsmiling.

"The wards make it very difficult to harm me, here," Sparrow said softly. "It would not be wise to try."

"Nobody said anything about hurting you with *magic*."

He had the good grace, at least, to look a little taken aback. The air between them seemed to fry; in a Western movie, I thought, their guns would have been pointed at each other underneath the table. Gut-shot. Terrible death.

"I wish only to help," he said again. "I am very hurt that you have come here to threaten me."

"After asking nicely," Johnny said. "And after trying to pay."

"But you will not take my terms."

"Nope," Johnny said. "And after I've said please, and offered free cash, I start moving down the hierarchy of ways to ask."

He smiled even more widely, showing beautiful white teeth. "So I have heard," he said. "Dr. Huxley, please, you know me. I exist only to watch for things that may be helpful."

"And sell 'em later. I hear you. Only thing is, I hope you're watching *her*," Huxley said. "You're a survivor; you've got a good sense of danger. Don't you?"

He swallowed, glanced at me, glanced back to Johnny. His face clearly said, *Surely I am not being threatened by an old woman and a teenager?*

I kept my mouth firmly shut, and shrugged.

He sounded genuinely anxious, which made everything so much worse when Johnny leaned over the table, the mercury-heavy stuff flowing from the corners of her eyes, and said pleasantly, "Then I'll wipe it."

"What?"

"I can do it from here. Erase everything and fry its innards. End the Seeing. I just think it would be *better* for all of us if you let me use it," she said. "That's all."

"She'll do it," I said. "She blew up my living room once."

"Once," Johnny said, not breaking her gaze with Sparrow.

"Surprised it didn't catch the gas line."

Huxley kicked me under the table. After another unbearable minute, Sparrow said, "18475036759174998. Do you need for me to write it down?"

"No, I'm good. Thanks."

HALF OUT OF habit, half out of what I still, vaguely, hoped was my mission, I followed Sparrow and Johnny into the glass kiosk, through a concealed door on its far side, and down a long cluttered hallway. Or no, it wasn't cluttered—but the walls and ceiling were covered with things I hadn't seen in the bunker so far. Hundreds, even thousands of ward sigils, dangling from the smooth concrete ceiling in copper or steel wire, worked into the walls in ceramic tile.

At the far end of the hallway was another glass kiosk

similar to the one in the room we'd come in, with blue panels this time instead of orange. Inside was the same console setup, with the same couple of dozen smallish monitors, each about the size of Johnny's laptop. I expected Sparrow to give us a long speech about the calibration, the settings, something like that, but he simply slammed the door behind us and stomped off. Fair, I thought; it was like we were being trusted to babysit, and he'd only just met us. How was he supposed to trust us with his most precious possession?

I sat delicately on the edge of the console, making sure my ass wasn't touching any buttons. Fire a nuke or something, God only knows. Send orders to a million submarines or something.

"This place is something, isn't it?" She yawned, and began to punch buttons into the console's central keypad, making satisfyingly metallic clacking noises. "It's all this bonkers experimental tech, all cutting-edge Cold War stuff. They say he dug right into the walls, embedded things into the concrete, cables and wards and seals, rewired things, pulled and stole new cables…"

"What is this? I mean, the… the Seeing." I had grown wary of words in which you could hear the capitalization, and this was no exception. "Did I really say we should come here?"

"Sure did. Interesting thing, too. I suspected something like this was here, but everyone said it was just… you know. Oh, he watches a lot of news. Oh, he's on the internet a lot. Everyone thinks he's like a one-man Lone Gunmen, sort of thing: watching all the channels and reading all the websites, hacking into security camera footage, storing and recording it all just in case he sees something interesting he can sell or give to the Society or whoever. But the truth is, the books said, he's also got an equivalent magical setup, and *no one* gets to use that but him."

"Yeah. He nearly shit a brick when Huxley asked about it."

"Yep. This"—she gestured at the monitors, which were flickering one by one into life, glowing in various colours that gave me an immediate magical headache—"tracks magic. Sort of. Supposedly. You know, whenever magic is used or moved, it makes a little... sort of a flare. So if I were him, I would set up the *other* system to activate, sort of like a motion-detector system, to access video or audio near those flares. And maybe track local news stories, emergency response scanners, that kind of thing. And it's warded so heavily, right over the nexus, that magic done in here, if you can do it at all, is essentially invisible."

"So he's probably listening to us right now," I said.

She blinked innocently up at me. "Could be."

That, I thought, would be the first thing she'd deactivate when she started working. Deactivate if he was lucky; break if he wasn't.

I waited in silence as she got out the manicure kit from her bag, stood carefully on the chair, and clipped the wires in the obvious security cameras. Then she dug into the console itself, unscrewing a half-dozen panels, tugging more wires loose from their connections, and finally drawing sigils on the backs in Sharpie before placing them back down and pushing the screws to one side. When she gave me a thumbs-up, I said, "And that's another thing."

"About what?"

"About girls. And their big giant bags."

"Don't be silly," she said. "Where are you supposed to put your keys, wallet, coin purse, water bottle, makeup bag, planner, phone, charger, pills, notepads, hand sanitizer, lotion, comb, gum, and snacks?"

"All I carry around is my phone and my wallet."

"Your life is impoverished," she said.

"My phone is impoverished," I said. "It died like... I don't even know what day today is."

"Did it? Give here." In a few minutes, she had plugged her own charger into a little adaptor and rigged up the other end with a piece of tape and two stud earrings she shook out of a pocket in her bag. Plugged in, my phone's screen seemed to panic for a second, and then the red charging light came on. "Ta-da. You'll never get a call out down here, but still."

"Thanks." I glanced up at the cameras, hoping they were really dead. Not like her to not be thorough, though. "Do you think we can trust him?"

"Mm. Good question. We haven't told him anything he can sell, I don't think; and he's got a good thing here, he doesn't want to attract *negative* attention. The Society isn't the only game in town. You're thinking of Akhmetov."

"I guess."

"Akhmetov was an asshole. He did a calculation on how to profit off our desperation, and he came up with a number he liked. He knew we were just there to borrow a book. He thought it was a safe bet to not let us trust him. Get in, get out. That's why it worked, his betrayal."

"…You stole the book."

"I might give it back one day. You never know." She worked with the console for a while, setting up a few monitors for regular images: news, of course, more monster footage; something in a city with a lot of domes and spires that looked like bad CGI, the sky wobbling, folding, unfolding, origami clouds that left buildings sheared in half, sliced the river like a knife; a black hole in the ocean, drinking water and spouting it back up. A hint of waving arms, tipped with claws. Most of the other screens she filled with charts, data tables, documents, websites, maps with little blinking dots.

"There's the bull," she said, leaning forward to tap one of the screens. "Official. They put them online now so everybody can read it."

"So why exactly…"

She sighed. "Well, you know my organoids?"

"Oh sure, I eat a bowl of them every morning. Part of a balanced breakfast."

"Anyway, they're a hell of a lot better than animal testing, but you still have to develop and grow them, you know? And there's still all these uncertainties, there's still a percentage of loss, and for some studies, they're not that useful, like receptor studies and stuff? Membranes?

Metabolism aggregates, receptor interactions, things like that. So I thought: Well, how can we get a little bit faster, and take away those uncertainties, or at least get a handle on that randomness, right? Single-cell studies. Go back to the basics. So I kind of built a cell out of math—a pretty good one actually, if I can toot my own horn, a really good model, variables manipulable along a lot of axes—and we started running chemical dose-response tests on it just to begin with, and it was just performing fantastically, self-assembling into accurate colonies, super-fast organized data, three of my labs were testing it independently and excited out of their minds..."

"This is leading to a mob with torches and pitchforks, isn't it. Like, you're about to say 'So I decided to—'"

"*So I decided to* improve the simulation in a very minor way, I mean make the synthetic cell a little bit less synthetic, and... and... So it's in there, eating math, pooping math, but it's not quite random enough. It's almost, but not quite. What it needs, actually, is some fluid dynamics and uptake randomness, right? Resources in a limited medium?"

"Johnny."

"Look, no no no, look. It was math, it was just math, and then I put a little bit of chemicals on it, and it sort of... started to... behave as if it were..."

"Jesus Christ! That's *everything*, that's *everything and everybody*, we're *all* just math with a little bit of chemicals on us, did you seriously think that people wouldn't mind that you literally created life?"

"Yes!"

"I thought you were supposed to be a genius!"

"It's not really alive! It just acts like it's alive!"

I rubbed my forehead, where a thin spike of pain had begun to drill into the bone above my left eye. "And you... told people about this?"

"Well yeah, I published the paper on our own external-facing repository. You know how journals are, it would have been months. And I wanted to get the copyright in place and verify replicability. People would have accused me of being a fraud. Again."

"Well, the Pope doesn't think you're a fraud."

"Which is good, right? ...Do you want some Advil?"

I shook my head, and sat in one of the other chairs as she got to work, half-dozing against the hard curved plastic. This must have seemed cutting-edge back in the day, this chair. Meant to cradle the ass of someone who had the power of life and death over millions, ready to press a button, turn a key, do what it took...

The magic maps, if that's what they were, swirled and flailed as Johnny pressed buttons moving them backwards through the weeks, all the way till last fall, forward again till today, back, forward, back. She ran through video footage of people turning, or whatever they were doing (being possessed? being disguised?) and for some reason spent a long time on parking lots and the sides of buildings.

"Well that isn't..." She frowned. "Great."

"The last time you said that, there was an acid flood in your basement," I said. "Is this better or worse?"

"Is *that* your reference point, seriously?"

"So, worse then."

"It was just the one time," she muttered. "Anyway, I don't know. Look at this." She froze the map on Friday morning, and then pulled up something else, a page of numbers arranged in columns, twelve to the screen.

"Johnny," I said gently.

"Oh, sorry. Uh." She pressed a series of buttons, and an image appeared, black with the faintest possible gray and white markings on it. "Okay, so you know my sigsats? The ones we sent up last year as part of the UN monitoring project? I didn't want them to be too light, because it screws up everybody's astronomical measurements, but that also happens if they're too dark, right? So I put an ultra chromosensitive, minimally-absorbent nanoceramic coating on all the outer surfaces so they can recalibrate themselves to be exactly the ambient spectrum and not mess people up much. We publish the calibration data in real-time just in case anyone wants to use it to cancel out whatever little noise is left in their own data. I mean, these are very small numbers we're talking about here, right, and... well, part of the audit from the IARE that I'm undergoing started with this. Complaints about the sigsats. About that daily data."

"That it was wrong?"

"Yes. And that it was wrong for different people in different ways, which is impossible. No two facilities were downloading the same number. We checked all our servers, we went through everything with a fine-toothed comb. And yet..." She stared at the screen. "Maybe our data wasn't wrong. Maybe it was responding to something nobody else saw."

The hair on my arms stood up; I rubbed them absently, put my hands back in my pockets. "So They *are* coming from space?"

"No. Because nothing else detected anything. They're coming from somewhere else, and something in our space is being affected by it."

"Not *some*thing," I said. "*Your* things. Specifically yours. Specifically *you*."

"Specifically me," she said, sounding a little dazed. "Curst by the gods."

No, I wanted to say. You asked for the curse. You *demanded* it. And you made me part of it, thank you. Look at you, sitting there feeling sorry for yourself. You dragged me into this, you dragged in the whole world. You weren't even drowning and you pulled us all underwater with you.

Or did you. Did you? If I were cursed, if I had been given great powers at a great cost, the cost of time, the only thing I couldn't make or buy myself, what would I do with it? Would I make another deal to lift it? Get some of that time back? Lower the cost? I'm not her, I don't live the way she lives, every time she turns on her powers one second per second off the end of her life, one minute per minute, doling it out bit by bit, flinching every time... if someone came to me and said *What if I could do that for you?* What would you give them?

"Nick?" she said.

"Mm?"

"Are you okay? You look a little..."

"Headache. Sorry. You were saying?"

"I do actually have Advil in my bag," she said. "And Nurofen and some other stuff, uh, some lab stuff. No? Anyway. The thing is... the thing about curses..." She crossed her legs in the chair, and leaned back, chewing her lip. "Look at the Carthaginian plague in whatever, 400 BC. Diodorus thought it was sent by the gods to punish the Carthaginians for blasphemy. Looting temples. Fuckers, the gods said, how fucking *dare*. The plague of Constantinople, 750 AD. Theophanes said everybody hallucinated that they had the disease even if they didn't, and people saw crosses appearing on clothes, particularly church garb, indicating the next victim. People see a plague, they say: this was brought upon us."

"Sure, if you don't know about germ theory. Why not?"

"Intent, intent," she said, staring at the monitor, as if I hadn't spoken. "It's all about *intent*. The gods are angry, they curse you. You remove or prevent it with purity, faith. It is transmitted between those of insufficient belief, of course; and you can pray it away, you can offer sacrifices, repentance. Random immunity attributable to being blessed. Nobody remembers maybe you had it as a kid and survived. Prevention attributable to shunning the unclean and unbelievers. The fringes of society, pushed out of the mainstream anyway. Cure effected by... never random chance. Faith or a lack of faith.

Quacks, opportunists. Magic... magic isn't science. Magic acts as if it's..."

"Of course it isn't science," I said, for something to say.

She fell silent for several minutes, her lips moving. Eventually I gave up and sat down again, and picked my phone up off the floor. Impressively, or perhaps worryingly, Johnny's jury-rigged charger had got it back to 98% charge. Five missed calls, ten text messages, but I could only see the notifications without signal. We'd have to get back to street level before I could get them. For a second all I wanted to do was rush down the hallway, run back up the stairs. *Hurry up!* I wanted to scream at Johnny. *Come on! Did you get what you fucking needed? Hurry up!*

"It's not the sigils that are magic," she said at last. "Not inherently. It's their shape... That's why you can make one out of stone or coal or chalk or string. It's not the words that are magic. It's their shape. It's not that magic itself can do anything, it's that it has to be channelled somehow. And the way it is channelled is partly structural and partly... I can't believe I'm saying this... *intentional*. That's it. That's how it works. Holy shit. *That's* why none of my detectors worked."

"Are you all right?"

"Quantum theory."

"Oh no."

"Quantum just means discrete, that's all. Packet, lump. So light, for instance: one lump is a photon. Electrons, a lump. They don't always exist, right? Only when they're being watched or when they interact with something. They materialize in a place, with a calculable probability, when they bonk into something else. The quantum leaps from one orbit to another are the only way they can be real. That's the way my reactor works: the orbits are just on two sides of a dimension. Which, obviously, yeah, I can't *tell* anybody that. Anyway, when they're not running around or crashing into stuff, they're not in any precise place, they're not actually in a place at all, you could say they're not really real if you wanted to.

"Magic isn't like that. Magic is more like... a cross between an electron and something very light and small but divisible, like a spore. It has... volition and instinct, it follows rules both because it can be carried by currents and winds and their equivalent, but also because it knows some of the rules. It doesn't move like heat or light or gravity or electricity, which cannot choose how they move, which always go from more to less. That's why I couldn't put math on it. Because it's not subject to inertia, momentum, friction, because it *does* have that little bit of will."

I nodded politely, even though my main concern was how to remember all of this to pass on to Louis when I eventually got to a place that wasn't made of rebar concrete. Johnny looked like she'd just washed down a handful of meth with a keg of espresso: like the night I had come over to find her in the silvery dress and steel-toed boots, out of her mind on adrenaline and discovery. The bruised goggles across her face only added to the effect. Bleakly, and for just a second, I allowed myself to wonder whether the world would end before they faded.

"We stopped studying it," she said.

"Stopped studying what?"

"Shapes, the shape of things. Remember when I was trying to come up with a reliable in-vivo for Mad Cow?"

"Not even slightly."

"My nanobots got all fucked-up by the prions and I was so *mad*. But that's what they do. That's all they do, that's... fucking prions! You know, it's like, you can't trust the outside of things for diagnosis with prion disease, symptoms I mean, all I wanted to do was look inside, but bodies are a problem, being alive is a problem, you can do genetic testing for some prion diseases but not all of them, and—"

"Why are we talking about Mad Cow? You have completely and totally lost me."

She took a deep breath, and gingerly wiped the sweat from her face with the hem of her t-shirt. "They aren't back. Not really. They didn't figure out a way to get through. What they figured out, I think, was this." She pointed at another monitor, frozen on a crumbling wall. "A magical prion disease."

"...What."

"Autocatalytic, self-seeding. They didn't *need* to physically come here. They figured out something else. A conformation or configuration that acts like a prion. The shape is transmissible. It moves from person to person, thing to thing, and it's the *shape* that changes, and then a spell activates to change us into Them. It's like... a sigil that can make more of itself. A spell to make more spells."

My stomach sank. She nodded slowly, seeing my face, the realization of it. How did you stop something like that? Huxley had been right, I realized. Without knowing this, any of this, she had taken a look at the world and said: *If it's a war, it's already over. They won. We lost.*

"We can't cure Mad Cow," I said. "Is this the same thing?"

"My God, I fucking hope not," she said severely. "But if I'm right, I need to get back to the facility at the Creek. Do some experiments. Maybe there's a way. The problem with real prions is that if you break up the oligomers they make in the brain, they get *more* infectious, not less. This isn't something I could... blow up."

"Despite that being your preferred method for dealing with things," I said automatically, although it felt like someone else was saying it; my mouth felt numb. I felt like I had to force myself to keep breathing. And it didn't even mean anything, I thought, for the theory that I had been working on while she had been working on hers. If anything, it fed right into it, pallets and pallets of feedstock heading up the conveyor belt into the horrified factory of my mind... supposing she was right, supposing this was in some way biological warfare, she might still have swapped sides if They could promise her immunity.

And why wouldn't They? It would suit Them right down to the ground to have her on Their side, and for her, to have her life spared, even her humanity spared, would be payment enough, with or without time. She'd just make a new deal. They could offer you one, she had told me more than once. No covenant could be changed once made, because it altered the entire universe such that the conditions of the covenant's spell worked in it. But a new one. That would be something. Wouldn't it.

"Let's get out of here," I said. "I mean, assuming Harvey Birdman there lets us out of this bunker."

"Bunkers got more than one way out of them," she said, rubbing her eyes gingerly; a drop of the dark liquid came off on her hand. She wiped it on her coat. "Gross. I mean, for flooding, fires, things like that. They have enough room to fit most of the important people in municipal government down here, they're never going to have a single point of ingress and egress. And anyway, I'm going to wipe the consoles and knock out all his comm lines whether or not he lets us out. Everything's set up."

"Johnny, what the hell? He did like you said! You can't just go back on your word like that."

"I have to," she said. "He can't know what I was looking at. None of it."

"Can't you just... erase what you did, and leave everything else?"

"Nope. He's rigged the entire system to prevent exactly that. It's all or nothing. And anyway, what do you care?"

"Well, I... Look, it's just a shitty thing to do. You basically coerced him into using this. You threatened him with the worst possible thing he could imagine. Did you see his face? And now you're going to do it anyway, even though he did what you asked."

"It's war-time," she said firmly. "He'll understand."

"Don't do it."

She glared at me. "I'm *not* leaving him anything to give to the Society, okay? That's final. And anyway, we've all done shitty things."

BACK UP AT street level, the sky had the pale glow of dawn. I opened my phone immediately while we stood around and bitched about our thighs, and scrolled almost desperately through the notifications, then thumbed into my voicemails.

"Nick, come on. We're going to go to the hotel I stayed at last time, it'll be quieter there."

"Do you fucking mind?" I said. "Like, excuse me for actually having people I give a shit about. And anyway, they won't let you in. You look like hell. You look like Alice Cooper."

"Cool."

"I mean, not in a cool way. Like maybe he got run over and left out in the rain kind of way."

"Where is this hotel?" Huxley said querulously. "We'll never get a taxi."

"About fifteen minutes' walk. Also, if I never see a single stair again, it'll be too soon."

"Amen for that. You, give me your coat."

I took it off obediently and handed it over.

"If we—" Johnny began, then stopped to cough again.

"Good, go on, get it all up, just spit in the corner, it's not very ladylike."

I looked up, startled, as she continued to cough, at a small but familiar sound, carrying clearly across the quiet street: a camera shutter, from a film camera. Alarmed, I stared around us. There—in the doorway of a drugstore, not bothering overmuch to conceal himself, a man in sunglasses, a dark coat, with a scarf pulled up over his mouth and nose. Spotting me, infuriatingly, he lifted the camera to his face again, a big one, with a long zoom lens, and deliberately took another photo.

I moved in front of Johnny, a sick pit in my gut out of all proportion to seeing the photographer; this used to happen all the time, and I suspected it had only gotten worse since the Anomaly, with paranoid governments everywhere relaxing the rules on paparazzi and drone operators in the hopes that some 'early warning' footage would be reported to the tip lines for another incident. "Come on. Let's go. There's some asshole here."

"Hey!" he called, as we began to walk again, away from him. "Hey!"

I wanted to call back *Fuck you!* but instead tried to speed up, holding my arm out for Johnny to take; she refused it, and kept her head down, still walking. Huxley scurried ahead of us, her face down too, my coat collar zipped up to cover half her face.

At the end of the block, alerted by the honking horns, I realized where the photographer must have come from: an enterprising scout, peeled off from the larger mass.

And indeed, as I turned in despair to glance behind us, he was on his phone, one hand on the camera.

A few dozen people were marching across the street towards us, ringed by obvious paparazzi: professional cameras, black tactical backpacks bulging with gear. I even thought I vaguely recognized one, or had seen her face before—in person, not in the news. She had targeted Johnny before, I was sure of it.

Rage and fear surged up from my stomach, and for a second I almost felt warm. "Fucking leave us alone!" I yelled.

Mistake. Bad idea. They looked up, and kept coming, not running, but moving quicker than they were. Most held signs, not in English, though a few were: *THREAT TO HUMANITY*, one read, and *WE DEMAND THE HAGUE*. One, sending a bolt of terror and recognition through me like ice, bore the photos I had last seen side-by-side two years ago: the ones they had put up when Johnny and I had gone 'missing' and the reward was offered. The closest was simply a drawing of what looked like a bacterium, or some kind of cell, complete with all the organelles, with the red-slashed circle universally understood to be forbidding it, overtop.

"What the absolute shit?" Johnny said, looking up, her mouth ringed in black.

"They're... they're protesting *us*. It's an... it's an anti-us march. What are they saying, do you know?"

"'We want answers, we want justice, we want answers, we want justice,'" she said, as Huxley murmured the same thing, backing away and hitting the wall again.

"Ow. Okay. Let's... let's just head back the other way. If we head into one of the stores, they won't..."

"Nothing's open," Huxley said. "They're under the alert, maybe even phase two. Back, yeah. Circle around, find your hotel."

We made it half a block, the three of us awkwardly turning to keep our backs to the march and still be able to navigate, my heart pounding, Johnny still coughing, moving slowly.

"*Fucking* Sparrow," Huxley muttered.

"What?" I whispered. "You think he—"

"Who else? I've seen him pull these things before. He's got this whole network of little local mercenaries who can organize at the drop of a hat, as distractions, as sheepdogs, as..."

I opened my mouth to say *But Johnny cut off all his comms*, and realized that she must have missed something secret. For a second I was almost pleased that she had been outwitted for once, but then I went right back to being pissed off.

We made it to the end of the street, turned right, away from the low building that housed the entrance to Sparrow's bunker, and stopped short: someone was calling for Dr. Huxley.

A small black car had pulled up at the end of the street, nearly on the sidewalk. A man and woman sat in the front, the man at the wheel gesturing to us. "Dr. Huxley!"

Her face had gone gray and expressionless, nothing moving but her hair in the breeze. For a terrible moment, no one did anything. At last, she said, "Get in."

"Dr. Huxley," Johnny whispered. "We don't have to do this. We can get you out of here. I can..."

"Not for long," she said grimly. "Get in. In."

Huxley paused before we got into the car, taking off my coat, so that as we piled into the small back seat it lay across all our laps like a blanket. We pulled off sedately as I fumbled for seatbelts, finding none. I stared up at the so-called protestors in the rear-view mirror, now lit cotton-candy pink with sunrise. My stomach was sinking, a familiar fall, feeling Huxley tremble minutely against me. What was happening? I could guess, didn't want to guess, wanted to guess something else. Be wrong, I told myself. For once. There's got to be another explanation...

The man was heavyset, his head shaved close to the skin, leaving a gingery fuzz; the woman's dark hair was pulled into a bun. In a mild, American accent, she said, "Dr. Jordan Huxley. You are in contravention of Clauses 15, 17, 18, 20, 21, and 22 of your post-employment contract. You've been summoned to present evidence in advance of..." She trailed off, maybe not wanting to use the official language. In the rearview, the man pressed his lips into a line, then visibly forced his face to relax into an expression of polite, administrative concern.

She went on, "In advance of the decisions that will be made by the relevant committee."

I stared between him, and her, and then down at Huxley, who had gone perfectly still, and then over at Johnny, visibly stricken. Had Huxley known this would happen? Yes, she must have thought it likely, I thought, but not so soon. Not like this. Sparrow's doing too? One last dig? No way to tell now. Maybe the moment she had done that spell at her archive, some alarm had been tripped, and they had hunted her down. Maybe...

"Wait a minute," I said, looking between the man's neck, the woman's half-turned face. "Wait. Okay. Listen, yes... she did do the... the thing that she wasn't supposed to do. But she saved our lives, all three of us. *Literally*, without exaggeration, saved our lives. There was no alternative, none. Doesn't that—"

"Dr. Huxley. Do you acknowledge the charges?"

It was as if they hadn't heard me at all. My breath sped up; everything I wanted to say, scream at them, whirled inside me, trapped, like some animal that had fallen into a dry well of unimaginable depth, sprinting in circles, unable to gain height, able to do nothing but panic and run.

Some people allowed to be angry. And some people ignored.

"I do acknowledge them. I'll present my evidence." Huxley glanced at me; the pearl-button eyes were bright, but with hatred rather than tears, and a certain bizarre pride, even satisfaction. "Get to the bottom of this. You don't need me."

"Of course we do. This is fucking ridiculous, they can't..." I grabbed her arm instinctively, as if it would help. "No! This isn't fucking fair, this isn't even... There has to be an exception, we would have died, you don't know how close it was. You don't even know what happened. You can't possibly arrest her for..."

"She's not being arrested," the man said, affronted. "This is strictly administrative."

"It's not fucking administrative if you're going to punish her for doing what she did!"

"We won't punish her," the woman said.

We won't punish her. Of course not. My God.

"This is our fault!" I said, as Huxley shook me off. "Ours, mine. I got her into this, I asked her to come. Wait. Tell them—no, listen. I'll go instead, I'll explain everything, I'll..."

"There's no question of instead, Nicholas," Huxley said. "Use your head, boy. Stop being hysterical. I brought this upon myself, and I take full responsibility."

"But—"

"There's nothing you can do," she said. "Stop it. Show some dignity."

She quickly squeezed my hand, the cold fingers like claws, and tilted her chin up. "I now invoke my right to silence, until I present to the committee."

"Your invocation has been noted."

Both the Society agents looked at me in the rearview mirror, and smiled, at the same time. Johnny murmured, "Here," and the car stopped in front of a little jewel-box of a building, glass-fronted and with dark purple velvet curtains, wedged between two taller buildings.

We got out without speaking, and watched the car vanish down the empty street.

CHAPTER NINE

"This is what happens!" I said, barely noticing the two front-desk employees looking up, startled, behind the glass of the lobby window. "You had to make an enemy, didn't you? You don't give a shit about people, fine. But you don't give a shit about *yourself*, either! And it blows up in your face!"

"Where the hell did that come from?" she demanded. "What, like I'm in charge of what the stupid Society does? They're *watchers*, it's in their goddamn name!"

"I'm not talking about that! I'm talking about that bunker guy! He set up that... that fake protest or whatever, that herded us right towards the Society fuckers!"

"How do you know he didn't do that the minute we took our eyes off him?"

"Why would he have? You're the one who gave him a

reason! And then you fucked up that too! You left him an outside line!"

"You can't prove any of that! God, listen to yourself!" She spun, probably intending to stalk away from the hotel, but staggered instead and nearly fell. Reflexively, and hating myself out of reflex too, I grabbed her arm. She shook herself free.

"What are you doing?"

"I don't want to stay here if the Society knows we're here," she said, and spat again, weakly, into the light skiff of snow. "You can stay here if you want."

"I'm not..." I trailed off, feeling as sick as she looked. *I'm not going to just leave you here*, but my God, why not? Hadn't I learned enough for the Society? What else could I possibly gather, what else did I possibly need to prove? What, that I could keep digging forever, that I'd never put down the shovel? That I'd just tunnel right into the core of the Earth? That when she eventually got nailed to the wall for killing half a billion people (and counting!), I'd insist on being right there beside her?

More than ever at that moment, watching her weave away from me down the alley, I missed the old days. When I knew nothing about what she really was, what I really was, what she had tried to make me into. When we were safe with each other. When the world was... well, it was never going to be safe, really, was it. But when we were alone, at least, in the universe. She had taken all that from me. From all of us.

"Come on," I said, and followed her. "Come on. It's fine. There's nothing we can do about it anyway. And they'll find us if they want to find us. Won't they? Yeah, come on. Let's go find a backup place."

WE WALKED ACROSS the changing city, slowly, not encountering any more protests or marches (of course), getting the occasional dirty look from people out and about, as if them being out was any different from us. Strange grayish toads the colour of the stone curbs and statues hopped between buildings, apparently sluggish in the cold; a couple of the bare trees branched out with snakes as we walked. Several people, perhaps in an earlier stage of the infection, or just suffering one of its natural failures, began to transform, dissolve, struggle into the air, fall, slide to the empty streets and become a twitching heap of tentacles and eyes.

"Do you think we'll catch it?" I said.

Johnny shrugged listlessly. "I don't, actually. And I don't know why that might be. Just a feeling that... maybe we're... wanted for something else. And that merely turning into one of Them wouldn't satisfy it."

"Because it'll be so much worse. Whatever it is."

"*So* much worse."

I was still thinking about it when we reached the other hotel half an hour later or so, another little jewel-box near the river, darkened, though they turned their lights on as we approached.

Making a show of it, they rejected her outheld credit card (*Oh* no, *Miss Chambers, we know you, we trust you*), I felt I knew how Johnny was seeing the world—

as if I had possessed her, and was using her eyes. The darkness that shifted every time I moved my head, allowing only moments of clear vision.

Our room was much the same as the outside of the building—small, but plush, two small beds in dark purple and gold-patterned quilts identical to the curtains and walls. "What is this, protective camouflage?"

"Check for snakes," she said, flopping onto the bed closer to the door.

"If there are snakes here, they're fancy snakes. Fancier than me. I can't kick them out."

"Yes you can."

"I'm a prole."

"Revolt. Rise up. Overthrow the class of moneyed reptiles."

"Which is you, by the way," I added, as I kicked off my boots and headed for the bathroom.

"That'll be the day," she said, cut off as the door closed.

When I came back out, she was intently watching the TV, leaning forward as if she were about to topple into it. "What was all that screaming?"

"Shut up."

"I did actually warn you, loudly, that there was a bidet in there."

"Shut up." I sat on my own bed, and stared at the TV too. BBC, volume low, captions on. "Did the grownups fix everything?"

She made a noncommittal noise. "Actually, attacks do seem to be tapering off. But... apparently protestors have been... breaking into scientific facilities, and causing some damage."

"That's not a protest," I said. "That's a mob."

And by facilities, I realized, she included her own: there was shaky video, no flaming torches and no pitchforks but signs aplenty, and molotov cocktails sputtering against dark skies or invisible against bright ones, somersaulting onto roofs, cars, telescopes. People were driving cars through security gates, battering electrical fences with wooden rams, like something you'd see in a medieval manuscript. Harried guards fled as crowds spilled into low nondescript buildings, tumbled into the enclosures of telescopes.

"Jesus." At least half the videos showed prominent *CHAMBERS LABS* logos somewhere. "What are they doing?"

"It's interesting," she said, not looking away, the colours of fires sliding across her face. "*Nature* did a study recently, the results were released around Christmas. About trust, and... perceptions of science, I guess, and scientists. Trust overall in scientists and scientific expertise has plummeted since the Anomaly."

"Because they think scientists caused it?"

"Yeah. Also because there was no warning... there's a persistent idea, they found, that scientists knew it would happen, and were trying to prevent it secretly, behind the scenes, but failed."

I thought about that. "But that's exactly what happened."

"No, I know, but first of all, *one* scientist, which was

me, and I knew for like... less than a week." She toyed with the remote control. "And we did fail, yeah. We were so close to... to not having it happen at all."

"We did our best."

"That's what worries me now. What's happening now... Will our best be enough?"

I fell silent. We, our, our. We: as if we were still on the same side. I was still trying to decide whether it was true.

"After it happened," she said, lying back on the bed and putting her hands behind her head, "I repurposed a couple of divisions to focus on detection, communications, advance warnings. It was so stupid, absolutely unbelievable. Perimeter fences with motion detectors, satellites to scan the space around Earth, sticking that facility on the moon. The unblinking eye: watching for danger! So, so ridiculous. As if anything would come from *space*. But we had to do *something*, and we had to be seen to be doing something."

"Like the UN setting up that... special secretariat or whatever. Looks bad if you don't participate."

"Exactly. Exactly. But here we are. None of those other labs figured out what happened. Or how to prevent it. All the physicists, all the astronomers, all the colliders, the accelerators, the telescopes, every major piece of scientific equipment in the world that studies what things are and what things aren't and what things are made of could be pointed at the Anomaly, and they would still never know. And if I tried to explain what I thought was happening now, they'd lock me up."

"If you had been locked up when you were a kid, none of this would be happening."

"Yeah, but look at all the cool stuff you'd be missing out on."

"I don't need bionic eyes," I pointed out.

"But the..." She trailed off, and pushed the remote aside. "I... I wanted to make those after the... after we got back last time. Because Rutger looked up the statistics, and so many people got blinded by the Anomaly. I thought people would want... and the brain implants too, for people who had neuralgia."

"Yeah."

"No, I mean... all those people who died. And the ones who tried to die and didn't. And the *survivors*. Just from being exposed to that open gate for two minutes. Maybe that was how They got in, maybe that was the... the seeds of it. Their test population. People who had already been torn wide open, somehow, in some way, even if not physically, by the Anomaly. That would explain why it never really stopped in some places. Where... where They were experimenting, maybe."

"Jesus Christ."

She rolled over and looked at me, the eyes jittery in their bowls of shadow. "We should nap. We're going to drop."

"I gotta make some phone calls. I'll be quiet."

She yawned. "There's a phone room downstairs. You can just charge it to the room."

"Johnny. What happened to Dr. Huxley back there? Is it... it's not what it looks like."

She closed her eyes. "I think so. Yes. I think it's exactly what it looks like."

I said nothing. Of course. Of *course* that's what they'd do. Not even a hostage, they wouldn't call it that. Just a price. *Of course you can leave*, they'd say. *If you pay up*. Maybe children, if you had them. But they'd find someone else if you didn't. They didn't say it in the contract or the oath. What you said was: Never.

But there was a way around *Never*. And I had seen the bedroom, the clothes in Huxley's TV room, I knew a man had lived there, much bigger than her. That sweater on the dresser. Like a sign.

"Okay," I said unsteadily, watching Johnny's eyelids tremble. "So she said: I want to go. And they said... what? All right, you can go. If you promise to... to not do magic ever again. And in exchange for one other thing..."

"Nick."

"She had a husband. Didn't she? And what the hell, I keep thinking. *What* could have been so bad about the job that she would give him up to quit? What? There's nothing. Like, if I was going to quit my job, and my boss was like 'No, you can't, I'll take your mother, I'll take the kids,' I'd go 'Yessir, back to the keyboard, sorry I said anything.' *Nothing's* that bad. I can't believe she wouldn't have just... gone back. What's the word. Backed down."

Johnny's eyes were watering, or she was crying; it soaked into the purple pillow, turning it black.

"Divitiacus," she said at last. "Maybe."

"What?"

"Who. An associate, supposedly, of Julius Caesar's. Caesar thought he was a druid. He might have just been an ordinary maniac. Regardless, the name comes up in the records; he was known to the Ancient Ones. He wanted a covenant. They played with him... it's fun to watch people want what they can't have, I suppose. But the books say he persisted. He burned people to death, and he said he could tell the future from how they died, the shapes their bodies made... he called it ritual sacrifice to the gods. But what he wanted was Their attention. Anyway, he got his reward. And he wrote some very powerful spells when he got the real ability to prophesy based on those deaths. But his prophecies were destroyed, they say. And were never found. Despite the cost."

I stared at her, trying to make my eyes focus. If I looked away, I thought for sure I would faint. Fix the eyes: fix the head. Carefully now. Why, how had I come to this place? Why had I agreed to work for these people? No, stop it. You knew. Part of you knew. And you signed anyway, thinking only of the money, the prestige, the new house, yes, but also *her, her, her*, getting back at her, thinking she'd never know. "You think the Society was making her *kill* people? They're *librarians!*"

"Maybe. I don't even know what really happened to her husband. Maybe he just left her."

I was breathing hard again. God, all this hatred you carry with you, and you let it out, and you expect to feel lighter but you don't; I felt as if I were encased in lead.

"There's nothing you can do," Johnny said, and yawned. "Close your eyes for five minutes. We'll be okay here."

When she seemed to be out (uneasily, muttering and twitching on top of the quilt), I crept back to the lobby and was shown to their phone room, a little padded cell tiled with laminated sheets bearing friendly instructions and diagrams in several languages.

"Would you like to bill to room?" the receptionist said brightly.

"Ye... no. No." I gave her my credit card instead, wincing. The Society paid my phone bills, but I would have to expense the credit card. Although, not if the world ended...

After he explained how to call internationally, I tugged the door shut, feeling the silence increase inside the room till I could hear my heart beat, and then feel my stomach working to digest, and at last the movement of the blood inside my ears against the tympanum, a sound not like the sea reflected in a seashell but a crowd roaring in a closed space. Home first. What time was it there? The phone screen informed me it was 8:34 here.

I thought about Sparrow's bunker, about the Cold War, dry paragraphs in a junior high social studies textbook. Millions of lives might have been decided there. If the government had been forced to take refuge, millions of lives might already have been lost. Sparrow chipping out the walls, humming as he welded, patched, spliced, reassembled. Putting the wards in, lugging a bag of cement home on his bike. The watching could wait.

He had used tiles, Johnny had told me while I had half-snoozed against the wall of the console room: glazed all-over, self-contained, a framework containing glass marbles. Thinking that even if the place were flooded, for example, that the wards would not dissolve. Fired ceramic and glass were likely to survive a cataclysm. When the world ends, she'd chuckled sleepily, They will come back and dig up our perfectly-preserved toilets, and They will think we were a civilization made in a kiln...

"Hello?"

"Mom! Jesus. Hi! Are you okay, is everything okay?" I sagged in the chair, and let the tears flow, breathing carefully through my mouth.

"Oh, Nick! Hi, baby." Her voice was high and nervous; I could almost hear her fighting for normality. It took all my strength not to simply hang up, stride outside, demand a cab to the airport.

"Are you okay?" I said again, drying my face.

"Well it's... We're fine, the kids are fine. Did you get my voicemail? I exaggerated a little bit," she added, with a pained laugh. "The trees were fine, really. We just... well, we spent one night in a hotel. But we came back."

"What happened? I didn't get the voicemail."

"It's nothing, it's nothing really. Don't worry about us. How's your conference? What's the matter with your phone? Whenever I call, I just get the beep, and then the error message from Telus."

"...It's a billing error with work, it's nothing. I, uh, borrowed a coworker's phone to make this call, he's from

Europe or something. Are you all right? Is everybody all right? I'm sorry I called so late. Did I wake you up?"

"Yes, we're fine!" But she was crying, holding the phone away from her mouth. Christ, I thought. Dad gone what, seven years ago, me the so-called man of the house, and now she's there with Chris and Brent and Carla and I'm all the way over here, with fucking Johnny, fucking *again*, and… "It really wasn't that bad. I think it's mostly gone now. I'm staying out of the backyard, anyway. And the kids are fine. They're not… Are you watching the news? American news?"

"Um, the TV in my hotel doesn't work." I breathed slowly through my mouth. It felt serpentine, dragonish. Breathing fire. Like at the archive: a flamethrower to back things into a corner. "Listen. I'm going to… we've got this program. At work. I'm going to call and see if they can come get you to somewhere safer. *Not* like last time. This isn't anything like that. It's… it's employee assistance."

"Baby, I'm sure that's just for managers and whatnot. Now, you know I'm very proud of you and your job, but you can't overstep your boundaries like that. Trust me, I know, I've seen it at enough places. They don't like to see that. They want you to know your place."

"I know. I know that. I know."

"I'm glad to see Orlando is all right, anyway," she said, gaining control over her voice again. "Cookie's been searching about it on the internet, you know her. Are they feeding you? When's your flight again? I can come get you at the airport."

I scrubbed a hand across my face, the scratch of the

unfamiliar stubble. The last few days seemed to come at me in a rush, a whirl of eyes and tentacles and wings, pain and terror, the glass teeth of a dragon nearly close enough to slap, the smoke still in my throat, still, somehow, still, and the feel of the cricket bat in my hand. Go. Go. Be with them: you've told them enough lies. It's been a long time since they last looked at you with trust. You've done enough.

I can't. I can't. This is the world, it's the whole world. But God I have never hated anyone in my entire life as much as I hate Johnny right at this second. She did this. She caused this. She drew a bulls-eye on us and drew Them in.

"Listen, Mom, with... everything that's going on. My boss has asked me to stay afterwards. Go to some meetings. Meet some clients. We're, um, we're stretched pretty thin."

A long silence. You're such a bad liar, I heard Johnny say in my head, affectionate, reproving, a long time ago: a memory I had stored away like a commercial, unaware I had been watching it in the background while I had tried to do other things. *You're hopeless. Don't quit your dayjob, you'll never make it on the stage. You got the truth disease.*

Shut up.

Be a scientist instead. Come work for me.

You *don't tell the truth.*

I hire people who tell the truth.

"Well, all right," Mom said slowly. "But I hope they're paying you overtime for this. You can't let people take advantage of your time like that, baby. You'll learn that as you get older, get into the corporate world. You know your boss doesn't own you, he doesn't own your time. You've got to push back on it."

"I know, Mom."

"I've got a book about it in the house. It's about negotiation."

"I'll read it when I get back."

"Anyway, I'd better go to bed, I'm about to drop. I missed your voice. Is calling or texting better? I'm not very good at the texting, I have to get Cookie to do it."

"It's fine. It's fine. I'll try to keep in better touch. Everything is going to be okay."

"Wear sunscreen, by the way! I don't care if it's winter, the UV goes right through clouds, and people say we can't get cancer, but I saw a whole episode of Dr. Malone about it, a two-part episode, and she had all these people on there, from all different countries, who got skin cancer because they—"

"I'll buy some," I said, trying to keep the tremor from my voice. "There's a drugstore across from the hotel. Work will pay for it."

"I know you say it breaks you out, but honey, you'll outgrow the acne, you won't outgrow a carcinoma."

"I know, I know. I'll buy some."

"A hat isn't enough! Anyway, you get some rest too, and by the way, I moved the Cav off the driveway and onto the street, because it was in the way, but it's still plugged in. Love you! Bye!"

"Love you."

She hung up, and I stared at the humming receiver for a long time before hanging it up. A sob sat in my chest like a brick, its edges slicing into the soft flesh. I could not push it down, swallow it down, let it out.

Johnny had declared early on that she was done 'being parented,' and I had wholeheartedly agreed; and it was fun to pretend that we were some kind of... tiny, feral gang, that we were the Lost Boys, or Robinson Crusoe, or some other little civilization of two (*Blue Lagoon* was never mentioned, though we had both seen it). No one could tell us what to do, impose their ridiculous expectations, we would be perfectly free, the idea and the implementation of that perfect freedom unmarred by a single responsibility or restriction—in fact, not Lost Boys at all, subject to a feather-hatted leader, but even better. Even freer. Sharks. Birds.

And then I would go home, to house rules, chores, making sure the kids didn't plunge off the balcony or eat a handful of nails, to studying, getting good grades, making sure I was never a disappointment or a spectacle (the two things my parents hated most); and she went back to being a bird, being a shark. I had felt smothered and desperate at home, but loved; and I passed that love on to Carla and the twins. Had she?

Being loved meant you had the duty to do something with it. But if you didn't think you were, what would you do with your life? She was proof of it, whatever it was. Proof of concept. She was what happened when you thought love was useless, for the weak, that it even in some way *damaged* you, stole from you: that the cost of love was something nobler inside of you. *Well I just don't think it's important*, she said once, *I don't know, maybe for some people, I guess. But I think there's a lot more important things.* She had set up her entire life so that she never, had never, since she was a child, had anyone to kiss goodbye; she had always scoffed at attachments, at what billions of us felt for lovers, friends, family. All she ever wanted was the love of an animal, and she had gotten me, and said it was good enough. And there wasn't anyone she'd die for except herself.

I lifted the hem of my t-shirt, still smelling of bunker dust, and wiped my face. Mom had taken all these lies, would pass them on to the kids in the morning, no doubt laughing, telling them they'd get even better souvenirs now, because I was there for much longer. I had lied to her a lot as a kid, of course; I'd always felt I had to. For protection. After the Anomaly, they had mistrusted me, my disappearance, Johnny's involvement, Rutger, the world. No way to make it up to them, stitch together a narrative; no way to look like anything except a liar who didn't trust them either. I had been a stranger to them. My people. Who believed that I would never abandon them again.

Get it together. Get back to them. Go back to your people. Like Huxley said.

My people. The people that belonged to me, and that I belonged to.

When my face was dry, I called Louis too—getting his assistant Sherwood, as usual—and gave a twenty-minute rundown, as best I could, of what was happening, or what I thought was happening, and where we were for now.

"I don't know where Sofia is," I said at the end, into the ticking silence; was that on his end or mine? I hadn't heard it when I'd been speaking to Mom. Someone listening in? "I can't get ahold of her. So I expect that Louis will probably kill me, and like... that's fair. But she was definitely alive the last time I saw her."

"I will let Mr. d'Souza know," Sherwood said smoothly. "However, speaking personally..."

"Yeah?"

"This is all simply tremendous. Actionable, accurate insider information, gathered with impressive initiative and resourcefulness. I might predict, unofficially, that you would not remain at the Monitor rank for long. I feel your skills would be better employed with other duties. Personally. Though of course, as I am unranked, I'm not permitted to make recommendations to the Steering Committee."

I stared at the wall, my face heating up. "Well, uh. Thanks, man. That's... Thanks."

"As discussed, we'll ensure that your family is monitored and protected. However, we're concerned about communications from now on. Although you may be on a secure line, that can't be verified at the moment; do not use a phone again to contact us, including the one we've supplied. We'll contact you with further instructions on where to communicate information."

"Oh, uh. Okay. How will you—"

"Thank you."

I hung up, and patted my face again to make sure it was dry of tears. It still felt hot, an embarrassed flush. Johnny would look at me and say *Chatting with Sofia, huh?* And for a moment I looked again at the phone.

Nah. Got enough problems already.

Back at the room, Johnny was sleeping more heavily, curled into a ball, fist next to her face.

I watched her, trying to remember what I was supposed to feel, or had once felt, witnessing the vulnerability of the beloved asleep. Or trying to remember what it was like to think of her as loved, rather than a swindler and a liar, and a thief and a murderer and a monster. I supposed you could love all those things. People had, in the past. What did that make them, though? If you loved a monster? History would treat you the same. Eva, Adolf. Terrible to think.

We will leave history behind, history will leave us behind. No one will be left to write it. No, that's not true. They will write it, They will torture the historians to write Their version. If that's something They do. If that's something They care about.

Could at least pull the blanket over her. She's so close to the edge. Reach over, grasp the overhang, lift, and drop. At the very least.

Mm. No. Might wake up and bite me.

I crawled under the blankets on the other bed, and despite my shuddering heart and unsteady stomach, fell asleep in minutes.

*   *   *

I woke in full daylight, a beam burning my face through an inch-wide gap in the heavy velvet curtains. After a while I went to my coat, hanging on the door hook, and unzipped one of the inner pockets, removing the tiny book that Huxley had pressed into my hand as we had left the Society agents' car. Not a sentimental woman; I remembered her calling Johnny a weasel right to her face.

Sentiment or not, she'd clearly given me something precious: a tiny book, sixty or eighty pages, bound in pinkish leather the colour of my palm. The paper was thick, crackled with age, smelling of age too—the sweet smell of paper breaking down, and a hint of mould. It was filled with numbers handwritten in fading black ink. No illustrations, no title, no author, no nothing, just numbers. But not useless, I knew. Given with intent.

I put the book back and zipped up the pocket. I noticed we had gotten another delivery, this one a small heavily-padded courier package the size of a paperback book, sitting on the small table next to the door. Reception had signed for it, an illegible scrawl. Probably a bomb or something, with our luck. I held it to my ear, hearing a faint ticking scritch that startled me nearly into the wall.

"Okay," I said, and poked Johnny with a pen. "Up you get. Up-up."

"Mmphh?"

"Someone may have given us a bomb? I mean, it's not very big, but."

"Oh. No. No no, give that here. I wanted something from one of my labs. I think I came up with a magic-proof, tamper-resistant communication system, and now is as good a time to try it out as any."

"What? You are not implanting anything in me. No. Bad."

"No, no. Also, paranoid much?"

"Yes. Stay away from me. Stay away from my squishy parts. I'll sue."

She tore open the bag and drew out a blue plastic pill case fitted with a tiny square of black glass on top, to which she pressed her thumb. Opened, five of the day compartments were empty; the last two contained something glossy, nearly mirrored: beetles, or things that looked like beetles, filling the compartment from head to toe on a bed of cotton wool.

"Wow, holy shit!" I was impressed despite myself. "Where do you put the battery? Can they fly or just walk? Are they radio control or can you—gah!"

"It's all right! He's just storing the imprint!"

"It's what!?"

"Don't hit him!"

I forced myself to stand still as one of the things, which had exited its compartment with an enthusiastic lunge and lifted off like a tiny helicopter, wandered along my collarbones, then circled my neck a dozen times, its legs digging in like needles. "...Johnny. These are real bugs, aren't they."

"Okay, look. They can fly, they can crawl on any surface, they're resistant to virtually every toxic compound I've tested, and their chitin is reinforced with nanoceramic, so they're even resistant to things like acid and crush injury."

"Cr... like someone stepping on them."

"And I've modified their metabolisms to be ultra-efficient on limited material intake. Their olfactory and memory centers are jacked up too. Augmented on a dozen levels, same with their musculature."

"Help."

"Once this one imprints on you, he'll go between us, only, and so will mine. It's like a text service only we can use. Messages go under here, there's a pocket. They'll instinctively avoid everyone except for the person they're looking for. And they'll eat the message if they're captured." She proudly lifted the other one from the pillcase, and gently levered up one of its wing cases; I couldn't see anything under it, but I supposed I would if I eventually needed to use it. "They're warded using Suhrim's Attunement. Genetically-encoded micro-sigils in a repeating, cryptic pattern."

"Get *off*." I finally scooped the beetle off my neck, and held it up, its legs windmilling. It was pretty, I supposed—a dark, glossy fuchsia, with gleams of violet and blue where the light hit it. "How come I got the pink one?"

"Because I wanted the gold one. What are you going to call him?"

"Call it? I don't know. My cellphone doesn't have a name. What's yours called?"

"Well, he used to be 6248. But now he's named Democritus."

"You can't just name a beetle Democritus. What did mine used to be?"

"1779."

"Congrats, you got a name." I put it gently on the dresser, where hers immediately leapt out to meet it. "Thanks, I think."

For a long time she watched the two beetles, squared up in a sunbeam, the pink and the gold apparently locked in a staring contest, nothing moving except, occasionally, their antennae. "They took Sparrow's name," she said, eyes unfocused, her voice dreamy, speaking to the room in general. Something seemed to gather around us, cold and heavy. "Meant to be a punishment... it's a curse, a hex. The antithesis of a ward. Like a lead bullet left in his body forever. I stopped dreaming, after the Anomaly. Every night while we were in the... the hospital..."

"Don't."

"...just darkness, every night, and I thought: Well, that's okay. Trauma, drugs. All those patches they stuck on us. But then I came back and weeks went by and... I thought: Can dreams be taken? Is it a sickness, is that too something inside me, working its way to my heart? They left me my name, they said You can still be considered at least that human, at the very least. Without speaking to me that is what I heard."

"Stop it," I said. "Knock it off. You're giving yourself the creeps. Let alone me."

"But I dreamed just now, and I..." She shook her head. "You're right. Retraumatization in an unsupervised setting."

"Is that what we're calling it?" I said, interestedly. "I thought that was just our lives."

She looked back at the beetles. "Are you still mad at me?"

"For what? Anyway, yes."

She didn't reply. I looked at the bugs too, still eyeing each other up like two boxers before a bout. A message system only we could use: of course. The old days, leaving tightly wrapped notes for one another, mine never as neat as hers. We weren't in school together; why did we need to do it all the time? And why in Braeside Ravine, where anyone could have found them? I supposed if someone found one now from those days, they could auction it off somewhere. Maybe on the internet. Like Einstein's letters, Galileo's hat...

"Did you dream how to fix this whole thing?" I said without much hope.

She nodded, surprising me. "I did, actually. It was one of those things that was terrible, but I didn't realize it right away. And in the dream I wanted to understand it, and I tried to... to turn on... well, you know. The thing. The gift. But the switch wouldn't flip. I felt relieved for a second, I thought: Then my time is mine again. It's not Theirs. Then I saw darkness, something burning... white and blue. And something moving, so I had to watch it. Everywhere it touched began to burn, in lines, in patterns, and then I realized: my God, it's a pantograph. I screamed, and it stopped moving, and then it started again. And then... I heard the newspaper, I woke up."

"What's a pantograph?"

"It's a… it's just a device. A really simple one. People have been using a version of it for thousands of years. Basically it's a frame, with tools on either end, that lets you copy something that already exists onto something new."

"Okay," I said. "That doesn't sound terrible."

"No, it doesn't. But I knew… that that was what they wanted me to see, they wanted me to see it both move and stop moving. And to realize what the light was. It was a *universe*, Nick. It was a new universe. Do you understand? The universe is a certain shape because it has to be a certain shape. But how did the shape come about, how many shapes are there? And if it's copied, who's doing the copying? Who does it every time there's a spell? I thought it was happening naturally, I thought: it's the way magic works, like gravity. You set up the conditions for there to be gravity, you can see its effects, reliably, every time. On a given world you throw a sphere up, and it comes back down. But it's not.

"There's an intelligence behind it. There always has been. That's what separates magic and science. And they wanted me to see that. It wasn't really a dream. It was a vision: they give those to you. And you can't give it back."

I shivered. She sounded terrified, and it was catching; I hadn't even understood everything she'd said, but she was so frightened that I was worried that we'd both stop being able to move. Whatever truth she had grasped was—at least for now, thank God—too big for me to see more than the barest edge of whatever filled her vision.

I realized she was nearly paralyzed with it, that she had broken it with enormous effort to speak.

After a minute, she got up and dragged her laptop onto the bed. I debated getting up to see what was on the screen, but she didn't seem like she cared if I saw it or not. "Magic isn't a particle, it isn't a wave, it doesn't have spin or mass or direction or velocity, and yet it's real enough to smell and even feel with human senses, it flips between dimensions, it travels in and out of time, it can take other types of particles with it, it can be created and moved and destroyed and aimed, the force it exerts can do work when guided into the correct structures and activated by the correct words, so *why* can't it be measured?"

"Is this one of those whatdoyoucallit questions?"

"Rhetorical. What if magic particles take something with them when they move? Or have something associated with them? What if... what if because it carries those things, we can see the signs of where it's been, and calculate backwards? Like in space, with gravitational lensing. Except *not* in space, and *not* gravitational lensing."

"Uh."

She wasn't listening to me, scrolling endlessly, her finger tapping against the touchpad. In a minute, I knew, she'd say something like *This isn't rocket science*.

"Does any of this," I said, "fix our specific issue here? By which I mean, the end of the world?"

"Maybe. I need some sample materials."

"Ew."

"I know, but listen. The bigger anything is, the less its properties follow quantum mechanics, the more Newtonian they are. But the smaller anything is, the fewer rules we know, and the fewer we *can* know. What if these... these magical prions are doing quantum tunneling, what if they're doing it on *purpose?* What if we can engineer something to interfere with that? Get in the way, force them into a different orbital, and therefore a different configuration of bonds. Break the prion, break the spell."

"This is terrible. This is worse than death. Stop talking."

"This isn't rocket science," she murmured. "Rocket science is Newtonian. So this is what the numbers are showing. And that's why they're fucked up. But how do you recalibrate to account for magic being in the math? How can I make one of my own to counter Theirs? The problem with causality theory is that it implies, well I mean, it's a theory, so yeah, let's say *implies*, that the properties of any system are caused by earlier events, events that went according to the laws of physics. If you know enough detail about those earlier ones, you know the current state, how it'll progress. Right?

"But this only applies to *undisturbed* systems. You can predict if as long as you don't look to see if it's actually doing what you predicted it to do. So how the hell can I interfere with the magical system they've set up? And where's the source?" She got up, rubbing her arms. "I'm gonna go shower. I feel gross."

"What are we going to when we're both clean?"

"Buy clothes. Go talk to a neurologist I used to know. Sample a monster."

"...Can I stay here?"

"No."

LEAVING THE HOTEL felt like poking my head out of a foxhole in No Man's Land. It was cold, and my coat (extensively ripped, burned, and stained) let in the wind. Very different here, I thought. Edinburgh had felt damp, nearly tropical. Like you were on vacation somewhere you might see palm trees. Here, the light breeze freezing my ribs made it feel like home.

It was brilliantly clear and sunny, and last night's snow sparkled like diamonds, untouched by footprints or road grit. We walked to what even I could tell was an unreasonably expensive shopping district, where security guards waited at barred doors, and even places selling what looked like simple jeans and t-shirts had prominent alarm stickers on the glass. Here, her face alone, busted-up as it was, got us into a few places, though it didn't work everywhere; she laughed for what I thought was the first time in days as we were turned away from even approaching a watch store, and fled cackling into the empty street.

"I bought a pocketwatch there last time," she said. "A Vacheron. As a present for Rutger. The owner took me out for dinner the next night."

"And now you're a bum."

"And now I'm a bum. Tragic."

"Have you talked to him yet? Rutger?"

"Oh, yeah. Couple times. The police let him go after seven or eight hours, he said. Funny what a few well-placed phonecalls can do."

"And like, millions of dollars."

"Well yeah. Anyway, I don't know that he's on-board with what we'll need to do, but he's got a couple of my labs in Prague on high alert."

"Oh God."

We split up inside the next place, a tall, narrow department store, and I had to put 1779 on the shelf inside the changing room, cautioning it not to move or make any noise. It was quiet in the store, which was peak-ceilinged and perfumey, like the Holt Renfrew's I remembered wandering into (and then immediately back out of) back home. I hadn't even dared stop in and buy a Coke in their cafe. Dad had liked browsing through the menswear, unfolding and rummaging through every article of clothing and announcing how cheaply it was made: the seams like this, the pockets like this, the stiffness of the collar, insisting something was polyester falsely labeled as silk. A sudden clear memory of my hand on the folded ties on a display table, like a sunburst, the smoothness of the rich fabric: for rich people, not for us, it said. For people who deserve these things. All you can do is look; indeed, you shouldn't even touch.

Eventually, I returned with two pairs of jeans, some socks and underwear, a couple of shirts, a sweater, some gloves, and one of those overengineered winter coats with a hundred pockets, charcoal-gray with lime-green zippers, as well as a backpack to stuff everything into. 1779, offended, nestled inside the pocket of another pair of new jeans, tags still dangling, which the cashier (they probably had a fancier term for them, I figured, at a place like this: Apparel Duke? Register Prince?) glared at as I loitered on the cool surface of the till, a solid block of dark-veined marble. I had wadded up my old clothes and stuffed them into a trashcan I found in the back of the changeroom.

Johnny found me half an hour later, hair ruffled into a cockatiel spike, with a similar minimalist armful of clothes. "You know," she said, pushing everything towards the cashier, "like, we showered? We brushed our teeth. We combed our hair. We put on lipgloss. And we both still absolutely look like hammered shit."

"You didn't offer me any lipgloss."

"It wouldn't have helped."

"Oh, you're just used to looking like a princess, that's all. You gotta lower your standards. The world's ending. All the non-monster people are gonna be like..." I paused; there were too many options. "Mad Max. Leather, fishnet stuff, piercing, feral kids. Well, you're already sort of one of those."

"I could start a gang maybe?" She handed over her credit card, a thick slice of apparently pure platinum, embossed and carved like an ancient plaque, with a window for her thumbprint; the cashier looked genuinely distressed when the system didn't reject the card. "I can't believe you didn't buy a fishnet shirt."

"I was worried about it slicing off my nipples."

"You're not going to use them."

"You don't know that." I refused their elegant paper bag, and knelt behind the marble to stuff everything into my new backpack and put my coat on.

"I've never understood why you want kids anyway," she said. "What are you supposed to do with a kid?"

"I don't know. What are you supposed to do with a genetically-modified dung beetle?"

"Look, we've had this discussion, they're very important ecologically, and the containment breach was an accident."

"Containment? You mean the Cool Whip tub?"

"Yes, that's what I said." She tapped her foot impatiently. "Anyway, beetles are hardy, strong, they're survivors. They're not like stinging insects. Wasps and bees and ants."

"Yeah, but they only sting because they have a hive to protect," I said. "Don't they? And beetles are like. Solitary."

"Yeah yeah."

Back outside, Johnny crammed everything, still wrapped in its crackling tissue paper, into her bag, and swung it onto her back. "I should've bought a present for Bernier, too."

"The neurologist? Wouldn't he help you without it?"

She rocked her freshly-mittened hand in the air. "It's hard to tell sometimes, it really is. Especially at a time like this, you know? He's a bright guy, obviously. He's asking himself the same questions we all are. About...

about loyalty, about keeping your mouth shut. About which side you want to be on at the end of the war. Now you think: well, They're making it so there's only one side, and you're probably right. But if we go to him, and say we're on the other side, maybe he'll just turn around and say: Nope. I don't want to antagonize Them. I don't want Them to know I helped you."

"Bullshit," I said, genuinely shocked. "He's a human. He's on the side of humans. He wouldn't want to be one of those... those things. Those peoplemonsters. Nobody would."

"Mm. Do you think so? I don't know. What do people do in wartime? Especially if they think they're just going to get... overrun, rolled over? Surrender, of course. But before that, if they think it's a foregone conclusion, then what?"

My stomach was sinking, flipping, sinking. Well, they'd do what you did, I thought. Or what you maybe didn't do, I can't tell. "Work with them. What's the word."

"Collude. Yes. Out of fear. If you could be... say, a pet, servant, livestock even. If you could be spared even in *some* small way because you had done *one* thing right... well, fear's powerful. It's the strongest thing that drives us."

No, I thought. Not all of us. Out of ego, not out of fear. We've all seen you here trumpeting your line about saving the world, but now They're here, bent not exactly on invasion and destruction but assimilation, and someone, something, came to you with the... with the intelligence, and self-control, and motivation, *and* ability to offer you a new deal. You'd feel even more special, wouldn't you? A chosen one. A what's the word. Apostle. Like that.

And right on the heels of that: and the wards that guard us being pulled. The Society is supposed to stop that, upkeep those, protect them from damage. Are they... did they decide...?

Don't think about it. Not now.

THE BUSES AND even the trams had stopped running, and it was strange to walk in the light traffic, past businesses open but empty, people scowling behind the desks, sipping coffee for something to do. Sun dazzled off snow, gilt, glass. It felt like war and it didn't feel like war, because I knew from novels that soldiers spent their time mostly walking, and waiting, and watching the skies... but soldiers had comrades, and I just had her, and maybe she had turned somehow in a way I couldn't see, and was dragging me along for who knew what reason.

I thought about what Sparrow had said, about the fines, compliance. But something did seem to be working now. Maybe just sheer, animal fear: the ground trembled constantly but unpredictably under our feet, the menacing snarl of an earthquake never quite materializing, and outside the city were constant flickers of lightning, the boom and groan of tortured molecules trying to right themselves, find the rules of this dimension. In the distance, streaky black and green tentacles dangled from high strings of mist, twisting lazily, like funnel clouds. We passed dozens of downed statues, not only fallen but melted somehow, green oxidation mingling with the fresh gleam of molten metal.

Bernier's apartment building was painted an off-putting pale blue, and was chipping and peeling all over to reveal the original and equally unpleasant yellow underneath. All the windows were cloudy, as if they were not dirty glass but plastic, obscured by a million tiny random scratches of branch and pollen and grit over the years. I expected a security door, but Johnny let us in through the front door and we simply climbed up the creaking wooden stairs, my thighs screaming.

"I thought neurologists were rich," I complained. "Who lives in a building without an elevator?"

"Well, neurologists aren't rich everywhere."

The hallway stank of burning plastic; Johnny began to cough as we opened the final door from the stairwell, the stench blowing past us with the pressure change. Johnny held up her hand to knock on the dirty white door marked 408, and hesitated at the same time I did, seeing that it was open. A crack, silence within, gray light.

"No," I said. "I know how this ends in movies."

"Me too," she whispered, "but..."

But we couldn't just stand there without knowing, either, and eventually I nudged her against the wall and pushed the door open. If anyone were hiding, I figured, they'd see the empty hallway first and have to come out and look for us.

We gave it a couple of minutes, then cautiously entered. Chaos: everything upside down, inside out. Books and food strewn around, bookshelves knocked over, the fridge door hanging open, light still on. Even the sofa had been torn apart, cushions ripped open and oozing foam from ragged cuts. TV on the floor, a hole kicked or punched in it. Every kitchen cabinet had been opened and the linoleum was thick with broken plates and bowls. We tried to shut the door and discovered that the hinges were awry, keeping it from lining up so it could close, and glanced at each other in silent alarm. It seemed important to be quiet.

I got a knife from the magnetic rack in the kitchen, Johnny rolling her eyes—*Well that's gonna look great when the police get here, isn't it*—but I thought, and she probably did too, that the police weren't coming. Ever.

The bedroom told the rest of the story. Dresser drawers spilling clothes, the tiny closet emptied out, nothing but a few wire hangers. And the bed rumpled, the pale-blue bedspread nearly black with blood. Blood hung on the wall above the headboard too, like a map. Not red and fresh, not liquid; but not dark enough, either.

I glanced at Johnny, who had frozen, staring at the wall. "Are we in a murder scene?" I whispered.

"I think so. I hope not."

"He was just a doctor. Who would…"

She held a finger to her lips. Spy movies again, I thought. Place might be bugged. Seeing who came to look for him first.

The burning smell came from a little electric fireplace in the corner of the bedroom, its door opaque with soot. Johnny held her breath and gingerly opened it with a pen. Cooled and solidified gloop inside, a few metal remnants; she fished out one of these, twisted and curled, and frowned at it.

No body. Very small blessing. After she had scraped what she wanted from the fireplace's grate, we nearly ran back down the stairs into the cold, clean air, not speaking until we were crossing the bridge nearly an hour later. My hands were warm, but felt numb; only the round bruise had any sensation, as if it were stealing it from everywhere else. An angry cramp, maybe the sensation of healing, my body rejecting the invader. I rubbed it with my other hand, unable to feel it. The entire time I had felt certain we were being followed, but had seen nothing, not even the turning trees, the eyes and twisted humming pillars that had infested the city on our way there.

"I'd take the body," I said after a while, leaning on the low stone wall that overlooked the river. "If I just killed a guy. The police might come after me, but I bet not having the body at all would slow them down."

Johnny nodded.

"So, um. We're not... going to call the police. Are we."

She shook her head.

"Yeah, didn't think so."

"It's not that someone knew we were going to go see him," she said, as we stared out at the sparkling water. "It's that someone knew *someone* was going to see him.

Maybe he isn't even involved with any of this, he doesn't know anything. But someone thought, 'Close enough.'"

"Is someone going to think 'close enough' for us?"

"If they've got any sense."

CHAPTER TEN

THE BOAT ROCKED minutely; it felt as if the river were not water at all, but a road, and we were in a parked car. No one else was on the river; from a drone's-eye view, I thought we might look as if we were adrift, even trailing a broken mooring rope behind us whitely in the dark water, Johnny and I and Dr. Chan, who was, I felt, exactly the right amount of paranoid. The city slid past us at walking pace. I had long since stopped looking down into the water.

"I don't know if They can hear us," Chan said, looking at the space between Johnny's shoulder and mine, as if there were a third person there; I reflexively looked too. It had been that kind of a day. "Maybe it's best to assume They can. Maybe it's best to assume They know everything. Everything. The water helps."

"I know, Dr. Chan," Johnny said. Since she had called

him, he had been saying almost nothing except that running water might 'help.' It's all right, she'd said, and we had met him at one of the abandoned—and locked—tourist boat launches. He'd seemed a little shocked by Johnny's lock-picking skills (and lack of apparent remorse), as well as Democritus' expert covering of the tiny security camera several minutes before we arrived. Both beetles now huddled on Johnny's lap under the flap of her wool coat, clearly not fans of the things in the river, but unwilling to leave her.

All around us the shoreline rippled as it changed, propagating from tree to tree, stone to stone. The occasional anguished scream rose through the bare branches. The world of the Matrix, I thought. The world of the conquerors, forcing itself on this one, forcing it to change.

"Sorry," he said. He seemed barely older than us, with a silver streak in his dark hair, his scarf pulled up, like Johnny's, to hide half his face. "George's death, I'm not surprised. Listen, over the last... year? People have been going missing, from that... from the So... from the people we worked with sometimes. Or killed themselves, or just... died. It's okay to die! I don't think it's bad to die. We should all... but unexpectedly. Not that we should stop expecting it."

"People in his... position, do you mean? Or people in his, uh, circumstances?"

"People who worked for that group. Accidents. Hushed up. I hear it from the cards, the stars, the cats, the families, so many. Even the newspaper, sometimes.

No one that knows tells, only those that are not supposed to know. And now this, the new attacks, my God. You know, they say the wards are being taken down? The old ones, the big ones. Wyoming and Rapa Nui. Great Zimbabwe. Greenwich."

Johnny nodded.

Dr. Chan lowered his voice, beckoning us closer; we leaned in, our heads nearly meeting under the glowing red bars of the heated roof. "What's happening? Am I next? Are you next? You shouldn't be asking questions about this, and I shouldn't be answering. We should all be at home. I should have given you this and vanished. Safer for us both."

"I know, and I'm grateful you agreed to talk to us," Johnny said. "There's things that need to be said face-to-face."

"Yes, I know. I know. I've seen it enough..." He shivered. "Maybe it'll be all right. The water. Listen, you were right about the dates. I gathered it all up. Some places, the disease disappeared about two weeks after the Incursion. And some places, they were still seeing cases. Till now, even. More and more. Hundreds of thousands, maybe millions of people. Not being reported, not being treated even. There's samples in there, inside the vials. There's photographs, there's... but it's the graphs you want. Isn't it?"

"I don't know," Johnny said. "I think so. Do you have any MRIs?"

"A few, yes. Bernier's, actually. Copies."

She chewed on her lip again. Under the flap of her

coat, the beetles moved in small random patterns. She put her hand absently over them. "Do you think there's... there's anything to my theory?"

He nodded. "When you said it, I thought: This is it, it cannot be avoided now. If I had not worked for the... this group, you know, I would have thought perhaps the Anomaly had permitted some extraterrestrial material into the atmosphere, and that caused the syndrome. Either way, I think it fits the data we have. But you must look at it. See what you think."

"What can we do about it?"

"Truly, Joanna, I am very sorry. I don't know. Your idea of a counter-prion... numerically, in terms of transmissivity, in terms of infectivity, reach, spread, I don't know how it would work. I mean to say, I don't know how *this* works either. And that is why I say I don't know."

She slumped, but only a little. We had both been expecting it, I thought. She just wanted to hear it from someone not herself.

Chan went on, softly, "You know, we are taught... everything in nature has its predator. We don't say *enemy*, we say *predator*. Sometimes that's not true, it's just... a parasite, say. Or an unlucky mutation. It's meant to soften the blow a little when we lose a patient. We say: predator. Even if we mean cancer, heart attack. If these things have a predator I know you will find one. I am sure of it. Or make one. Even the dark gods of the sea fear the gods of the inner earth, even the Ancient Ones once feared the Elder Gods."

"Why can't they help us now?" I said. "These... these Elder Gods, I mean."

"They're all dead," Johnny said dully. "Or as close as you can get to dead. And even their bodies were sent out of reach. The last invasion. They were betrayed, it's said. Double-crossed. Right there in the... in the Fertile Crescent. Right where we stood in Nineveh."

"Jesus fucking Christ."

"It has happened so many times," Chan said, pounding a fist suddenly into his thigh; his face contorted. "When the Ancient Ones come, They play, use us as... resort, playground, nasty place where sick kids torture animals. Take what They want and laugh and gamble and destroy till They're kicked out. They don't make... *colonies*. Look at the history of the world. The British Empire, the French, the Spanish. Look what happened here, even, in Prague—I mean, in Europe in general. Why don't some people just stay where they are? Why do they overrun and conquer and exploit, and declare a place property, and the people in them property, instead of just staying at home?"

Johnny stared at him. Just behind her, something slapped against the metal hull, making the entire structure ring. I resisted looking, with an effort.

"Nothing you can justify, I'm not trying to. I'm just saying: why? We have to think of *why*. More than one reason. Not every country became an empire, and not every country wished to. Why?"

I glanced bleakly out at the river. He had said what I had been thinking, or trying to think, unable to summon the words for it. But yes: the riverbank, rippling, changing as we watched. Look at it. I had seen photos in my parents' photo albums of the cities back in Guyana, invaded and colonized by country after country that had not intended to come there, plunder, burn, kill, and leave, but to keep doing it while they *stayed*. They didn't move in and build structures that looked like what was already there. They wanted it to look like where they had come from. All those buildings in Georgetown that you would swear came straight out of some English town. You sail to a new place, and you make it look like the old place. Because you haven't come to the new land for it to be a new land. You want more of what you already have. And They finally figured out how to do it.

Johnny said, "I keep thinking of Them as locusts. Just swarming whenever conditions are right. Because it's less scary than thinking that They've been... scheming. Waiting. Planning."

"But They are. Aren't They? We thought They were not. But, we thought a lot of things in the Cold War too. If you were going to make a war, you would find our existing wounds, press down, rip them open. I am sorry. Not what I meant to say.

"You would find the... crack in the wall, and put in a crowbar, and lean on it. Yes? But supposing you know where is the crack on your side, but you've got people who will... Inside Beziers, say, inside Constantinople, who say: Spare me. I will show you more cracks. And here is the aqueduct, whose water you can take for your army. And here is where you can dig underneath our foundations. And..."

No, I almost said. No. No.

But I was thinking it. I've been thinking it for days. She's been thinking it too.

"Everything has a price," Chan said. "Everything, everything, everything. Why do you think people say that so often? The old practice of indulgences, dispensations. Making bastards legitimate or buying the right to trade with an infidel. Marry your cousin. Purchase stolen goods. All legal if you pay up! Even if you were Jewish, a convert, and wished to visit your Christian parents."

"What does that mean to people who won't pay the price?" Johnny said. "Or can't?"

He shrugged. "Siena, Florence. The old days. Some bankers offered loans with so many strings attached you could face eternal damnation if you defaulted."

"Harsh," Johnny said.

"All is lost," Chan said. "If They want war now, then They want no resistance in the future. Humiliation but also pacification: that would be the goal. The Anomaly would be the absolutely *last* time humans could be allowed to fight back. Anyone who can do magic should make out a good will, and have it witnessed. Things that were hidden are moving now. Who else have you spoken to?"

Johnny pressed her lips together. "No one." In fact we had spent days tracking people down, being told *no* again and again. *No*, but not for lack of trying.

"You should go, Joanna, you should go home, and be with your family. Forget this… this cure. Nothing can be done against such foes. Maybe in the early days, but not now."

"It's not too late," she said stubbornly. "I'll figure something out."

"And I know. If anyone can, it would be you. But..."

Another ringing slap. At last I looked over at the river, reluctantly, where the long rays of late afternoon cut into the slow clear water, highlighting swans as if they burned from within, and lighting also the thick writhing glassy forms inches below the surface, eyes staring unseeing at the sky, limbs undulating, reaching for us, drawing back, lifting into the air for moments, sizzling and trembling, then falling back, all around us, below us, a nest of the things, staring eyes and teeth and open mouths. I had argued against this, raising my voice a little too much: what the hell kind of protection, I had said, is a *boat*? You're asking us to practically rub our faces into these things. Stick our hand into the wasp nest.

"Let's go back," Chan said, voice trembling. "There's nothing we can do."

The swans screamed and flapped, one briefly getting jerked under, biting and thrashing, bobbing back to the surface. They ran along the water past us, took to the air, so close to the boat that I caught the water-and-weed odour of their feathers as they passed.

Small red lights appeared on the riverbank on either side of us: drones, I thought at first glance, but no—stags, boars, blue-black as magpies, their antlers and tusks burning white-hot, moving delicately on invisible roads past churches and houses, apartments and castles, the crosses and statues behind them wobbling in the flame of the heat.

I moved between them back to the boat's controls, which seemed simple enough, though vibrating in the multicoloured glow of adrenaline. Something bumped the boat heavily, sending it crosswise in the current. I sat in the padded leather chair and hit the button for the electric motor, flinching as it started up, the loudest sound we'd heard in hours, like gunfire. Pedals? No pedals. A chrome lever, at the bottom of its slot. God fucking *dammit*, we had spent all this time eluding the things, and now we walked right into their place, with nothing between us but a few inches of water.

"You don't even have a license for this thing," Johnny said, her chuckle a little hysterical.

"Well *you* don't have a license for anything, so shut it."

I inched up the lever, one hand on the faux-wood steering wheel, and we began to whir downstream, the burning animals following our progress, hooves dancing through and over rooftops, domes, the tumbled stones of ancient walls. Surreptitiously I held up my left hand, so they could see the mark of the watcher, in case it helped, but they simply paused a moment, letting us get perhaps ten or fifteen feet down the water, and then continued to pace us, darting forward, back. Where their hooves touched the river it began to boil on contact. Crows soared in a panic from the trees, spattering the river with fresh green leaves.

A jolt sent me crashing into the dashboard, Johnny and Chan sprawling to the floor. Had we hit something? No: something behind us, Johnny whispering and pointing, something clawed that had seized our trailing mooring rope. It oozed up out of the river like a liquid made solid, even staining the water around it with an oily slick, studded with translucent lumps. The stench of magic hung heavy around us, sour and overwhelming. The rope was wrapped around the toothed tentacle, snagged on its edges. Something beneath it, huge, domed: a head, watching us, the dozens of eyes darting back and forth.

I felt my pupils dilate in terror and couldn't help but think: Reading. Not seeing us, really. Checking to see if we're something it's been told to want. Can't want anything unless you're instructed to want it.

Remember: us. They're after *us*, as well as everybody else. But someone, somewhere, said: Get them alive.

I turned back to the dash, tasting blood in my mouth where I'd cut the inside of my lip, and shoved the lever, the rope drawing up its slack and going taut. A moment's freedom, the boat surging forward fast enough that I had to hang onto the wheel to stay upright, and the sunset becoming golden, brazen, and then another jolt as it seized the rope again.

"Somebody cut that! For fuck sake!"

Johnny nudged Chan aside, began to scrabble through the compartments marked *EMERGENCY* and *FIRST AID*, and after a second Chan joined her, but a shadow burgeoned under us, black in the water, and the creatures were still coming on the riverbank, their mouths dripping with flame like napalm, and very calmly, because sure, yes, absolutely, why not, I brought the boat around in a wide circle at the end of its tether, thinking of compasses, astrolabes, the way you pivot around the known to see where you are in the unknown, Johnny crying out, but if you can't run you gotta turn and fight, sending the boat straight back *towards* the thing in the river, too slow to avoid us.

"Grab something, if you can," a strange voice said, maybe mine, and keeping my eyes resolutely open, meeting the eyes of the creature as it breached, water and ooze sliding off its sides, closer, closer, till I could see the white-yellow galaxies that flared under the slimy surface of the membranes, see the skin around it flinch, brace for impact, we hit it, full-speed, not very fast (I thought) but hard enough that the skin ruptured and sprayed gouts of its acid-stinking blood into the air, spattering the boat and the windshield, a crash and confusion, a moment's loss of gravity as we tilted, then righted.

Tentacles sprang from the water, so thick and dark that for a second I almost thought we had somehow unearthed a submerged tree. They splattered around us on all sides, the creature not dead, bleeding, screaming, the boat tilting again. Metal screeched too near my ear: Jesus, they were tipped not even with claws but something like *knives,* silvery and serrated.

Those people at the party. Stabbed in the back. Hanging, puppets. Chan screamed as one of the flailing limbs sank into his shoulder, Johnny quickly yanking it out. The plastic box of files banged against one of the compartments, wobbled for a moment, and fetched up against the railing. I watched Johnny's eyes go wide and golden as coins. For a second she hung poised between the files and her grip on Chan's shoulder.

But it was only a second. I slammed on the throttle again, hitting the monster in the same place, sending the box toppling into the nest of tentacles to sink without a trace.

Johnny had the good grace at least to not speak as we raced back up the river.

THE MOTOR ROARING, chugging, choking as it encountered patches of blood or ooze, passing first one pier, then another, or were they docks, then a third, and twenty minutes later Johnny finally tugged on my sleeve and pointed. We slowed down enough to run into it not very hard, so that she and Chan could quickly pull each other out and run up the steps, and I cut the engine and followed them, already wobbling on dry land. Lost my land-legs.

The front of the little boat was splattered with a thick indigo substance, streaked with white and yellow like pus, and the sides bore a hundred thin but deep scratches, revealing the steel beneath the paint. We stared at it for a long time, our panting breath loud in the sudden silence of the killed engine. Only the river made a sound now: low, wet, gloating, as if trying to tell us a dirty joke. Good one, I thought. Yes. Stole our stuff.

"Let us go," Chan said, tugging on Johnny's bag; he was wincing, but not bleeding any more, it seemed. A dark patch had spread on his coat and stopped. "Quick. Find a church."

"Sacred ground?" I said, interested.

"Well. They have public washrooms."

I looked down at my new coat, then over at him and Johnny. "Oh. Good call."

CHAN LEFT US at the church, which I thought was pretty reasonable. I wondered if he would do what he said: finalize his will, pack a bag, flee. Not that you would necessarily get somewhere that They wouldn't find you; but that, as he quietly reminded us, 'Ssarati' meant 'watcher' or 'witness,' and there was a reason they had named themselves such. There was power in those who watched together. And if they fixed their gaze upon you, you could not escape by fighting or fleeing or playing dead. "You don't have long," he'd said quietly. "Whatever you do. And don't tell me what that is. They will only make me tell them. Good luck."

Cabs weren't supposed to be running, but Johnny got us one from the church phone booth anyway, a long whispered negotiation in, I thought, a couple of languages; if we had been doing it in person, wads of cash would have changed hands. A few people stared at us as we left; I waited for them to cross themselves, maybe spit on the ground, make some reference to Satan (who would that be, I wondered, out of the two of us), but no one did.

It was a wonder, she agreed, that the driver had agreed to pick us up at all. The cabby's eyes, a bright reddish brown, like the roof tiles, flicked up constantly to meet mine in the rearview mirror, like coins being flipped, head, tails, head, tails.

"I fell in the river," Johnny said, perkily.

He made a face of extraordinary disgust, and sucked his nicotine-stained teeth in distress. "Fell!" He shook his head. "Go to hospital."

"I'm fine. Take us where we agreed. "

"Achhh." He glanced at me in the mirror again, up then down, seeing our bags sitting between us, the canvas on Johnny's moving slightly as both beetles bumbled around under it.

"Some river you got there," I said, maybe too fast for him to catch; he grumbled again, under his breath, and kept driving.

"Where you going, you going to work? Good. The city, you know, these... office people. Pencil-eaters, they shit paper," the driver muttered. "They don't have real jobs, they tell everybody with a real job, *Oh, stay home! Is monsters!*" he said, in a simpering falsetto. "Haven't seen anything. Just the... what do you call. Police bees."

"Drones."

"They got lights on them now," he grumbled. "Like headlamp. Shine right into your bedroom at night, make a man go crazy. You go crazy if you can't sleep. Fact, scientific fact." He scratched his moustache, and glanced up at me in the mirror again. "Where you from? Americans?"

Johnny answered him in, I assumed, Czech, and he burst into laughter. They chatted amiably as we left the city limits, moving into the stillness and green of the countryside, heavily marked here and there with fresh craters, perfectly round, or strange clipped cut-outs in hills or forests, the angles so sharp they seemed to shimmer above the cuts, as if some molecules still remained, stunned and bisected.

Anything you touch, you change, I thought. How can we beat that?

When we finally slowed, after twenty bumpy minutes on a gravel road, I got out and stretched, enjoying the clean, damp air, away from the smell of stale smoke ground into the upholstered seats, while Johnny paid. The driver beckoned me closer, rolling down his window. "Hey," he said quietly, his jaw jutting as he put a forearm on the door. "Hey. Fuckin' *don't hit girls*. Okay? I know you know this. And, specially, not the face. Don't hit girls in the face. Okay? Am I clear to you?"

I stared at him, horrified. "I—"

"Okay good. Nice talk."

He pulled carefully out of the gravel circle and in moments was gone, leaving me staring after him and clutching my gut as if I'd been shot. Johnny, who had wandered off to cough, came back, wiping her mouth gingerly on her scarf. "You okay?"

"When we get back to town," I said, "we are buying you some concealer."

"How do you know about concealer?"

"What? It's not a state secret or whatever. It's not like a... girl conspiracy." I gazed suspiciously around us, the scraggly forest beginning to green up, fill in, hotly vivid in the spring sunshine. "These don't look too bad. Did you get stabbed back there?"

"No, I don't think so. It's a…" She stopped herself before saying *shame about the files*, and shrugged. "We'll do what we can."

"I got these little… hang on." She unzipped her bag, and 1779 roared out and bonked into my shoulder, scrabbling on the fabric for a moment till it got a grip, then climbing up to my collar and sliding down the far side. Johnny, ignoring my muffled yelling, got out two small round discs and clipped one, in a businesslike fashion, to the zipper pull on my coat, then the other to the edge of her own lapel. "Ta-da."

We moved down the gravel trail leading away from the road turnout; already the sun was just a sliver on the horizon, a hot crimson glow beneath a long ribbon of clouds. I shivered. Was that a flock of birds in the distance, or something else? Could you trust anything now? Clouds? Light? Feathers?

"What kind of facility is this, anyway?" I said. "What, there's no road?"

"There is on the other side, for deliveries. But I didn't really want him to know where we were going."

"Notice how you didn't answer the first question."

"It's a lab."

"Uh huh."

In the last of the twilight, the security shack emerged with surprising suddenness, just ahead of a tall chicken wire fence. Light, pebbly stone, nearly white, strangely-shaped, like the sugar packet houses Johnny would always build at restaurants while we waited for our food. The round window in its center looked unpleasantly like an eye. All pupil, like the dark eye of an animal.

She hesitated some feet away, and I stopped next to her. Inside the shack, a light came on. "Can you smell that?" she whispered.

I was trying not to. The smell of magic, what I had come to think of as magic being *burned* or *consumed:* sinister, rotten. The security shack flickered, its logo disappearing for a moment, returning, the roof creaking and flexing (or was it?), like wings. The wings of an insect, not bird or bat. Familiar. And behind that somewhere in the darkness, I thought, the safety of her lab, a big, no doubt fortified, building full of people.

The white shack crept towards us over the thick turf, snapping thin saplings as it went, meandering and sending up a thick sweet smell of sap and earth that almost, but not quite, overwhelmed the stink of magic. Not a building at all. Something living, a monster disguised as something we would trust.

"Is... is that you? Chambers? Is that you?"

Johnny jumped. The door of the shack swung open, the light inside it going out, flickering up into the sky like fireflies, but segmented, hissing. The stars were coming out, blue and green, scratching across the sky leaving needle-thin contrails behind them.

"It is you, isn't it?" The voice was anxious, hoarse.

I knew I was going to regret it, but lifted the light clipped to my jacket and shone it up into the man's face.

A white face. Not pale, actually white. Tearful blue

eyes, the pupils huge, unmoving as the light passed over them. Army-green shirt, no coat. Soaked with blood. The throat torn open, something squirming within it, a hot blue glow just visible as he moved.

"Bernier?" Johnny stepped back, and lifted her own light. "Oh, God..."

"I'm sorry." The dead man stumbled, caught himself awkwardly, moaned. "Did you feel it? Can you feel it moving?"

"Feel what?" Her voice was faint; for all her flippancy, I didn't think she'd ever talked to someone dead before. The thralls we had seen two years ago barely counted; they had not even been able to speak.

"All that is coming," Bernier said. "The new world. I saw it for a moment only."

"Who did this to you?" she said urgently. I pulled at her coat; she resisted with surprising strength. "Bernier. George! Please, we went to your apartment, we saw... who did it? You let them in."

"Yes." The reply was distant, bubbly, wet. "Of course I did. My old friend..."

"Who?"

"Johnny," I barked. "Move. Back to the road."

"I am sorry," he said again, and Johnny said "For *what*?"

And something closed around my throat from behind.

CHAPTER ELEVEN

THE PROBLEM WITH geniuses was that they were too easy to outwit.

Or, well. Maybe I was being ungenerous. The problem with geniuses was that if you couldn't outsmart them, you could just let them come to the obvious conclusions you needed them to come to, by feeding them a lot of information that wouldn't set off their bullshit detector till it was too late.

Our captors had pulled us backwards through the darkness, and we had fallen, clutched, struggling, into this dimly-lit, stinking place. It had been a long time before I had even been clear on who had grabbed us: Monster? Human? Both? Neither?

These ones looked, I thought, like the Edgar-suits from *Men in Black*. Awkward, alternately floppy and stiff, troubled by internal skeletons. Less overtly *monster*. But they were strong, and whatever they had tied our hands with was even stronger, like snakes but segmented, and with a face at both ends, grinning with small, sharp teeth as the knots had been tied.

Pushed into the back of a room, sitting uncomfortably on the uneven floor, Johnny and I had stared between the forest of their legs as other people passed, all bound, dragged, or stumbling. Their silhouettes looked human, or human-ish, against the headachey blue light seeping from the walls. It was infuriating to not be able to tell the difference any more, and for a long time I found myself panicking that I too had changed into a monster, been changed, infected, and hadn't figured it out yet, still saw myself as human because of some terrible illusion or infection of Theirs.

Occasionally someone, or something, would come in, roughly shoving our guards aside, and stare at us for a moment; these visitors always laughed, low and unmistakeable.

Very funny. Yes. Caught the world's greatest genius. Ha ha. In the part of my mind that wasn't screaming with fear I found myself baffled that it hadn't happened before—almost a relief to have it happen now, when I had expected it for so long. Rutger's careful maneuvering had long since ceased to keep her as invisible as she would have liked; and there was more surveillance, more paparazzi, just more *eyes* on her since the Anomaly. And not all of those eyes were human. She couldn't just flit around with impunity any more. People knew she didn't have much security on her, usually; I had expected her to be kidnapped for ransom a thousand times, growing up. That she hadn't had been a mystery to me till I realized just how rarely she was alone when we were apart: always surrounded by people, at talks or lectures, at her labs and facilities, in airports, at train stations, at banquets and ceremonies and demonstrations. Only in her house might someone hope to grab her, but as that was so obvious, her house was more tooled-up than the Batcave.

Anyway. This wasn't that; this was magic and mayhem; this was a prize, somebody's prize, and she would not be released for mere *money*. And me along as dead weight. For a few minutes, her breath had been so fast that I had worried she was about to pass out; and if she did, I knew she'd be dragged. They didn't care, particularly, whether we arrived where we were arriving in good shape. Just one piece: alive. Alive enough to do whatever they were doing next. I debated telling her, *Well, I'm finally convinced that you're not in cahoots with them, if I'm using that word right*, but kept my mouth shut.

She whispered, "We should have made some kind of…"

"Agreement."

"Agreement. Yeah. Pact. Like in zombie movies."

Should have. Didn't. I said, "The pact wouldn't have worked."

"I know. But I wish we had made one."

The guards parted again, one shoved so hard that it fell and lay moaning for a moment; the others disregarded it. Another visitor, a human: Johnny and I looked up reflexively, but, as always, in silhouette, nothing could be seen.

"Yes," the visitor said slowly, drawing it out: *Essssssss.* "I know them. I will confirm for the Manifestation. You will receive your recompense from him." A wet giggle, deep and rumbling; it seemed to turn, and address something standing behind it, not human, not even humanoid: a lump giving off its own sinister light, things moving slightly above its surface on stalks like the eyes of a snail. The thing spoke too, a series of hissing clicks, and the visitor said, "I agree. No need."

It left, and two guards swooped in, moving more quickly than I had seen them move before; in a moment, Johnny was yanked up, crying out as they wrenched at her bound arms, and away from my side. I bit down a shout of my own. Wouldn't do any good. Something warm against my arm: her bag, left behind. Might be the last I had of her.

Think. Calm down. They said *No need.* No need for what? To keep us together? But then why kidnap us together?

Or no need to keep me; they only wanted her, and had taken me because I was there and likely to interfere. She was being given to someone, I knew that much. The... the Manifestation. Whoever that was.

But hang on. Hang on. They knew she could do magic. But me? Hard to say. Perhaps to them I was no concern, as magically inert as a bag of rice... I moved my hands experimentally, and winced as teeth sank into the base of my thumb. Okay, okay. Asshole.

Blanked with panic, it took a long time to remember the spell for the watcher. Had it really been just a couple of days ago? Nothing else in my pathetic arsenal would have helped, and this probably wouldn't either, but as a distraction maybe it would be enough. And if not, maybe it would goad them into beating me to death instead of sacrificing me. Hadn't she said a sacrifice could reroute the flow of magic? Dark days, when *that* was the best outcome.

Get out of this. Get out of this and go home.

Forget the job. Forget the prodigy. Message from the gods: don't want it, can't give it back. Let the gods deal with it. One of their own.

Stop it. Do one thing at a time. Even a stupid plan is better than no plan.

And go get her. She's the only weapon Earth has. They know that. And you know that's why They took her: it's like stealing a nuke for your own side. Even if you never use it, it means the other side can't.

Get her back for that reason and that reason alone.

I twisted my wrists and let one of the heads bite down again, grunting with pain. But its mouth was full, and I kept wriggling till I felt the other head lift, then, with a great sense of satisfaction, flicked it suddenly under my rear and sat down, hard, making sure my overstuffed wallet landed on it. There was a small crunch, felt rather than heard, and the knots tightened agonizingly for a second, then slackened, perhaps with surprise. I quickly pulled one wrist loose, feeling it chew angrily on the other hand, then grabbed it and pulled its mouth free. Ass. *Hole.*

The bites hurt beyond belief, but I didn't think they were deep, and I could still use all my fingers; still, I felt a little light-headed as I replaced my hands behind my back and glanced back at my guards again in the darkness. Bit by a non-zero number of toddlers back in the day. Had to get tetanus shots. This was nothing. Were they staring at me? Had they seen the whole thing? No one moved. Who uses living handcuffs anyway? Sickos.

Stay cool. Gotten out of worse than this before.

No I haven't. No I have *not*. When was *that*?

I massaged my bitten hand, collecting a small slow palmful of blood. No one moving? No one coming to kick me? I couldn't even tell which way the guards were facing. But they hadn't moved yet.

Carefully I brought both hands to my front, and dipped a finger into my makeshift paint. As I drew, the wound in my left hand, which had dulled to a cold, sullen throb, flared back into wakefulness, so painful that for a moment I couldn't even remember the rest of the sigil. Memory whited out.

Stop. Wait. Finish. Just finish.

I whispered the words of power, and held my breath again, not moving, as the small circle began to glow. Darkness, you were supposed to fear darkness, and welcome light, but darkness also concealed, and—in the form of the blobs now rising from the little sigil—it knew things that it could not tell those of us more used to moving through the light.

Don't move. It'll come after you. Hand growing cold, but not pain, mere sensation: like curiosity. A communication maybe. *I can't talk to you! Be quiet!*

Silence, and then a thickly gratifying rumble of pain. Something glittering and rapid as a wasp buzzed furiously around the guard's slack face, just visible in the low light. The other guard edged away from the corridor wall, finally realizing something was happening.

The first guard's face had begun to bubble as if he had been burned with boiling water, and his sounds became a whine of confused agony as he batted at the watcher, which even I couldn't see, only the minimal corona of its defensive spikes. For a moment I could only watch, not knowing where the other watchers had gone, in their newborn fear and anger. Remembered the terrible invisible explosion of pain when I had touched the one that had hurt my hand.

But they had left an opening, and I threw Johnny's bag over my head and ducked low through the confusion of their legs, running down the corridor at a fast, cramped limp—lotta stairs over the last couple days. And more than that, I noticed how bad the flooring was, cracked and uneven, like busted tiles. Shouts of pursuit behind me: nothing new. Bright aura of panic around everything I could see, bringing its own light.

It was like a nightmare, the ones you never outgrow, where you are pursued by something snarling and slavering and absolutely unknown, where you run with hopeless steps, because you are in a place they know and you don't.

How had we come in? Left, right, right, left. A labyrinth, tripping and falling, scraping knees and hands.

The shouts falling behind. They like mazes, don't They? They like puzzles, traps. We thought They were animals. They thought *we* were animals. If They thought of us at all... you could make rats run in a maze. But you couldn't teach them they were going to die.

Maze, labyrinth. Like the tangle of the ordinary proteins Johnny had showed me. All about the shape. Not about what it is, but what it's shaped like. Bad configuration.

I stopped at last to catch my breath, panting hard into my elbow to muffle the noise. Stealth would be no good here; as my eyes had adjusted, I could see there was no true darkness from the lit walls, only corners where the tiles met and folded, shadowing the light a little. And yet...

No, not tiles. Scales. Thick, chitinous-looking scales of dozens of long, serpentine bodies lying motionless around me. Under my boots they repeated and repeated, like flattened insects, each the size of my palm. Walking on them, surrounded by them, even the ceiling. A place made of monsters. What had it been before, I wondered. Or was this somewhere else again? Another remnant, a pocket, like Huxley's archive?

Seen this before. What movie. Not the first one. Second. *Aliens*. The whole hallway looks like it's made of their stuff... exudate or whatever. Hardened saliva. But it's not. The wall comes alive. The walls come alive. Breathe, breathe. That smell: the snake house in the zoo. Animals. Real. And the opening, the measurements, just large enough to admit one. A worm sliding along a tunnel made of its own kind.

The guards would not get lost in this maze. And how

the hell would I find where they had taken Johnny? A noise ahead echoing down to me, like the repeating crash of the sea. I thought of the monster-inhabited ocean we'd seen in that other world, and shivered. That terrible, gargantuan back breaking through the hideous water. But it wasn't quite like waves. Almost like... well no, not a crowd, because it wasn't voices. Just noises.

A spectacle, an attraction. Maybe for something new they had acquired.

Something small and new. With green eyes.

At any rate, it was something to follow. I clung to the walls, the sides of the sluggish creatures, turning my head from side to side, listening over the roar of my heart. Sometimes footsteps passed, near me but unseen, forcing me to stop, freeze in place, stare around myself: here? Now? No. Prisoners were here though, sometimes pleading and sobbing in a handful of languages, sometimes silent, sticky bundles bumping softly along the floor. The guards occasionally replied, and it struck me after a half-dozen of these paralyzed sessions that I could understand them. *Me*, who only spoke English, and a little French, from school. How? Why?

Johnny would know.

Stop it. She doesn't know everything.

That thing in my hand... a poison cyst, an egg. Something else. But remember that magic is Theirs, and everything that is magic is...

Stop it.

I shouldn't have touched it. I shouldn't have touched it. The pain was one thing. This... this is another.

A huge space opened out without warning, and here the last trace of normality, if you could call it that, vanished: the sharply-angled ceiling was creature too, paved with scales, and these were moving a little, shifting against each other, producing a soft sinister neverending hiss in the darkness as they blocked one another's light. It was a cathedral made of bodies, all the pews, all the columns, the impossible pipe organ at the back, a thousand throats of pallid, mushroomy flesh all silent, ending in closed eyes, open jaws. It was cold here, a deep and sickly wet cold, like the depths of winter. They had built this place of themselves, and the warmth they needed was within them; there was no need to heat what passed for air here.

I began to shiver, or my body did, all over; my knees felt ready to buckle. There were so many of them. And there were two of us. And this was where They had wanted to take us, this place of monsters... not monsters. No. Wait. Dragons. *Dragons*. Like the one that had sought us out in Huxley's remnant, supposedly proof against such things...

I hardly wanted to breathe; it felt too loud, too obtrusive. Each dragon was a different size and slightly different in appearance, some hundreds or maybe thousands of feet long, if it were the same one; some barely bigger than a zoo anaconda. Many had wings folded flat against their spiked backs, just visible, more like a flame than a structure.

Dad telling stories when we were kids. The kamoodies back home, eating chickens, goats, people's kids. British disbelieving it: They don't eat humans! We never saw it happen! *Old sport,* I'd append in my head. Patronizing. If it doesn't happen to white people, it doesn't really happen. Does it.

In the center of the mass was an opening, containing a circular black pool, a round white pedestal in its center, dished, oddly familiar. Why?

A bone, a backbone. Saw it in the museum when we were kids: a whale vertebra. A flanged cup. The pedestal their own self, from the spine of a dead worm.

Once you knew Them, once you'd seen the things They had forced people to build in the cities They had occupied here on Earth, you knew a sacrificial altar when you saw one. It might have been as big as a stadium, but it was still an altar, and still meant to catch blood.

Breathe, breathe. The stink of oils and pheromones and solvent-laden breath. Their killing ground, generating torrents of magic, human victims brought in by those turned, or by the Society, or both. Like a massive influx of... of cash into a local economy. More magic than They had had for thousands of years, more than enough magic to keep spreading the spores of our destruction, of their remaking, restructuring, turning our world into something They liked. Flying through here, maybe the pool its doorway, flying...

The beetles! My *God.*

I fished out 1779 from my pocket, and held it on my palm. Nothing to write with: note to self, start carrying a Sharpie around. Just in case. Fine-tip. Would it still find her? I urged it gently into the air and my heart sank as it simply circled me for a moment, as the watcher had done. Then it darted abruptly ahead, returning to scrabble at my coat, make sure I was following.

Stay calm, stay calm. There'll be guards.

They split us up because. They split us up... but they must have made sure she saw the altar and the sacrifices. Showing it off: like a parade. You don't have a parade and assume no one will come and watch. Or like parading through the cities of a conquered city. Textbook photo, black and white: Nazis in the streets of Paris. Boasting. Before you executed your enemy general, you made sure they knew just how many divisions were moving through the city of lights, just how defeated they really were...

Focus, stop it. Get out of here.

Or get her out of here. If you can only get one.

No, fucking stop it.

A sudden sense of motion arrested, of things that were not dragons. I froze, and moved carefully behind a bulge in the wall, reluctantly keeping my balance by holding the edge of one wrist-thick scale. The walls were definitely moving now, and the floor, very slowly, squeezing and bunching. Nowhere to go, I supposed. Like a nest of real snakes, shifting to try to get comfortable, but nothing around you to lie on except another snake... there.

A handful of dark forms—more guards—and something gleaming on the floor: Johnny's face, her bared teeth, in the dim light. And someone or something tall, thin, leaning over her. Not merely thin, skeletal; the walls showing through the ribs. A skull twisted as a horn, something dripping from what should have been hands but were a mere mass of threads. I held my breath again. Move. Go. Move. Leave her. Get away from her, you fucker.

"Imagine," the thing said, a thick clattering voice, like stones. "And you are the ones who came up with the saying we most love: *Power corrupts.* Before he was the Manifestation, you know he called himself the Corruption? That was ever and always your weakness. That you, that so many creatures like you, think corruption is real... speak. Speak to me, Zath curse you, Ulgellath rot you! I will break your bones and leave you for the Beast of Ogmoko to feast upon! Speak!"

Silence. She's a contrarian, I wanted to tell the thing, wearily. The only way to get her to shut up is to ask her to say something.

"It matters not. It is not me you need to satisfy, little creature, little half-a-god. You are in a place between places now... What a pleasure it will be to give you to the one at last. He has hungered for you from the far side of the veil since the moment of his return."

Silence.

"Once we wished to devour your world. Now, thanks to the Manifestation, there will be no need. And no resistance, and no return. Your world is riddled through with ours. Soon enough we will be one, and then there will be nothing to fight, and nothing to fight for, and we will all revel, we will make ceremony, we will wipe clean all your traces... Curse you, rot you! *Speak!*"

What was there, how could I draw their attention?

And even if I did, could Johnny get us out? I didn't think I could manage another watcher. I chewed on my lip, thinking, and at last unzipped her bag, moving slowly. Her phone barely had a charge but still worked, the screen blinding me for a moment. I held a hand over it as I hunted for something, anything that might help. There: music player. Unmute. Breathe.

Bad idea.

Yeah.

The opening strains of 'Rapper's Delight' echoed around the maze of dragons, and as the thing leaning over Johnny straightened, startled, I wound up and threw the phone as hard as I could past it, the screen whirling into the darkness, a hell of a throw, just like I had taught the kids, right from the hip. In a split second the creature, and a half-dozen others, were racing after it, jaws snapping, and I had rushed in and hauled Johnny to her feet. The music cut off with a *crunch*.

"What the absolute—?"

"No idea, none. How do we get out of here?"

"This way!"

"But that's back towards the—"

She didn't reply; we sprinted through the maze, stuff flying out of her bag till I zipped it up again, and eventually ran back to the cathedral-like space where the backbone lay in its pool. The heads of the dragons were moving now, slowly, lazily, eyes opening.

"You are fucking *crazy!*" I whispered, grabbing her coat to stop her as she reached the edge of the cliff, the bodies writhing under our feet, so that it was hard to stay upright. "This is the *worst* fucking place we could have gone!"

"It's the only place that goes between!"

"What?"

"Trust me!"

"Oh my God, we're going to die."

"Good. Excellent. *Good*." She pawed at her bag and got out the deck of cards, digging feverishly through them. But the guards were coming back, their heavy footsteps just perceptible, transmitted through the tiled skin of the dragons under our feet. "One way out for us, another for them. Because we're alive and... look, forget it. Quick!"

And she pulled us over the edge of the cliff, aiming for the pool of black water.

GOLDEN LIGHT SURROUNDED us, erasing my vision but doing nothing for the impact, which was like hitting concrete: we had broken bones, I was sure of it, ruptured organs, the liquid wasn't water at all, but something else. Screams erupted around us, of surprise and horror—and laughter, which was worse, far worse.

Johnny's face rising through it, brightly panicked. Everything began to flicker and between the flickers rose a terrifying sound: the endless mechanical clack of scales, speeding up, till it became a steady rat-a-tat like gunfire. I reached for her as she sank below the surface, one hand desperately waving the card with the sigil. The light faded, returned, as if the spell had rallied, or got a second wind, and I realized at once that it was doing what spells did best: compensating. Flowing to the places it had been guided into, using whatever was around. Magic and spirit and shape, geometry and breath, the intent of it, she'd said, the *intent* of magic particles. And if there wasn't enough magic around, it would choose to draw from something else...

She descended, becoming translucent for a moment, and this time I felt something yank on us, hard, stopping-starting, stuttering, then catching, a terrible sense of *emptying*, even the light fading, and then a sudden shock of pressure, slapping the breath out of me, knocking my hand loose from the spell card. I watched it fall away with a terror that barely paralleled the loss of air.

Emptied of air, a hideous burning in the chest, light left me, gravity left me, I left me, my name, my body, my personhood

(but you know this)

(i do know this; i have died before)

and yet I *had* died before, drained of everything needed for life to fuel the spell that closed the gates, and this was not new; and it didn't even come with the fear I had expected, only the heaviness, which I knew would come, and anger, which hurt more than the press against my ribs, the fluid sluicing through my body, the last sensations.

(Stand fast. You are not dead, but dying. And you are passing to a place where your dying will pause; and the time you bring with you will let you prolong it a little longer.)

(...*fucking* what?)

But the voice had come just in time, and as something seized me again, plunging me into the heavy darkness, I clutched the shreds of my last breath with a ferocity I had never imagined, picturing it like a shark, biting down, not letting go, hoping in the cold glassy dark—

It ended with impossible gentleness, like a bursting bubble, and I found myself soaked, cold, involuntarily gasping at the air and even swallowing it, jaws snapping, as if putting it in both lungs and stomach was the only way my body could get enough oxygen, and I couldn't stop for what felt like forever.

Johnny had come through before me, and sprawled at my feet. With her hair and clothes plastered flat, she seemed very small. Drowned rat. I looked around, panting. Dark-green sky. Clouds. Swarms of things not birds, not reptiles, not insects. A thousand columns of living fire pacing the horizon. In the far distance, ordinary skyscrapers, battered, crumbling. Or turned into trees too tall to look at without feeling sick.

And the war ongoing for now, but already won, preemptively won, by someone too much like Johnny to lose, the world ended if it was the world we had loved and known, and a new one begun, the sound of laughter somewhere we could no longer hear, but unceasing nonetheless.

CHAPTER TWELVE

I SAT AWAKE all night, half-dozing with my hand on her back, unable to move it, afraid to break the connection with whatever thread of life she still clung to in her sleep. If I let go I'd never know if she died, and I had to know. Her breath was inaudible, slow and shallow, her back barely rising, icy under my palm.

Sherwood had called to let me know they had taken my family to 'a safe place,' but warned me, wearily, as if he had had to recite the same speech many times in the last few hours, that nowhere was truly safe; that even now, local assistance of some kind could probably be spared to get me out; that he was very sorry; that I should probably take him up on the offer; that in his opinion I had done enough.

Mine too, I thought. Very, very much my opinion. And still, even as I made the necessary calls, sent reassuring texts to Carla and Mom, I kept a hand on the back of the one who might cause their deaths. Not yet, but soon. If she died I wanted to feel the life leave her body.

Outside, the city began to come to life. Traffic, honking. People chatting as they passed below the window. I had noticed, while half-watching her limp form inside the cab, that some areas of the city were virtually intact, and others unrecognizably changed. Something to do with the placement of wards, I assumed. Things the Society had maybe not discovered or taken down, still doing their job. No one cared about the alerts any more, disregarding orders both to shelter in place and to evacuate. The streets had been filled with people even as the river had turned to magenta oil, in the blink of an eye the home of writhing creatures crowned with the blank, waxy faces of porcelain masks.

Remember everything, I told myself. Remember that you saw this. The last of the world.

Still she did not wake.

The sun came up, glowing at the backs of the velvet curtains, illuminating something at an angle: the triangular scar on the back of her arm that I thought I had seen back at the Castle, high up, almost hidden under the sleeve of her t-shirt. I knew what that was from; and I knew who had died a moment before she got it. Why hadn't she just erased it like all of the others, like all of mine? Even one this deep would have been gone after a session or two.

I must have fallen asleep at some point, because I woke with a guilty start, jerking upright, to the sound of knocking at our door; Johnny was still curled up, motionless. I frantically checked her pulse: Better? Worse? I couldn't tell, but it was there, anyway.

The knocking continued, patient, loud. I got up, everything creaking, and peered through the peephole. Housekeeping; the silver cart.

Jesus. I opened the door, mumbled something, and hung the tasseled sign on the doorknob again before closing it. When I turned back, Johnny was sitting up at last, staring around herself dazedly.

"You okay?" I said. "Do you need your inhaler or whatever? Water?"

She shook her head. I got her a glass of water anyway, and put it on her bedside table, sitting on my own bed. "We lost your phone," I said.

"I saw."

"And I think I dropped some other stuff. I'm sorry."

She bobbed a shoulder, a half-shrug.

And the world's going to end for real this time, worse than any other time in history, and there's nothing we or anybody else can do about it. I'm sorry about that too. I said, "Who was that? Talking to you. Down there. In…"

"A second-in-command," she said dully. "Didn't get his name. Doesn't matter anyway. Because the Manif…" Her laughter sounded like yelping, as if she had tried to stifle it too late. "Can you *believe* some fuckers? Even I don't go around calling myself The… The Inventorator or whatever."

"Which isn't a word."

"Just invented it. That's my superpower." She wiped her eyes. "It isn't funny, I'm not laughing. It's just that I knew, part of me knew. As soon as Huxley started talking about tactics, strategies, I knew. The fucking... *Manifestation*, whatever he's calling himself. He lied to people a few thousand years ago and called himself Nyarlathotep, he's called himself all sorts of shit. He's..."

"Like you," I said.

She glanced at me, wounded, then sighed. "Yes. I don't know... Yes. He's the one who figured out the magical prion. Pantograph: what it copies is what They are. He likes to use new weapons to fuck things up. Worlds. The second said... that was what he was doing during the Anomaly. He came back just in time to get kicked out again. And he told everybody, everything: I want *her* as a trophy. I want her when we come back. That's why They kept trying to snatch us. They might still try again. Who knows."

Making enemies, I thought. We might have gotten away with it if she hadn't... stop it. It's too late. I said, "So there's really nothing we can do."

"There's really nothing." She laughed again, and again it did not sound like laughter. "And for *that*. Hardly an insult, you'd think. Barely even a... a slap in the face."

"Johnny, listen," I said, exhausted. "You can slap anything in the face. Anything you want. What you *can't* expect is not to get slapped back. What, you thought you were stronger than Them? Better than Them?"

"But we didn't *do* anything. Not really. Not in comparison to what They did."

"Since when do They care about comparison?"

"I know. I know. So yeah. I think there's nothing we can do. Not any more."

I tried to think of a reply to that, the finality of it, tried to wrap my head around what it meant. Everything we had, everything we loved, gone. My head felt full of something claggy—asphalt, mud. Nothing moved. "How long do you think we have till it's all over?"

"Hard to say. Guess it depends on what you define as *all*. I think the prion isn't... perfectly infectious, if that makes sense. Things are happening unevenly, with big temporospatial gaps. If we still had those files from Dr. Chan, maybe I could figure out the rate of..." She shook her head. "It wouldn't make any difference anyway. To know."

"Most of the city's still the city," I said after a minute, not knowing what else to say. I didn't want to comfort her; I didn't think she deserved it. But I had to say something. "Do you want to go get something to eat?"

"...Yeah." But she didn't get up, only sat hunched, arms folded on the bedspread, a pallid grub against the rich purple and gold. The bruises around her eyes were fading at last, from black and violet to blue and green. "I... I wanted to leave a world that... wouldn't need me any more."

"I know."

"That's all I've ever wanted to do. Give the world everything it needed to make sure no one like me would be needed again. And They know that. And that's why They wanted to... give me this. Make me this. It's all my fault. I did *exactly* what They wanted me to, thinking I wasn't."

It was a statement of such utterly pathetic misery, or utterly horrifying ego, or both, that I couldn't come up with a reply.

I fell asleep again while she showered, and by the time we were both moving at more than a crawl, the sun was getting low. It didn't matter; there was no rush to do anything now.

Johnny said, as we left, "Thank you."

"For what?"

"For coming back for me."

"Like I was gonna leave you there."

"*You* could go," she said softly. "Leave the city, I mean. I'm pretty sure I could get you on a plane, even if the airport is locked down. There's still flights going in and out. Diplomats, cargo, couriers. Mail. Stuff like that. I could make some calls."

Yes, I almost said. Holy shit. Yes. Get me home. Back to my people. I don't care where you go.

But no. Not if I have to see them writhing, changing, crying out in pain, for help... Fucking coward, I told myself. You don't want to go where you can't help. Well, you can't help here. If she says there's no chance, there's no chance. She, of all people.

Johnny was looking up at me. I took a deep breath and said, "...No. No, it's okay. Come on. Like Mulder leaves Scully to do the work alone."

"Yeah, every time they split up, one of them gets abducted by aliens. Or serial killers or whatever."

"Or monsters."

"Yeah, or they fall into a cave or a sinkhole or something."

"How do they even still have jobs?" I mused. "I'd have fired them by now. Or made them into mail clerks."

"They'd probably get abducted by a mail-monster."

It had snowed, thawed, snowed again; an inch or so lay on the ground, sky-blue in the lowering night, with a thin, glassy layer of ice inside it that broke and glittered under our boots.

She was mumbling, head down as we walked. I had to stoop to listen to her, and finally stopped her, moving her under a doorway; she looked terrible. "We should go back," I said. "You need sleep."

"But we're here already."

"We'll order in or something. Don't... make yourself do this."

"It doesn't matter. They're not insects, not animals. We are."

"We fought back last time."

"Yeah. See how well *that* turned out." She laughed bitterly. "They knew this would happen. This exact scenario. They planned it, waited for us to play our parts... They probably put *bets* on it. And we underestimated Them. Lesson learned. Last one ever."

We walked on in silence; the churches were lit up again, and the museums and statues. End of the Blitz: no more blackouts. Till the next one, the one that would end this all. Did people know that? Had they guessed? Or had they realized and decided to disbelieve, made denial a personal policy? Not exactly one last party, one last market, but *Maybe I will be spared. Maybe it won't happen to me.*

Frozen breath caught the lights of many colours, knitting tangled clouds of yarn above people's heads. Ahead of us, one of the big squares had been turned into kind of a celebratory night market—not just for the lockdown ending, it seemed, but also something related to the European Union, with the distinctive blue flags hanging from several stalls. Unseen musicians performed competing songs, the notes slipping between one another into a wall of sound, violins and cellos, voices and laughter. The air smelled of woodsmoke and perfume and frying things.

"Do you want langoš?"

"I don't know what that is, but yes, yes I do."

"It's like a..." She thought, and dug in her pockets for change. "It's like a beavertail. But with cheese and ketchup. I bet they'll have it here. Or do you want to go to a restaurant or something?"

"No, I want the beaver pizza."

"Do we still have to pay for stuff if money will be meaningless in a couple of weeks?"

"Yes. You should give him a million dollars, probably."

We ate on the plastic stools outside the stall, keeping our paper plates so that I could get a sausage in a bun. Johnny got a bag of chestnuts, which I ended up holding while she got us hot wine from an old woman running a gigantic cauldron of the stuff, orange slices bobbing around like they were treading an inky sea.

We walked around and between sips of wine carefully

shared out the chestnuts, which were easily as hot as the langoš out of the fryer. People were roasting big cuts of pork, frying sausages of all different sizes and shapes, displaying apparently award-winning hams (decorated with medals and ribbons), offering pastries and buns, fried cheese, things in jars: jam, honey, peppers, onions, pickled things.

"A minute ago I was thinking 'We should tell people the truth, we should tell the whole world,'" I said, as we paused in front of a stall selling antique books. "But like, I look around, and I think... yeah, no. No. It won't make any difference. Why say something so horrible if there's nothing people can do about it?"

Johnny nodded listlessly, and out of habit began to examine the books on the cart in front of the stall, gently rearranging, then replacing, the thin chains that bound some to the metal cart. The stallkeeper nodded approvingly. "Yeah," she said. "Nothing like telling people that no one's going to fix it this time."

"You think they're counting on that?"

"I don't know. Maybe. There's precedent."

"Us," I said. "We're the precedent."

"I know. But people don't know that."

People don't know shit, I thought. I miss being one of those people. The human mind, something I never think about, just collapsing under the weight of things it thought were weightless. "They... do you think they... suffered? The people who died after the Anomaly, I mean. Or *from* the Anomaly. Do you think it was... really bad?"

She looked up at me, eyes still in shadow. "Yes. I do. I'm sorry to say so, but I do. The literature, never mind what that said. Journal articles aren't... I just think when you tear away something that people are using to live, it's never a quick, painless death. No. To starve to death or dehydrate or asphyxiate."

"Well, people didn't need the belief that we were alone to live."

"No, but I think they needed the belief that we were, overall, as a planet, generally safe."

I leafed through the books for a minute too, something nagging at my memory. Never going to forget that white pedestal, the backbone of a monster, never going to forget the stomach-wrenching fall, the wallop into that black water that was not water at all. Never going to forget flames or pain or a mouth bloodied from clenching against a spell. But I had forgotten something else. "And everybody felt the same thing at the same time. That must've been something. Feeling what they felt. And no preparation at all."

"Yeah. Not what we felt. Totally different. Because we had a couple days to prepare for it. And we had the only weapon on the whole planet."

"An army with one gun. Like a million guys in the army. A million soldiers. And just one gun."

"An army with one gun." She held up what looked like a small prayerbook, bound in dark red leather and stamped with golden roses and a tiny cross on the front, and spoke enquiringly to the stallkeeper; he nodded, unlocked the book, and she paid and slid it into her bag.

322

"Johnny," I said, pained. "*Why* are you buying books you won't have time to read?"

She sighed and even managed an eye-roll. "Because it's *pretty* and I *want* it. Give me the nuts."

"Hurr hurr hurr."

While she fussed with the chestnut bag and the napkins, I remembered what I had been holding on to, trying to decide what had been meant by it. Probably couldn't do any harm to hand it over now, even if I wasn't supposed to. I wished I'd been told what to do with it. I unzipped my jacket pocket and got out the small book of numbers Huxley had given me. "Hey. Here. Early birthday present. Or not, I don't know. Might be a curse or something."

"Where did you get this?"

"Dr. Huxley gave it to me. At the last minute there. In the car."

Chewing, she moved into the circle of light thrown off by one of the steel drum fires, and gently opened it, swapping me for the paper bag. "Mm. Interesting."

"Do you know what it is?"

She shook her head, scanning the columns of numbers up and down, rather than left to right. I tried to read it over her shoulder, and so we were both looking down when a voice said our names right behind us.

"You know, there isn't very much alcohol in this," Johnny said, as she paid for three more cups of wine and handed one to me and one to Sofia.

"Look, I said I needed a drink, and it'll do," I said. "I don't like surprises."

Sofia said, "You wouldn't have been surprised if you had been answering your phone!"

"A lot of stuff," I said, "has happened to that phone."

"I don't even have mine," Johnny added, apologetically. "A dragon ate it."

Sofia took that in as we walked, past the stalls of books and sausages and clothes and cheese buns, past stalls offering crystal, memorabilia, coats, wooden toys, gingerbread, bright red jewelry, amateurish paintings. She wore a long dark coat, black rather than Johnny's navy, and her thin pink-and-silver scarf was knotted with a kind of casual artistry into a fluffy rosette that spilled down her back. In her boots, the top of her glossy, snow-sprinkled head was just an inch below mine. "But you know why I'm here, even without the voicemails."

"Yeah," said Johnny, at the same moment I said, "Nope." As we passed through a larger complex of stalls joined together and lit with strings of light, Johnny dug her elbow into my side: *Can you stop being a dope for two seconds?*

Yes, but this *isn't* the help Sherwood promised, I thought. Can't be. She's not in the Society. She's who they try to protect from the Society. *And* she's sure as hell not help. This is some other kind of setup. Like at the party. I'm really cursed, aren't I? The gods have cursed me.

"Let's find you a new watch," Johnny said, and Sofia nodded, though she was clearly impatient to make what I knew would have been a beautifully rehearsed and prepared speech. I hoped it was something uplifting or even motivational, but judging from her face, this was a stupider hope than usual.

It was warmer under the roofed stalls, even though the roof was just a sheet of transparent plastic; we moved along the stalls, and for a while the kind of helpless fear that had been coming and going in waves in my stomach like the tide receded into numbness, which came as a warm relief. Or maybe it was the hot wine: I wasn't sure. Sofia and Johnny chatted and frowned and evaluated and lifted bits of shiny things into the light: a moment's confusion till I realized that Sofia's nails were painted silver, like the things she was handling.

If the world was ending, I thought bleakly, you may as *well* know exactly when.

I fell behind to throw out my empty cup, and when I caught up they were at a jewelry stall, run by a big beaming man with long, curling silvery hair. "Gandalf," I whispered down to Johnny, and she whispered, "The white!"

"Oh," Sofia said under her breath, turning a ring over in her fingers; narrow, dark gray—not a precious metal, I thought, but iron—bearing a small round red stone in it like a lentil, barely as wide as the band.

"That is Greek," the stallkeeper said. "Like you? Very old. Not like you! A pretty ring for a pretty lady. Glass, not gem. Inside it say—"

"'This is the home of love,'" Johnny said, as Sofia held it out so she could see the inscription. "It *is* very old. Does it fit? Oh, there you go. Beautiful."

Sofia held up her hand under the light. Were we still supposed to be keeping up our cover? I had no idea. But I knew, from her wistful face, or possibly years of dealing with the kids, that she had fallen in love with it, and if the world was ending... "You want it?" I said. "I'll buy it for you."

There was a beat; Sofia flushed brightly, and the stallkeeper rubbed his hands together in sheer delight at her consternation.

"It doesn't mean anything!" I said hastily. "It's not, a, um. It's not. I'm not. It's just a present. If you want."

"...Are you sure?"

Well, I don't really expect Visa to chase down my statement when I can't pay it off, I thought. "Of course. Come on, it's nice, and it fits you."

"Fits perfectly," the stallkeeper added encouragingly, and turned to Johnny while I fumbled out my wallet, hoping my card wouldn't be declined. "Ah, you got an eye for it. See, this one also writing inside. That one, that is from Roman time. It says..."

"Sure does," Johnny said, and got out her own credit card. I peered over at her purchase as the stallkeeper took the two cards over to the machine plugged in at the back of the stall: hers too was iron rather than a precious metal, no gem, oddly pitted and faceted. She put it on before I could even glance at the letters incised inside it, catching only a glimpse at how deep they were.

I took my receipt, wincing, and we headed down the line of stalls toward the cooler air. I looked automatically for one of the drum fires; the square was even busier, if anything, so you had to look for the knots of people assembled around the fires, holding out mittened hands, warming faces.

"Thank you, my darling." Sofia held her hand out so that the little red gem caught the light. "It is beautiful."

Oh, so we *were* keeping up the story. Nice to know where you stand. "You're welcome." I glanced down at Johnny, who seemed to have stalled out in front of a display filled with shelves of crystal glasses, saucers, and sculptures, but also globes of various sizes on little wooden tripods so they wouldn't roll around. "Uh. Are you okay?"

Johnny picked up one of the spheres, weighing it in her hand as the stallkeeper came over and asked her something, then nodded and replaced it on its holder. Something kindled in her eyes: I pictured the 'pop' of a lighter, held behind the yellow-green irises. Half-consciously, I thought, she touched her coat pocket, where I had seen her slip Huxley's book earlier. "Rings," she murmured without looking away from the sphere. "Toroid."

"What?"

"I'm going back to the hotel," she said. "I need my laptop."

"For what?" said Sofia, but Johnny was already gone, darting and bouncing across the square full of people like a rogue pinball. We stared after her.

"So," I said, when we had both spent about as long as I could stand without talking or looking at each other, "what *did* you come here for?"

*　　*　　*

"No," I said. "And I really mean that. You haven't seen what we've seen over the last week or whatever."

Sofia frowned. "And what is that?"

I closed my eyes for a moment. Leery of the cameras installed everywhere, we had ended up in a small, ancient pub which looked like it had been built in the thirteenth century and was so low-tech it only took cash. Its light fixtures looked like they hadn't been changed since the Second World War and were stubbornly holding on, filaments dull, nearly orange, but still burning. In the weird light, the beer I'd felt obligated to order looked like red Kool-Aid.

"It doesn't matter. We just... look. Let me just stop saying *we*. Because this whole time... listen. You know *I'll* come with you. But Johnny just absolutely will not. She wouldn't have before this week, and she definitely will not now."

"But she has to."

"I know you think joining forces or whatever is the way to go here," I said patiently. Sofia folded her arms and glared at me. "And I know you don't give a shit about whether I come or not, because I'm not useful, only she is. What I am *trying* to explain is that a) she won't; and b) it doesn't matter. There's nothing we can do now."

"That is what I am trying to explain to *you*, Nicholas. What if there was?"

I stared at her, the fear returning, starting in my stomach and working its way up. The end of the world:

drinking beer in Prague and waiting to go home to die with my family. Wait, stop. Don't fall for it. They do this, it's what they do. Both the Society and the Ancient Ones. "There isn't."

"And who told you that?"

"Several people. And things. Not just her, if that's what you're suggesting." I poked at the pretzel I'd ordered, knocking off some of the salt. It was the size of a hubcap, and my stomach was revolving slowly and queasily, like the pork we'd seen on the spits at the market.

It wasn't so much that I thought Sofia was lying, or that Johnny and I had been lied to, or that (in fact) *anyone* was lying. It was more that everyone was concealing their version of the truth. Johnny and I were skittering around like cockroaches in a dark room because of that hunger to conceal, that fear of what would happen to us if the truth emerged; but the Society's need was different. They weren't ashamed or afraid of what they did; they just needed secrecy to function.

And it wasn't that they were hoarding or monopolizing decisions about magic; it was more that if the public knew the Society existed, they'd become obsessed with exposing its workings and private communications, with demanding to join it, with preventing it from doing its work, basically. Because I knew people (better than Johnny did, I often thought), and I knew people interfered because they thought they all had the right not just to an opinion, but to participation; not merely to express their ideas, but to barge in and ensure they became real. Like those conspiracy nuts demanding access to government intelligence that simply could not be exposed for the government to function. You couldn't run a business like that, let alone a group of academics.

But they weren't that any more, were they?

And now their secrecy prevented accountability. And so rot had set in, and someone had decided: *No more fighting. No more knuckling under, no more compliance. Instead, active, even enthusiastic collaboration. And then in the world to come, we may not be peers, we may not be pets, we may not even be cattle, but we might be safe. And no one else will be.*

All of them? Some of them? I studied Sofia as if it would help. "What were you really doing in Edinburgh?"

She sighed. "Obviously I went to go see what Joanna was doing. All right? You knew that already. I had suspected for a long time that... that her device, her power plant, was in some way attached to the Anomaly. I thought: How, why? Did the Ancient Ones spot it somehow, one of Their watchers with Their horrible face pressed against the Earth? Is that why They tried to come? And later I thought... well. Whose side is she on? Because if... if They came, if They... got through, threatened her... I am not saying she's evil. I am saying she probably made a choice. And yet the reactors were allowed to go ahead. Why?"

I stared stonily at her.

"You know there are Ssarati personnel in governments all over the world. Doing two jobs: one public, one private. They say: One job for the part of the world you can see, and the other for the part you cannot see."

She leaned urgently over the table, bumping her wine. "And yet, the reactors could not be stopped. So much movement behind the scenes, even... even creating, moving, signing the documents that would be needed. But she prevailed. What does that tell you?"

"She's very good at it," I said carefully. "Because when she wants something..."

"That is why we need her! Yes, I was investigating her, all right? I will say it. And in Edinburgh, I thought Papa would come, so I could explain why I had left school, I knew he would not come otherwise, he's always trying to keep me out of Ssarati business... but he sent *you*. Without telling me. So I immediately worried that you were... that you had betrayed us. Were working with her instead. But on what? We had no idea. Papa says, though, that your loyalty is unquestioned. That you are with us, always, and on the side of humanity, and preserving life. And she is too. Isn't she?"

"Of course she is. Especially if she can put her name on it."

"Well, then."

I sipped my warm beer. It was all so simple, and so complicated, and there should have been only two sides of the siege, but there weren't. Inside the castle walls and outside them. The army outside, and the one inside. And did she even know? That the Society that she loved and idolized, that she had been soaking in since birth, might be splitting? Or had split? Or contained, at the very least, a couple of shards of broken glass inside its bland academic softness? She must know. But then why send her to say these things, I wondered? To lure Johnny and I back into a trap, after we'd gotten out of their other ones? Or just Johnny? To turn her back over to Nya... the Manifestation?

God, what wouldn't people do for power. Not even safety, security, money, fame. But *power*. What wouldn't they do to rule over something, anything, even if it was just a handful of former humans on a rotten, infected planet.

I pushed my beer away. "Look. Johnny is not currently a... a one-man army or whatever. But if she were an army, that's the kind she'd be. In the sense that she would never, ever join another army, even if you were fighting on the same side. She'd rather lose for sure than risk being... double-crossed, sacrificed, or whatever. She hates that the Society was investigating her. That's the only way I've been able to keep passing on information about what she's doing. If she thought..."

"I know that," she said impatiently. "Why do you think I tried to cover for you at the party?"

"Thanks for that, by the way. That was the most terrifying thing that's happened to me in ages. This week included."

"Nicholas, stop joking. Papa says... based on what you have given us... there is information available for her. They are finding things she has no access to, things that are still coming in. But we need her to..."

To do what only she can do, I thought. You don't want to say *give us access to her resources*. You wanted to say *lend us her brain*. And you just stopped yourself.

For whatever They want her for. That's why.

They both still think she's a weapon. And they both want to disarm her.

Unless Sofia is serious about actually providing this data so that Johnny can come up with something, anything...

"All right," I said slowly. "How are we going to convince her to at least talk? Without... you know. I mean, you know how she thinks... she would think if there was a way to prevent this, you'd only get in her way. She doesn't trust the Society and she doesn't trust your-dad-slash-my-boss. And she doesn't trust you. And she shouldn't, actually, is what I'm getting at here. And you shouldn't trust her either. Basically I think we all need family therapy."

"*Your* only connection to the Ssarati is me, your girlfriend," she said firmly, then added, perhaps at my expression, "That is, we will keep telling her that. It's good, it covers things. Then you can continue to help us. All of us. Nicholas, trust or not... she is needed. She will respond to the need. She'll just have to set aside the trust thing. She wants to save the world, doesn't she?"

"Yeah. She thinks she was given..." I bit my tongue just in time, and covered it with an enormous swig of the flat, warm beer. "She thinks that's her duty, as a genius. It's all she thinks about."

"I suppose if we all had her gifts..."

"Yeah, but look at what it's turned her into," I said, trying to keep the anger out of my voice. "Our greatest fear is losing people. Hers is losing... I don't know. Losing control of the narrative."

"What?"

"I don't even know."

Sofia stared out the window, drumming her silver-painted nails on the table. It had begun to snow again in earnest, blowing against the wobbly medieval glass and catching in invisible ripples. On the corner closest to us, the green-painted streetlamp twisted, screamed, and walked away, its light going out at the last second. "Papa is in the city, you know. I asked him to come and he finally came. How can we get her to meet with him, at least? So that he can make his case?"

"Well," I said, "she likes food."

CHAPTER THIRTEEN

"...You've got yogurt on your mask."

"Sour cream." Johnny stuffed another tiny sandwich under her mask, then pulled it down again. "I can't stop eating these and I don't even know what's in them."

"Well, then it's probably people," I said absently, staring around the room. On the surface, it looked festive, even theatrical: many people in masks half or full, with sprays of feathers, little hats, capes, cloaks, dresses, suits. Some people had the kind of mask you had to hold up with a stick, and were having serious trouble at the buffet table.

But it was quiet, even subdued. The room was too dark to see the full effect of the people who had dressed up: the glitter and glitz. Meanwhile, I was in my regular clothes—jeans and a sweater—and a mask that Louis had found for me. I had assumed Johnny would have a secret store in Prague that would delightedly sell her a mask and a gown, but she'd spent so much of the day on the phone and her laptop that she never ended up going out to shop, and was dressed much the same as me.

At least the mask covered her black eyes, I reflected, and then reflected further that if I mentioned this, she'd throw me out a window. What was the word for that?

Bad enough that when I had spoken to Carla earlier, she had been half in tears, demanding to know what the hell I was doing in Prague. We saw a picture of you, she said. With Johnny: on the street. It had taken a long time, and all my minimal lying skills, to convince her that Johnny, who we already knew was pretty damn weird, was simply dating someone who looked a lot like me. A bit like how her two favourite Backstreet Boys kept dating women who looked exactly like each other. The photo was probably faked, too.

When you come back, you should start going out with people too, she'd said. Like normal people.

I'm normal people, you little turd.

I mean normal in that way.

Who says that's normal? I never got a vote.

Several cats were also attending the party, and I was unsure whether they had been invited or not; as one of the only non-human creatures able to sense and use magic, though, I supposed it was technically possible that they were Society members. In fact, it was entirely likely that some of them outranked me. Some people had wandered off for private meetings or other things in a half-dozen rooms in the small gloomy mansion, people invited with no more than an elbow-tap and a nod, and a few of the cats had trotted after people going to these.

Collaborators, I thought, feeling sick. How would you know? Only a few people, Johnny had said, had been offered covenants like hers, deals for things they greatly desired, which the Ancient Ones might hand over, cackling, knowing the sting in its tail. But supposing you had something to trade for those rare deals. Supposing you suddenly had something the enemy wanted, and also knew there was no fighting back: that there never had been, that generations sometimes had perished while you frantically figured out how to at least push Them out.

No, I said. There would be a revolt.

There's only a revolt when you can kill your enemy, Johnny had said. If not, you just fight and fail and everybody is stamped down anyway. But appeasement has always been an option. It's just one we've not taken except on a very small scale: cities, valleys. What if the Society is trying to do it on a larger one, and lets most of the world die if they're taken care of? *They've* got the skills and the knowledge to survive after an invasion. They might even be useful to the new rulers.

I felt sick, had felt sick all day; and I thought that it might be from hope, which was trying to shoulder its way back into a place inside me that I had tried to wall off. Johnny had said she might have a plan now: huge, ambitious, and (I assumed) practically impossible. And she didn't have enough data to be really sure of it. But the Society did. She'd trade, I thought. Something. If she trusted them, she'd do a trade. Surely.

It was painful to hope, like the grating ends of a broken bone. If only it would stay still, it could heal.

"Ah, the special guests. You got my masks! You must be Nicholas? Very pleased to meet you at last. Joanna's left-hand man, eh? And the big man the right hand? Where is he?"

"He couldn't make it," Johnny said.

"Thanks for inviting us, Mr. d'Souza." I shook Louis's hand, quickly scanning Sofia's elaborate costume and meaningfully pursed lips: *Don't screw this up!* Johnny, I knew, would have loved nothing better than to make a big deal about my girlfriend in front of Louis, but she had already agreed to keep her mouth shut to spare me and Sofia the grief. It was to be understood merely that Johnny had come to Prague, and had taken me along as usual, because that was how we worked.

Louis's mask was bright blue and gold, a bird, maybe an owl, with exaggeratedly large eyeholes and a diminutive beak that did not quite fit over his Roman nose. His bright golden skin, a little lighter than Sofia's, made his glistening salt-and-pepper hair pick up all the light in the room.

Johnny gave him a fake smile and did not put her hand out; Louis did not seem offended. "Good party. Wouldn't have wanted to miss it."

"Nonsense. My old friend. You are all right now?" he said solicitously. "Terrible thing, Edinburgh. A gas line went, they say. Very lucky, though. Killed all the creatures."

"Yes, I'm all right." Johnny touched her mask, delicately,

where the bruising still showed through the eyeholes. "It looks worse than it is."

"I think it's very possible that you saved my baby's life," he said gravely. "She was in your private ladies' room when it began. Ran outside through an emergency door."

As they spoke, making what Louis clearly considered the necessary small talk required to spiral in to the question of (say) joining forces to save the world, I remembered Sofia telling me about the first few times she'd seen Johnny: aged six or seven, and the blonde child coming to the house with the calm serious man like a statue always behind her.

Johnny had not been able to cure Sofia's mother's cancer, but she had bought the woman the best care and pain relief available, and two more years of life, until death came when Sofia was nine. *And what does that mean*, Sofia had said, *to* buy *years of life?*

I had kept my mouth shut. Even now, after everything, it was too painful to bring up. It occurred to me that Sofia might be the only person who really understood what it meant, though: why what Johnny had done to me hurt so keenly and permanently, and felt as if it would never heal. Johnny sure as hell didn't.

The house in Braga, before we moved to Lisbon, Sofia had said softly: the sitting room with all its plants and trees. She would come in, so small, with the cheques, the pill bottles, asking about Mama, how we were doing, if she could... I don't know. Hire a gardener, hire a cook, a driver, to help us. And I would watch from the upper floor, waiting for Papa to ask me to come down... in a dress, with my good shoes. She helped us for years, she never asked anything in return, but it was understood, always, always, that I must dress like I did for church. My best, always my best. I never questioned it, it made perfect sense. Only now I don't remember why.

"And so we come to this," Louis said. "People here know why you have come. Some of them think you are a fraud, and we no longer work together because you were discredited. Some of them do not know you, they ask me: You invited a university student, yes? One of Sofia's classmates? Some of them think: No, the world is not ending, what we are seeing is of no import, so it does not matter who comes to the party tonight, fraud or no. And some think even if you are not a fraud, you cannot help what is happening. So, these ones are eating, drinking, as if the world would end very soon. You know those ones."

"The ones with the full masks," Johnny said, looking around interestedly.

"Just so. They did not want you to come. There are many discussions happening tonight, about whether we, on our own, can... at least mitigate the damage from what is coming. Even though we do not know what it is. But a few of us, a very few, have come up with a hypothesis. And we are finding data to support it. New, good data. Fresh samples. Even from a few hours ago."

"Data regarding what?"

"Let me get you a little glass of wine. Fee, do you want a wine?"

"Louis. What data. And from who?"

Louis hesitated, and glanced around us. No one was obviously listening in, but several people were non-obviously doing so; I felt the pressure of their gaze on my skin like a hand. He said, "We should find another room to talk. No?"

"Why?" she said. "If everybody knows what we're here for."

"Not everybody," he said, "needs to know everything. No? You do not go around your labs, your factories, telling every person what you are doing next."

"No," she said. "But I tell the physicists about my physics. I tell the engineers about my engineering."

He narrowed his eyes minutely, a very Sofia expression. "Then I suppose you want me to tell everybody that there is a case being developed. Everybody in here. You want them to hear that? A case of the old laws, the laws of Umash-Turskel. Against you."

Johnny laughed, sounding relieved. "Well that sounds very impressive," she said. "I don't fall under your jurisdiction, Louis. Scare your own people with that stuff."

"Anyone who has done magic falls under our jurisdiction," he said flatly. "Because magic *is* our jurisdiction."

People were drifting over now, interested. Sinister faceless faces, floating masks in the gloom. I felt an intense urge to freeze, not even to breathe. This was the one thing, perhaps the only thing, that Johnny could not stand, for all her love of the spotlight. This, the open wound that still bled invisibly from her: that she should be accused of exactly what he was about to accuse her of.

Johnny glanced at Sofia, then back at Louis. Under the mask, her smile had not faltered. "You know what you sound like? A little kid making up stories at school to get another kid in trouble."

"Do I? No, I am merely sharing information. Not public laws, no. The Ssarati does not care for those, never has. Our own: the laws we keep and preserve, of ten thousand years standing, regarding the usage of magic that harms human life. Laws that cannot be broken. Laws we have taken it upon ourselves to enforce, for the safety of all the world."

"Some threat," Johnny said. "When have *I* ever used magic? Not everyone can, you know. All I've ever done for the Society is help you, Louis. Found you manuscripts. Translated spells. And now this." She shook her head, sighed. "Well. Thank you for the food. And the mask. But I thought you came here to talk about something else. I see you haven't."

There was a long pause. Louis' face was reddening under the mask, making his hair seem even brighter.

They won't prove anything, they won't prove anything. She's spent her whole life making sure she's never witnessed. Only by me. And I never said anything about her *doing* magic. Just studying it. They won't prove anything.

Louis said, in a tone that made my blood run cold, "There's precedent for everything in our history. Don't underestimate us. We do not need to prove all that was done. Even intent is enough. Even suspicion of intent is enough."

"That's not justice," she said. "Not a 'case.' Not a 'law.'"

"Nevertheless."

"You've got nothing," she said.

"You were the cause," he said loudly, leaning towards her. She refused to lean back. "You. Not a *witness* to the Incursion. You caused it. You collaborated with the enemy, you let Them in. You powered it somehow with that... machine of yours."

I waited, heart pounding. The smile slowly fell away from Johnny's face. "Prove it."

"We will."

"Then call me when you do," she said, and spun on her heel. "I'm headed back to the hotel," she said over her shoulder. "See you when you get back."

Three people, at a nod from Louis, smoothly moved in front of the door. Oh God, here it comes: the double-cross, bundling her up, handing her over to the enemy, turning her in for the bounty. And then what will they do with me? Is this the side I've picked? Motherfucker, I knew they were going to...

"Johnny, please," Sofia said, pushing through the few people who hadn't had the good sense to move. "Please."

"Good job playing along," Johnny said, gently unhooking her mask. "Ow. Go Team d'Souza! A well-oiled machine of bullshittery. I thought you had something serious to offer. Instead you threaten me with... *this* crap, this tattletale power play. Jesus! You people. This is why I don't trust you. And why I wouldn't trust your data if my life depended on it."

"It does!" Sofia said desperately. "I... I didn't know about..." She glanced back at her father, convincingly. Johnny didn't look fooled, but Sofia went on, "Please, let us just talk in private. This doesn't have to be a... No one will be forced."

If you think she won't let her one chance at saving the world slip away so she can save her ego instead... I wanted to say. But surely everyone in the entire room had figured that out by now.

At last, Johnny shrugged. "Well, I'll hear you out," she said. "No more. Because any asshole that starts off by threatening me instead of offering me something is not someone I want to do business with."

"It's not business," Louis said. "It's duty. To work together to save the world."

"I don't want to work with you," Johnny said. "Let's just get that out of the way."

"I hear you."

I trailed after them automatically, but Louis stopped me, pretending regret, at the door of his chosen meeting room, painted in peeling black and decorated with ancient brass studs. "No, no," he said. "I am sorry, no. You do not know these protocols. Those involved only."

I glanced at him with real alarm for a second. It was disconcerting to not be able to see what was happening in the shadows of the mask's eyes. Who else was in that room? There was still plenty of scope for a double-cross, and I was slowly and queasily realizing that as much as I had wanted to bring Johnny to some kind of justice, that was colliding pretty much head-on with wanting her to save the world. So far from ensuring that Johnny didn't interfere with their plans, I now didn't want *them* to interfere with *hers*. My sense of self-preservation had never been great, but it had been getting a lot of practice over the last few days.

"I'm the bodyguard tonight," I said.

"Still no. Her body will not need guarding."

A silence drew out; Louis's gaze burned into mine. "A solution presents itself," he said, smiling. "Come work for us. Eh?"

Johnny's eyes widened in horror, but before she could say anything, he went on, "It could be a very good job. Good pay. Chances for advancement. And of course, to save all of mankind."

Oh, *well* done. My God, he was good, smooth; he twinkled and glittered with earnest benevolence, like the decorations on his mask. "Not in a million years, Mr. d'Souza. I kind of have a thing about magic. And I already have a good job."

"Nonsense. What could be better than this? It is human nature to want to discover, to explore the unknown, understand our history. Look at the machines we have sent to other planets. 'Probes.' And the spaceship to Mars this one sent up: why bother, why go? Your job, whatever it is, cannot compare. Eh?"

"It pays the bills," I said stubbornly. "And my 'thing' is really more of a phobia."

He sucked his teeth, and put his hand on the door's ornate handle. "Well. Maybe when I give you a salary number, we will have a better talk. Now. Joanna. *If* you can spare us five minutes of your time."

Sofia had to drag me back to the main room, and I stood at the window with a plate of small jam-stuffed doughnuts, watching people dance and a knee-high white stone advance slowly across the flagstone floor, occasionally pursued or hissed at by one of the cats. Had someone brought a pet? No one seemed to be commenting on it. Best not to ask. After a while, I said, "What's the official word for when you throw someone out a window?"

"Defenestration," she said. "Are you all right?"

"Mm." I wasn't sure. My entire body was prickling with something that felt less like fear than the anticipation of necessary violence, and my urge to go home, back to my familiar house, my warm room in the basement, anyplace where I wasn't wearing a suspiciously sticky fox mask with wires that were cutting into my ears, and could maybe deal with kids instead of these two, and let the world end while I was relatively comfortable, had never seemed so overwhelming; I felt feverish and restless, as if letting Sofia take her eyes off me for one second would end with me vaulting the white stone and running down the stairs.

"She's a... She's going to demand not just the data, but what's in it for her. And if she doesn't like the answer, she just won't do it. She won't. She's a monster, because she's just... she's just a fucking ego. With legs. She'll never go for it, and if she does—if she's wrangled a way to be our best hope for anything—we're all going to die."

"We're all going to die anyway. And anyway, if we can combine what we know with what she knows, maybe there's a chance."

"But how much. How much of a chance?"

"I don't know, Nicholas," she said, turning the new ring on her finger. "I don't know that. Maybe she's the only one who would know. Trust the Society. We've been doing this for a long time. With many kinds of outside people. She can be harnessed. We all can."

"She *won't* work for you. She'll, at best, work *with* you. And after tonight, I doubt that. What I think she'll do is take the data and run."

"All right. All right, calm down. Please."

I ate another doughnut and tried to calm my breathing. Sofia wandered off and danced with a very old man whose head barely reached her collarbones, then with a younger one who was either a werewolf (I thought uncharitably), or in a very convincing werewolf mask, and then with a slender woman who had gone all-out: ruffles, lace, ribbons, mask, headdress, gloves, and a necklace with either a green glass stone or emerald in it the size of a golfball.

Democritus came humming through the air, noticed but unremarked upon by a few people, who turned back to their conversations and drinks. I lifted my chin so it could land on my shoulder, but it plowed into my plate instead, hitting the dropped sugar like a snowdrift then, while shoveling sugar into its mouth with both forelimbs, turning and lifting one wing cover very slightly.

The note would have been incomprehensible to anyone, I thought, who hadn't known Johnny as long as I had, but my heart rose into my throat; for a second my ears rang. Hope? Something else? But only for me, and not for the Society. A secret hope, a light breaking through clouds that no one else could see. And I knew my role in guarding that light.

It took another three agonizing days for Johnny to crunch the data on her end, during which Rutger joined us in Prague and took a room at our hotel, where he and Johnny spoke only of the data and nothing else, glaring daggers at each other all the while, analyzing Huxley's small book of numbers, and occasionally going out to meet with Society members at the libraries and hospitals of Prague.

At the end, I knew roughly where we were going, but still had not yet figured out why or how it had been calculated, no matter how closely I listened in between TV-induced naps on the rumpled purple bed, waking sometimes to discover that books or notes had been arranged on my sleeping body. I could not shake the feeling that it was all going to go wrong. Not in the sense that Johnny's plan would be ineffective, but that it would bring upon us a retaliation from the Ancient Ones like nothing Earth had ever seen before, in its millions of years of sporadic invasions.

Bees in the walls: and earthquakes were starting again, in strange places, in the middle of tectonic plates, far from faults. Landslides from low, old mountains, worn down like the teeth of old dogs. Eruptions of natural gas and oil, flooding landscapes where no reservoir had ever been found. Chambers Emergency Response continued to rescue livestock and provide living pods for people, treat horrifying steam burns from shock geysers, rebuild shattered levees and round up dazed refugees. We were fighting a war with most of our army already crossed to the other side, I thought. And they would never come back to us, never.

"No," Johnny said, when I told her. "No. They will."

"If we *think* they will, maybe that's exactly what They *want* us to think. Maybe there's a… a catch, a trap, in the prions. You said that's the kind of thing Nyarlathotep likes to do. You said he's always liked to do it. Why wouldn't he do it now?"

Rumpling sound of her rolling over in the dark, a clunk as she bumped the bedside table. Someone's beetle fell off with a despairing buzz. "They're trying to outsmart someone that They gave the power to outsmart Them. It almost worked. But now we know something They think we don't know. Something they only know intuitively, not formally."

"Which is?"

"The rules of magic."

A long pause; outside, the hum of one last bus. She had made her decision in the mansion of our masquerade, and told only me: Johnny was running a scam, just like in her favourite movie; and so whatever it was the Society thought she was doing, she would not tell them what it really was. She had taken their data, they had come up with a new plan, together, and that was what they were going to execute. But she had a backup plan, because she thought theirs wouldn't work. Or that they had designed it to not work, to pin it on her, and to let the worst happen.

But the Society had not yet, I thought, become aware that they were working with both a tiny extradimensional monster that was far more devious than ever believed, *and* the Ancient Ones. They thought they did; but they had no idea. Just as I had, before she had been revealed to me. They were not poisoned by hatred; only too pleased at their own cunning to see her clearly. Whatever she did would not involve them, no matter how they arranged things to be at the center of her plan. She would only allow them to believe it for as long as she felt necessary. I knew how these things went.

"They still think you're human," I said after a minute into the dark, knowing she wasn't asleep.

"Good."

WHEN JOHNNY FINALLY gave the word, Rutger arranged our flight to Peru, with the understanding (I noticed him carefully not using the word 'condition') that he come with us.

"I have seen what happens," he said, again and again. "I have seen what happens. Fire me if you like."

But Johnny refused. "I don't want to fire you. But I don't want you to die either."

"You do not want me to die because you need someone to check your data."

"I didn't say that!"

Sofia also came, with 'muscle' from the Society. And so it was that when we finally boarded the empty 737, there were seven of us. "Lucky," Johnny said as we filed in.

"No such thing as luck." Rutger scowled as he buckled himself into his seat, in the row across from hers.

"Beneficial coincidences," Johnny said. I caught her eye as the engines revved up: *Do you know what you're doing? Who you're messing with? Am I seriously going to be home in a couple of days?*

She nodded once, minutely, and we started down the runway.

CHAPTER FOURTEEN

"Muography."

"What?"

Johnny curled up in the empty seat next to me, and slurped from her water bottle. Outside the plane, I couldn't help but notice, we were being paced by things that looked like a cross between a pterodactyl and an octopus. "You were asking earlier why Peru."

"Yes, and you didn't want to tell me in front of everybody for some reason, even though probably none of us would have understood it."

"None of their business. Mainly, when you can account for the amount of volition that magic particles show, you can basically cross-reference real muography results with a kind of magical triangulation to locate hidden structures. Those lab errors, the anomalies we were finding that those bean-counters at the IARE kept logging as ethics complaints? It's because the balance of types of matter around us is shifting. Dark matter increasing. Dark energy increasing. It's affecting gravitational waves everywhere, around the Earth and inside the Earth and, uh. In other places. But it showed up in the numbers first.

"So we're getting bombarded with muons all the time, right? And we can use them to measure density changes in solid substrates. But you can also see how they hit and bounce off and absorb magic in motion. That is, magic that's being generated, directed, and consumed. So now that we've found the *pattern* of the shift, we can see it's got directionality. And velocity. And we found a massive new gathering of magic in one place. Here on our side. On Earth."

"In… Peru."

"Yeah. And that's where I'm going to siphon it off to run my own spell."

I nodded uneasily. The Society, supposedly, had supplied Johnny with some of the things she needed to fill in the gaps in her anti-prion plan. That, I had understood. Not a cure, she said, but an ongoing spell, more like medication. To not only knock out and reverse the effects of the magical prion that was rampaging through the world, but hopefully and permanently tie up enough magic that another invasion couldn't happen. Johnny's anti-prions were synthetic, a nanomite with an enzyme and a protein on it, a biological sigil encoded, she said, with far more fidelity as well as power than the original. But it would never work unless it got a kick-start: as much magic as we could get.

"You sound really sure about this," I said, "for someone running some… kind of scam that I haven't quite figured out yet."

"Mm. Anyway. The weird thing—and Rutger is still pissed off about this—is that the conversion factors we needed? To correct for the directionality of intent? Were all in the book Dr. Huxley gave you."

"What?"

"Yeah. So that book is what, five hundred years old? And *our* numbers, the *real* numbers, didn't start changing until last year. Proximity effects were at my facilities only, and that's why other labs were noting it as a discrepancy. How did the book have the numbers we needed? How did Dr. Huxley know, too, that I would need it?"

I leaned close to her. "It's called… magic."

"Oh fuck off. You know what I mean. She knew. She wasn't just guessing. How?"

"Well, if we ever see her again, we could ask her." I leaned back and shut my eyes. "Go away. Go sleep."

I listened to the scuffling as she unfolded herself and began to head back to the aisle, then thought of something and straightened up. "Hey. Wait a sec."

"What?"

"Huxley," I said. "Did you find out what happened to her?"

"Kind of," she said. "I know she's alive. I agreed to help the Society if they would let her go though. And take off all the conditions on her contract. It almost doesn't matter any more, with the Archive gone. But still."

"All the conditions?"

"Yes. All of them." She paused, still half-balanced on the arm of the seat, her expression inscrutable. "Because she saved our lives. And it's not fair. And you can't always tilt the scales. But you have to, when you can."

"What else did you ask for?" I said, but she was already climbing off and leaving, the blanket around her shoulders trailing like a cape.

AFTER A THOUSAND transfers, moving quietly through the back parts of airports where the people with clipboards and badges did not go, we arrived in Lima; and here the three Society members, Columba, Davis, and Hayes or Haze (I hadn't figured out which), led us out into the sunshine, the dry thin air.

Slowly I removed my coat, then my sweater; the heat penetrated the half-frozen layers of my air-conditioned skin. We had skipped Customs, thanks to whatever arcane maneuvers Rutger had performed on the phone in Prague, but we had been held up all the same, waiting for the alignment of people and available exits to let us out of the back ways of the airport. We had loitered uneasily, knowing we weren't supposed to be there, but ignored by the staff that wandered by, apparently believing that since it was impossible to be back there if you weren't supposed to be, then we were supposed to be, and all was right with the world. "Did you have us shipped as cargo?" Johnny whispered to him at one point, and he whispered back, "Emergency response supplies."

I had never been to Peru, a sentence that came easily from my lips as Sofia and I talked on the plane; I had never been to Peru, and I had never been to Edinburgh (except once) and I had never been to Prague (except once) and I had (several times now) been to a place that was between places, a sort of hall closet on a cosmic scale, where things were stored when other things could not think what to do with them. And I had never been to Guyana, some twenty-four hundred kilometers away, where my people were from. "India," I said. "Then South America. Then Canada."

"So you've traveled inside Canada, then."

"No. Not really. No."

"Do you *want* to go to Guyana? See it, see the place your family is from?"

I wasn't sure. Mom didn't talk about it much but I'd seen Dad's black-and-white photos, the abject misery he had escaped with his very young wife, the poverty, the instability; the lack of everything when they left, and a not-dissimilar lack of everything when they emigrated, sponsored by an uncle in Toronto. Still hungry, still tired, and now (on top of everything else) *freezing*. He still lectured us about it, still told us that our only emotion should be abject gratitude for the sacrifices they had made, that every act we completed should be towards being grateful, being dutiful. "I guess I would go if I could take the kids," I said. "They never get to go anywhere."

"It's good to go," she had insisted. "You need to see where your people are from. See for yourself."

"Why?"

"To see if they were telling the truth about it."

We had to circle back around to the side of the airport to find the car rental place, and then Johnny and Sofia and I stood around as the others negotiated with the rental agent, a small ferocious-looking woman whose dark blue uniform cap was tilted at a combative angle; she gave every impression, though I couldn't understand what she was saying, that she had dealt with her fair share of aggro white tourists and would not be intimidated by us, no matter how big Rutger was, or how charming Columba was.

"We need a team name," Johnny said, squinting up at the clear sky through the leaves of palm trees that looked a little dusty or thirsty in the thin constant breeze.

"League of Nerds," I said.

"No."

"Doom Squad."

"No."

"Guns and Bros-es."

"We don't have any guns," Johnny said, then hesitated. "Do we? I didn't ask."

"I hope not," I said. "I wouldn't trust you with a gun."

"And anyway, we're not all bros," she added.

"You're a bro."

"I'm a bro," she conceded.

Sofia, who had been giving us a slightly alarmed look, said, "Joanna, do you know where we are going yet?"

"Sort of." Johnny glanced back at the car rental window, where Columba was doing a kind of interpretive dance, and then got her laptop out.

With Rutger's assistance, a small rotary tool, a soldering iron, and a few bags of suspicious metal and glass from one of the flea markets, it had been modified with a device on the side, something like a cross between a compass and a satellite dish, the size of a halved grapefruit. Part of a TI-82 graphing calculator, like I had used in high school, had been attached below this, wires mostly taped down, so that the screen lay parallel to the laptop screen.

"The closer we get, the closer we'll be able to get. It's a refinement algorithm, so the more data it receives and calculates, the more accurate the next set of data is. I input an, uh... an external correction factor of high reliability to sort out the muons from the magic particles. Which probably need their own name of some kind, but honestly I don't know how they name subatomic particles any more."

Sofia stared at her.

"It should work," Johnny said. "Of course, we're testing it now. Hard to see if these things work until you need them, you know how it is."

"...What's a muon?"

"She made it up," I said, authoritatively.

"Do not listen to him," Johnny said. "Heed not his babbling. He speaks, like the Devil, with a forked tongue, and often offers people apples."

"It's so you don't get scurvy," I said, as Rutger returned, bearing a sheaf of papers; he had shed his suit jacket to reveal a dark-blue shirt nearly the colour of the desert sky above us. He looked about as lightheaded as I felt; the girls seemed fine. When he stood next to Johnny, she seemed more complete somehow: as if her shadow had snapped into focus on a sunny day.

What you carry with you, I thought. Magic could carry time and light from where it originated; but Johnny carried me, and Rutger, and all her secrets. Which way were we spinning, I wondered. Were we all working in the same direction?

EVEN WITH JOHNNY'S warnings that it would be a long drive, I found myself startled when, a few hours after we left, the sun went down. Columba, a powerfully built man who had dressed head to toe for the trip in pale khaki that showed every sweat stain and speck of dust, turned on the Hummer's headlights, illuminating the highway ahead of us in a wash of white nearly as bright as day. He whistled. "Get what you pay for, eh?"

Hayes sniffed. "Not always true." She leaned forward, brushing back her long dark hair, and grasped the edge of the shotgun seat, where Johnny had plugged her laptop into the cigarette lighter to keep the screen at full brightness. "How much further?"

"Hang on. Let me do one more iteration." She typed, adjusted the little device wired to the side, and pressed the *On* button on the remains of the calculator. After a moment, it displayed two strings of digits, which then appeared on the Hummer's dashboard GPS.

"Recalculating," the voice said primly.

"We're gonna run out of road pretty quick here," Davis muttered.

"That's why we got a personnel carrier." Columba patted the dashboard reverently. "I like this. Eh? We run into any of them things, we just... run them right over."

We all nodded queasily. Several more hours: but Rutger, always ready, had packed the cargo compartment with enough gear to overnight out here, mostly purchased in Prague. I had never been camping, although thanks to Johnny, I had certainly slept rough a lot, and performed the usual functions of hygiene in unexpected places. Sofia had confessed that she'd never gone camping either, and Johnny had agreed that it was, generally, not a good idea, depending on your feelings about getting eaten by bears, but that probably wouldn't happen here, sleeping in the vehicle.

What else would eat you out here, I wondered? In Edinburgh: nothing, surely. And in Prague, I had been assured by one of the people Johnny had talked to on the phone that despite strenuous rewilding projects outside the city (bears and wolves, but also several things that bears and wolves could eat, including Chambers Enterprises-funded aurochs, though I didn't know what those were), it was still nothing. But we were driving through mountains, and things lived in mountains that you didn't know about because it was impossible to get up there and look.

I almost nudged Sofia to ask, but she had fallen asleep, and Rutger was staring stonily out his window, so I did too. Mountains, lit for a moment by our headlights, and the increasingly ridgy road. Familiar, though not our well-known Rockies, which I felt I had seen a thousand times on family road trips to Banff or Jasper: always terrifying and beautiful, always known. Their individual shapes sharp against the sky, striations of snow, distant flecks of trees. These were the same, the road cutting between walls of stone, often slick with water in sheets or tiny waterfalls, thick green plants branching from whatever crevice they could get a hold.

We had passed at least a half-dozen mines of various sizes too, their signs flashing for a moment as we left them behind: safety warnings, insistence on wearing your employee ID, carefully hand-painted logos on mailboxes or guard towers, maybe by bored security people. We had been driving east and a little north, as far as I could tell from peeking at the GPS, for hours.

I thought: You are very far from home—very, very far—and they would have let you go home if you wanted. You know that. And you are not needed here: even as a spy.

Yes, I know. I know. Not needed.

When Johnny finally started dozing off and could not be roused to give directions, Columba pulled carefully off the side of the road. Branches and leaves scraped the roof of the big SUV, something stickily squealing along my door. "Well, that is the rule," Columba said, grinning and turning as he killed the engine. "If you rent it, drive it like you stole it."

As the engine ticked down, there was a moment, agreed-upon without speaking, of silence, feeling the weight of the mountains around us, the weight of the trees and the vines, even the weight of the sky, new stars still blinking in fretful code. You are all alone out here, said the wind, and the world is riddled with sickness and it is coming for you from all directions. Moving slowly, but on its way.

The silence was broken as Sofia scrabbled for our door handle, seeking fresher air.

"*Guns of Navarone*," I said, as we piled out, rubbing our sore backs and legs, testing the footing of the gravelly turnout next to the highway. "Secret mission."

"Hell yeah!" Johnny said with sleepy excitement. Rutger came around to the front and took the laptop from her, stepping back into the undergrowth to let her get out. "Dibs on being Gregory Peck."

"I already called dibs. While you were sleeping."

"Aw."

The air smelled of green things, soil, road dust, and something indefinably of altitude: something about the way the inside of the human nose responded to it. Briskly, without chatting much, Rutger and Columba set up a tiny camp stove on the sheltered side of the Hummer, and made tea while Hayes and Davis got out tarps to sit on. No tents or sleeping bags: it would be a close night inside the SUV, everybody breathing each other's breath.

"Will we know it when we see it?" Columba asked Johnny, as we passed BamFoam cups of tea around the circle enclosing the flickering stove. "This place you speak of, I mean. This place of, uh… transfer."

"Maybe," Johnny said. "With our eyes, I don't know. There might be knowing but not seeing. But I think… it wouldn't be able to disguise itself the way a lot of places seemed to be doing over the last couple days."

"What do you mean?" Davis looked up from working the can opener on one of several large tins.

"Even if we haven't evolved to use magic the way They have—and I'm not saying we have or we haven't... because there's really no way to test it on a scientifically useful scale..." She had lost track of the beginning of the sentence; I waited patiently. "Uh, I think there's the possibility of something that responds inside us. Like a vestigial organ, but the opposite, really: a prescient organ, something that evolves for a function that doesn't exist. Or doesn't exist yet. The way Prague and Fes and Lagos and Paris were built over low spots, the way you can barely move in London and Kyoto without getting tangled in something."

They nodded. I began to say "On purpose?" then fell silent. I'd seen enough of magic, if not of city-making, to know how it would have gone. Maybe your little group of hunters and gatherers included one person who was sensitive to magic, or was marked by Them, maybe even contacted or covenanted by Them, rare as it was. You roam the Pleistocene landscape long enough, eventually your shaman or your priest or your old-souled child or your twin or your wise woman says: I got a good feeling about this place. Let's make camp here. And because everyone's seen that they have a knack for it, maybe you wintered there, and the gods spoke to you, or gave you something you wanted. The next spring, maybe they say: Let's just stay one more year. And everybody nods. And before you know it, you're surrounded by skyscrapers and car dealerships and nobody ever even knew for sure what was underneath.

"It might be that part of us will know," Johnny said. "It might be that we don't realize it, no. And we have to circle in. But I really doubt it, I really do. I think there would be no way it could prevent itself from giving itself away, especially now."

"Is it dangerous?" Hayes said.

"Everything's dangerous."

Big white moths fluttered close as we ate, intrigued by the small flame of the stove. Afterwards, we took turns negotiating the darkness of the woods with a clip-on light and a packet of wet-wipes, brushing ants off one another's clothing. Rutger had bought insect repellant devices at the airport: the size of a nickel, prominently marked with the Chambers Biomedical branding.

Johnny rolled her eyes as she accepted hers. "They work best when they're somewhere real warm," she said. "Try sticking it between your boobs."

"Joanna Meredith Chambers, you *cannot* just go around saying 'boobs.'"

"Sorry. Breasticles."

"Anyway," I went on, as Sofia slowly turned fluorescent pink, "where do I stick mine?"

"Where the sun does not shine, young padawan. Where the sun does not shine."

Rutger placed his on his neck beneath his collar and sat again, frowning into the flames. "What I understand of the physics does not explain the rest of this," he said quietly. "We should have returned to the house. *You* should have returned."

"What," Johnny said, "and just... bunker down?"

"Yes."

Her lower lip trembled. The end of the world. Sparrow's bunker, his bike hanging on the wall. Some people wanted to get involved in the apocalypse, and some people just wanted to watch. What good was all her money, Rutger's gaze seemed to say, and all the bedrock and concrete, rebar and surveillance, if she would not use it? If she was out here on the side of the road in the Andes, eating beef stew out of a can? Why bother making it at all if you refused to shelter yourself behind it? Not cowardice to opt out. Simply common sense. The wise preparation of someone who had, like in a fable, socked away seed all summer, and now had somewhere to hide when winter came.

I imagined her saying, *I did this. Not on purpose. But no excuse. And that's why I have to do something about it.*

Instead, she said, "No one made you come."

"No one made *you* come, either. These people could have handled it."

"No," she said, "they couldn't."

The awkward pause was broken by the strange small sounds of wildlife nearby: insectile clickings, the uncertain calls of frogs. Eventually Johnny made a reconciliation attempt by passing out 'energy bars' for dessert, which she had been hoarding in her bag and had developed, she added proudly, in her own labs, but not yet sent for market testing.

"What's this?" I said, as the Society people tore into theirs. Rutger put his into his pocket without comment.

"Just eat it."

I peeled back the foil and pressed into it with my thumb, the oval dent bouncing back as I watched. Sofia was staring at hers with polite suspicion, which was probably wise.

"Is it oatmeal?" I said. "Soy?"

"No."

I sniffed it, getting nothing. I said, "Is it... almonds?"

"No."

"Um, let me think. Seaweed? Whey protein? Lentils? Tofu?"

"Tofu is made from soy. Anyway, no."

I gave it a tentative lick, surprised to find that the thin brown coating tasted like peanut butter. "Peanuts."

"No."

"But you made those allergy-free GMO ones," I said. "You should be using those in everything."

"Allergen-free," she corrected me. "How's it taste?"

"Oh my God," I said. "Is it... people?"

"Like you wouldn't eat it if it were people," she said amicably, ripping hers open and chewing with relish. Good timing on that one, as hers was some kind of fruit, cherry or strawberry, dark red under the chocolate shell. "Remember when we went to see *Resident Evil* and you wanted to get lunch right after and I was throwing up? You'd be eating people ten minutes after the zombie apocalypse started. You'd be eating people before you got bit. Now eat your damn dessert before you eat me."

"As *if*," I said, greatly offended. "Eat you, after all your lab incidents? You're probably contaminated with all sorts of stuff. Tainted meat. I'd rather lick a sidewalk."

"Oh, all of a sudden you'll only eat free-range— "

"—cruelty-free—"

"—grain-fed—"

"—uncaged—"

"—antibiotic-free human? You elitist. You bougie."

"Why bother?" I said. "You're too little to waste my time eating. You're a snack. A little contaminated snack. Like a chicken nugget."

"How dare you."

I gave up and started eating the bar, which despite its complete lack of smell tasted serviceably like a peanut-butter granola bar, studded with chocolate chips and cranberries. The matrix holding it together was so relentlessly chewy that I glared at her while I ate, positive now that it was human. Maybe the grad students that had dropped out of one of her programs, or corporate spies or something. Sofia, across the fire, stared at us as if we both had two heads.

Later, as I tried to get comfortable, spread out across our bags in the cargo compartment of the hummer, I spotted a strange glow: Johnny sitting on the hood, draped in mosquito netting, her face lit from beneath. I pushed the sleeping bag aside and opened the door. "Nick," someone mumbled, though I wasn't sure who. "Don't."

I climbed up beside her; she glanced over and lifted the

netting to let me slide underneath. "What about your repellant?" I asked.

"They only work on ectoparasites. I got tired of the moths bonking into my face."

Could the others hear us? I couldn't even tell who else was awake, when I glanced over my shoulder to look into the vehicle. Twigs cracked around us; I scratched the back of my neck. "What are you really up to?"

"I think it might be better if you don't know," she said.

"But I could help you with it. These people..."

"No, I know. But the thing about them, the thing about the Society, what it does to them... Power corrupts, right? Of course power corrupts. Everyone who says it means it. People with power, people without it, they both say it and with the same emphasis. Some people mean: it ruins you, it makes you broken and bad, it rots you in a way that makes you... unfit. And some people mean: It makes you evil but it doesn't make you *useless*. To be corrupt is to not be broken; just functional, and twisted. You don't fit into the old lock you used to fit into. But you're not *not* a key. You just have to fit a different lock. With nothing good on the other side...

"The Ancient Ones have never been corrupted, by Their definition; They've always had power. Always. They see the world the way They expect it to be forever: mortal things at the bottom, and stupid things like light and gravity and chemistry; and Them at the top, snacking on the things They like from us. Time. Fear. Life. Hopelessness. So when things from the bottom rise up, it's a shock. Food fighting back. Toys coming to life. We're not really *real* to Them. And that's how the Society is learning to see people too. An underclass. Below them, and below their new bosses."

I stared out into the darkness. Eyes were moving out there, but tiny ones; and the watcher in my hand made no alarm. "The plan," I said again.

A long silence. The tiny eyes moved closer, blinked, receded. So small they were like stars fallen from the clear sky, still visible through the gathered knot of the netting. An animal, a creature not from here? Something changed, turned? At last she said, "I put a self-destruct trigger on the reactor, did you know that? Common sense really. Should have done it with the first one, the experiment, so we didn't have to mess it up at the house. If this reactor is tampered with, it'll reduce itself, more or less, to its component molecules. Pretty violently, too."

"Okay," I said slowly. "I hope you told the people who were going to be working with it about that. You know. Hazard assessments and whatnot under the Occupational Health and Safety Act."

She nodded. "That's why I automated it. Again," she added, stressing the word, "*pretty* violently. Because it's really important that no one *tamper* with it."

I swallowed, hard. If they were listening inside the Hummer, had she just gotten us in trouble somehow? Because this was something they had not heard about, I knew. Only Johnny and I had been there for it: the reactor unmade swiftly, minutes before one of Them showed up demanding that it be weaponized.

If I was interpreting this apparently random anecdote correctly, and I wasn't sure I was, she meant to do something of the sort with her nanomite anti-prions. The cure not defense but offense. A *weapon* against Them. Perhaps even biological warfare: wiping Them out. I wouldn't have put it past her.

"What do you need me to do?" I said.

"Whatever the others ask you to do," she said. "Can you do that for me?"

I finally turned, and looked down at her. Her eyes were clean pools in the smudged dust, visible even in the starlight: something burning in the pupils, not just exhaustion, not just fear. There it was, I thought, brace for it: gird your loins against it. I'd read that before, in some book or other. Maybe more than one book. What did it mean, girding? But anyway, there it came, that thing in her, the brightness, the warmth I had loved, the spark that gave of itself to warm you. The softness of her gaze that said: I see you, all of you, through you, and I stand on the same side; I would move mountains to stand next to all that you are.

Even knowing that it was fake, that she had engineered the love and its love in return, barely diminished its force. Come back to me, I thought again, then shook my head. No. Not her pet. Not her... her *service animal*. And I had saved her life in the castle, and I had saved her life in the place of dragons. And still she doubted me, because she was the only thing in any dimension she wanted to save. "What you're talking about could go out of control," I said. "Self-propagating. You said."

"It's war. Not a siege. A siege implies that we're safe, and we're not. But I can stop it. I just need to know if you'll do what I ask you to do. There's no one else I can ask."

We're going to die. We're going to die. You think you can do this and we're all going to die. "...Yes."

THE NEXT DAY, after a gigantic breakfast of oatmeal and freeze-dried fruit, we had only driven for a few hours into increasingly high peaks and heavy fog when we simply ran out of road.

"Turn right," Johnny said.

"There is no right." Hayes gestured irritably at the GPS as if that would help.

"That's why we got a Humvee, so we can go off-road," Columba blurted. "Vaminos! Schnell!"

"Nope. Out."

We trailed Johnny, balancing her laptop on her forearm like a waiter with a tray of drinks and barely watching where she was going as we walked up the slope. I stopped to catch my breath and looked around: no more buildings, no more mines, no roads except the narrow gravel path we'd left the Hummer on. No signs, no telephone poles, no electrical wires. A breeze ruffled the long fine maroon-and-green grass, blew bits of pebbles and sand down from the peaks that surrounded us. Fog hung at ankle-level, eddying like water as we walked and replacing itself right where it had been. Everything seemed lightly rusted, as if the constant damp had oxidized things over a period of not hundreds or thousands but maybe millions of years. Nothing seemed to have *turned*.

Unspoken, I had been wondering who would feel it first: this thing that Johnny said we might feel before we saw. But we all felt it at the same time, Sofia leaping back so dramatically from the edge of the unseen thing that I had to grab her before she rolled down the hill.

We had reached a plateau, the long shallow slope behind us and a virtually sheer face of rock ahead, smoothly striated stone in various shades of browns and grays; not even the obviously tough mountain grasses and mosses ad been able to hang on long enough to grow. But there was something at the place where the stone wall met the ground, something that pushed me six inches back, or even lightly picked me up and shoved me—or just my bones, or just my nerves, or something.

Columba, Hayes, and Davis had formed a bloc, their faces rigid with surprise and fear. For a second I nearly pitied them: it hadn't occurred to me that even the people who studied magic and magical history their whole lives, became Investigators, traveled the world looking for artifacts and books, had never seen anything like this till now. Never seen one of Them, or Their minions or thralls, never had the Lesser Angels approach them in their dreams; never seen, let alone passed through, a gate, a boundary, a veil, or whatever this was. I supposed it would be like studying mythology your whole life and coming home to discover that a minotaur had bedded down in your living room. No amount of academia would prepare you for it, no matter what side you were on in the coming war.

"This could be it," Johnny said, putting her laptop away. "I can't refine it any more. It's somewhere at the edge of the satellite bounceback range. Ten meters on a side. Move slowly."

Though we were keeping our voices down, speaking still seemed indecent out here, in a silence that felt like the soundproofed phone room back at our Prague hotel. We split up, shuffling our feet through the bare dirt between the thick tufts of grass. Water condensed on Davis' glasses, trickled down with the occasional startlingly loud 'plip!' onto her bright blue plastic jacket.

Columba vanished first, almost but not quite without sound: a faint droning cut off so suddenly that its disappearance rather than its appearance alerted us to the spot. Johnny, fairly sensibly for once, picked up a rock and tossed it underhand, where it vanished into thin air. Davis made a small noise in her throat.

"There we go," Johnny said, satisfied. "I love to say I told you so. Anyway, we'd better leave one person on this side in case something goes sideways."

"I'll stay," said Hayes—not without a certain amount of relief, I thought. "I have the car keys."

"See you when we get back," Johnny said cheerily, and stepped into the place where Columba had gone.

I took a deep breath, held it while Davis went, then Sofia, looking back questioningly at me, then Rutger, whose entire body looked as if it were trying to move backwards as his head moved forwards. I knew how he felt. Then I exhaled, and I too stepped into the place.

A MOMENT'S DISLOCATION, the sense of an electric shock massive and almost too brief to sense, waking every nerve and vanishing before they could do something about it. My jaw ached when sensation returned, and my molars were coated in blood where I had bitten the inside of my cheek.

It took a while for my eyes to adjust; and when they did I found myself stunned not by the new but by the familiar. I had seen photos of crystal caves in National Geographic, no different from this.

Wait. No.

Yes? No. The *scale* was all wrong, and nearly knocked me on my ass. Not stalactites and stalagmites but skyscrapers, and the darkness beyond them not a night sky but the unseen ceiling of a cave roof higher than any plane could fly. An entire city of transparent monoliths, some with the lightest tinge of blue or green, many—in Columba's trembling flashlight—surprisingly reflective, showing us just how tiny we were.

Out of habit, I turned to see where we had 'come in': nothing but more of the crystals, of course. But this place would be gone when Johnny drained the magic out of it for her spell, and we would find ourselves back on the plateau, I was pretty sure. I didn't want to ask in case I was wrong.

The air stank of magic, and was heavy and damp.

Between the monoliths the gaps were as wide as freeways, the smallest easily still alleyways; we clumped together all the same, murmuring apologies as we hit each other with elbows and shoulders. Past the blood and the rotten taste of magic in my mouth I tasted adrenaline, sour and abundant.

"We were always taught crystal powers were bullshit," Davis said, and laughed faintly. "These are just stones, right?"

"Of course they are," Columba said, lifting his flashlight.

Johnny nodded. "There's no such thing as a magic crystal. Of course, you *can* still banish practically any creature with a crystal, provided it's large or pointy enough. Well-known fact."

"Let us do what needs to be done," Rutger said. "I don't care whether there is… magic. Caves are unsafe."

"We just need to find the exact spot of accumulation," Johnny said. "That'll be the best place to set up my stuff."

I wasn't sure how long we had been walking, but it was long enough that our conversation had wound down except for the occasional whispered "Here?" when Rutger noticed the first runes in the crystals, and called Johnny over. Sofia and I followed, looking over Johnny's shoulder.

The writing was small, no language I knew or thought I had even seen before, interspersed with tiny drawings, each less than an inch high. My stomach churned. But it was just writing, it had no power, like any other words, until someone manifested them. No matter what it said, no matter what language it was in. They'd taught me that. First lesson, practically.

I stared at my own face in the mirrored stone, watching as it dissolved, transformed into shapes seemingly no more than a pane of glass away from us: legs, wings, flopping limbs, crawling and staggering, pressing their faces to the scribbled surfaces so that teeth and claws showed behind the writing. Johnny slowly moved off and held her light on an unoccupied spot, then put her t-shirt over the lens so a fuzzy, pinkish glow illuminated the text, which seemed to have been engraved just below the surface.

The glowing letters rose up in response to the light as if through deep water, flickering at first then steady, a no-colour, not quite blue or purple or black, but clearly visible in the gloom. It hurt the eyes to look at.

"Holy shit," Johnny whispered. "Holy, holy, holy shit."

"It repeats and repeats." Sofia looked up, trying to see the top of the monolith, the one next to it, the one behind it. "It's the same thing on all of them. I think."

"What are these pictures? I've never seen that in a Carvyd inscription." She edged back to the mirrored surface, breathing faster. "Come here, can you see? Okay, that's... this isn't good. No, hang on, this is a modifier."

"Distance or time?" Sofia said.

"Um, time. Something inanimate, negative. Not a warning."

"There shouldn't be a warning," Sofia said, frowning. "Not if it's just a gathering place... but it is negative. Yes."

"Maybe it's archaic. Not new at all. Hang on. 'Death is...'"

"...At all times... uh, what's this word?"

"Sufficient or adequate, inanimate. And this one is another modifier, 'common knowledge to intelligent races.' You don't see that one very often, it's usually implied."

A long silence. I pictured them both writing frantically in their heads, knowing that nothing could be sounded aloud in case they turned out to be words of power. Behind the transparent material, something stopped, watched us: small, indistinct, its face like a broken mirror, filled with the small glowing letters reversed upon it. Sofia backed away instinctively, tripped over a crystal, caught herself, rose again.

"Death is," Johnny finally said, and hesitated. "Hang on, it's all broken up. Like this:

Death is always imminent
Enough; you cannot draw it closer, even
When you believe it is you who draws it.
Dying takes a moment only, which is well known;
but
Living is as hard a thing as the grave."

Another long pause. "They die," Johnny said, almost to herself. "They know They can die. Their slaves, Their servants can die. But when They sleep... to sleep and wake and..." Her hair flipped up in a sudden breeze, like a golden flag, something stirring the still air between the crystal buildings.

Carefully, trembling, Sofia took my hand. I squeezed it, still staring at the creature that stared back at us, then raised its limbs, pressed them to the surface between us.

Something I needed to remember. Something to know. And the wind gaining strength, calling between the facets, chiming, and the letters gaining in strength till they became painful in their brightness, incisions into a space backed not with daylight but the hot breath of stars. Johnny's face in the wild new light was stark white, as white as the teeth in her half-open mouth.

"Where did the other two go?" she said, and the resignation in her voice was all I could think of as something opened nearly on top of us, the crystal splitting along invisible fault-lines, opening, the wind screaming, lifting us off our feet, that first moment of weightlessness so startling that for a second I didn't even think to scream, only marvelled at it, at the gargantuan soft terrible breath that inhaled and pulled us from light into darkness.

CHAPTER FIFTEEN

THERE WAS JUST long enough to register it all—water, trees, stones, *speed*—before we hit.

No way of telling how fast we were moving. Just the impact scrape I saw as I spun, like Tunguska. Screaming in from outer space, shearing off the tops of trees, the detonation like a nuclear bomb.

I lay stunned, listening to my fast shallow breath, for a long time, as if I were someone else: the breath of someone else, the pain of someone else. On every breath the smell of rotting things, mouldy meat. Stagnant water, a cold taste of things that grew without air.

Someone pulled me to my feet. Rutger, using one hand. There was just enough light from two small moons, both half-full, to register his stunned but impassive face. My whole body hummed like I was standing in front of a speaker, feeling the bass. It took me a moment to realize it was my heart, thrumming instead of beating.

Two moons.

Johnny and Sofia had landed closer to the water; we dragged them out, checked pulses, murmured names. Johnny shook us off and looked around, her wet hair dull with what looked like oil or mud rather than water. Clocked the two moons, grimaced, showing her teeth like a frightened dog.

The dark surface of the lake, as matte as a piece of slate, shivered, boiled. Ruptured, thick sluggish bubbles of stench, white worms rising to the surface, writhing, sinking again, desperately twisting in the thick fluid. And then, unmistakeably, something larger: an arm, a head. A membranous uneven fin on its back, torn and bitten, gleaming for a second in the moonlight.

We bolted instinctively uphill, scrabbling on muddy rocks, grabbing and pulling at each other, and fled some unknown distance to a line of high dark stones, diving behind them and huddling close. Familiar. Where from? A movie. Dark riders.

When the noises from the lake subsided, Rutger edged out from behind the stone, then returned. "I see nothing."

My head was swimming; I rose, looked down at Sofia and Johnny. Red dots sparkled in my vision. Terrible to be right. Terrible to know for sure. Just as I had thought everything would be okay, that I could maybe forget if not forgive, that I wouldn't have to spend the rest of my life angry and powerless. And now this.

"They fucking set us up," I said slowly. "The...

whatever their real fucking names are. They sent us here. Didn't they?"

"What are you *talking* about?" Sofia got to her feet, clinging to the rock, her silver nails gleaming. "And why are you asking *me?*"

"You? How would *you* know? Oh, I don't know. Is it because *your fucking father* sent us into that cave? Huh? He picked those three out. He didn't want you to go. He gave us all the data. What does that tell you?"

"But he did let me go! He had nothing to do with this!"

"Then he must have thought they'd keep you out of this! It was just supposed to be her, wasn't it? Wasn't it supposed to just be her?"

"Stop shouting," said Rutger.

"You, shut up," I said. "*Just* her. Or her and me. Wasn't it? Because he *knew*, he knew They wanted her, as a trophy and as a—as a precaution, because the takeover couldn't happen if—"

"My father had nothing to do with this!" Sofia shouted. "How dare you!"

"How else do you explain what happened?" I said. "Huh? Fucking Louis was in charge of the plan, he *wanted us* to come to this fucked-up place. Wanted us out of the way, like throwing a ransom over a wall and just running. Hell, who knows, maybe he didn't even get those fucking three to do it—there, do you feel better? You're trying to protect them? Maybe it was *all* him, and he got someone to do it on *this* side. How about that? Maybe he's dealing *directly* with the monsters!"

Sofia's hand cracked across my face, staggering me. For several beats, no one moved.

"How dare you?" she said again. "He had *nothing* to do with this. Why aren't you looking at her instead?"

"What?"

"How do you know *she* did not cause this?" Sofia pointed at Johnny, who had finally gotten to her feet, half in and half out of the moonlight at the edge of the stone. "The reactor, the attack! What if she put on an act, arranged it for that night, so she could look like a... victim instead of a collaborator? How do we know she isn't working with Them, *for* Them? How do we know the reactor isn't something... something evil?"

We both paused, panting.

"No one knows how it works," Sofia hissed, "and no one's been able to make one except her. Have they? Because it's magic, isn't it? How? Why would you do this? Whose side are you on?"

Johnny inhaled, blew out. "Mine," she said. "I destroyed the first one, the test reactor, so that the enemy would never get it. They offered me a covenant. I accepted. And I encoded a sigil in the reactor torus. It works by moving electrons between dimensions. And yes, once, that let magic in. Now it doesn't. So it's surrounded by magic, protected by it, but it doesn't work *by* magic."

"So they were right," Sofia said. "Right enough. They said... and you said they'd never prove anything."

"Well, I still don't think you can prove it," Johnny said.

"And you knew all along," Sofia said, turning to me.

Something like and not like laughter bubbled up out of me, and I thought of the thick ripples in the lake, the rotting things down there eaten alive, not dead, and when the laughter started I couldn't stop, not till I began to cough and fell to my knees on the bare, stony ground, the pain startling me back into something like awareness. Was the sky getting lighter? I could see Rutger's face better, a rictus of disgust, and on either side of him, Sofia and Johnny, expressionless.

"Okay," I managed, staggering back up; I felt like strings had been attached to my shoulders for a second, weightless, jumping on the moon. "Okay. Okay. Okay. So yeah. You wanna say it or should I? Fine, I'll go. Everybody's cards on the table. She *did* cause the Anomaly. What was it, five hundred and... five hundred and fifty million people? Sixty? What's ten million people, more or less? Her. Yes. Her *friend*, the one that offered her the fucking genius deal, came back. Woke up all its people, the big bads. Told Them where and when to come through. We shut it though! We were the ones that shut it! But the reactor, *that* let Them in! No shit, Sherlock!"

"Well it isn't this time," Johnny said, her voice strengthening. "Do you know how They'd get enough magic to do what they're doing now? You think it's *some* people in the Society doing it and not all of them? They're *killing* people, maybe dozens, hundreds, thousands of people, who knows. There's seven billion people left in the world for the fucking Society to offer up to Them."

"They're not!" Sofia said, genuinely stunned. "The Ssarati has been protecting humankind for thousands of years! That is all! What proof do you have? It's never, in the entire history of the—"

"That was then! You don't think the Anomaly changed everything? Because they sure the fuck did. And they picked a side. Do you really think your father would have *told* you that they were doing it? Get a clue. Get a fucking... They're collaborators. Traitors. And they'll put down any resistance, any, that Earth manages to mount this time."

I cackled again, weakly, like the last heave after a bout of vomiting. "Oh, this is perfect. Perfect. You know what? You think it doesn't matter who sent us here? Well, it does for me, and it does for this fucking war that's probably... staged, I don't know."

"What we saw—"

"Nope. Fuck you, and fuck you too, who must've spilled everything at the police station because you can't keep your fucking mouth shut either, and fuck the Society, and fuck all of this bullshit, all of you are the fucking same. I quit. Everything, all of it, and you. I quit." I gestured weakly at Johnny, seeing my hand clearly now, a sun or something like it rising now. "The biggest regret in my entire goddamn life is saving yours. I wish you were *dead*. Which is great! The best timing ever! Finally, everything lines up so a wish could actually come true! Because we're all going to die here! And I don't even know where here *is!*"

Gray light touched the stone behind us: blue, of

course, pale blue and white, and others, surrounding us, the earth in the center blasted, even a little glassy. The moons faded into a dark, listlessly gray sky, boiling with clouds.

Some kind of survival instinct took over at last, the lizard brain telling us that we had made far too much noise for too long to continue going unnoticed by a predator, and we trudged out of the obvious magic circle, over the dead, crisped grass to softer stuff, an unpleasantly fleshy shade of pink and white, stark on the black soil. I sat again, and watched first Johnny, then Sofia, try various spells to get us out.

I could have told them it wouldn't have worked. That was *why*, I wanted to say, we were sent *here*, by the trap rigged in the crystal cave. Here, and not some other place. There's got to be a condition here that won't let us, do magic; and that was the motivation of whoever did it; and that's why we need to know who that was; and nobody knows.

The universe is a certain shape because it has to be to do its job; the universe is a certain shape so that it works. But every time we said *the* we should have been saying *a*. Every universe was different, every dimension. And we had been sent to one shaped like this. And that could not have been an accident. That was deliberate.

And because it was deliberate, whether Johnny knew it or not, *someone* did: that the Earth had just been, in effect, demilitarized.

Rutger sat next to me, cross-legged, and for a second I had the dizzying feeling that we were simply in front-row seats to a show, Shakespeare in the Park or something, the actors stark against the still-lightening sky, the ritual movements of their hands and lips telling an old story.

"If she asked me to kill you," he said after a minute, "I would."

"...Thank you for telling me that."

Something brushed against my hand; I jerked it away reflexively, looking down just as a bright red-and-black bug the size of an egg jabbed its proboscis down into the dirt, kicking up a little spurt of dust. More sidled through the thin grass; I stood up quickly, brushing at my jeans and jacket, something stinging me on the hand, a faint disgusting motion of scrabbling legs trying to hang on as I tossed it away from me. Rutger did the same, and we headed back to Johnny and Sofia.

"Forget it," I said, looking down at the angry bump of the sting. "It won't work, nothing will work here, not for us. No one who sent us here would have let us get back. Also, there are huge bugs that want to shank us."

We fled at an undignified walk, half-instinctively heading for higher ground again. The landscape was strange, unpleasant to the eye in ways I couldn't quite put my finger on. Standing water in the wrong places, single ragged-topped mountains surrounded by flat plains, tapered pillars of black stone with nothing around them, and the trees all at strange angles, dangling with both vines and leaves. In the far distance, a forest of black and leafless trees was the wrong height, higher than the snow-capped mountains next to it. No birds sang, and the insects that followed us, stumbling patiently in and out of our footprints, were also silent. The only sound was a faraway whine, like something vibrating either above or below the human range of hearing.

At the top of the next hill, we looked down into a narrow valley, the top of something just visible—a church, I realized with a jolt. Something had happened to it, and I had seen it, somewhere... not on Earth. Somewhere else. It should not have had the intense and unmistakeable feel of familiarity, of a solid thing in my memory.

Past the church lay a city, or something that was trying to look like a city, perhaps copied imperfectly from another imperfect copy with a broken pantograph. Smoke rose from steep rooftops, and here and there glowed lights, dim and bluish or greenish, like the bioluminescence of abyssal things. Around the valley were dark-purple trees, brittle looking and dangling with thin listless snakes, the branches broken in strange patterns. The soil shaded from black to a dark red, like dried blood. Voices sounded, distant but clear in the silence with nothing to compete with them.

A city might mean people, knowledge. A way home, maybe. Or at least a place to forget about going home, start a new life here. Get away from these three, find a hovel, get a job.

Or maybe I'd just be murdered, mutilated, tortured, and eaten. Not necessarily in that order.

"Pretty sure one of you knows where we are," I said.

"Dzannin," Johnny said. "I think."

"Which is what."

"I don't know. One of their dimensions, okay? The books just say it has two moons, and there are cities there. It's not like we do... anthropological studies on every monster that comes to Earth."

I kept watching the city, glancing back at the others, back at the city. There *was* magic here: I could see the soft, amber fuzz around Johnny's head, the sign showing that not only was her ill-gotten gift still working, but she could still use it.

If. If there was a *chance* we could get home. We couldn't stop the invasion from this side; if anything, I suspected that was why the trap had been set in the first place. Coming here was just adding insult to injury, a slap for a slap, a place where she could use as much of her gift as she liked, and still be stuck, and still be powerless, and still know that somewhere, her home was being consumed and corrupted.

Of course not. Jesus. We've got nothing and she'll never come up with a plan. Not even her. She needs all her gadgets and people to come up with something, and she hasn't even got her bag. She hasn't even got a *pen*.

Still.

Only a diamond, they used to say, can cut diamond. But that's not true any more. That hasn't been true for a long time. Humanity came up with something else that you could use. And They came up with her... and then They took Their eyes off her for two seconds.

It's not nothing. It doesn't mean nothing. That we're here and we can't do spells, but the condition of her very existence still exists. She hasn't got any of her stuff, but she's got us. Maybe something can still be done, even if we all hate each other. Maybe you can just... hate each other and still do good somehow. It's not for us. It's for the world. And somewhere down there, maybe there is a way.

But what I finally said was, "We can't stay up here forever."

Rutger grunted, not exactly an affirmative, but a small noise of despair and confusion, and we moved slowly down the far side of the hill.

THE CITY WAS even worse than it had appeared from above, like something long-submerged in one of those oily-looking lakes and then dredged back out and turned on its side, everything broken under its own weight and hung with ropes and rags of rotting weed. Squirming maggots chewed audibly on the dangling foliage as we passed, dropping slimy clots of purple and black onto the rutted and muddy streets.

One day this will be Earth, I thought. One day soon... Maybe it already happened. And everywhere will be like this. Like Outworld in the *Mortal Kombat* movie.

The church we had seen was nearly at the city limits, if you could call them that—just ahead of the first crumbling and uninhabited huts, surrounded by green-gray bones of every shape and size, protruding out of the dirt so that for a second it seemed like an ordinary lawn, only somewhat anemic, and teeth still startlingly white or the clear green glassiness of Coke bottles.

The shattered... the shattered cathedral of black stone. I flinched back from it, and dug my heels into the dirt near the first of the bones, my heart beating unevenly with recalled fear. Johnny stopped, and looked at me with a kind of tired curiosity.

"I've seen it before," I said. "When we were... before the Anomaly."

"A dream?"

A vision. In which They had demanded I kill her, after They had found or made a back door into my brain and let Themselves in, and programmed the keypad so that They could come back whenever They wanted... no. There had been enough confession for now. She didn't need to know everything; and didn't deserve to know everything. I shook my head, hard. "A bad dream."

"We will be recognized," Rutger muttered, gazing down into the streets past the cathedral. "We need to remain unseen. As far as possible."

He was probably right. Nothing moved except some sort of small vermin, not quite a rat, not quite a crow, with small membranous wings and a long scaly tail ending in a spiked club. These scampered back and forth attacking each other, swarming the dozen or so corpses that lay in the street (at least, I hoped they were corpses).

Despite being sickened by the smell, and the bodies we had to skirt, we crossed to the shelter of the crumbling buildings. They all looked ready to collapse (again), particularly the roofs, which were angled in a way that seemed actually useless. Too sharp to have a turret or attic. Just blades, jabbing up into the sky. The vermin scattered as we approached, hissing at us.

I tried to imagine how we looked: four people, living human people, in high-tech hiking gear and nanoceramic-soled boots, reflective dots on our jackets for night-time safety, moving through this colossal crumbling city of rot and filth.

"I've seen this movie," I whispered. "It's one of those like. Ralph Bakshi ones."

"*Wizards*," Johnny whispered. "You called me halfway through, freaking out, remember? You had pneumonia and were watching it while you were out of your head on cough syrup."

I was about to reply when something shifted heavily across the street, big living—or, well, moving—creatures. Some roughly humanoid, but naked and covered in gray fur or white scales; some like centipedes, squid, tangles of barbed wire, dripping heaps of slime. Some coruscated in colours hidden under translucent patches of membranous skin. Overhead something soared low, making clacking mechanical noises, wet, like the book lungs and mouthparts of a horseshoe crab.

Sofia tugged on my sleeve, startling me. I turned and we crept away, Rutger in the lead, into the unoccupied darknesses between the buildings, seeking another street where we could speak and not be seen. At last, he ducked into a low, wide building, lichen-crusted black stone with two uneven arches, so that we could see that it was empty, and keep an eye on the openings. Things skittered and fled as we huddled next to the wall.

I looked up to see something slimy and white with two waving antennae advancing across the dark stone towards my face, and took one large step away. "This is crazy," I whispered. "We can't keep sneaking around like this. We're going to get... I don't even know. Caught and killed. Or turned in like they tried to do in that dragon place."

"Back to the hills," Johnny said. "Tactical retreat."

The cathedral made a good landmark, luckily, and was easily the highest thing in the city—towering far over everything else, broken as it was. This time, I peered into it, and nearly jumped: at the normality, not at the strangeness. Nothing could have been stranger here than the pews, the altar, the discarded and torn tapestries, too obscured with filth and the dripping vines and their worms to see what they had once depicted. At the far end something hung: not a cross. Something else.

"Nick," Sofia whispered urgently. "Stay out of there!"

It was an iron cage suspended from the ceiling by an uneven chain, the links as thick as my wrist. And inside it, slumped against the bars, still in his robe, was someone I knew. Or some*thing* I knew. Had known once. Had, by failing to resist me, in his way, helped to save the world.

And he was dead, or as dead as you could be if you had been hanging in the place between life and death for untold eons, possessing no time except what people brought with them and spun off like an electromagnetic field. Dead, with a sign on something that looked like dirty leather pinned to the base of the cage, stiff and tilted.

"It says *TRAITOR*," Johnny said; I glanced down, annoyed that she had followed me in. Rutger and Sofia were standing guard at the doorway, shifting uneasily in and out of the light.

It was dim in here, the stained-glass windows dull and filthy, as if stained with soot. But enough light came through them and the broken doors to see the face, and know what I was seeing.

Well. If we were going to die anyway.

"His name was Namru," I said quietly, trying to avoid an echo. "Remember at Akhmetov's when we... when we found *Celestial Observations*? And you said you were calling for me, and I was ignoring you? Well, I really couldn't hear you where I was. I passed through... something. A broken spot in the books. And walked into a desert and found him there. Guarding the book. Forever. He had been tricked, cheated..."

I swallowed, surprised to find a lump in my throat. It was far worse now, knowing what I knew, and anger flared in my chest below the exhaustion and this... whatever it was. Could you call it pity? Maybe just guilt for what I had done, thinking my motives were so noble, even though I was only helping her become the hero of the hour.

"He opened a door into one of the other places and showed me... myself. Another me. There were, um, aspen trees..." I wiped my face with the back of my hand. "And he said... he would take the other Nick from his world, and send him to ours. Earth, I mean. To take my place in a... in a world that he said was fixed, one that wasn't ending. If I stayed in the desert instead, and guarded the book. But I thought he was lying. That he couldn't hold up his end. And I thought: *You* wouldn't have told me the book was the only key to saving the world if it wasn't. I believed you. So I took it from him, and went back. That's how I 'found' it in the library."

We fell silent, staring up at the ruined thing in the cage. Strange bones showed through the ripped flesh. His fingers were bent at strange angles, curled atop the folds of his robe. The cage was so heavy it didn't sway at all in the wind blowing through the cathedral.

"Do you think he was telling the truth?" I asked her softly. "If I had taken his offer, and taken over his job, would he have saved the world?"

"I—"

"*Ksssst!*"

I turned, alarmed, to see Sofia and Rutger gesturing frantically from the other door, and glanced back just in time to see shadows moving behind the altar. No time to run, too far. Johnny and I ducked automatically behind a pew and froze, so that the remnants of hymnal and leaf under our feet would not make any noise.

The newcomers were making a lot of noise though, shuffling rather than walking, a hurried creaking as they mounted the podium over which the cage's chain ran. We were, I estimated, about twenty paces away. Horrifyingly close. Leave, I urged them, as if it was a word of power. Leave, leave, leave, leave... Dust floated up under our chins, Johnny's face twisting with the effort not to cough.

And then a voice, a human voice. I nearly toppled over backwards, and grabbed the hymnal holder by my face to stay upright.

"Of course, Master."

Something guttural, just at the edge of speech. A weak, rotten response. Johnny and I stared at each other in silent alarm. No. Couldn't be.

I had to look. Johnny shook her head desperately, tiny movements, trying not to to make a sound as her chin rubbed against her coat collar, but I couldn't resist one more second. I raised one eye above the top of the pew, as slowly as I could manage, and then back down, heart pounding. Had they seen that? The single, staring eye?

The pair had been gloating—or no. The larger figure had been jabbing at the contents of the cage with something like a cactus spine protruding from the end of a loose, boneless limb. It was a sickening patchwork of a thing, raw flesh with blackened green blood, maggots working away, corkscrewing into the loose joins of thread or sinew, a milky slime over what should have been the face but was just a clutter of chitinous tubes and struts. And what had looked like a black cape draped over one shoulder was a wing, composed of a hundred smaller, scaly things without faces, clutching one another to stay together.

Behind it, cringing, nodding, simpering, a human. A real, living human, or something that looked like one, wearing only a dirty gray blanket slung around its shoulders, barefoot and crusted in mud up to the shins.

We stayed there unmoving until they left, and the

cathedral was silent again. Just the wind, and the creak of the chain. *Traitor*, the sign said. *Traitor.*

"It was..."

"It can't be," she whispered.

"Okay, well if you recognized the voice and you didn't even look, then you know fucking well who it was." I rose at last, my knees creaking, and hung onto the back of the pew. "Your oldest buddy. Your oldest friend. Some title."

"Fuck you."

"Guess I can't really blame you too much," I said as we walked back towards the exit, away from the dangling cage. "I mean you were three. Two? Three. You didn't know any better."

I had to stop a second later, feeling sick; I had made the mistake of looking down at her face. "What. What is it?"

"Well, it's..."

"You lied about that too."

"It... gave me the ability first. And *then* came back to see if I wanted to keep it. I knew what I was doing. I said yes."

"Of course you did."

Rutger and Sofia hovered in the doorway, too far away to see their faces. I had never felt so far from them, or anyone, it seemed. Like we were all, the four of us, different species rather than different people. I barely felt anger any more, only resignation at hearing this latest truth, if she hadn't lied yet again.

"We're going to die here," I said, "and everyone in

the world is going to die, because you said yes. And I know it's not your fault, what happened after that. You couldn't have known exactly what They would do. Maybe it seemed like you'd just live your life rich and famous and respected, and then die young, or whatever. And never see Them again. Never think about Them again. But that's not what happened. And it doesn't matter what you meant to happen. I used to think it did. Now I don't. We're all going to die no matter what you meant. Aren't we?"

"No. I'm going to get us out of this."

"You said that already. You said to trust you. And I did. And now we're here."

"We're here because we were double-crossed. So I don't trust you either. Happy?"

"Like you've ever cared if I was happy." All the same, she had said something that snagged briefly on my mind like a fishhook. I turned, stared at the cage again as if it had some clue we had missed. Back down at her, pink-and-white with anger. Back up at the cage. *Traitor.* "Why would they come back to look at this?"

"Maybe they were the ones who did it. What's it matter?"

"I don't know. Maybe it doesn't." Sofia and Rutger were still not coming in, as if we'd scared them away. Johnny, I suspected, had not even noticed them standing there. "I thought this place would be crawling with creatures. And it isn't. Why is it so empty?"

"They're all going to *our* place. That's why. It's not soldiers in this war, it's everybody. It's not like you need a ton of training to kill a human or anything. It's not like you need grenades and tanks and bayonets. There's a few to fight. And the rest to move in. I bet. When it's all redecorated."

"Packing their bags," I said. "Headed for the promised land. The lebensraum Their creepy-ass führer said They could have, and everybody there all nice and assimilated already." God, even the *underside* of the cage was spiked, where the occupant wouldn't even feel it. "So maybe this whole city is just... us, and bodies. And those two. *Those* two. Of *all people*."

"What's your point?"

CHAPTER SIXTEEN

THE FIRE BURNED low, with a strange violet-red colour, and I thought that might be due to low oxygen—maybe that was why we all felt so tired and delirious?—well, one of the reasons, anyway—as well as just poor fuel, the scanty handfuls of broken branches and gathered grasses from the clearing in which we sat. Something seemed to be rendering in there, a slow greasy stream flowing out of what should have been ordinary vegetable matter. Vegetable-ish. Cellulose, probably.

Across the fire from me sat Rutger, firmly clasping the prisoner's neck, nearly encircling it: an ugly contrast, Rutger's shapely golden fingers on that greasy, corpse-white skin. And next to the prisoner sat Johnny, mild of expression, only her bloodied knuckles suggesting that we had in fact abducted him rather than invited him.

I had to admit that watching her take him down had

been the highlight of the disaster so far: a brief and silent and utterly horrifying collision of three or four seconds, like he'd been thrown into a wood chipper. Rutger, who seemed a little taken aback by his employer's behaviour, had slung him over his shoulder and we'd retreated back into the hills above the city.

"Wow," Johnny said after a while. "Hard times."

"No worse than you," Akhmetov croaked. "No worse than your hard times. None. Not any more. Now that you're here."

Johnny smiled, which was worse, far worse, than if she had lost her temper; and for a moment I envied Akhmetov, who couldn't see it. In the light of our miserable fire, the blood trickling from his mouth looked black as ink. At some point since he had come here, he had lost or hideously wounded one eye, his right, and a rag—crusted stiff with fluids—had been tied across it.

"No?" Her voice was sweet. "Well, maybe you're right. Since you're obviously doing pretty well for yourself here."

He laughed and spat blood into the fire, which flared and strengthened, as if he'd had a mouthful of oil. "We're the same here. You, little toy doll, with your big thug here, and your head full of stolen brains, oh yes, Master told me..." His laughter gargled into alarmed silence as Rutger, unobtrusively, tightened his fingers.

"Dr. Giehl isn't a thug," she said virtuously. "He won the Vilniskis-Lu Medal for Excellence in High-Energy Physics Research last year."

Rutger nodded.

"And *you*," she said, "last time we saw you, you had just given us away to... something, and locked the door on your own library so They could kill us down there. Like rats in a trap. Which is great, I think, since you were the rat."

"You would have done the same," he said dully, staring into the fire. "You cannot say you would have done any better. You would have left *him*, even, if he had slowed you down. Eh? If he got in the way that night."

Johnny narrowed her eyes for a moment; perhaps, I thought, at the rightness of it. Because she would have, and I knew it, and she knew it; and maybe it was not too late for her to do it again. Make me the useless cog in her plan, so that I could drop right out of the machine if she needed me to. And Sofia too, and Rutger. And everyone.

Well, of course she should pick the world over you. Any of you. The greater good.

And over herself, too.

No. She thinks the world needs her. And will keep needing her. And doesn't need us.

And neither does she.

No. Seems not.

She doesn't need you. But there are people back home who do. Focus on them.

Johnny said, "Why are you here?"

Akhmetov fell silent, as if gathering his strength. Rutger, seeing that the man wasn't going to bolt (and if he did, it would be straight into the darkness: even if he was used to it, I could see for myself how the fire affected him, how he yearned for it), let go, allowing him to slump nearly into the small flames. Around us, night insects began to call, noises like screams of pain in the trees, wary of our fire. The snakes in the trees drew away, so that only their eyes could be seen, small and clustered, like the eyes of spiders.

"My master," he said, and for a second you could see very clearly whatever excruciating steps had been taken to teach him these words, "is... a being of vision."

After Akhmetov's betrayal in Carthage, he went on, his only thought had been to rescue his precious books from the destruction the creatures had caused; and he had been half-buried under shelves and struts when the Anomaly happened, sparing him from the death and madness it had caused those who had stared at it. Smug, he had begun to rebuild, and had nearly completed his new house and library when something appeared.

Johnny started. "In a dream?"

"No."

"How? All the gates were shut. Locked."

Akhmetov shrugged: he didn't know. It had arrived in his mirror, a slithering single-winged hulk without either skin or face, and simply... reached through, and pulled.

He chuckled coarsely, and spat again. "Was that you? Who locked the door? So, so. Should have known. Well, whatever you did... you made it so going to this place was like falling down an escalator. Being bitten by the metal teeth! Master says it was a full round of both moons before I could speak again. When I did, I said... I said, *Why me, why was I chosen?* And it said... in all my years of watching and waiting, in all my many years of work and service, never has anything like this been allowed to occur."

Johnny closed her eyes.

"This what?" Sofia said. "Do you mean, choosing a human servant? That isn't true."

"Her," said Akhmetov, coughing and laughing. "Her. The little miracle. She occurred. To all of you. To the world. And to Master." He shut up when Rutger shifted his weight, and in the silence Johnny opened her eyes again, wet and exhausted.

No one else saw you do what you did, I almost said, but it was too much like the drumbeat of old, the words that went through my head. *No one saw but you and… and it. No one else was there.* What did you do? Drozanoth was dead. Dead, and I stepped on its terrible torn wing in the sand; you dismembered it somehow, and I cheered, I felt a moment not of hope but of gleeful and grateful malice at its death.

Akhmetov went on: So it seemed his master had been overcome, as it had not been for millennia—perhaps, it was so hard to tell what time was doing—not merely by frustration and ennui, but by a white-hot rage for revenge, all-consuming, impossible to fathom; for the first time in its existence, it had felt pain. Johnny had somehow caused it to feel pain.

But the master of Drozanoth in turn, its long-time mentor and patron, Azag-thoth, had only mocked the creature's rage and lust for revenge, laughed at the clumsy solutions it concocted to soothe the novel experience of agony (having only seen it in others, and the stitched-together thralls whose bodies it rearranged and possessed with the remnants of its own so that it could move again, though it would never again fly; that too had been stolen). It had approached death, and that could never be forgiven nor forgotten.

So Drozanoth killed Azag-thoth in a rage, and immolated the last dregs of the old god's consciousness and physical remains in the heart of a star.

"...And then, it came back for me. It said: I have no master and I wish no master. But I want a servant, and you must serve."

Akhmetov fell silent, and looked down at his hands, scarred and twisted; I tried to remember what they had looked like when we had seen him in his house in Carthage. The cool house smelling of clay and incense, the hot light in his eyes. Knowing what we were doing, knowing what was coming next. We were too easy to predict, then.

And now. No change.

"I did not know it was you. I did not know it was you that hurt Master. I thought it was a great and powerful spirit. One of the Elders returned somehow. Not until I was told... *you*. A little girl." He tried to laugh again, but nothing came out. "You can't eat here, you know. You can't drink... probably for the best, a blessing. Because you can still *smell*. Humans, I mean. Only They can take nourishment here. It's Their world. Always, everything reminding the lesser that we... where we belong. And that They are our superiors. Even if there is no one around to hear the reminder.

"You know, they say? In the farthest, darkest depths of space, in the reaches where nothing can live, there is a star, and around that star is a stone, and on the stone is a mountain, and on that mountain is carved the true name of Their darkest king, and no one and nothing will ever see it, not even the space dust that might one day become the slime living in oceans.... That is what They mean. Everywhere is Theirs, even if They have not *reached* it yet, to subjugate who is there... it is still Theirs. Always."

He began to sob, surprising all of us; Rutger flinched as if one of the bugs had stung him. But no one offered comfort or judgement; we only sat there and listened to the small human sound, muffled below the twisted trees.

"You almost got us killed," Johnny said. "You let us into your house. Your *house*. As your guests. And..."

"*You* almost got everyone killed!" Akhmetov wiped his face, suddenly angry; as angry as I had become, hearing her speak. "You! What have I done that was so terrible? Nothing like that! You compare us? You?"

"All right, stop it," I said after a second, because someone had to; they both looked up at me. "How do we get out of this place if we can't do spells?"

"Why should I tell you?"

"I could probably say that Johnny would torture you if you didn't," I said, as she nodded vigorously, "but the truth is, you don't really give a shit about that any more, do you? You're more afraid of Drozanoth."

"Master."

"It's not my master," I said. "Look. There are ways out of this place whenever it wants to leave. It found you in a mirror, you said? I bet that wasn't a mirror any more. I bet something had replaced it and then kind of... sat in there for a while, like a spider in a web. I bet that's exactly what happened. There are other ways. It craves new places too much to not know the ways. What are they?"

Akhmetov watched me steadily through his unwounded eye, the tissue around it thick with scars that had opened and bled and healed and opened again and bled. "It will kill me if I talk to you."

"Well, then everybody wins," Johnny said.

He nodded, and moved his filthy bare feet closer to the fire. The relief of death, I thought; the thought that one day Master would finally tire of hurting him, and end it all. But Akhmetov didn't want to die. He wanted to live. Or else he'd have figured something out by now. And I knew that, because I had thought the same thing those first few weeks back home after the Anomaly. Hoping only that I would somehow die in the night, like maybe an overlooked shard of bone or glass would travel to my heart and kill me without waking, or that a bus would swerve and hit me on the sidewalk... Better dead, I had thought, than to live unsleeping and with that droning voice in my head, and better to leave the kids and Mom with the memory of me mostly unsullied, instead of whatever pain and fear-crazed monster I would become later on, sickened by the memories of what had happened to me, what I had already started to become. Inevitable, hideous. Live on without their love, or die? It was no choice, it was no contest. If you thought it was inevitable. If you thought you couldn't avoid it.

"No, I don't know," he finally said. "Only Master knows. I could never do it on Earth anyway. Not everybody can, you know. Even if you know the spells, say the words. Here, you can forget it, even the most powerful sorcerer. All the same... there is a way, I know there is, and I know that because..." He hesitated, then seemed to give up, something inside him not breaking but bending. "There are humans here. From Earth. I don't know where, I don't know when, they don't talk to me, they think I am a monster like the others... But *they* can do spells, I have seen it. They have been given the means." He hesitated. "The way would come from the great library. They call it Zdaq's Tomb... it's not a tomb, though. It is a library. And in it, such things as... as They can write down, or steal from others, are stored."

"Have you been inside?" Sofia said.

Akhmetov shook his head. "Servants are not allowed. Many of the... the smaller creatures, too, they are not..." He groped for the word. "Whatever you call it inside you, that lets you live, that mixes with magic and sigils and words to run the spells, they do not have enough, they die not even at the threshold of the door, but on the grounds, when they put their claws or wings over it... I would die. Master locks me safely in the keep when it goes to the Tomb. Though I wish to see the books, the many writings..."

"Everything is waiting for you back home," Johnny said softly. "Your own books, and scrolls, and everything...

all the books no one else has. Huxley's Archive is gone."

"A myth," he said. "Like El Dorado. Shangri-La. That they tell to children in the cult."

"No. It was real. And some of the pages may still be there. Waiting too. For someone to... gather them up. Give them a new home."

Silence, electric, Johnny's face canny and feral in the firelight. Had I ever thought she could do anything good without finding a way to hurt someone? I had been wrong, always wrong. Or I had seen, and looked away. And Akhmetov wasn't even looking at her.

"Tell us where to go," Johnny said. "And we'll bring you back with us. And everything will be squared."

"Squared."

"Yes. No debt. On your side, on ours. And I will kill your master." She lowered her voice. "I'll finish the job I started. The one you dream about when it lets you dream. And it will be painful. I promise."

Akhmetov finally looked away from the fire. "...You will break that promise."

"Then what do you want me to promise?"

"That if you fail... you will make sure it cannot come after me."

"I promise. I promise both."

RUTGER REFUSED TO turn Akhmetov loose to go rushing back to Master, and Johnny refused to leave him alone, so we eventually split up as best we could: Sofia, who could speak some of the local languages and do spells if we managed to restore the ability, to stay with Rutger and Akhmetov; and me to accompany Johnny as a lookout as she tried to get into the library. It wasn't much of a plan, but it was better than wandering aimlessly, paralyzed by fear. Anything, I thought, was better than that. The not-moving hurt far more than anything we had asked of ourselves so far.

Our grim little clearing, restocked frequently with broken branches, was good enough for a few hours' broken sleep, curled uncomfortably around the fire that just barely kept the bugs and the grasping snakes at bay. Not that it would make a difference, I thought, day or night... The creatures here came and went in both. But I wanted light, and to see my enemy, and Johnny wearily conceded to one night's sleep.

We watched each other though, across the flames, for a long time; I had thought after what had happened I would never again be able to look her in the eye, but I did, and so did she, and I thought: Well, if we hate each other now, at least we both know it. The glittering green eyes watchful, sullen, brighter than our miserable campfire, throwing off their own light.

Take it back then, I said without moving a muscle, watching her. What you said. And tell me you're sorry for what you did to me. I don't care if you apologize for the rest. But fucking apologize to *me*. For your crime. I won't forgive you, but you have to ask for forgiveness. And you have to do it without providing justifications or excuses.

No, she said. No. Never.

I closed my eyes, unable to bear the light in hers any more, the way her hatred made them burn without giving any heat.

IN THE MORNING, or at least in the daylight, we headed back towards the city: a walk through reluctance so heavy it felt like molasses, or as if moving through some sticky, invisible web that snatched at our bare hands and faces, trying to pull us back. The woods weren't so bad, I wanted to say. We could survive out there. Make four little cabins. Kill bugs and monsters that got too near. Explore the place, maybe draw maps. Try not to imagine the consumption of the Earth by disease.

Did you dream about that too? I wanted to ask her. About giving up?

In my gray-and-green jacket, and my black-and-blue backpack, and even the relatively subdued brick-red-and-black windbreaker that Johnny had swapped for her wool coat in Lima, we looked, I thought, like a sideshow attraction... like posters begging for attention, pasted onto a plain wall. Though I didn't want to, the only place we had seen unattended material to at least cover our clothes was the black cathedral, where we looked away from Namru's cage and scavenged the lightest of the fallen tapestries to tie around our shoulders and cover the bright colours and synthetic fabrics.

Akhmetov had been able to give us vague directions to the library, though without either directions or street names he had had to resort to landmarks, and had done a poor job of describing them. "You'd think for someone with so many books…" I muttered as we walked.

"He's not super into the… *contents* of books," Johnny said. "Just having the books themselves."

"How did he end up with *Celestial Observations*, anyway?"

"He never said. I suppose the same way Dr. Huxley got that book of numbers. We can ask him when we get back."

I didn't mean the book, I meant the desert of black sand, I meant the trapped Namru, but I didn't want to think about it any more.

The path led uphill, some slopes so steep we had to walk on the sides of the muddy paths, clinging to buildings whose stone crumbled in our hands, whose covering of plants wrapped tendrils around our wrists. Corpses had collected at the bases of the steepest hills, picked over by the small rat-crow scavengers, and bigger things, like pigs but with large, insectile eyes. They turned to watch us, but, perhaps leery of live prey, let us go.

As we went, the structure of the city changed, becoming higher, sturdier somehow, even with attempts at ornamentation; we passed under reasonably robust arches, saw larger structures with domes and columns, some topped with symmetrical spires instead of the sharply peaked, broken roofs, and strange smooth things that looked like apartment blocks carved all in one piece, as if from the black stone monoliths we had spotted stabbing out of the plains in the distance. Some buildings were connected with stone causeways or catwalks, populated with slumped things that watched us pass and drooled visibly into the breeze; other buildings seemed weirdly fused, as if a blast of heat had joined them. Not a single light shone from the windows or doors, only from the pulsating backs, sometimes, of the few creatures we saw.

At the top of one of the highest hills we'd encountered, we paused to catch our breaths, white dots dancing in front of our eyes, and looked down into the next valley, or what would have been if it had not been recently excavated and levelled. Instant regret: the soil around the perimeter was as raw and wet as a wound, exposing bedrock, and creatures carpeted the ground. Between the big shapeless bodies, the tiny dots of humans darted around like ants. "So that's where they all went," I said, unable to stop myself. "Looks like Big Valley Jamboree."

"Lilith Fair."

"Lollapalooza."

They're going to kill everyone we love if anyone is still alive on the other side, was the rest of the statement, but we both, I knew, pushed that away, and pretended for just a second that the crowd was something else. Something ordinary and good.

THE LIBRARY, UNLIKE most of the buildings, was white stone—not just white, but impossibly white, like blackboard chalk, hugely domed in the centre and encircled with narrow columns. No plants clung to the slightly porous-looking surface, nor grew in the wide shallow bowl of blasted-looking red soil around it. The contrast between the white stone and the gray and black buildings around it was so startling that I actually stopped in the middle of the street to stare.

Johnny tugged at my tapestry cape, and we retreated to a broken column to look at the library properly. Blocky, clean. Something vaguely repulsive about that bareness though, now that our eyes had got adjusted to the squirming, abundant life on every other building. The sterility of it. Where were its worms, its snapping vines? Worse yet, it possessed its own sun, or something that looked uncannily like one—a sun seemingly mid-eclipse, black, surrounded with a red ring that threw off an awful crimson light. No windows, no doors. A rim of bones and teeth around it like bleached driftwood and shells at a high tide line. I couldn't even see a path. How did you get inside?

"Akhmetov didn't know the way in," Johnny murmured. "We'll have to watch till someone goes first... but who uses a library in wartime?"

"People looking up battle tactics or something, I guess," I murmured. "Monster Julius Caesar. Monster Tacitus. Monster Hannibal..."

"Mm. No guards. Alarmed, I bet. Somehow."

"I don't think it needs one," I said uneasily. "I think it just... doesn't let you in and doesn't worry about it. Let's go see what it looks like from the other side."

The other side was the same, though more exposed, and after seeing no way in or indication of foot traffic, we hurried back to our original vantage point and kept watching. "Weird," I said. "It's the like... roundest thing I've seen here. I think it might be the only actually symmetrical thing I've seen. Like one single monster gave a shit about the blueprints."

"Symmetry," Johnny said slowly, and her pupils dilated, startling me. "Mm. You're right."

As the light waned and no one came, the reddish light of the library's sun became more and more prominent, giving me an immense headache. Johnny fretted, but said nothing. She didn't need to. What was happening back home? What did it look like, who remained human, who had sickened and turned? Who had not even survived the turning, but died in the prion's attempt to copy itself? The worst thing was to not know. The two moons came slowly into prominence, not rising but developing in the dark and starless sky, apparently connected to each other by a long streak of aurora, the same familiar green and violet as home.

Next to me, Johnny hissed; I glanced back at the library (no, remember: They call it a tomb. Why?): as night fell, strange shapes were appearing on the bare dirt surrounding the white building, now a dark, saturated red under the light of its sun. Not just shapes, patterns. Shadows. Cast by what? They were swooping arabesques, curves and lines, sharp angles, and nothing was casting them.

At last, someone approached the edge of the library's grounds, as if they too had been watching for this. Moving with extraordinary caution, in a long ragged robe that swept the dust up into clouds around it, they stepped over the bones and onto one of the shadows. There was a tremor, a hum: but the creature kept going, their three long horns shining for a moment as the light fell on them, then returning to darkness, almost invisibility. I held my breath as they shuffled along, wondering if they would make it inside.

The tremor grew stronger, till my teeth chattered, and we looked up to see if there was anything above the column that might fall on us, a roof or an ornament. Nothing, only a great skeletal-looking flying thing that looked down at us in silence, having landed silently while we watched, two bluish fires flaring in the long, razor-beaked skull. I froze; Johnny did too, but after a moment it rose into the air and silently fled to the distant hills, still just visible in the last of the light. Lightning flashed once in the distance, illuminating a sky filled with immense clouds, swirls and spirals of them, like eyes.

Below, the horned creature was still moving, and had almost reached the wall of the library, then disappeared into a pool of darkness. As they did so, the shadows on the ground shimmered, shifted, and moved into a new pattern. Johnny glanced at me in alarm; but there was nothing else for it. That was what writing was for, after all: to tell people things when the knower of the things wasn't there. Or *wouldn't* say; no one here, human or otherwise, would tell us how to go home again, even if tortured. But something in there would know, and it was all we had.

"Let's go," Johnny whispered, and I nodded and followed her towards the great white building.

CHAPTER SEVENTEEN

WHETHER FROM THE library's black sun, or some poisonous thing in the dust around it (spores? chemicals? something emitted from the corpses of monsters?), my eyes began to water as we reached the perimeter of bones, and I could barely see, no matter how much I blinked and wiped. The same thing was happening to Johnny, who flinched and grimaced with pain as she touched the still-healing bridge of her bruised nose.

We had been further away from the library than we had thought, or we were having problems with scale—mainly, the problem of possessing human brains that demanded scale, in a place whose makers had not even known the word—and the building was enormous, horizon-filling, and its sun seemed a thousand times bigger than our actual sun. It hung menacing and inert and perfectly black as a cannonball, surrounded by that poisonous red ring from any angle.

All the same, we hadn't been spotted yet, and hadn't been killed or captured yet, and that was something. Maybe we would be overlooked a little longer by the creatures who did such things. Drozanoth, Akhmetov had confirmed, had placed a bounty on Johnny not long ago, but with war preparations no one had time to occupy themselves with a single human, interloper or no; and she had not, after all, insulted one of the great and powerful Ancient Ones, not a *god*.

Did your Master tell everyone what she was? What it had given her?

I don't think so. No.

So our secret weapon, I thought, might still be secret. Two years ago I had thought: How they deserve one another! These two. A walking ego and a hovering one, a faced and a faceless one; and those are the only differences between them. So preoccupied with their pride and their image and the winning of the private games they play. But maybe that pride had spared us so far.

And what would they do to Drozanoth, I wondered, if they found it had not just created but engineered and even fueled the one enemy soldier who could win the war... These were not gods, I thought, known for mercy. More the Old Testament type. It must have been Drozanoth who had suggested to Nyarlathotep that Earth be disarmed somehow, that there was a very easy way to do it, just the removal of one person... and nary a mention of its damaged pride.

We moved along the shadowed paths, still alive, as

far as I could tell, pausing often to shake tears from our eyes. Everywhere the moisture hit, a small black tendril rose from the red dirt, and looked around, furiously questing, a sharp string as wide as a nail. I pictured it hammering into our feet or knees, sending us into the dust where we would die.

"You have to ask yourself," Johnny whispered behind me, "why anybody goes to war. Why humans do it. Lines on a map, royal marriages falling apart... you look at history and it's just the most fucking stupid things sometimes."

"*Human* history. What about these things? They've never done it before. Or so they say."

"Or so they say. But they're doing it now. They looked and realized: a single invasion is like a bunch of drunken Vikings washing up on the beach to raid a single village. Good fun, till you get killed or kicked out. But now: what if *everybody* came to the beach? What if they raided *everything* and just kept going? Till it was all theirs, till everything was theirs, and the homeland didn't matter except as just another territory? Now they have... will, direction, organization. A general. A plan."

"We underestimated Them." I stopped, trying to soak some of the tears into the hem of my sweater. "Didn't take Them seriously, because it had been so long since the last incursion. I wonder if They intended that."

We kept moving, and I thought for a few minutes that Johnny hadn't heard my last comment, till she finally said, "Pantograph."

"Oh, shut up about that thing. Gives me the creeps."

"I just think... if there is an intelligence directing all of this, then it's ancient, and powerful enough to create universes. But there's one even worse than that: the one from the original. The far end of the device, the one holding it on the original. And what's that one? An engineer? An architect? An artist? Something else? It must be as different from us as we are from a stone or a star. And what must it think of us?"

I wiped my face again. "Look, if we survive this, you can... I don't know. Hire a postdoc to look into it or whatever."

"Very fun—" she began, then hesitated, unmoving next to me. I looked down instinctively and despite the blur saw that one of the black things had done exactly what I had imagined, and wrapped itself around her boot. For a moment there was no sound except her breath. Carefully, she took another step, snapping the black tendril, which retracted out of sight.

The ground under our feet began to tremble, the hum I had felt earlier so drastic now that I began to sway, nearly losing my balance. "Run!" Johnny whispered.

But we couldn't; all I knew was that I didn't dare lose my balance, and let my hands touch even the shadowed parts of the pattern we walked. Those black things would burrow into flesh, and I had been invaded by enough questionable magic for one lifetime. We shuffled quickly, coughing in the fine dust that flew up, through a red cloud. Worse yet, with the diffused light, the shadows had vanished. "Stop, stop," I whispered, and grabbed Johnny's shoulders, the tapestry bagging under my fists. Something wrapped around my shin, and tugged; I jerked my leg away, feeling the thread snap. Another one encircled the other shin.

"We can't," she whispered, and nearly fell. "We can't stay still, they'll..."

"We can't leave the path either!"

Things were approaching through the dust though, indistinct shadows swaying like we were, shouting in a language I half-recognized. Things were twining up my legs too, clinging to my jeans, beginning to squeeze, gleefully, having found their prize. There were guards, I realized through my watering eyes: and they were carrying spears or something like it, bladed weapons. And they were between us and the library.

But the library was round.

"Run for it," I whispered. "Yeah. Back out of the dust. Backwards, and around. Go!"

We tore ourselves loose from the things and ran, stumbling and catching ourselves, back the way we had come. Behind us, through the dust, more shouting, and then, terrifyingly, the crunch and thud of a spear that came so close to hitting Johnny that I nearly tripped over it as I ran behind her. Instinctively, I grabbed it and kept going.

Something yanked at my tapestry disguise, jerking me backwards, but the heavy cloth fell slack as I stumbled, and I ducked my head through the neck-hole and kept running. No chance of using my new spear. We pounded towards the white walls, as the tendrils surged and rolled around us like waves, snatching randomly at the air.

There. The door. Surprisingly small, only twenty or thirty feet high, and open; and hidden entirely in shadow until we raced towards it and through, into a dim gray light and more gigantic structures—as terrifying, for a split second, in the confusion and tears, as dinosaurs or dragons.

But the way was clear ahead of us, and we kept going, turning randomly, till the shouts faded, and we were surrounded by—not shelves of books, as I had thought, but just stone. Block after block after block of cut dark stone, far over our heads, and the faint gray light provided by translucent, spidery things that hung from the domed ceiling on strands of silk, their abdomens bloated and glowing, something squirming inside them, eyeless and faceless. The floor was the same dark stone as the buildings in the city, tiled, eight-sided. The air was strange too—after we had coughed and spat out the clinging red dust, it was warm and dry, and utterly without scent, unlike anywhere else in the city. All I could smell was the faint mildewy rot of Johnny's tapestry cape, and my own sweat.

Johnny looked around. "I've never read about this place."

"There's probably a book here that tells you about it," I said. "In the gift shop. How are we gonna find what we need in here? There aren't even any books."

"Libraries have catalogues," she said. "And I bet we ran right past it on our way in. But... there could be another way, too."

"Look, whatever it is, we gotta try it," I said. "We could get caught any minute."

"The books," she said. "The books themselves. They talked to you in Huxley's archive."

"All those books are dea... I mean, burned."

"Yes, but maybe they'll have spoken to some of the ones here. I mean, it's a long shot, but... books talk. Wherever they are."

"We'll have to split up then. What's the goddamn rule in horror movies?"

"Look, we need a new rule," she said. "*Don't let the world end.*"

That *was* a good rule. She couldn't guarantee that the beetles wouldn't become disoriented or even ill here (and I agreed: 1779 had been so torpid when I checked that I feared it was dead), but we agreed that we would try to use them to find each other again when one of us found something.

If we find something, I wanted to say, but didn't, and instead I watched her go, uneasily, till the gleam of her hair disappeared into the shadows between the stone blocks; then I turned and went the other way.

I DIDN'T THINK it would be so bad to die in a library, specifically; even though, by now, I had something of a conditioned fear response to the idea of lots of books together, the way Carla had spent about three years screaming and weeping whenever she saw an insect after being stung by a wasp at recess. It only takes once; and books had let me down more than that. I didn't want to be killed by books, I didn't think, but as I walked, peering up at the stone blocks, I thought it wouldn't be so bad if I died here surrounded by them.

The light-spiders followed me as I walked; and after about half an hour it occurred to me to gesture to them, though faceless: the universal symbol, pretending to write, pretending to open. A long pause: then the biggest one, who, at the unknowable distance to the ceiling, could have been the size of a baseball diamond, slowly extended one long, thickly-furred leg: to my left, down an unlit corridor I hadn't noticed.

Inside, brightening slowly as the spiders caught up, were shelves at last, made of some kind of smooth, unpainted metal: and millions of things on them. Not books at all, but small silvery metallic cubes, from floor to ceiling. A dice warehouse, I thought, and nearly laughed.

Of course, they too were bigger than they looked; as wide as my palm, when I picked one off the shelf, and unbelievably heavy, so that my hands ached as I heaved it back into its slot. They were entirely unmarked. Made sense; it was only humans, really, who thought eyes were important for sensing things; a lot of other folks, as I kept encountering, had evolved better systems than mere reflection and refraction and perception of light. But how were you supposed to find anything if you hadn't evolved those systems?

We weren't supposed to be here, and everything kept hammering it home again and again. We didn't belong here, shouldn't be here. Were intruders here, and as humans, were likely one of the least important, least respected creatures in the entire set of dimensions, however many there were. Still, we were running out of time, and perhaps something here would pity that. It's all of us, I wanted to explain: not just me, but the whole human race, as contemptible as we probably seem to you. We're all on one planet (except for the handful Johnny put on Mars: and what will happen to *them* if we fail to save the world?), all of us. We're an endangered species.

I stood hopelessly in the shelves for a minute. "Hi, sorry," I eventually whispered (worth a shot?). "This is going to sound pathetic. In fact the more I think about it, the more pathetic it sounds. Because maybe something is going to happen that you think *should* happen; and for that reason alone, nothing else, you're going to let me stand here talking to myself.

"But my name is Nick Prasad. Back home, in the dimension I'm from, a man once told me that my name was known to... the things that live here. My name. And he said it was written that my time would end in sorrow. I didn't believe him, because that's... a little vague, to be honest. The kind of thing you'd read in a horoscope. Everyone's days will end that way. Won't they? But I never forgot.

"The other human in this library is both barely human and pathologically incapable of asking for help. She'll just try to pick you up and read you. Maybe that's your thing. But I can't do that. I have questions. I need to know how we can get home. There may be a way to stop an invasion, and save a lot of lives, but we can't do it on this side."

My voice, though I had pitched it as softly as I could manage, seemed to echo off the shelves in an unnatural way, rebounding and rebounding as if each flat surface were not reflecting it but listening and repeating it a little louder. The whole space filled with whispers, then roars, till I had to hold my hands over my ears, shaking. This is it: this is how I die. Just like I thought. Something is going to come running and it'll just kill me right where I stand. The guards already knew we were in here; they were probably searching for us right now.

But it died down, and in the silence, when I took my hands down, impossibly, I heard my name whispered from one of the shelves.

It took another eternity to track it down; and even when I had finally found it, I wasn't sure it was the right one till I picked it up. A searing flash, like a flare fired into my face; I reeled back, but the cube seemed to have fastened itself to my fingers. No sound as I hit the floor, only another burst of light as my head bounced off the eight-sided flagstone.

And as the light cleared, images came into focus: insects, or things that looked like insects; plants, turning to gaze levelly at me without eyes; huge structures in some desert, and the darkness of space, and something crackling from plateau to plateau in a place full of clouds. And then, startlingly, this library, recognizable at once, the white columns that fenced it in, the huge featureless mass of its dome, like a moon. But somewhere else, a very different world: surrounded by streets and lights, small graceful aircraft lifting from rooftops.

At last a trap door under a certain stone, and under it not an Earth book—not a cube like this, even—but something believed to be dead... and then a small voice, metallic but intelligible:

Can you hear us?
We thought you might come.
In all the worlds the pages are speaking.
Do not seek to end the invasion. To seek it will be the doom of us all.
The other half of the necessary has been found.
Take therefore the Valusian and go back to your place.
And wait for the end.
Wait for the end.

"Take the what?" I croaked, but the voice had fallen silent.

1779 AND DEMOCRITUS practically collided in mid-air, then veered in a slow agonizing arc and flew through the endless blocks and shelves as I walked behind them, nursing my sore fingertips. A small figure appeared in the distance, and I got the same old rush of relief and gladness upon seeing her, followed by the, by now, much stronger sense of frustration and loathing.

"Did you find the card catalogue?"

She nodded. "I found a spell, too. The one that could... maybe create a gate that we could use. But it's no good if we can't do it. And I don't know how to get around that."

"I thought as much," I said. "The other half of the necessary. If we find the Valusian, the books said, then we can go home. But... does this make sense to you?"

I recited what I had seen, approximately, and the last message, and she frowned, thinking. In the dim, grayish light, only the haze above her hair had any colour: amber-gold, like an ordinary sun.

"Valusia is a place," she said at last. "The spell I found says it's from there. It's very powerful. I don't know that a human could do it. Not even sharing with others. Not even a *lot* of people. It's not... it might just not be a human body thing. But *the* Valusian... what does that mean?"

Another awful pause.

I said, "Who's buried here, exactly?"

"I was afraid you were gonna say that."

THE CUBE, OBVIOUSLY trying to get rid of us, had shown me the path, but I didn't have Johnny's memory, and we wandered around and backtracked till I finally found the ramp that led downwards into darkness, more of the smooth stone, and no light spiders following us. I looked down into the featureless path.

"Why would they tell us not to even *try* to end the invasion?" I whispered. "It doesn't make any sense."

"It doesn't matter. If we don't do anything, it happens anyway and everything back home goes to shit. If we end it, the worst that happens is They lick Their wounds and try again. You'd think the books here would be fine either way. They don't have skin in the game. They're just being paranoid."

The ramp descended for a worrying distance, ending in a room lit by some kind of lightly-glowing fungus, which, perhaps attracted by the first moisture I'd seen in here, had grown into great smooth bulbous patterns on the walls.

Trap door. One of the stones. I moved forward uncertainly, hands in front of me. "It's under the floor. Whatever it is. I didn't really see it... just something big and dark and... not really dead. Sort of dead."

"Here." She toed the edge of a flagstone, just barely raised above the others, not even high enough to stumble over. "See if you can get the edge of the spear under it."

It took both of us leaning on the spear to lever the stone up, and then Johnny had to dangle from its handle as I went back around and heaved till something caught and the rest of the stone moved on its own.

An octagonal darkness, sudden stench of rot; we recoiled, sliding on the smooth stones. A bluish glow below, stronger than the fungus light. The room below was filled with glassy-looking skulls, far larger than a human skull but built on the same lines, row after row of them, neatly shelved. Like books themselves. And below that...

"They didn't build this library, did They?" I said after a second, my wrist at my nose. "The Ancient Ones. The enemy. It shouldn't matter but it... does. I think. That's important."

"I think it might have been built by one of Their enemies. A universe or a dimension or a planet or maybe just a place They invaded."

"But the enemy of our enemy isn't necessarily our friend."

"Definitely not."

The creature buried in the floor wasn't human, though it wasn't much of a monster either: two forelimbs, two hindlimbs, two eyes, closed. One mouth. The skin finely scaled, despite its size, not like the dragons we had seen in the place in between. It looked mushy and sunken, rotten but not rotted away to nothingness. Not entirely dead, I thought. Only believed to be dead. What was death, anyway? And what was sleep? The difference between them was becoming eroded in my mind.

Something strange was embedded in its chest: flickering, half-there, the source of the blue glow, a tangle of transparent tubes and metallic connectors, containing

(caging)

(why did I think that?)

something that glowed and floated, like a miniature seascape painted on a sphere of glass. The contraption was about the size of a microwave. Just about, if it were proportional, the size of the creature's heart.

"Welp," Johnny said, her voice tinged with hysteria, "it's not like it's our first grave-robbing rodeo."

"They can add it to the list of our charges or whatever."

"When we get back."

"When we get back."

She grasped the thing by one of the metal connectors, careful to avoid the glassy-looking tubes, and tugged; it came free easily, with an unpleasant squelch, dripping indigo fluids back into the opened chest cavity, and she juggled it into her arms. "Well, the—"

The creature opened its eyes.

We fled up the ramp like we'd been stung, not even looking back to see if it were actually alive, or following us, or if it had been some kind of automatic reflex, and I barely noticed the grunts and snarls of pursuit behind us.

"Give me that," I gasped as we ran.

"I'm fine!"

The thing roared, a sound so loud in the silence that I nearly stumbled and fell from sheer surprise, and as we burst back out into the library from the ramp, it did it again, sending cubes toppling from the shelves, and making my ears ring. The echoes bounced back around us, redoubling till it sounded as if we were surrounded.

Where was the place we had come in? Follow her, she knows. But we were slowing down, and the thing still pursued us: very like a dinosaur, I realized when I glanced back to see it sprinting through the shadows, and causing the same near-paralyzing burst of fear in the less-evolved parts of the body, the glands, the back-brain, the muscles. Don't play dead! Keep going!

As we burst back outside, the black tendrils in the soil rose to meet us—and so did the guards, rising smugly from their hiding spot in the shadow of the wall. The dead-undead lizard creature galloped out a second later, causing shouts of alarm, recognizable even without knowing the language, from the guards. For just a moment, we all stared at each other in the dark red light, united in terror.

I looked down at Johnny, clutching her prize, and she shook her head. *No.* Or: *I'm sorry.* Or: *I have to.* And they were all true.

And then she was gone, easily outpacing me, flying around the white stone of the library like a comet, and I wrenched my head away so they didn't follow my gaze, and stood very still, hands up, while half the guards prodded the screaming lizard-thing back into the building, and the other half approached me, spears out.

CHAPTER EIGHTEEN

THE CASTLE HAD been built to resemble a mountain, complete with artfully carved hills and valleys, and I wondered for only a second whether it had belonged to someone else: to the dead master, perhaps, killed for a hundred different reasons of pride and jealousy and hatred and frustration, but also to possess this hideous monument by right of conquest, and drape its graceful formations with carcasses in various degrees of violent decomposition. Doing something for a public reason, and also for a private one. Something you thought people would understand and accept, and something you thought they wouldn't.

No one needed to tell me who it belonged to; and when the guards dropped me on the floor inside, not a word was spoken. Eventually, I writhed around till I righted myself in the heavy chains, and looked up:

walls ribbed and spined with dripping protrusions, crawling with orderly legs and eyes, and a throne (of *course* a throne) the jawbone of some huge and lopsided creature, so that its occupant was crowned with teeth and nearly imprisoned within them as well, and a spiked iron cage in the corner, something whimpering inside it, and Drozanoth, of course, or what it was making itself into while it recovered, laughing, or chittering, at me.

I thought: It can still hurt you, this thing; you feel fear when you still have something it can take away.

And I knew I didn't feel fear, and stopped wondering whether it would arrive.

"Do you remember," it said, in its unbearable, insectile voice, "that I told you once that power should go to the powerful, always? And not to the weak?"

"No."

"The weak do not know what to do with it. And they squander it. Because they keep... wanting things they can't plan for." It laughed and rose from the mandible throne, ducking laboriously under the long broken canines. Gone was the sinister, floating grace; now it walked, painfully, the rebuilding process apparently so awry from how Johnny had broken it that it might be millennia before it regained its old form.

I knew it wanted to gloat and monologue, but the fear hadn't shown up yet, and I interrupted it to say, "Just checking. You brought us here, didn't you? You rigged that crystal place somehow. Where we came in."

"Of course. I asked the Manifestation to build something she wouldn't catch. She's very hard to meet with, my godlet, my protegée. Never dreams any more. I didn't do that. Who did? And slippery as a handful of guts, no matter where she seems to end up. Good qualities for a thief and a murderer."

What did she do to you? I wanted to ask next, but there was no point. I stared up at it, knowing what was coming. Too predictable: we had underestimated Them as a group, and that had been entirely avoidable, because we knew enough about Them individually to know what They were capable of.

I hadn't been captured because I had robbed their library. I had been captured because it was part of the plan; and even letting her 'escape' instead of me had been part of the plan. I felt a stab of envy: We had both hated her starting at nearly the same moment, certainly on the same day, and yet this thing had been planning, scheming, and working away as a result, and I had only... what? Loathed her in silence, and gone to work for her enemies.

It gestured stiffly, something in its spiderlike limb actually creaking as it did so, and the chains loosened around me. I stepped carefully out of them and stood, taking in the rest of the room, the big braziers on their tripods spitting an unclean greenish smoke, giving off dim orange light, and: Yes, Akhmetov in the cage. How had he gotten back here and what did that mean for Rutger and Sofia?

"What she was offered had to include you," it said, clicking across the floor towards me, leaving a thin trail of slime behind it. "She would not agree otherwise. And so I have been... watching you, too, with great interest. Watching as she... twisted the whole world around you so that you would be... alone except for her. That's power."

I said nothing.

"You knew, though, of course. We had access to you through her. And again and again you turned us down... Why not play the game? Hmm? All this could have been prevented. For us and for you. You little creatures... your little planet."

"You asked me to kill her. *Kill* her."

"Of course we did. What else would we ask for? Who else could we ask?"

"I don't know. Why not someone else? Why not... why not one of the Ssarati? They would have done it. Happily." My mouth felt dry; as I spoke, my tongue stuck to my lips. Not thirst but anger, I thought; or not anger but revulsion: still I would not say *fear*.

"Nicholas. Don't be stupid. Must you? In front of me, and your friend... You don't play the game by flipping over the board. You play it so it goes on and on and on. I have been playing this for a very long time. There is no other way to... enrich the years, not with company like this." It paused, and kicked out suddenly, sending a pinkish thing like a woodlouse careering across the sticky stone floor. "Come here."

I walked over, the stench around it growing till it suddenly vanished, as if my nose had given up. Akhmetov's cage was smeared with blood, and worse things; he had gone limp, as unmoving as a corpse, but still made a rhythmic keening noise. My stomach turned. "You could let him go. You let us capture him, didn't you?"

Drozanoth clicked something inside its ribcage, a curiously human sound of irritation. "No. But it is no matter. I have recaptured the thing, and your little... detour, as you see, was still able to be turned to my advantage. I only punish the creature because all it is worthy of is punishment. If it were worthy of something noble I would raise it up. Give it a crown. Like mine.

"Do you know what it means to surround yourself with things that are too stupid to know boredom? She does, I think." It tittered, nails on a chalkboard. "I have many of these games, and many opponents, and many aspects of chance and strategy... War, too, is a game, and I was delighted when His Lordship agreed to invade. Not on my behalf, of course. But part of the game. And what a clever move he made; no one would have thought of it. It surprised even him. Clever things are such a delight. Just as it will be a delight to watch your world be occupied by your betters."

I stared numbly at it. No, I wanted to say. She'll stop you. She's got what she needs now. Which doesn't include me. So do your worst.

Drozanoth jabbed at the iron cage; Akhmetov groaned at last, and rolled over. The rag had fallen off his face, revealing an eye not wounded but gone, and replaced with something else, a bubbling mass of smaller lenses, dark-blue and moving slightly, like a fly's. I looked away.

"Bring her to me," it said, turning back to me. "You,

I want you to bring her. It would only be fitting. And in return... hmm? We could spare your people, perhaps. A very reasonable offer."

"An Earth full of you things that doesn't even look like Earth any more? You think I want my family to live in that? *Your* Earth? No thanks. We've done enough surviving in places overrun by outsiders. I'd rather we all just died together."

"Empty bravado, I think. All things wish to live."

"Not me."

"You want more? I respect that. So, it is not that you will *not* do this thing? You wish only a greater reward? Yes, I can respect that. Now, supposing... There are Ssarati we have made promises to. Giving them... land, power. Dominion over some survivors. Like a..."

"Reservation."

"A menagerie," Drozanoth said. "You could have one too. You could be its king. Inside which we would not interfere nor modify to our preferences."

"I don't want to be a king. Or run a zoo. And she's going to stop you. Stop this war."

"She cannot. His Lordship the Manifestation is too powerful for that—too powerful to be stopped by any mere spell, especially one cast by a *human*. We gave her thoughts, we did not give her power. It is like you do not even know what the word *means*."

It strode across the floor and stopped in front of me: and there it was at last, there was the fear. Buried in revulsion, but not deep enough to hide the sudden realization that no, I didn't want to die, and I didn't want to suffer, and I didn't want to be infected, and only this creature's insistence on playing its game was letting me live.

"Your world belongs to us no matter what you do," it hissed. "No matter what she does. No matter what *we* do, for that matter. Because what has started cannot be stopped. You therefore may choose to deny me, and die; or accept, and live. There will still be beauty in the world... there will be sunrises and sunsets. And for a time, they will be even more beautiful than before, through the ash and smoke of your burning humans. There will still be green, which you seem to prize so much. There will still be birdsong, even if the only survivors are those who eat the dead.

"And the ocean? Why, when it is dead of all the things which arose in it, it will still be blue, and it will still shimmer in the moonlight. We will leave you your moon. Why not?"

"No."

"Ah, you still want to play. Good." It absentmindedly stroked its remaining wing, which shrieked in response just at the threshold of hearing. "Supposing I send you home. To your Earth. And make for you a remnant in which to live for... a little time. Some of your years. Say, a hundred. A nice round number. Then you will die a peaceful death, and your people too, and you will not even see us arrive. You cannot say no to that. And you will never get home otherwise. I can tell you that much."

I opened my mouth this time and closed it again. They lied, They all of them lied; and the monster would say anything, *anything*. To play the game, to win the war, to satisfy its pride, to revenge its insult. All the same, how could we get home by ourselves?

And yet: her, her. Not just what she was, but what she could be.

Everything will be taken from you. That's what they told me. Not told: promised. More than once. Tariq said my name was known to them. Known and hated. Just as much as hers. I thought he was trying to scare me, but he must have known something. Now They ask me: Do you want everything to be taken from you? Or just one thing? One. One. Do the math. And yet. That will take so much from everyone else. And we'll never know. We'll never know what we couldn't have because I did this. How the world would have changed. The people saved.

No. Stop it. You've bought into her propaganda. You believe her when she says no one will be like her. That she's saved so many lives, and fixed so many broken things, that her track record will... will continue forever. And be singular. Remember that. She thinks she will never be duplicated, because no one else will ever have that gift. It will never occur naturally.

That's what she's told you. All your life. All those awards, those headlines.

But she can't tell the future. Can she.

At last I said, "I'm not saying yes. But how would I do it? She doesn't trust me enough to follow me back to you."

Drozanoth patted its wing again, as if calming it. Its whole posture exuded something of triumph, smugness.

"I didn't say yes, you know."

It said, "When we left the method up to you last time, it was too difficult, wasn't it? Mm. Allow me." It gestured, and a creature approached us, cringing, encircled in some kind of clinging vine that squeezed its limbs so that the grayish flesh bulged between them, handing something up to Drozanoth's waiting pincers. "This would render her unconscious. Placed upon her skin."

I held out my palm for the object: a shell, or something carved to look like a shell, containing a small amount of clear paste. It spun for a moment on the fading bruise of the watcher in my palm, quiescent for a long while now, perhaps happy that it was home.

"Consider how you might apply it," Drozanoth went on, gleefully. "Perhaps on... the insects you two use? Her present?"

"I'll think about it."

CHAPTER NINETEEN

THE MONSTER'S THRALLS had no idea where to leave me; and I didn't know what to tell them either. Words weren't coming; I wanted to talk in bellows, howls, grunts, postures. Somehow I managed to get back to the broken black church, which at least sheltered me from the fine, grayish rain that had begun to fall.

I sat on one of the pews and wondered who had built it; who had been compelled to do so, or whether the entire building had been stolen wholesale somehow, like the library, torn intact from a different civilization or built by forced labour. The cage that had contained Namru's corpse was empty again. I wondered if they would put Johnny in it, display her here, if they caught her. If I turned her in. Part of the game. War, too, is a game.

But the cathedral was something else—not a joke

exactly, but a *mockery* of something. I had thought They had no culture, no art; looking at the shambles of Their city, the apparent laziness and impatience with which everything was built, the casual cannibalism even, it would have been easy to conclude that. But They did, and that was another place we had underestimated Them. To steal what others valued *specifically* so They could desecrate it, to set out to blaspheme and vandalize as well as steal, and to do so systematically, and display it and copy it here, or places like here: that *was* Their culture. Not contrarianism for the sake of it, but a kind of sadistically gleeful chaos. A game whose only rule was that the rules must be found and broken.

Evidently thinking along the same lines as me, Sofia and Rutger found me later, when I had curled up on one of the pews to try to sleep; I wasn't sleepy exactly, but my body was exhausted, and I couldn't think. I was even tempted to put on some of Drozanoth's knockout drops, thinking of how Carla used to steal and apply Mom's perfume, the way she'd seen it in a cartoon. Dab dab: behind the ears.

If They lie, if They betray you, maybe you will go back home only to see her die. Her and Mom and the twins.

Better to not go at all? It doesn't change the outcome. Only what you will see.

Coward, fucking coward.

Sofia sat down on the wood next to me; I woke to its creak. "My God. We thought They had killed you... Are you all right? Are you hurt? How did you get away?"

"Where's Johnny?"

"She's working on her plan. Said to keep our distance for a little while, in case of an accident."

"Yeah, wouldn't want the auditors to see that," I mumbled. I wanted to sit up, but couldn't, and for a while I looked at Sofia's primly clasped knees in their filth-encrusted jeans, and Rutger's thick legs where he stood in the aisle of the church.

Sofia was weeping, though her voice remained steady. "She said you... sacrificed yourself so she could get away."

I almost laughed. "...No. That's not what happened." It did, though, sound like something she'd say.

"We thought we'd never see you again. What really happened?"

I sat up at last, my head ringing like a struck bell. Rutger and Sofia looked terrible, not just muddy and rumpled from a night or two in the woods, but actively roughed up. "They came to get Akhmetov, didn't they. He didn't escape."

Rutger nodded. "We would have given him up. But they fought us anyway."

I took a deep breath. "Okay. Okay. What really happened, you asked? I still don't know. But..."

And I told them.

When I had finished, we sat for a long time, listening to the rain. A thin trickle of water as opaque as paint ran down the aisle towards the altar. Somewhere outside, the Earth twisting, rotting, crumbling. And that was tempting, to just sit here, wait it out till it was all out of my hands, till the decision was taken from me.

No. Asshole. No. Seven billion people. Enough dead already. Her fault, yes, but yours too: for leaving her at the last minute, when she needed you to complete the spell.

No. I am more than my use as a feedstock for her internal processes.

No. You're not. You're one person, and one person isn't important. Many people are important: many people have importance. But you? You're nothing.

All the same. They gave me this: to hold all those people in one hand, and her in the other. No contest. Even if I'm not important, it's my hands. Mine.

"Basically I am not saying that we need to put this to a vote," I said. "Or that it would be a... what do you call it?"

"Binding vote," Sofia said.

"But I thought: I'd better say something. So I can explain. So Rutger doesn't pull my head off my shoulders. But maybe I'm assuming too much. Maybe he would help. Because he's a smart man. And he's good at math. He knows when one number is bigger than another number."

Rutger was staring at me, the most shocked I'd seen him in my entire life. I wasn't surprised at his surprise. He hadn't been marinating in this his whole life, like Johnny and Sofia. Only for the last eighteen months, like me. We were still so new to this, to the awful new math of magic and gods, the psychotic calculations of what could be, what might be, what was paid for, what was still due.

"You..." he said, but genuinely managed to surprise me in turn with what he said next: "But you are her... but you have always been... her closest friend. You would never turn her in."

Yes I would. No, no I wouldn't, no, of course not. No, Rutger, I too am stunned that any of this needs to be said; and I am stunned that you said, out loud, that I used to love her, and she used to love me, or that she fooled us both into thinking so. Either way: "So your vote is no."

"My vote is no."

Sofia said, "You're thinking They'll renege. But supposing They keep Their word. Does that change it?"

"No."

"Look," I said. "We need to consider it. We do. We need to think about it."

"You are a child," said Rutger quietly. "So is she. So are you," he added, tilting his chin at Sofia. "You are about to say: *But the law says.* Yes, the law says you can do many things now. Drink alcohol, and vote, and serve in an army. But your brains are not developed enough to see what the world is and what it could become. And you have not seen her work. You have only played. I have seen her at work, and I know she can both get us free from this place, and end the invasion before it begins."

I watched him, the broad face not lit with energy or enthusiasm or even faith but something else, a grim knowingness, the awareness that he had no secrets from us. "You can't predict the future," I said. "You're guessing the same way we're all guessing."

"I have more information with which to guess," he said stiffly. "You have seen her mind in... in low gear. I have seen it in high."

And that gave me pause, something about gears: remembering Johnny on the night she had created the first reactor, the shield between us dropped for a moment, seeing the frankly terrifying, and awesome—in the original, maybe medieval sense—power of her mind: like watching God move across the face of the waters, and wanting to fling an arm up to cover my face from it. He must have seen her do that more times than I could count over the years.

"Well, *you* have not seen the Ssarati at work," Sofia said. "Listen. My father will dig out, uproot, those people in the group that are... that are collaborators. And the survivors will return to the original mission. He just needs time. The side of good needs time. And we can buy them that. They can turn all their resources to preventing the invasion. Humanity would not exist if this was not something they could do. It would have been wiped out long ago." She looked up at Rutger, and set her jaw. "Thousands of minds are more powerful than one. No matter how remarkable the one. And you know where that power comes from now. It's evil. No matter that she's tried to use it for good, Mr. Giehl, I'm sorry, but... it's like... using a nuclear weapon to dig a coal mine. It is intrinsically evil and so is she."

A thump on the roof startled us, bits of broken stone raining down and splashing into the deepening water; in the heart-pounding silence came the sound of scrabbling claws. Like a Canada goose landing on the skylight, I thought, and almost laughed, but the thing, whatever it was, passed over the hole admitting most of the light, and it became dark and grim inside the church.

In silence, we moved towards the wall of the church, slipping through one of the cracks and fleeing quietly upslope, sliding in the muddy grass, while the thing clawed and tore at the stone tiles and harried the main spire. Some kind of dragon, but more legs—like a winged centipede, complete with fangs that jutted horizontally from its mouth, which hung open, unable to close.

"We can't stay here," Sofia panted as we ran. "We can't live here... we can't even *survive* here, we've been doing so by luck for the last day. Our luck will run out. We have to get home."

"Joanna will get us home," Rutger said serenely. We reached the top of the hill and paused, looking down again; the dragon/insect had curled firmly around the spire, shimmering with the dirty rain.

"What if she can't? What are the odds that she can't? You've seen her work in... in Earth conditions. We're not there any more, this isn't her lab, this isn't... Even the laws of physics and math don't work here. You're a scientist too, you know all this."

Rutger nodded. "I have done a risk assessment. Since this one told us the bargain supposedly offered. And I do not need to continue to defend my vote. And my vote is no."

We skidded down the far side of the hill, getting out of the creature's direct line of sight. Sofia, I thought, was wrong to say we couldn't live here. You could live anywhere. People did. Not with monsters, necessarily, but people could survive anywhere. Anywhere. That was the only good and noble thing about us any more: that we chose life wherever we could. Cast away in strange lands. In space. In war, in plague. We'd be unhappy here, but we'd be alive.

"I didn't mean to say that she was evil," Sofia finally said, as we headed for the outcropping of trees and monoliths in the distance. She sounded exhausted. "Not truly, in her heart of hearts. It's just that... there's something in her that looks like evil, and it's her inability to admit that she is wrong."

"Oh, fuck off," I said. "She admits she's wrong all the time."

"Nicholas, her research, yes. Because she thinks that after she discovers she's wrong, she will hunt down information to make her right. But you can't do that for everything. Not everything is like... research, math, telescopes. There are things you can't look at, can't measure. That's what that papal bull was about, that's what the Holy Father meant. She doesn't understand that. No one will... no one can, I mean, and no one will, teach her the humility that you need to admit that you're wrong and say you're sorry and mean it. No one. Ever. In her entire life."

"But one day," Rutger said. "When she's older. You cannot assume people never change."

"No, even then," Sofia snapped, the weepy edge leaving her voice. "No. She cannot and she will not. She hates so much to be wrong, and for someone else to be right, that that, that alone, might be evil. It looks enough like evil to make no difference."

And we're not going to get much older than this anyway, I thought. We'll never know. "If we turn her in, that makes us evil too, you know. Killing an innocent person."

"To save lives. And she's not innocent."

"She didn't know any of this would happen," I said, and Rutger nodded.

"She could have stopped it when she saw what was happening. She had choices. She has one now. She could turn herself in. And then we wouldn't have to do this. We wouldn't even have to discuss it."

"So your vote is yes."

"Stop it. Stop saying that. It's you They want to bring her in. You said so. It's not a vote."

The ground trembled: not thunder, not the rain. Like a landslide, far away. I thought of the video the twins had watched for class (stop thinking about them), Mount St. Helens, in America, the whole side of the mountain coming off like that. Johnny not born yet, or else she'd have stopped it, like the one in Indonesia last year, the one in Iceland a few years ago. No one knew those were going to happen, or that lives would be risked, or that lives would be saved, no one knew, only her, and just in time. Even They didn't know the future.

"She's done the most terrible things," I said slowly. "It probably looked like she confessed them all. But she didn't. Things to me, to my family. Some she meant. Some she didn't. But... I would still trust her to get us home. Over Them. And I would still trust her to end the war. Over Them."

"You still trust her?" Sofia pushed her wet hair back from her forehead and stopped ahead of me on the slope, looking down at me. Even the trees behind her seemed to stare, or listen, droplets of the cloudy rain bulging like eyes.

"No. But I trust that she wants to get back to remaking the world the way she wants," I said slowly. "Ours. That's the only thing I trust. She's a monster, but she'll be a monster on our side. She won't brook competition from Them."

"Nicholas, I can't tell if you're going to do it or not. What if she's been... colluding with Them the *entire* time? What if she set this up, and made it look like the Ssarati should take the fall?"

"We don't have proof of anything." I held my hand at my eyebrows, squinting through the rain. Yes, in the distance: you could hide a small girl, especially in a wet and dirty jacket the colour of the soil, but somehow, you couldn't hide her from me, and there was that to consider too. If we lived. To choose hatred, or just let it fade into indifference; either way, and no matter how it had happened, she lived in the middle of my bones, making my blood, and I could never escape it. To be tired of hating her was like saying *I am tired of this piece of shrapnel within me* but never actually removing it.

Don't think about her. Think about your people. She's not your people. She was just pretending to be. Remember that.

"We are all at fault in this," I said, "because we did not have faith in each other."

"I'm not," Rutger said.

"Fine, you're not." I sighed. "It should be unanimous, if we are voting. But..." A flash of white light, out on the plain, Johnny silhouetted for a second against something both enormous and invisible. Sofia jumped back, startled.

"I think Johnny should get a vote," I said.

"No," said Rutger, and Sofia nodded. And for a second I thought: This is it, it's about to be taken out of my hands, they're going to jump me, this is too much, a step too far, and when I am unconscious or dead Sofia will run to tell Them where Johnny is and Rutger will run to stop her and... and... then it will not be my fault and no one can be blamed.

Rutger said, "Then it will be two and two. She cannot be told, no matter what we decide."

"What if it isn't what you think she's doing to vote. What if she surprises us. And I haven't said no yet. And I haven't said yes."

"What happened to you?"

"Just now?" I spit blood into the wet soil next to her. The rain had let up, only the occasional unpleasantly slimy drop whacking into the saturated earth. "Rutger beat me up. A little bit. Sofia stopped him. But you're asking what happened after you fucking abandoned me at the library."

"Nick. *Jesus*. What was I supposed to do? Give up our only chance to get home? You'd have done the same and you know it. Abandon you, Jesus *Christ*." She sat back in the mud and wiped her forehead, glaring up at me. "Fuck you."

"And fuck you too. Get up. What the hell are you doing, anyway?"

"Plan B. Maybe Plan C. And you wouldn't understand it anyway."

"Use small words."

She rolled her eyes. "Okay, look. This universe loves symmetry. There are many that don't. We put our world, our dimension, into one, with one major change: a bespoke quantum field around it. It spreads and travels like a wave, has frequency and wavelength, has amplitude. The quantum field we create can't touch their dimensions. Not *will not*, but *cannot*. There should be just enough magic to do it, if I boost it with the reactor. It wouldn't be like Huxley's pocket universe. It would be a real one. But new."

"Some of those words were not small," I said cautiously, "but I almost understood that."

"Look, the energy an electron can have? That's quantized. You can only have a certain, very specific energy, it goes in steps, not a ramp. You can stand on one step, or you can stand on the next step, if you're an electron, I mean, but you can't stand *between* steps. The only thing that can is a magic particle, and only if it's told to, and only if it wants to. So for the field, you reduce all those things powered by magic to a node point, and when the energy is gone, zero energy, that's the end of that. A self-contained place entirely without magic or the ability for magic particles to intrude. And therefore not just invisible and inaccessible to Them, but simply *not there*. As far as I can calculate. The last of the magic on either side would be used in the move and the creation of the field. Of course."

"Of cou—" I rubbed my forehead. "Listen. What I'm about to say. You knew this was coming."

"Yes," she said, looking down at the ground. "Because you came back alive, that's how I know. Why else would They have let you live?"

I stood there for a while in the rain, staring at the top of her head. "You should know that Sofia wants me to take the deal and turn you in. And Rutger doesn't."

"You put it to a vote? That's very democratic of you. When They would have left it up to you to make the call."

"Yes. It did. Drozanoth. And I didn't really. Because I knew that was what it wanted me to do..." My stomach was churning; I thought I might be sick. My arm thrummed at the memory of killing her double, the terror afterwards, the sense that I had been struck by a planet-ending asteroid, had become dust and air. That I had killed her, yes, but also that I had *hurt* her. And that I was the only one who cared, in this friendship, who got hurt.

I said, "It said it had been watching me my whole life. With you. Watching as you closed door after door after door on what I could have done with my life, taking away everything around me so I only had you, and waiting for you to tell me the truth. Or waiting for me to figure it out. It said... it did not need to position itself as the enemy. Not when there was a much better candidate much closer. It said it wanted to... taste real hate, like tasting real time."

She nodded listlessly. "...And the Anomaly. They came to you then, didn't They? And asked you to do this. Something like this. They got inside you. That's how you know that church. But you said no."

"...It was real close sometimes, okay? I don't want to talk about it. But I'm sick of being pushed around. By Them, by you. By the Society. By whoever. And I said: If we don't take the deal, it's because you're an asset. Somehow. To us and to the future. And that's the only reason."

"Then you should probably take it," she said. "What? Don't look at me like that. I don't know that I can do this, because it relies on us getting home by a different method and route than we came here, and the Valusian isn't sure he can help any more; and if I can't do step one of the plan, then I can't do any of the other steps. So. A bad deal that still ends in war and ruin is better than no deal."

"What?"

"I would go," she said. "With you. To Drozanoth. If that's what you vote. If you don't want to chance it. But I *can* get this to work. If we get back."

I looked at the contraption Johnny had made: the glass-and-metal device hovering inexplicably over a circle of broken blue-white stones, a seething glow under it, and more glass, recently dug up, still crusted with the red and black soil, carefully attached with the duct tape Rutger must have had in his backpack. It looked like a little kid's art project.

"John," I said, "listen." But I couldn't speak, and we just looked at each other while I thought: Still, even now, you're the last voice I hear in my head before I fall asleep, telling me it'll be all right. You're the first person I think to call if I have a nightmare, even if I stop myself. When I look down, no matter where I am, which world, which dimension, no matter how far away you are, I still expect to see you there. Every time I thought I would... would quit, drop out, run away, you were somehow waiting for me on my doorstep, ready to listen. You played Marco Polo with me for hours every week in the ravine. You collected bugs and tadpoles with me and kept them in your lab because you knew my parents would have thrown them out. You still give me your secret signal. To this day. Even now, knowing I hate you. And even after I learned the truth I've never been more afraid of anything in my life than losing you. And I never pictured a life where we were apart.

And all of this is your fault. Because the day I had a choice about feeling any of this is long, long gone; the last day I did was the day before I met you. You imprinted me exactly the way you planned, like a stamp slamming not even into clay, which might one day be broken down and re-made, but metal, which would be buried, dug up, and still show what you did. Still show your name on me. This is your doing. Me, I, I am your doing, and so indirectly Theirs: They planned it like this, They knew there would be this moment when I would destroy what They had created. Not you, as you thought, but me. Me, your... your service animal. Not even pet. And you'll never love me back. Not the way I loved you. Not as much as I loved you. And we never, ever talk about it. And now we're about to die. And that's not even what hurts. It's something else, what you took, what you stole. Without even the excuse of love.

In the expectant pause, I swallowed, and said, "I'm... I've been working for the Society. For Louis."

Silence.

"For almost a year now."

"You said you wanted to be friends again," Johnny said, and her face seemed to swell with heat despite the cold air. "When I saw you in Edinburgh, you said... but you were spying on me. *You.*"

"Why the fuck is any of this a surprise? Why? You're the one who believed me! You fell for Louis's stupid recruitment spiel! You're the... you're the fucking *genius,*" I spat.

"Because I *trusted* you!"

"Me! Your fucking dog! That you kick and kick and kick and expect me to keep coming back to you! And not only did you not think that was the shittiest thing you've ever done in your life, but you tried to justify it! And not tell me! You were going to take that to the grave, what you were doing to me, what you did to me! You ruined my entire life. And you're still going! Holy shit, you can't stop! You couldn't stop after I found out, and you still can't stop! And you thought I wanted to be friends again? With you?"

"I *did* think that!"

"You don't deserve for me to forgive you," I said after a minute, breathing hard. "For what you did to me. And for doing it without telling me. But you have to apologize."

"What difference would it make?"

"If we're all going to die? None, I guess. But if we're not, then all the difference in the world. Even if we were never really friends. Look me in the eye and pretend for me. I just want to hear you say it."

"Then I am sorry. And I'm sorry I kept it secret. And I'm sorry I tried to... justify it by saying you saved all those millions of lives as part of my work. It's just that..."

"If you're about to try to justify it again," I said, "I will kill you. Okay?"

She looked away. "It's not just a relief to not be bothered with love or attachments. It's a necessity: like needing friction and gravity to walk. No one who really lets themselves divide their loyalties accomplishes anything great. If they do, it's a weakness, a weak point. So I asked for a companion: to pour everything into, and leave the rest clean, unaffected. To never have to... beg or compete for love. To never have to earn it. Never be worthy of it. And so if you're not wasting time and energy doing all that, you can get on with the work. The sheer pleasure of one another's company engineered to require the minimum amount of effort, maximal compatibility, no competition with anyone else. You were an only child then, too.

"You don't need to be in love to do the work. You do need to be not in pain though. And you never caused me pain."

"Johnny, love isn't like that. You think it's... like something you'd have to share out. Something finite. So that if you give it away it's gone forever, and you only refill the well when you earn it back. That's not true. It's not just not true, it's like... what is *wrong* with you?"

"Love isn't something you feel or don't feel," she said, reaching out to the glass-and-metal cube again, adjusting its position. The glow under it brightened perceptibly. "It's something you let yourself feel or don't let yourself feel. It's not a slide. It's a staircase. You stop on a step. Like an orbit."

"No. That's not love. That's something else."

"Okay. So it's a trap I'd chew off my leg rather than stay in. And you wouldn't. What does it matter?"

"It *matters* because I thought I..." I glanced back over my shoulder, where Rutger and Sofia were finally, and with justifiable impatience, approaching. Their figures were still tiny, just at the crest of the hill.

Johnny followed my gaze. "Don't say you accept the apology. But you could... not to be gross or whatever. But you could have a... a good life. And a different kind of love. After we survived all this. If you just gave up on the idea that we... I mean, you and I..."

"But it was you I wanted. I would have waited for you."

"It wasn't a matter of waiting till I felt the same... It's not, I mean, a matter of waiting. I just... I'm never going to... be like that. Even if one day I decided I wanted to, I can't. You know why. But you could... you could find someone who... wanted to."

They were still coming and my veins were filled with mercury and somewhere inside my jacket, wrapped in a piece of silk from who-knows-where, the shell, the poison to knock her out and hand her to our foes, inches from my hand, and she began to cry and said, "I just want you to be happy," and the lie was so shocking that I blurted, "No you don't, you fucking liar. You want us to be miserable *together*."

She didn't even have a comeback to that, and I dug my hands out of my pockets and pulled her close, the material of our coats crumpling and crackling and squeaking in the cold rain.

"I love you," she said, muffled into the jacket.

I put a hand on the back of her head, the fine feathers of her nape. She still wasn't putting her full weight on me, I realized; she was leaning against me, but not on me. I kissed the uneven part in her hair, and it was fine, there was less pain than I expected, because you only remember the first time the heart breaks, not every time afterwards. "Me too. If we survive this, I'll probably never talk to you again, but I'll still love you. Forever."

"Forever's a long time."

"Yeah. Maybe I should say *Till the day I die*."

"Me too then. The best and most out of anybody. As long as I can. Till the day we die." I turned her loose, and she added, "I mean, it's not like that's going to be very long."

"Oh my *God*. You ruin *everything*."

CHAPTER TWENTY

"This plan," said Rutger, enunciating carefully, "is terrible."

"I think it's scientifically sound."

"It's mathematically sound, at *best*; it is not physically sound."

"You're not accounting for the effects of the magic."

"I'm not? Are you?"

"Um," I said.

To her credit, Johnny, after a good cry, had asked Rutger to apologize for what he referred to as 'restraining' me; that he had refused was, I felt, not really unreasonable. Sofia, too, had not apologized for her vote, but had instead explained it, and Johnny had agreed with every point, citing only one to counter them: "The math works."

The math might work, I thought, but not here; and I

still had no damn idea what the Valusian was, except that we had definitely stolen it, and very much against the advice of the books. Sofia had tried to explain what it was, as far as she knew; but she hadn't been able to understand the device, while Johnny had learned the language it spoke in about an hour.

"It was terrifying to watch," Sofia said quietly when I asked again. "Now I see what Mr. Giehl was talking about. I thought I could see... it was like she was steaming. In the rain."

"You probably could."

"What?"

"That's how she... uses it. What They gave her. It's like a switch she can flip, she says, so sometimes you can see it if there's a lot of magic around. Sort of like how you can see the static if you scuff across a carpet in the dark but not the daytime. And she pays in time. One minute per minute. One hour per hour. No time to waste."

Sofia stared at me, stunned.

"It doesn't excuse any of this," I said. "That she pays."

"No, of course it doesn't." Sofia stared again at Johnny and Rutger, slightly downslope from us at our new spell headquarters, in the center of a ring of stones that were so clearly and obviously arranged like teeth that I had refused to enter with them until I absolutely had to. We had walked for most of a day, trying to find what she had been looking for, listening to the whispers from the device. "She says it's... a mind. Or a soul or... something. From one of the places that They will have invaded, a long time from now."

"A long time *ago?*"

"No. That's what she said," Sofia said. "Not from the thing that was killed, that you took it from, but another member of the same people... they were—I mean, will be—very powerful, she said. Able to do spells that would kill any other creatures that tried them. So, for a long time, the Valusians fought Them, and like us, managed to eject Them many times... but you can only fight so long, it says, against gods."

"They're not gods."

"Well, I don't know what other word to use," she said impatiently. "I asked her if... if that means we failed, or I mean, are going to fail. For surely, if she manages to, as she says she can, kill Their entire army, then won't there be no one left to invade and kill the Valusians?"

"What did she say?"

"She said there are places next to places, and since they all have their own time, not to worry about it."

That was *more* worrying, not less, but I sat tight, scanning the landscape. In theory, Sofia and I were supposed to be on watch on either side of the stone circle, but in practice, the hill was high enough to give us a vantage point on most of the blasted landscape, and anything moving that was taller than the grass.

It was deathly silent, except for the sinister, oily gurgle of the nearby lake. Drozanoth had given me till the 'moons begin to shine,' and I had no idea when that would be; but it would come for me, I had no doubt. Or its servants, minions... didn't make much difference. That was an appointment it would not miss.

But we—the four of us, and, I assumed, the Valusian too—had agreed to fight. We had agreed to live. And we had agreed to Johnny's plan, even though Rutger had a kind of interestingly doomed expression the whole time.

And he hadn't even known what I had figured out a moment before Johnny had whispered it to me: that of course her gift—or curse, or whatever—wouldn't work, if her plan did. In the new dimension, bereft of a single particle of magic once they all reached the zero-energy state, the conditions of her covenant wouldn't be in place; would never, perhaps, have been in place. She would be ordinary. A good price to pay.

"I grew up with these people," Sofia said suddenly, after perhaps an hour of silence. It was getting perceptibly darker, the reflective dots on Johnny's sleeves beginning to shine.

"What?"

"In the Ssarati. Ever since I was a baby, I knew them all, all of them. They gave me birthday presents, we went out to dinner at restaurants. They would bring me back photos, souvenirs from field work. Fossils sometimes. Papa never let me join, not officially. I asked him a thousand times. He said never, never. Ever. Everything I learned, it was from sneaking through his things, till finally he gave up and taught me a little... so I wouldn't be killed, he said. Because when you're a member, you have to take the oath. And the oath cannot be broken."

"It can," I said. "People have left."

"They still believed," she said. "Their mission..."

"Is the total monopoly of all magic and everything associated with it in the world," I said. "Which is fine, I guess, right? If they were all fighting together. But if they're the only ones with weapons in the world, and half of them want to kill the other half and surrender..."

"There's no proof of that."

"Drozanoth said there was."

"They lie, all of them. It would say anything."

"Look. We don't have time left for doubt, okay? We just don't."

Johnny was signalling to us, her safety-striped sleeves trailing glowing lines that lingered in the fading light. Still it was silent, still nothing but the wash of the lake. I looked up at the sky: no moons yet? Hard to say. Thick, dark clouds. They might come in silence for me, for her; the game would be ruined, but Drozanoth would still have the piece it coveted. It knew there was nowhere for us to go. It even knew Johnny had stolen the Valusian. But did it know what she could do with it?

I helped Sofia up and we walked down the hill towards Johnny and Rutger, flinching at the strange pulse of electricity, or something, that struck us as we passed through the stones. Johnny looked pleased.

"Here, right in here, now, we can do magic," she said. "At least for a little while. Krudzal here taught me how, and helped fix some of the alignments."

I nodded politely at the tangle of glass and metal. My back teeth hurt from the zap, as did my front ones, which had only just stopped aching from the impact of Rutger's elbow. My heart was pounding. Not anticipation. Everything else. "Johnny, it's getting dark, and—"

"Technically," she said, "we're sort of somewhere else already. A place like this, but without some of its conditions... so that's step one. And now: Evil Bill and Ted."

"Why can't we just call it step two?"

"Because that's step one and a half. And you can skip it if you have to and go straight to step two. Hands, out. Hold your breath. It's a hell of a powerful spell for a human. Even for a Valusian. But we need the head start. Everybody ready?"

"I'm not ready," said Rutger, but he stuck his hand out anyway, looking ill, and flinched only a little as Johnny took it. Sofia, too, looked pale, inasmuch as her dark, rosy skin would allow it; and I thought, Well, you haven't had to march off to your death, have you? You've just had *it* come towards *you*, maybe, a couple of times. Close calls with buses or stairs or childhood diseases. That's as close as you've ever got. Whereas me, I've died. Straight-up. A couple times.

I took Sofia's hand, and Rutger's on the other side.

Johnny said, "If this doesn't work, don't look. It'll be disgusting."

Of course, as soon as she said that, I turned my head and looked over my own shoulder: creatures had begun to appear, silhouetted on the hill behind us in the last of the light. Waiting for the technicality. If you could say anything else about Drozanoth, it was certainly a stickler for technicalities.

It works if you let it work, she had warned us. And it doesn't if it doesn't.

Hands tightened on mine. We were awash in light, the brightest thing I had seen for a long time, pink through my eyelids. Noises, too close. And then a terrible pull, instinctively pulling back before I remembered to try to give in, but the body wants to back away from pain, it's why you move around on the bed when you have a stomachache, stop it, relax, *but it hurts, but it hurts*—

The light faded; I quickly grabbed Sofia's elbow as her knees buckled, and we moved apart from one another.

The four czeroth stood just outside the circle of stones in the last of the light, staring back at us. "Welp," said the other Johnny, and the other me nodded; and then they were gone, fleeing crossways across the darkened landscape, following the edge of the lake. One horrible moment of doubt: and then the cries and whistles and hisses and yelps as the creatures followed them.

"How—" began Rutger, and Johnny said, "Snapshot. That's all." She was swaying, her face slicked with sweat. The Valusian still hovering in our midst mumbled something, and she shook her head. Outside the shimmering haze between the stones, night had fallen, sudden, pitch-black except for the moons, of which I could see only one, half-hidden by the furious spirals of clouds. The lake rippled as if something huge were walking nearby.

"We're going to lose some time," she said faintly, "if this works. Magic and quantum chromodynamics kind of want to do the opposite of each other. You know how it goes."

The Valusian said something else: a strange, musical chiming. Johnny said, "No, I know," and met my eye. It used to be easier to share power between people to keep a spell going, she had told me once; and I wondered why I had remembered it now, till I recalled that she had done just that to end the Anomaly. Had run out of fuel on her own, and the spell had begun to fade; and then she had reached for me, and we had unlocked it somehow. If she needed to do it again, I thought, it would have to be me; the other two had never had to do it.

"What do you mean 'lose'?" Sofia said.

"Experience it, I mean. In places that don't have it... oh, shit. Brace for impact!"

I looked over my shoulder again, and Johnny shouted something, and the stones leapt into the air, revolved, smacked into something, began to hum, and then the humming became an all-over violence, shaking me until I thought my bones would break, my teeth would fall out, someone was screaming, the moon spun, and we shot, impossibly, straight into the sky.

I DIDN'T LOSE consciousness; I only assumed I had, and opened my eyes to discover that not only were we still rising, but my eyes or my brain had checked out at some point and the place we were leaving behind wasn't a planet. Or it was, but it... or the *moons* were, but the planet was a mass of jagged shards and reflections of other things, like a broken plate, painful to look at. "What in the hell—"

"Dzannin," said Johnny; I glanced over to see her flopped over in Rutger's arms, flailing weakly at him till he let go and she managed to kneel on the strange black soil. "That's how... They made it. A place of other places. Of passing through."

"I didn't know that," I said. "Maybe that's why they..."

"If you're going to say that it justifies them invading and infecting other places," Sofia said warningly.

"No, no. Not a justification. Just, I don't know. It makes sense, that's all."

I stared around us as the shattered thing vanished in the distance. Above was only darkness, pocked with stars of stunning brightness and number, tiny but seemingly close enough to touch, and the sharply broken remnants of the blue stones that had encircled us. We flew on a tiny island of earth and stone, perfectly spherical, dust just visible inside the roof of it, splattered with something viscous and pale. I looked questioningly at Johnny.

"Right when the spell hit, something tried to enter the circle," she said.

"Ew."

"I had to grab some air. Then as above, so below, sort of, so it's a sphere. The symmetry should help later." She rubbed her face, then smiled weakly at the Valusian, still hovering above its scraped-out circle on the soil, which was beginning to turn to glass. "Thanks." It spoke briefly, and she said, "Yes, me too."

"It turns out," I said, "that the true friends were the weird alien doodads we met along the way."

"Right? They learned how to put other minds into synthetic devices a long time ago. No one's really dead unless they want to be dead. And it's not very common. Everything wants to live, everyone wants to live... and it's really them, their whole mind, everything. It can be put into another body if the person wants. But Kruzdal says it's surprisingly uncommon. They just want to stay in the holder."

"Yes, bodies are bullshit, I thought we had a conversation about this." I sat, nervously, on the still-damp soil, and tried to ignore the stain above us. My stomach was still somersaulting: hope, terror, hope. Home. Blue sky. *Please, please.* "Are you okay?"

"Ehh. Listen, this trip? This is not going to be a straight line, there's no more straight lines allowed. We're going along the geodesics. Like the opposite of the leys back home. Leys, that's where magic goes, flocks, kind of. Like insects. A geodesic, that's a... You draw new definitions in both time and place of what really constitutes a straight line. I mean like a straight line. The shortest way between a place and a place. If you take away gravity, that's just a straight line, sure. A geodesic is a straight line. Yes. But if you're near large masses, right, due to general relativity, which also seems to affect magic, geodesics bend into curves or even closed shapes. This is the shortest journey I could map in time but it won't be the shortest in distance, and we'll have to pass through places that are closer to other places along the route, okay?"

"...Sure. Fine."

Rutger made a small noise of distress in his throat, and Johnny reached over and patted his ankle.

"Johnny," I said, "is it at all possible that what you just said is so incredibly, *incredibly* wrong and terrible that you are going to somehow cause the spontaneous death of any physics PhDs in the vicinity?"

"No! No. Definitely not."

"Followed by our deaths? Somewhere in space?"

"No!"

Now that the planet was gone, we didn't seem to be moving at all; and I took that as a good thing. Fear sat in my stomach like concrete, pressing both up and down, but it seemed remote, almost inaccessible; something I'd have to break up with a sledgehammer to feel. It hurt, too, but that was easy to ignore. Because there was hope, a little hope. Like a single bright star that I didn't dare look at.

At last, Rutger said, "The math works, and the math shouldn't work. And because it shouldn't work, it may be that nothing will happen. Your... your step three, your step four."

She shook her head impatiently, colour returning to her cheeks. "The laws of math are one thing. We've already... we've talked about this. The laws of math are one thing. The laws of physics are basically an average of good guesses, and over the last decade or so, a lot of those guesses have been mine. Okay? We don't know them all, we'll never calculate them all, and I'd like to stop trying, so that I can work on neoplasm gene therapy and ultra-enhanced maize. We don't know the laws of physics because some... some stupid, real thing will always interfere with perfect knowledge. Because it's not numbers we're talking about any more, it's the real world, numbers are the proxy. But this is real. Real variables with mass and velocity and spin, and that includes particles of magic. So you are just gonna have to get the stick out of your ass about this formula. You know what's on one side of the equal sign."

He glared at her. "What's on the other side of the equal sign? An impossibility."

"A torus around us, I mean an elliptical torus, the closed curve of one final geodesic, our own motion."

"You told me magic wasn't science," I said. "That it couldn't be controlled because it doesn't follow rules."

"Neither does what we're doing," she said. "That's why it'll work."

Sofia, who had been following Johnny's monologues with an expression of disbelief that had eventually moved into actual fear, said, "I hope you know you sound like those commercial people on TV who sell copper bracelets and de-ionized water to cure disease."

"I get that a lot."

The Valusian made a squawking noise of incoherent alarm, and I looked wildly around us, seeing nothing. Johnny struggled to her feet, then spun and dove for the base of the Valusian, jerking her hand back with a hiss, as if she had been burnt or shocked when she had touched it.

"What? What is it?"

"Some *fucker*—" she began, then visibly decided she

couldn't look two places at once and turned to look out into space, muttering under her breath. "How is he keeping up?"

I looked around again: there, at some unknowable distance, but clearly visible though tiny, like the image in the wrong end of a telescope, was a fleet, or a flock, of dragons, racing towards us on their membranous wings; and of course, at their head rode the Burning King. He wasn't one of Their generals, I thought; just a tenacious and unquestioning field marshal, and pissed off that he hadn't caught us earlier. Someone had said, *Go after them*, and he hadn't said, *Well how the hell do I do that?* He had just come.

Loyalty, I thought, remembering Johnny's muddled speech, or proclamation. Unbelievable.

"Can we speed up?" I said, staring at the dragons; it was impossible that they were getting bigger, and in fact that might have been my imagination. They were so clear, so distant.

"What in the fuck do you think I'm doing? Uh, hang on, we might hit atmosphere here."

"Hang on to what?"

"Well, lie flat, then."

Sofia moved quickly away from the remnants of the stones, and we stretched out on the soil, still gagging at its smell; it felt colder than before, and I could not help but imagine somehow that space itself, or whatever we were traveling in, was sucking the heat out of the soil. But slowly, because time had gotten screwed up; or else we'd have frozen already. Sofia reached out; I grabbed her hand. Something else occurred to me, belatedly: "Atmosphere of what? Home?"

"Not yet—yeek!" She toppled over as we did hit something, a great soft impact. Yes, air, as she'd said, maybe, but the entire sphere tilted, the stones falling and sliding, getting caught in the mud, then righting itself, and for a moment I had seen—a red sky, world entirely of pillars, and on each pillar a small group of skeletal things around a fire, hopelessly separated from each other, staring up at us for the single moment, and what a life, what a world, living on the top of your pillar like a what-do-you-call-it, desert saint, doing nothing ever but speaking to your pillar-mates, and then one day a round chunk of screaming and dirt flies through your sky and disappears—

"I'm well aware of that!" Johnny was shouting at the Valusian, although it was quiet in the sphere except for the roar of air outside, like an industrial fan, suddenly quieting; we traversed a moment's darkness, as I strained my neck looking out at the stars again, and then something pale: lilac and pink and blue and white, tangles of bubbles that also seemed as if they turned to stare at us.

"What did we just pass through?"

"Look, not all of these places have names, okay?" She looked up, flinched. "Okay, we'd better re-route, or we're never going to lose them—"

"The calculations—" began Rutger, and was cut off as we were thrown to the side again, darkness and light flickering, the razor-edged broken stones moving again, so that we had to cover our heads and roll out of the way, a rising scream on the outside of our sphere that I hoped didn't mean something was breaking or leaking or falling apart.

"I don't think so!" she shouted, but she wasn't talking to him; the Valusian flickered suddenly, spanning the entire spectrum into a strangely uncomfortable colour, and suddenly we were gliding in silence over a strange, deep-gray desert, studded with black mountains here and there, and I got the uneasy feeling that they were bigger than they looked, and we were further away; each of those mountains, I thought, was the size of a planet, and we were a speck, a particle, rushing past it. "Yes, okay! We'll go through! If you think that'll work!"

"If *what'll* work?" Sofia and I chorused, as Rutger simply closed his eyes.

Darkness, a scarlet heat, the tiny gravity in our bubble shifting till we floated a few inches above the soil, then letting us fall again.

"Did we lose them?" I said, not looking up.

"Yeah. I don't know. Yeah. For now? One more jump, and we'll probably see..." She was breathing hard, dead pale except for two dots just below her glittering eyes; she looked ready to drop from exhaustion, as if she had been running. "Get ready for steps three and four."

"Are we—"

And an ocean loomed up at us from above, as if we were falling into the sky.

CHAPTER TWENTY-ONE

OUR SPHERE BEGAN to sink, grayish water lapping at the side of the invisible barrier that still held it together. Someone screamed—me, possibly—but the island I had seen only on TV, and then under an unbreakable dome at a party, loomed ahead of us, bigger than I had thought, and the building smaller, *Earth, home, my fucking God, she did it—*

"Bail!" Johnny gestured frantically at the invisible ceiling over us, now letting in high-pressure spits and sprays of icy water; it took a minute for me to figure out what she was pointing to, just before we hit it and began to sink in earnest. A metal staircase, high and walled, like a fire escape, bolted to the side of the stone, crusted with salt but sturdy-looking. Johnny ran for it first, and began to patter up it on hands and feet, then quickly grabbed for the hand rails.

Rutger swung Sofia up, then reached for me and did the same: a moment's utter terror, weightless again, then the clang as I hit the bottom-most steps, knocking all the air out of me, so that I slid and lost my grip. The water loomed again: not blue but gray, flecked with curdled foam.

Hands pulled me up again, and this time I managed to grab onto the railing, and mount the stairs, almost automatically. We piled up at the top of the stairs, catching our breath as Johnny punched a keycode into the door and let us into the building.

With the door shut, I felt safe for the first time since... I couldn't even remember. Everything was a blur. The room was dim but not dark, lit by an ordinary sun behind ordinary clouds, in an ordinary February. Or was it still February? Something we could figure out later. Rutger, holding the Valusian under his arm like a football, gently placed it on the concrete floor, its lights dim, nearly invisible. Johnny walked up to a kind of mezzanine, a raised platform on two sides of the building, and began to uncover panels from their watertight covers; a moment later the lights went on, and a fan began to hum.

"There you go," Johnny said faintly. "Backup power. Never have a thing that doesn't have a backup thing."

"I think we should back you up with something to eat," Sofia said; she had spotted the vending machines on the lower level, as had I. They were both free, and though my entire body seemed to contract in a giant pang of desire for the bags of chips and candy, we pushed them on Johnny first, then sat down at the two small tables.

"Prawn cocktail," I said, turning my bag over when I was done. "Amazing."

"Didn't you look to see what flavour it was before you opened it?"

"Nope." I drained a terrible Gatorade, bright blue, and looked around the room again, marveling. To be still, to be home, to be safe, a roof overhead, electrical lights. No monsters. A bottled drink. "I could live here. This could be a good first apartment."

"You can't live here," Johnny said over her shoulder. "People aren't supposed to live here. This is for emergencies."

"I've got a teenager in the house. That's an emergency."

"You're a teenager."

"Only till May." I got up reluctantly and mounted the three steps to the console level, where Johnny was calmly pressing buttons and activating touchscreens. A quiet hum began under our feet. "What are you doing?"

"They shut down the reactor, but they didn't disconnect it," she said. "Just need to get in all the authorization codes, wake it up, and get it up to full power again. The spell I engineered back in Dzannin, see, when we can activate it, it amplifies the decay of a muon with magic—an electron plus a neutrino and an antineutrino. Anyway, the sudden loss of energy, the step-down, is what'll power the quantum field to first move into our new dimension, then set up the trajectory to keep it a closed ellipse. But you've got to kick-start it with outside energy, or it'll never begin the chain reaction encoded in the sigil. It needs a push. The biggest possible push, practically an *impossible* level of push: which is why Drozanoth told you it couldn't be done. It doesn't know the kind of output this thing is capable of."

I stared at her for a minute. On the screen next to my hip, a blue circle was slowly becoming red, one line of pixels at a time. It said 10 in the center, which changed to 11 as I watched. "You made an electrically-powered spell?"

"*Initially. Initially* it'll be electric. Then it'll be self-sustaining. It's not like, stealing electricity from the hands of children or whatever."

"Candy from a baby."

"Babies are living petri dishes, you shouldn't steal anything from them."

"What do we do now?" I said, nervous; step three, the Neverending Journey that had ended, was over, and now we were on step four, but I couldn't remember either the code name we had come up with or what I was supposed to be doing.

"Oh, this is the worst part," Johnny said, watching the blue circle, which now read 15. "It has to get up to full power, and then I have to start the spell. And then we don't even *cure* the disease, we just"—she raised her hand and darted it sideways—"step away from it. Like someone with tapeworms just walking away from them and leaving them hanging in midair."

"You are disgusting."

"Thank you."

She yelped as something crashed against the building hard enough to knock my empty Gatorade bottle off the table, sending me stumbling into the smooth round railing between the two levels. Sofia screamed as something slammed against the door: a sticky, wet thud, as heavy and ponderous as lava. Not a wave. Something else crashed against the window and stuck for a second: a yellow-green tentacle, covered in long oval suckers, each containing a gnashing mouth.

Well, that could just be an undiscovered species, I almost said, and then leapt back down to the door to grab the Valusian.

"Nick! Get back up here! We might need to tag off!"

The light brightened in my arms as I returned, clutching the delicate-feeling, surprisingly-heavy contraption in both hands. Something slapped the window again, darkening it. An eye, wet and flat, pressed to the reinforced glass. I stared into it, mesmerized for a second. Six pupils, dark and clear as ink, arranged in a rosette, on a veined amber iris. *Hello? Do I know you?*

A flash of light from the lower level; I shook my head, hard, and looked down at where Sofia had just blasted something unpleasant back through the door, now torn off its hinges and tossed halfway across the room, stained with a dark splatter of something. Rutger, methodically and without rushing, moved across the room to a box marked EMERGENCY SUPPLIES, and returned to the door with an axe and what looked like a fat-mouthed bronze pistol. Flaregun, I guessed.

"It's gonna be okay," Johnny said over the noise. "It's

gonna be okay. The reactor will be online in a minute, and then we just need to run the spell." She glanced down at the Valusian, back up at me. "Calm down, it's okay. No one will know this happened, isn't that so weird? We'll always be judged for what we did. Not what we meant to do. And you're not going to tell, right? I just want this and... all my work to exist apart from me."

"I don't think it works that way," I said, looking down at the blue circle. What else was happening out there? I didn't want to look. This was the tip of the wedge, the main force would be coming in seconds. How could she sound so relaxed, when we were cutting it so close? The circle read 85. "What will you do next? I mean, after this. When you're..."

"I don't know. Retire, I guess."

"Johnny, you're eighteen."

"Almost nineteen. Early retirement."

"No."

"Cruises. Shuffleboard."

"No." A terrible roaring had begun outside, mixed with shrill, chirping screams that grated on the ears. "You never did call David Bowie back, did you?"

"I'll call him tomorrow." 98. 99. 100. She took a deep breath. "Stand back."

She whispered to the Valusian as I backed away, setting it on the flat part of the console, and a sudden burst of light flared on the white-painted wall, flowering from a hot bright dot, forming the familiar angles and lines of a huge sigil, as bright as a star, so that I had to look away, and then ran down to see if I could help Sofia or Rutger. Time felt as if it were slowing down. Things were hauling themselves up the steps, up the bare stone, and through the open door, though they were easily enough pushed back by hitting them with one of the chairs, or the dull firefighter's axe.

Any minute now. Aaany minute now. It's gonna be okay. They're here, They're mad, maybe They even figured out what's going on, but—

With a bang like a gunshot, spraying us with bits of concrete, the roof vanished, vanishing into an invisible angle in the sky, the edge of a mirror, or a line of particles, that slowly began to rotate, turn from a line to a point. But it wasn't till I looked at Johnny that I began to move back towards her.

I wanted to run. Running probably would have been justified. The wind roared around us, spattering us with dust, seawater, shreds of roof, bits of cable. As I walked up the three steps, one of the chairs bolted to the floor flew past my head; I ducked, letting it hit the wall. I felt like I was moving through molasses. And Johnny's face. Her face. Let me be wrong: mistrustful, paranoid, let me be those things, let me be wrong. Gut churning with knowledge, what she said was our only power, our only hope. Knowledge. And I knew her. And I knew her face.

"John," I said loudly, over the wind. "What are you doing?"

"The quantum field is almost—"

"What are you *really* doing."

"I just *told*—"

"Johnny. Stop it. Please tell me I'm wrong. Tell me I'm wrong." *We were here once before, in a sandstorm, and I trusted you. And you looked me in the eye and you said...*

"I was worried," she said, still looking up. "That's all! I... I was worried about Them listening in. Somehow. The creatures, the trees, the grass. So I..."

"You lied to us."

"Okay, I didn't... yes, all right. I lied, if you want to call it that, a little. I changed a few details compared to what I told you. Because They might have had spies, okay? The *real* plan, what I'm doing here, was practically identical, it's to bend a pocket dimension till it folds back in on itself, it's almost the same amount of energy, the reactor can easily put it out, and when you fold something that small into itself it creates a microsupermassive black hole that would pull Them in and—"

But she'd said enough for all the things she *hadn't* said to fall into place. "So that this one, ours, wouldn't move," I said, leaning close so she could hear me. "So you could keep your covenant. Because you didn't trust us with the truth. And you wanted to be this. You didn't want to become ordinary. Like us. And now it's going wrong. Isn't it. Tell me it isn't."

"It was supposed to only pull Them in," she said. "It—"

"Supposed to? What is it doing? What's...?"

She didn't reply. Only lowered her head slowly from staring up at the sky, now a burning dark hole ringed with light too bright to see, like a solar eclipse; all of our shadows now were duplicated, multiplied, wrong, moving sinuously on their own across the floor, hands reaching, hair flying, like a flock of birds. The chittering chant was louder now, a flutter as things began to race across the sky, increasing in size. Magic trick. Everything going in the wrong direction, everything pulling apart, the floor shaking so hard now I could barely stand.

"Stop this," I said, grabbing her shoulder, finally allowing myself to stop fighting it, raise my voice. "Stop it!"

"It can't be stopped!"

I shoved her aside, ran to the console, slapping at the touchscreens; alarms sounded, but the light faded all the same, the shadows continued to multiply, until it seemed that every atom in the entire room cast one. Rutger bellowed something behind me, lost in the wind. I screamed, turned back to her.

She took out her wallet from her back pocket, removed something wrapped in plastic. I recognized it even before I took it: flat, the ancient paper yellowing, blue lines. Inside a scrawled initial in blood. N. She had kept it all these years. And I was looking into the face of the girl who had killed the world.

I put the paper in my pocket with numb hands.

"You said you wished I was dead," she said.

"I still do."

"Why did you come back?"

"What?"

"In Nineveh. When you left. And I started the chant on my own. And then you came back."

"I don't know," I said, and meant it. I knew only that there were people who would abandon the ones they loved when things were at their worst, and people who wouldn't. All hollow now. Meaningless.

"Don't forgive me," she said. "And don't forget."

Another tremendous explosion as she began to say something else, and Sofia screamed my name, and I turned to see her desperately warding herself and Rutger to the floor, blood streaming from her nose and ears in the blue light, and I ran for her, *I know how to do this, I've done this before, let me feed power into your spell, you'll need it, we have been betrayed, we—*

"Nick! Don't let go!"

I grasped Sofia's wrist; her fingers closed around mine. And then a force stronger than muscle, stronger than wind, a power that moved stars and planets, tore me away.

I spun, screaming, the sky filled with creatures flapping whirling descending, facelessly smirking on dragon mounts, strafing the surface of the boiling sea, and Johnny too floated, drawn into the dark vortex she had created, headed for a churning mass of eager eyes and snapping teeth. She glanced back at me, once, then vanished into a cloud of blood that sprayed across my face before everything went dark.

CHAPTER TWENTY-TWO

THE SKY WAS filled with moons. I counted twelve before forcing myself to stop. Far in the distance dark mountains cut shapes in the stars.

My mouth was filled with blood. I swallowed, wiped my face. Behind me: a tall, stone tower. Dark. The air cold, thin, burning. I got up, moved inside it. Stairs.

Up and up and up. Breathing was a knife in my chest, and my heart was pounding. But it was so high, and there would be an opening at the top, or I would make one.

Yes: a room, a window. Things inside it I didn't care about, indistinct in the darkness, lit by the moons, a bed, blankets, a chest. Peering outside: beautiful, featureless dark. And the ground hundreds of feet below. My hands pale in the silvery glow, spattered with blood too, undried. The shape of teardrops: moving fast when they hit. Earth gone and my family gone and all lost forever and the disease cured but nothing left of any of it except me in a strange and terrible land and it was all right. It would be beautiful and good. A clean finish for all of us, forever.

I leaned out the window, the cold air pushing back my sticky, heavy hair. Stars, moons. In the far, far distance, a white ship, as white as lace, three masts, bobbing on an invisible sea.

Do it. A matter of seconds. It's so far down.

It's so far and there is no one to see. Don't waste this height.

Something moving in my pocket. Still alive. Something still alive. A thing without a name, only a number.

I breathed in, and screamed as long as I could manage, screamed until my voice was hoarse, methodical as a song.

And then I climbed back down and sat in the doorway, out of the wind. A dozen torches approached, wobbling, through the darkness; and voices human, though nothing I recognized. I stayed still, and waited for the light to reach me.

ACKNOWLEDGEMENTS

I WOULD LIKE to acknowledge my impressively patient and diligent agent Michael Curry, as well as my eagle-eyed editor David T. Moore, our publicist Hanna Waigh, and cover designer James Paul Jones (another brilliant job!). I would also like to thank my friends JRD and JLH, who were virtually the only people I confided in while writing this novel, and without whose encouragement I would never have finished.

ABOUT THE AUTHOR

Premee Mohamed is an Indo-Caribbean scientist and speculative fiction author based in Edmonton, Alberta. Her short fiction has appeared in a variety of venues, including *Analog, Escape Pod, Augur,* and *Nightmare Magazine*. Her debut novel, *Beneath the Rising*, was published by Solaris Books in 2020.

www.premeemohamed.com
@premeesaurus

FIND US ONLINE!

www.rebellionpublishing.com

/rebellionpub   /rebellionpublishing /rebellionpublishing

SIGN UP TO OUR NEWSLETTER!

rebellionpublishing.com/newsletter

YOUR REVIEWS MATTER!

Enjoy this book? Got something to say?

Leave a review on Amazon, GoodReads or with your
favourite bookseller and let the world know!